MW01166651

FORGOT TO SAY GOODBYE

New York Times **Bestselling Author**
S.L. SCOTT

ISBN: 979-8-9878634-7-3

*Visit my website for warnings. Please note this page contains spoilers.

FOLLOW ME

To keep up to date with her writing and more, visit S.L. Scott's website: **www.slscottauthor.com**

To receive the newsletter about all of her publishing adventures, free books, giveaways, steals and more:

https://geni.us/intheknow

Follow me on TikTok: https://geni.us/SLTikTok
Follow on IG: https://geni.us/IGSLS
Follow on Bookbub: https://geni.us/SLScottBB

ALSO BY S.L. SCOTT

To keep up to date with her writing and more, visit her website: www.slscottauthor.com

To receive the scoop about all of her publishing adventures, free books, giveaways, steals and more:

Visit www.slscottauthor.com

Join S.L.'s Facebook group here: S.L. Scott Books

Read the Bestselling Book that's been called **"The Most Romantic Book Ever"** by readers and have them raving. We Were Once is now available and FREE in Kindle Unlimited.

We Were Once

You do not want to miss the international sensation, **Best I Ever Had.** This book has won readers over with its emotion and soul deep love. **Best I Ever Had** is now available in ebook, audio, and paperback, and is Free in Kindle Unlimited.

Best I Ever Had

Audiobooks on Audible - CLICK HERE

The Westcott Family Series (Stand-alones)

Swear on My Life

Never Saw You Coming

Noah Westcott's Book

Marina Westcott's Book

The Everest Brothers (Stand-Alones)

FORGOT TO SAY GOODBYE

S.L. SCOTT

S.L. SCOTT

PROLOGUE

Noah Westcott

THEN

LIV.

That's all I got.

A name is also all I gave.

First names were enough when we tipped the last of the bottles back. Letting the whiskey and wine take hold, we agreed not to attach any strings.

I regret making that pact.

I don't want just one night.

I want more than only the coming hours, craving a last name, maybe her age, where she's from, or why she's here in the Hamptons this weekend.

But that's not the deal we made.

Dark brown hair falls like silk over my legs, her luscious lips wrapped around my dick that's slick from her mouth and swollen. Despite the long strokes of her tongue and the heat she's creating as she consumes me, I suspect the eyes that beg for my attention match mine in the daylight.

It's too tempting to drop my head back and savor the suction of her glorious mouth, the way she takes me so deep that I hit the back of her throat. But the trust she gives in her gaze should never be taken lightly, so I keep my eyes fixed on hers.

I'm the opposite of someone who has a right to behold it, but since she's offering, I'm enough of an asshole to take anything she's willing to give.

I don't hold back and give into the ecstasy. Twisting my fingers through her hair, I keep her steady until I fall apart, giving her all of me and more than she can handle. She slips back on her heels, the palms of her hands hot against my knees.

Swollen lips, glassy eyes, a look of contentment settles through her fine features as she tries to catch her breath.

Dropping to my knees before her, I grasp her face in my hands, coming so close, I could kiss her. I don't. Instead, I say, "You're fucking gorgeous, you know that?" I then kiss her and those lips that pulse with the sexual energy flowing between us.

She grabs my shoulders and pulls back, her breath heavy against my neck. "It's been . . ."

Her words grab my attention as much as the way her nails dig into my skin. I tilt back to look into the eyes that try to hide what she was so close to saying. "It's been what?"

With the slightest shake of her head, she looks down. "It's just been a long time since I've been with anyone . . . intimately."

I didn't take her for shy based on the fact we met just a few hours ago. She had no qualms taking charge of the situation as soon as she removed my swim trunks. So opposite of who she is from what I've seen.

No way will I let her sit and worry about a reaction from me. Every other guy's loss is my gain. That I even get to share a night with her makes me feel damn lucky.

Tucking a finger under her chin, I lift it until our eyes meet again. "That's a damn shame." I kiss the corner of her lips as a smile grows beneath. Lifting her to her feet when I stand, I say, "Get on the bed. It's my turn."

She crawls onto the mattress giving me a quick flash of that fine ass before she turns to lie before me like a steak presented to a man on a hunger strike. My mouth waters for her as I wedge my hands between her knees.

Butterflying open for me, she bites her bottom lip and watches as I go down ready to devour her. Her back arches, her moans growing in frequency, the sound of my tongue fucking her before I nip at her clit has her thighs squeezing together with my head in the middle of them.

It doesn't take but a few minutes to have her bucking and begging for me to make her come. I lap between her lips and kiss, sucking her sweetness until her body begins to tremble under my tongue.

There's something about feeling her, *hearing her*, fall to pieces . . . my name escaping her lips . . . her body clenching around my tongue . . . her hand holding mine until it becomes too much.

It's too much for me to hang on for long. *Again.* I'm hard and in desperate need of relief. I won't take this from her, though. Placing one last kiss on her lower lips, I replace my tongue with my fingers and trail kisses down her thigh, lifting her knee and stroking under the bend as if I were still lapping at her clit with my tongue.

Fingers fisting the sheets.

Toes digging into the mattress.

Her belly taut with building tension.

I sit back to watch this gorgeous goddess come for me. When her eyes open, I lean to kiss her knee before climbing beside her and lying still.

Our breaths fill the void though the ache of my dick is visceral, causing mine to tense before releasing again.

When her body stills, I prop myself up, leaning over to kiss her mouth, but am quick to fall back again. Reaching for me, she whispers, "That's never happened before."

I grin, my ego fed and satisfied.

Turning to her, our eyes meet and the wave that just ripped through her is replaced with a calmer sunset. "That long, huh?"

Her gaze rolls to the ceiling. Our arms press together before her pinky wraps around mine. "It's been never." With a flutter of her lids, her eyes close.

I can't stop thinking about "never" and what she means by that, but I don't want to disrupt our peaceful state to ask. Rolling to my side, I kiss under her jaw, then her chin before covering the column of her graceful neck, taking my time to appreciate the intimacy.

Intimacy isn't something I've ever wanted. That urge is never present. *With Liv, I crave it.* I don't want this night to end.

My dick finds an ounce of relief in the contact between us, but nothing will ease the hunger growing inside until I'm buried deep within her. But her breathing deepens as if exhaustion has finally taken hold of her without permission.

My chest is as twisted as my thoughts lying beside her. It's probably the whiskey, the late hour, and the woman. It's probably best if I get some sleep like she's finding.

Bury the thoughts, the twist, the desire of wanting more from her. Sleep. It doesn't take long for me to give in like she has ...

I'm not sure how long I'm out but when I force my eyes open, I stay quiet in bed, spying on Liv leaning against the frame of the balcony door. The wind catches the ends of her hair, sending them into a tiny mess while the ocean grows louder in the morning hours.

Ice crumbles against the sides of her glass, and condensation gathers, threatening to fall against her creamy skin. She's stunning in the moonlight, the silhouette of her body —great tits, that ass that I bit for her attention, the curve of her lower back my hands grazed over, and the softness of her belly that I kissed just after making her come. She'd probably hate that I notice the details of her body, but it's not about seeing them now.

It's about memorizing, remembering everything about this night for later ... a night alone, an urge that needs an image to accompany it, a dating drought. That's never happened, but there's a first for everything.

Those urges come roaring back from the sight of her body, mine on full alert. Sleeping didn't ease the discomfort of wanting something more from her. Is it the way I'm not allowed into her thoughts or how she appears aloof that keeps me magnetized by her presence? Or maybe it's that the only thing I definitively know about her is three letters. *Liv.* I'm not used to being shut out, yet she's doing a great job of keeping things surface.

She takes another sip, the shift of the glass causing a droplet to hit her chest and run toward the slight of her breast, threatening to coat her nipple. The chill sends a shiver of goose bumps across her skin. I follow the water as it trickles over her skin, the trail glistening in the moonlight.

My dick stirs, the sight summoning me to her. If I'm only getting one night with her, I plan to make the most of every minute of it. And I can't wait another fucking second to taste her again.

Pushing up from the bed, I walk to her, needing to touch her in a way that causes an eruption of awakening within her. I run my hand over her hip and dip to kiss the curve until I reach the spot behind her ear that makes her tremble in the most delicious way.

Without telling anyone, we left a bonfire only a few hours earlier and made our way back to the house.

If she would have had her way, I would have been inside her as soon as we crossed the threshold, but we kissed instead. Not sure when I grew a conscience, but I slowed things down trying to win over her mind as much as her body. She appeared to be on a mission of her own, though. I wasn't hard to convince. We did little talking thereafter, losing ourselves in the exploration of each other's bodies, hands scrambling to undress each other as we headed for the bedroom.

I can't say I didn't try to be a gentleman.

But now the mood has changed. I'm sure she feels the shift as much as I do. She remains quiet, keeping her thoughts to herself, and her lips wet from another sip of water.

Since we're both standing here naked, bare to each other, I whisper, "We don't have to leave as strangers." I sacrifice another effort to make something from nothing.

The tips of her fingers, cold from the glass, tap my cheek as a smile graces her face. The moonlight dances in her eyes as she stares into mine. "That would go against our agreement."

Chuckling under my breath, I move in, anchoring a

hand above her head while staring into those gorgeous eyes of hers. "We made the rules, babe. We can break them as well."

I slide my fingers between her legs, slipping them in the slick welcome of her pussy. "What do you say?" I ask, then kiss the side of her mouth.

I pull back and brush her hair away from her face, admiring her beauty and the innocence before fucking her with my fingers.

Her head tilts back, eyes closed and mouth open. I cover it, swallowing her breath and giving her life. Pulling back, I watch her chest rising and falling through jagged breaths. When she peeks, she whispers, "Noah." She wraps her arms around my neck to hold me closer. Kissing the side of my mouth, she adds, "Let's not ruin a good time."

That's the last time I ask. If she only wants sex, I'm more than happy to give her what she wants. I'll fuck her so that's all she remembers when she leaves tomorrow, all she feels when she walks away from me.

"You're so wet for me, baby." I pull my hand back, bringing my finger to my mouth, hungry for a taste of her more than I need my next breath. *Fuuuck.* So good.

Picking her up, I press her back to the doorframe. With the moon bearing witness and the ocean drowning our moans, I position myself at her entrance. I'm ready to have her wrapped around me, to feel her body take all of me to the hilt. As soon as she looks at me, a question lingers with bated breath between us. I hold myself still though it's becoming impossible to keep from doing what I know will give me the relief I'm desperately craving.

She rubs the back of my neck and takes a deep breath. "I want this, but it's been a while—"

God, there's something so fucking sweet about the way

she's looking at me—innocence buried deep in her gaze. I can't stop myself from kissing her and then again. "Do you want me to go slow?" I ask, studying her pretty face. Though her features are delicate, a scar lies just above her right eyebrow. It's nice to see the perfection broken by something natural.

The slightest of nods accompanies her arms holding me tighter. "Just to start."

"I can do that for you just to start." I push in slowly, kissing her again, this time my breath catching in my chest. The heat of her body consumes any thoughts I had before that this is any other chick. "Fuck," I growl, my head dipping down to her shoulder and sinking as deep as I can. *It's not enough.*

I need more.

I need all of her.

Lifting her higher, I wrap her legs around me, her ankles clasping behind my back. A pant breaks the wordless connection of our lips, and then a mewl tickles my skin. "You feel . . ." It's just another whisper drifting past my ear, but I hear her. "So good."

"You think you can handle more of me?"

Above widening eyes, her brows pinch together as color floods her cheeks. "I thought that was—*Oh my God.*" She sucks her harsh breath deep into her lungs, her eyes clamping closed, and her jaw slacking. "Yes. Feels so good. More. Harder."

I'm not gentle, and I'm not kind. I fuck hard, making sure to decimate any stupid notion of this being anything more than a one-night stand. "So fucking amazing."

She exhales. "Oh God, yeah." Her hands fist as if she's restraining herself from digging into my skin. Sucking in a breath, she drops her head so we can stare into each other's eyes.

There's so much more to this, more to us than a physical connection. I don't say anything, though my thoughts collide with the sensations of pleasure we're sharing. I stumble as gratification enters the horizon. "Fuck, I'm coming," I confess, caught in a state between failure and victory.

Gripping tighter, I pump and thrust, fuck, and kiss her shoulder as if she's the balm to heal this aching thunder ripping through me. My body betrays me. Not able to hold on any longer, I clamp down on the same shoulder I just left kisses, groan, and then give in to instinct.

An earthquake shakes her core and sends tremors through her body. She embraces my dick as much as my outside. My name rattles from her tongue in a chant of rhythm and cause.

The sound of her embeds in my memories.

It's easy to lose myself in her darkness, her moans, the heat of her passion, and the sanctuary of her song. Her beauty and the downfall of what comes next. That's not something I've ever concerned myself with prior. With her, I can't rest knowing the end is part of our beginning.

As our bodies sag in the aftermath, our breathing yet to catch up. I kiss just behind her ear, and then carry her to the bed. Setting her down, she falls back as if she's too weak to move. "Want to stay?"

"I can for a little while."

Thumbing toward the bathroom, I add, "I'll be right back unless you want to go first."

"No. You go." A giggle bubbles. "I don't think I could stand up if I wanted to."

"Guess you're stuck with me."

She turns her head as if something more meaningful was said. A graceful smile full of sincerity breaks her free. "There are worse places to be."

"Yeah." It's tempting to linger, but I don't. I go to the bathroom.

When I walk back out, she startles, whipping around at the dresser. Her hands grip the wood and guilt covers her face. "You robbing me?" I tease, keeping a straight face while I climb under the covers. I can't stop from grinning, though. Anchoring my hands under my head, I watch as her shoulders ease, and she laughs.

"I don't need the money."

"What do you need, Liv?"

That beautiful smile returns. "Nothing more than you've already given me."

My eyes are drawn to the dresser behind her when she sets a pen down on the surface. "It's been a good night." Before she crosses the room, she adds, "It has."

"Are you leaving me your number?" I wish I were still joking but hope infiltrates my voice.

Light on her feet and giving me a flash of her ass as she spins into the en suite bathroom, laughter trickles through the air. Holding the side of the door, she replies, "Thank you, Noah."

I never know what to say when women thank me for fucking them. It's not like I didn't get something from it. I shoot her a wink. "Trust me, the pleasure was mine."

"If I've learned one thing in life, it's that I don't trust anyone who tells me to trust them."

"Wise woman." I chuckle. "Because I'm a fucking cad."

She bursts out laughing. "So what you're saying is I shouldn't trust you at all?"

"Probably best."

As the lightness of the conversation fades, so does her smile. Our eyes remain locked on each other as she worries her bottom lip.

I prefer the fun over the heaviness drifting between us, but I don't fill the silence lingering in the air. Instead, I give her my best smile. "Don't be long, okay?"

Liv nods before looking down and pulls the door to close it, but she stops and glances back at me. Questions populate the distance, but words aren't exchanged. I'm not sure what I'd say anyway. The reality is we agreed when morning comes, she'll go her way and I'll go mine. But what if the rules are worth breaking this time?

"NOAH, GET UP!"

I bolt upright in bed, my heart pounding in my chest. My eyes are blurry and burning from the lack of sleep, so I clamp them closed again. Peeking open one and then the other, I realize the daylight floods the room, though the French doors to the balcony make it worse.

"Noah." The voice rings in my ears, and before I have a chance to make out the woman scurrying around the bedroom, I already know who it is. And it's not Liv.

Shit.

Blinking rapidly, I move to cover her, but I fall flat on my face. My vision clears, but I don't need to see to know she's already long gone. *Fuck.*

Here I am, the idiot who thought we had a good time.

Things were looking good before I fell asleep waiting for her to come out of the bathroom. Guess I'm the fool now.

As the realization sets in that I have nothing other than

her first name, I grow irritated. "What are you doing here, Marina?"

My sister drags her arm across the top of the chest, dumping the stuff littering the surface into my duffel bag.

"Mom and Dad aren't even thirty minutes behind me. Get up. They'll kill you if they find out you're using the Hamptons house as your sex lair."

Dropping to my back, I roll my eyes before draping my arm over them. "I'm not in the mood for jokes."

"What part of Mom and Dad finding you here basking in your post-coital—*ew*." She shivers, scrunching her face. "I don't even want to think about my brother doing those things." She dumps my bag at the door, and says, "You have ten minutes to make a clean getaway, Noah. Go."

I drop my arm to the bed beside me and sit up. "You're not joking, are you?"

"Nope."

"You do know that I'm an adult, right? I'm fairly certain our parents know that, too."

"Yep." She shrugs, taking the doorknob in hand. "If you're okay explaining why this place smells of bad moves and booze, then stay. It will only add to my entertainment since I'm stuck hanging out with them for the next three days."

"Could be worse."

"How?"

"You could have just been woken up by your sister only to find that your . . ." What is Liv to me? A hookup, one-night stand, date, friend, or overnight guest? "Friend disappeared sometime during the night."

Her smile softens, the corners of her eyes lowering. "Sorry, can't win them all, big brother."

Why'd I tell her? Why do I care? Liv and I said no strings

attached. That's what we got. Although we made the agreement last night, I just wish it didn't make me feel like shit this morning.

I sit up again. "Don't be too concerned for me. It was just sex." I lie to her *and myself*. Plastering on a fake smile, I add, "Now scram so I can get dressed."

Apparently, I narrowly miss my parents' arrival. Marina said she put on a good show to cover for the mess I left because she's awesome and now I owe her two hundred bucks.

I don't mind paying for her silence in this situation. I just wish I could pretend last night never happened. I mistakenly thought there was something more between us or could be. I was wrong.

She stuck to the agreement.

That leaves me no other option but to move on like it never even happened.

End of story.

1

Noah

Now

Two Years Later . . .

I make this look easy.

A job offer on the table two months before graduation.

A sweet package with a six-figure salary and stacked bonuses based on performance.

A three-bedroom apartment with a view in Midtown Manhattan.

Yep. At twenty-five, I'm living the dream.

I was called the golden child my whole life. *I don't see the lie.*

Straightening my tie, I step off the elevator.

"You're late." That's not the greeting I expected, but it's the one I get the moment I enter the lobby.

Bancroft & Lowe, a pillar—*literally*—in the New York City skyline, occupies the entire forty-sixth floor. The gold lettering greeting guests and employees alike gleams under the spray of light from the recessed lighting. It's a not-so-subtle reminder of their golden reputation and, for me, not to fuck up this opportunity.

I chose my best suit—tailor-made, silk tie, Italian leather shoes. I felt like a million bucks until my plan got punctured by the accusation. Checking my watch, I'm five minutes early.

So the woman impatiently tapping her heel as if I'm keeping her from something more important doesn't sit well with me. Jet-black hair with a purple streak matches the purple collar of her fitted black dress. Pushing boundaries within the confines of corporate America? I'll give her props for individuality.

A smile eases from her tightened lips despite the stern welcoming, and after tugging the waistband of her skirt, taking in a few deep breaths before releasing, she says, "We should start walking." She grabs the door beside her desk and pulls it open. "Welcome to Bancroft & Lowe." Holding her hands out like a game show presenter, she has a quick pace despite the rushed tour of the facilities. "The top marketing firm in the city, winning three . . ." Her words fade as I realize I've really made it.

I accomplished my career goals on the first day of work. I got the job that my magna cum laude grad school degree earned me. I didn't nail an interview because I never had one. I was recruited to the big leagues, skipping the minors altogether.

The higher pitch of her tone squeaks back into my head. "And that's how we ended up baking bread in the oven on the roof."

How long was I gone? "Baking bread?"

She laughs. "I knew you weren't listening. It's all in the handbook, but I'm sure you've already studied everything you need to know about the company, considering you're the first person they've hired straight out of college. They usually only hire seasoned pros into the marketing positions."

"Graduate school," I correct, kindly, of course. "And technically, Olivia Bancroft was the first person the company hired straight from university."

"I knew you'd know the basics, but does the boss's daughter really count?" She snaps her mouth closed. "Talking about the Ice Queen will land me in trouble. Keep that comment between us. Okay? I'm not looking to get fired, so I shouldn't have said anything. Just consider it a warning." This woman doesn't appear much older than me, but she's far more comfortable than I'd be gossiping about the boss's daughter to a total stranger.

This does make me curious about how the Ice Queen got her name, but I sense some bad blood with this woman, so I'm not asking questions. "You're safe with me."

She grins, and it's not the first time I've seen a flash like that in a woman's eyes, the dilation of their pupils as they take in the sight of me. Women flirt with me all the time. My mom and sister call it the "Noah Effect."

An extra button has already popped open since my arrival, and she suddenly appears to have all the time in the world for me. I have no intention of having sex with anyone at the office. Those kinds of entanglements can ruin a career, and I'm just launching mine.

She stops just outside a conference room with a plaque engraved with CR 1. "The meeting has already started, Mr. Westcott." She briefly glances back. "As I said, you're late.

Make a quick apology and then agree with whatever they're saying. That's how I get by, and it works every time."

I could let the slight regarding tardiness go, but since she's said it twice, I feel the need to defend myself. "I was told nine o'clock."

"I know," she replies, tapping her watch. Giving me half her attention, she adds, "They like to test the new hires."

"Great." I sigh under my breath. I've already blown it.

"Nine oh three." I'm hit with a devious glint in her eyes. "Good luck."

A wall obscures the contents of the room, so I ask, "Why do I need luck?"

"With that attitude, you're going to need all the luck you can get. This isn't the small pond of fishies you're used to swimming with at Beacon University." A click of her tongue escorts her eyebrow shooting up. "This is the ocean. You're swimming with sharks now." She opens the door without so much as a warning, and announces, "Noah Westcott." With a quick whip of her head toward the door, she adds, "Start swimming."

As if she's been glued to the wood of the door, I dip my head in to see a room full of eyes staring at me and not a smile in the crowd. *Shit.*

The sharks are ready to eat.

I force my feet forward, throwing my hand up to the side of me like I'm the new guy, basically like an idiot, and wave. "Hello."

I'm met with silence.

She's right. This is not the same pond I'm used to ruling.

"Mr. Westcott." A voice pulls my eyes to the far side of the room. Lawrence Bancroft, graying around the temples and sporting less hair than his online photos, stands with a friendly grin. "Welcome aboard."

"Thank you, I'm happy—" I reply to the only familiar face I spy in the room after a quick scan until my eyes land on *her*.

My heart lurches to a stop and drops to the pit of my stomach. My hands sweat, and despite my usual knack of keeping my cool around women, my breath chokes in my chest. When my throat dries from the sight of her, only one word slips out. "Liv."

"Ah! You know my daughter, Olivia?"

Olivia.

Olivia.

Liv ...

Liv is Olivia Bancroft.

Fuck.

His words spin around my head not making sense as I watch her chest fill with a jagged breath as her hands fist the edge of her jacket. She squeezes her eyelids closed, but then a burst of energy shoots through, and she bolts upright ... next to her father. "Why don't we let everyone get back to work?" Her eyes are trained on her father as if she's afraid to look away.

Daughter. Father ... *Bancroft.*

Fuck. Fuck. Fuck.

He turns back to the filled room and claps his hands. "Remember. Give them hell out there. Now get to work."

Not exactly the warm and fuzzy, go get 'em team speech, but I guess everyone has their own form of motivation. I can't dwell on what makes him tick. I just need a minute to process this situation, to process that I'm staring at a woman who I've not only seen naked but also fucked like there was no tomorrow.

There wasn't supposed to be. We made an agreement

that night, and even when I slipped a little possibility into the equation, she stuck to the deal.

Fuck that.

I wasted not just minutes but hours and days over the past couple of years thinking about what I could have done differently to make her stay. Or why she snuck out in the first place.

I was a fool to believe that night was special.

Fuck special just like she fucked me over. I gather my wits about me, remembering how that one encounter fucked with my brain chemistry. I traveled through the stages of grief in record speed until I landed in anger. That stage served me well for a while. Fucking became a mission. I fucked with abandon. It didn't matter. *Not at that time.*

I should probably apologize to a few of the girls I dated back then, but they were calculated in my downfall since they were having their own needs met. Yeah, there were no complaints. I was used in other ways. Being on the arm of a Westcott was enough in our small town of Beacon to gain recognition. And they reveled in that attention.

Maybe I'm still lingering in that stage because I'm fucking furious right now. Unfortunately, I'm a new hire standing in front of his boss. He repeats, "So you already know Olivia?"

I compose myself, straightening my jacket and turning to her. Staring right into those eyes of hers, I reply. "No, I don't know her at all."

"You called her Liv, so I assumed—"

Returning my attention to him, I grin my award winner. "Only from the company website. I wanted to learn everything I could about the company smart enough to hire me."

He chuckles. "I like you already, Westcott." With his hand on her back, he says, "This is the guy I was telling you about. Whip smart, a real coup in acquisitions for Bancroft & Lowe."

Liv . . . *Olivia* clears her throat and raises her chin as soon as her hand shoots out. "It's . . ." She steals a quick breath but then her shoulders sag on the exhale as if she's lost the energy for this charade. Tell me about it . . . She finally continues. "I'm not sure where to start." She glances at her father first before turning to me, and adding, "My father is happy to have you joining the company."

Nice workaround.

And I solidly catch the drift regarding her feelings of seeing me again.

Same boat, sweetheart.

The difference is, I'm here to shine. Seeing her again won't break my stride straight to the top. "I appreciate that, *Olivia*."

I clasp her hand in mine. The electricity conjured the night we met shoots straight through me, along with memories better left out of the office. That night with her was nothing more than another one-night stand. I'd be better off if I remember that instead. I drop her hand and shove mine into my pocket.

As if forgetting that night ever existed would be that easy when I find myself staring at her, the white top she's wearing reminiscent of the lace covering those perfect tits I couldn't wait to unwrap. Her hair is pulled back into a sleek twist at the base of her head, but I remember how it waterfalled through my fingers. Her eyes, those hazel eyes that have haunted me for years, widen for a split second before she averts them out the large windows to the passing cloud momentarily darkening the conference room.

Out of all the companies in Manhattan, I'm hired into

this one. Olivia Bancroft. *What the fuck?* How is this even possible?

I anchor my eyes on her father, not daring to give her the pleasure of my attention again, and clap my hands together. "Let's get started."

He laughs. "I like the eagerness, but I'm sure HR will have some paperwork for you to sign." He turns to his daughter. "The sooner we can get you settled in, the sooner we can start this new chapter."

"New chapter?" I ask, intent on proving my value to the company.

"We've restructured. Times are changing, and we need to change with it. Fresh blood means fresh ideas. I look forward to hearing yours." He walks toward the door. "Olivia will show you to your office."

"I have a call," she says so casually that I question if I was imagining her reacting the same as me. Nothing about her demeanor now holds an ounce of care for my presence. She's not tense or rude. She's calm and collected as she heads for the door like her father. Just before she rounds the corner, she smirks. "I'm sure he'll have no problem finding the door with his name on it."

"Jennifer?" He calls into the hall. I make my way toward the exit just as he turns to me to add, "Mr. Lowe is in Chicago. You'll meet him when he returns in a few days. Jennifer?"

Late thirties, early forties, put together with her hair in a low ponytail at the base of her head, a maroon suit and black shirt with sensible black heels, Jennifer bounces her eyes from me to him upon arrival. "Yes, Mr. Bancroft?"

"Show Mr. Westcott to HR."

Yes, sir."

He leaves without another word. Sympathy coats her expression when we're left alone. "He's a bit impatient."

"I gathered."

She starts to walk. "HR is up here on the left." I follow her but stop at the corner when the space opens to killer views of the city on one side and a row of desks with a slew of assistants staring at monitors on the other. I just catch Bancroft entering his office and closing the door down the corridor from where we're standing.

Jennifer says, "You've made quite the impression on him."

"Have I?"

We cut through the large, sunlit room full of cubicles. "He doesn't spend time with people he doesn't see potential in, so take it as a compliment that he remained standing there, especially after the recent turnover."

"What happened?"

"Spies. Two of our employees were working for the competition. They stole some clients with intel they acquired while here." She stops and turns on her short heels. "We all have trust issues now."

"They didn't have NDAs in place?"

"I assume the money was worth the risk." She shrugs before opening a door at the far end of the cubicles. "Here we are. Human Resources."

"Thanks."

After spending the next hour filling out more paper-work, I'm shown to my office. "Hope this will do," the HR rep says before rushing back to his office.

"Thank you," I reply before opening the door. Greeted by a view that definitely doesn't feel legal to give a kid right out of grad school, I cross my arms and grin. This will most definitely do.

As soon as I walk in, I'm struck with glaring hazel eyes and pursed red lips. She sits forward in *my* chair, resting her elbows on *my* desk. "Did you really think you'd waltz into this company like nothing happened between us?"

"I didn't waltz, sweetheart. I was recruited. Let me break that down for you. That means—"

"I know what it means." She stands, her fingertips whitening from the pressure against the desktop. "I don't need you to explain anything to me." Coming around, she adds, "Here's what's going to happen. Tomorrow, you're going to quit."

"Quit?" I struggle to keep my eyes from bugging out. She won't get the best of me . . . like she once did. I approach the desk, and volley right back, "You've got a lot of nerve to tell me how this is going to play out."

"It took more than nerves to make it to where I am in this company." She comes around and pats me on the chest. "*Sweetheart.*"

I catch her hand before it slides away. She double steps back, which brings us face-to-face. "I'm not quitting to make you more comfortable. If you remember—"

"Oh, I remember." She holds my gaze with her glare. "I remember everything despite spending two years trying to forget that night altogether."

Forget that night? Why the fuck does she even care when she was the one who walked away? "So let me get this straight. You sneak out in the middle of the night, but somehow, I'm the bad guy? That's rich, *Olivia.*"

Her eyes dip to the bond between us before she yanks her hand away. She also makes sure to get a last dig in by poking me in the chest. "Say my name while you can, but make sure it's on the way out the door." Her fake smile falls as fast as her face did when she saw me in the conference room.

How the fuck did this turn into a war in the office?

No warm welcome, but a chill in the air permeating off her icy exterior. It's irritating that I'm still stuck on the details of her when she's well over me.

I shouldn't be, but there's no denying how attractive she is with her heart-shaped face and lips that swell from kisses and run the coloring from pink to softer red. Hazel eyes that could set the world on fire with one pointed look at the delicate line of her nose to counteract her fury.

Fucking hell. I'm as drawn to her as I was that night.

Taking my time to enjoy every inch of her again, I lower my gaze to a tailored white shirt squeezing the same tits I once did, a black leather belt wrapping around her waist that I held on to, and not a hair out of place, making me want to see the ends blowing in the wind again. Besides black lashes, her makeup is subtle against a summer tan, except for the eye-catching apple-red lips.

Fuck me.

I haven't been able to get her off my mind since we met, so it would be easy to let my imagination run wild through the memories of her naked body, but it seems she's an enemy in the flesh instead.

"We've slept together, so you know as well as I do that this could never work." She takes the knob in hand, but the door stays closed as she examines my face. "We shouldn't ruin our professional lives, careers that we're both still trying to build."

"How does that night affect our present-day circumstances? It doesn't. I'll happily admit that it was a good night I enjoyed very much. Judging by how many times you screamed my name, it's safe to say you did as well. So why are you so bothered now? You afraid you can't keep your hands to yourself, Liv?"

Her confidence has been infuriating, but now she falters under a joke of a question. Her gaze drops to her feet as she tugs her lower lip under her teeth. For a moment, I can still see her leaning against the door to the balcony, moonlight highlighting her beauty for me to study.

"I'm not sure what you think you're doing here, Noah, but I suggest you do it elsewhere."

"You act like I'm here to ruin your career. It's not about you at all." Whether she's Liv, a one-night stand, or Olivia, the boss's daughter, doesn't affect the course of my life, so I add, "So do whatever helps you get over this because I'm not going anywhere."

Tugging the door open, she narrows her eyes over pursed lips. Still so fucking beautiful it's become frustratingly annoying. Her gaze swings away from me, and I catch the minutest of nods before she takes a step forward, pauses, and then leaves.

At least she has the courtesy to shut the door behind her.

Fuck.

2

Olivia Bancroft

NOAH WESTCOTT CHANGED the course of my life forever.

I rush to my office, carefully closing the door behind me as if I could act normal under these circumstances. Scrambling to grab my phone from my purse in the drawer, I push the number in my contacts.

"Mom?" I say before she has a chance to greet me.

"What's wrong?" Panic shreds her tone.

"I didn't mean to alarm you." I try to calm the shake to my voice before I worry her more than needed. What kind of concern is required in this situation because this feels like a four-alarm fire. *Steady, Liv.* "He's here."

"Who's here?"

"Him."

Silence begins to stretch before she asks, "What do you mean him? Maxwell is napping right now." My heart clenches. *Maxwell.* My sweet boy.

Shaking my head, I can feel my hands doing the same. "No, not Maxwell. Noah."

"Honey, who's Noah?"

I hold the phone tight in my hand and walk to the window to pace in some feeble attempt to calm myself. "No-*ah*, Mom."

"You can say it as slow as you want, but I still don't know who you're talking—" She doesn't have to finish that sentence for me to know that she's realized exactly who I'm talking about. I hear her breath on a slow exhale before she asks, "How? Why? Did you know?"

I'm still shaking my head in disbelief. I finally take a deep breath and stop, staring at the Financial District's skyline. Lowering my voice, I reply, "He's the new accounts rep. Dad hired him, recruited actually." I can't stop annoyance from coating my tongue. It's not fair that I feel betrayed. I know my father had no idea who he was hiring, but that one decision has major consequences for my life.

"I don't know what to say, Olivia."

"Me either." When my knees buckle, I sink into my desk chair and drop my head into my hand. With the phone still pressed to my ear, I whisper, "I can't lose him."

"You won't. I promise."

"He's . . ." Tears fill my eyes, but I tilt my head back, hoping they won't fall. "He's my whole world, Mom."

"I know. I know, honey. Don't do anything rash. We'll figure this out when you get home."

"And by rash, you mean try to convince him to quit on his first day of work? If that's rash, it's too late."

"You've spoken?"

"I panicked. It's all I could think to do."

"Okay." She sighs and pauses. I don't have to see her to know she's pacing like I was seconds ago. Much like me, I'm sure my mom has all the scenarios playing out in her head. I wonder if any of hers come with a happier ending than I'm envisioning. "Until we can make a plan, you need to avoid him. Do you understand?"

"Should I call my lawyer?"

"No. Let's not escalate the situation before we know what we're dealing with."

"And who we're dealing with." I nod again, knowing I have at least one ally, my mom, in my corner. Relief doesn't wash over me, but it does trickle through me. "You're right. We'll get a plan together before I need to tell him that he has a son."

"Olivia?"

"Yes?"

"It's going to be okay."

I know she can't see me nodding, but those damn tears roll down my cheeks from the reassurance my mom has always given me. I'm lucky to have her.

She says, "I'll see you tonight."

"Love you."

"I love you, too, honey."

A rap on my door startles me before I have a chance to hang up. "One moment," I call out just as I hit the end button.

I'm wiping my tears away when the door opens. "Hey, Liv—"

Dammit. I spin around, hiding my face from Noah. I refuse to give him the pleasure of seeing me upset. "Don't walk into my office without permission."

"I thought you said to come in."

"I didn't. I said one moment."

"Are you okay?" I hate how nice he sounds, like he actually cares about me.

After a quick double swipe across my cheeks, I spin back, holding my chin up. "I'm fine. What do you need?"

"Need?" The word sparks something in his eyes—an idea, a rogue thought, or maybe it's revenge he seeks. He looks like the type with his great-fitting suit and smirk that sends butterflies scattering in my stomach. The only thing I can't force myself to be mad about is the color of his eyes. They're so close to the ones I love that I'll never tire of staring into the wealth of colors that make up my son's.

He says, "I don't need anything."

"Are you here to tell me you're quitting?"

"Now, why would I do that?"

I shrug. "Figured you want to do what's best for the company."

"Best for the company?" He bursts out laughing. "Look, Liv—"

"It's Olivia."

"Olivia. *Oliv-vi-a.*" He rolls my name around on his tongue like he's tasting it for the first time. "Look, Olivia, I'm not sure why you want me gone, but we need to talk about what's really going on here."

"What's really going on is that you invited yourself into my world without even so much as a hello—"

"Interesting requirement since you struggle with goodbyes."

I laugh just to mimic, to stay on even footing, though there's no humor or believability in it. Not even to me. I'm the worst faker, even if it would serve me better after having the rug pulled out from under me.

"Hello." His voice is calm, too comfortable for someone who shouldn't feel that at home here, much less act like he has the upper hand. But moreover, why does he have to look so handsome in his arrogance?

It takes me a second, but then I realize what he's doing. *He's toying with me.*

I can't even look at him without anger taking over. Walking to the window, I tighten my hands to my arms because if I don't, I'll be fisting them again, and I refuse to show him that weakness. "Look, Noah . . ." I start, sounding calmer at least. Keeping my eyes set on the avenue below, I shift, lowering my arms just before turning to face him. "This may be a joke to you, but it's my life, my career, and my reputation that will be ruined in an instant if—"

"If word gets out that we slept together? Is that what you think I'd do?" He stands on the other side of my desk, an ease in my presence taking over his hard body. "You think I'd tell everyone about our night in the Hamptons, gossip about that night just to win them over as if this is a competition and only one of us survives?"

"I don't know what you'd do because I don't know you. Sleeping with you—"

"We didn't sleep together." His voice is firm, the edges of his patience tested in the reply. "I fell asleep waiting for you, so you don't have to dance around the act of sex to make it more palatable. Just call it what it was."

"What was it?"

"Fucking." His eyes leave mine as his temper flares—the tic of his jaw, the hard lines of his shoulders returning when he stands.

"I can't argue with that, but I need it to stay in the past forever." I sit back down and pull myself forward. Clasping my hands together on the desk, I say, "I've worked hard to get where I am. It's not been easy. In fact, the hoops I had to jump through to prove my value to this company and to my own father would have deterred most people. But I jumped. So if anyone finds out, it will set me back again and—"

Staring at me, not a blink shared between us, he sets his

phone down and presses his palms to my desk, lowering himself until he's eye level with me. "I won't tell anyone."

"Thank you."

He straightens his back and pulls at the front of his suit jacket. "But you need to work through whatever has you so hell-bent on me leaving this company because I'm not quitting, Olivia." I shoot daggers when he turns his back to me. Opening the door, he adds, "You'll have to excuse me. I have a meeting."

When he walks out, he closes the door behind him.

I suck in a harsh breath, not realizing I had stopped breathing when he was so close. I want to hate him . . . so much. But the best I can muster is hating him for turning my world upside down twice. Though I can't hate the outcome.

Feeling a smile cross my face, I turn back to look out the window again. My gaze travels the three blocks, and my smile grows, my chest feeling lighter as joy fills me with images of my son. "It will be okay, Liv." I jump, my smile wiped away before I could find comfort. Noah adds, "I forgot my phone."

Our eyes go to the desk between us. He slips the phone from the surface and tucks it in his pocket. He says, "We don't have to be enemies."

Enemies? Is that what I'm making him?

I just worry about the damage he could do If I even open the door an inch to let him in. Until I know the man behind the smirk, the sexy swagger, and who he is on the inside, Noah Westcott is the key to my demise.

Moving to the door, he looks back over his shoulder at me. I ask, "Is there any other option?"

His chest fills, and his shoulders rise before he exhales slowly. He doesn't bother hiding the disappointment. I'd know that look anywhere. I'm used to it from my father. Noah's eyes leave mine, and he walks out the door again without another word shared between us.

I'd say that's calculated on his part, but a feeling in my gut has me believing it was a genuine reaction. How did Noah manage to turn this around so I'm feeling sorry for him?

Don't second-guess yourself, Liv. I can't take the risk. I won't lower my guard to make him feel better. Most importantly, I refuse to leave my son's future to chance with a man I once barely connected with.

"DEFINE RASH FOR ME AGAIN?" Frustration rolls through me as I push my apartment door closed behind me and set my purse down on the bench in the entry. I kick off my shoes and continue down the hall.

"Oh no," echoes down the hall, my mom's voice reaching me before I see them. As soon as I enter the living room, my mom looks up from the floor. With her perfectly coiffed brown bob and light touch makeup, my mom is always put together and tasteful. Wearing ankle-length pants in navy and a shock of pink sweater, she puts me to shame when I'm home with Maxwell. "What happened?"

My gaze pivots to my baby, who squeals in delight when he sees me. Best welcome home ever. While I wash my hands, he balances vicariously while holding the edge of the couch. "Look at you." He's pure happiness for my soul. "Who's my big boy?" I ask, drying my hands quickly so I can hug my little munchkin.

I slip off my jacket, draping it over the back of the couch as I rush around, making sure not to disrupt the balance he looks so proud of accomplishing. Sitting on the couch, I bend to lift him in my arms and smother his chubby cheeks in kisses before embracing him. I close my eyes, soaking in his goodness and reveling in his baby smell and the way his fingers twist in my hair . . . just before he tugs.

When I pull back, his toothy grin is on full display and his eyes are bright just looking at me. "Everyone should be this lucky," I say, planting another kiss on him.

"He does give great greetings."

"He sure does." His smile fills every gray day with pure sunshine. "Has he eaten?"

She reaches over and tickles his belly. "He's eaten, we went for a walk around the apartment, and I suspect he'll want some playtime before bed." Getting to her feet, Mom kisses my head. "Tell me what happened at work."

Maxwell loves to bounce on the couch cushions, and it keeps him busy while we talk. "Noah Westcott is just so infuriating, Mom."

"Most men are, honey." She laughs, but I'm not sure she's joking. She and my dad have been divorced for more than five years, but she seems content not dating. She could and gets out regularly if she's not stretching the truth. I believe her. She's a former beauty queen and was modeling when she met my dad. She's also been mistaken as my baby's mother. I'd like to think someone was flattering her and that we don't look the same age, but she does look amazing and her zest for life keeps her youthful.

My dad is the opposite. You'd think he was twenty years older than his age. She kept him younger.

She comes to sit next to me, taking hold of Maxwell from behind to keep him bouncing and laughing and giving my arms a much-needed reprieve from the workout. Leaning to the side, she looks at me. "Did you say Westcott?"

"Yeah, that's his last name." I rest back, tapping on his toes which elicits a joyous laugh. "Why?"

"There aren't many Westcotts around, but I know a family. They're from Beacon, but they have a home here. Delta Westcott works with a lot of charitable organizations. Lovely woman."

Maxwell flops on his butt, so I lean over him and blow raspberries on his belly. Looking up, I say, "I'm sure that's just a coincidence. That last name doesn't seem that unique."

"I'm sure it's not."

Setting him back on his play mat on the floor, I sit beside him but turn to my mom. "Doesn't seem like he's willing to quit, even when I laid out the facts."

"The facts being?"

"How his presence affects me professionally." I shrug as if I'm justifying it to myself. "We have a past, a brief history—"

"A baby together."

My heart stops, an ache replacing the beats that existed prior in my chest. I look at my baby with worry taking over again. A dry throat causes me to clear it, but it doesn't seem to help. "I need water." I get up and move into the kitchen. I can feel my mom's eyes on me, so I huff. "Just say it, Mom."

Resting her arm on the back of the couch, she asks, "Are you going to tell him?"

I pull the pitcher from the fridge but stand at the counter with my thoughts consumed by this fated question. "If it's the right thing to do, which I assume it is . . ." I sprinkle in some sarcasm and an eye roll to keep myself from tearing up again.

"You know it's the right thing to do."

"I know." I reach for a glass and fill it with water. "But if it's right, why does it feel so wrong?"

"Because you don't know him. We don't know what he's capable of or if he even wants a child."

"My fear is the opposite. That he'll take him away from me." I drink the water like it'll be ripped away from me if I don't. The cool liquid soothes the panic racing through my veins.

"You'll fight. You'll win. You've been his only parent and have done an amazing job. But now that you know who the father is—"

"I knew who the father was, Mom. I hadn't slept with anyone else in a year."

"I meant, you didn't know his last name or how to find him." She stands and comes around the couch. "You did everything you could to find him, to tell him." She takes my hand between both of hers. "You did everything to give Maxwell a father figure. When that didn't pan out, you went through it alone. He's an amazing baby, Olivia. Don't let the presence of this Noah shake you. If you need to fight, you're not alone. But what if you don't?"

"What if he wants to co-parent? How can I let him walk out of here with my baby?"

"If he wants to co-parent and put in the work to earn the title of parent and dad, Maxwell wins."

I refill the glass and take another sip. Eyeing Maxwell again, I nod. "You're right. It's about him and what's best for his life." I return to the baby and pick him up. Anchoring him on my hip, I walk to the hall, where my mom slips on her shoes and her purse. "I don't have to rush into it, right? I think I need to see how he is, who he is, and judge from there the best method to handle the situation."

"I think that's fair." She brushes Maxwell's front curl to

the side. Her eyes return to mine, and she smiles. "But I have a feeling he's not as horrible as you're hoping he is. Don't build a case against him too fast. You found him charming enough to woo you into bed—"

"Okay. Okay. That's enough. I don't need to talk about that night with my mom. Thanks for watching Maxwell today."

She starts to laugh. "My pleasure. Cassandra said she got her appointments taken care of and will be back in the morning."

My nanny is amazing, but I'm so fortunate to have my mom in my corner.

She kisses the baby and then adds, "He also must be very attractive, considering how handsome my grandson is."

"Mom," I whine, embarrassed about discussing this with her. At twenty-seven years old, I shouldn't be, but it just hits some raw nerves. She's still getting a good laugh in when she walks out the door. Just before closing it, I add, "He was and still is."

She turns around and stops, smiling like she's watching me perform my first ballet. Blowing me a kiss, she says, "I love you. I love you both."

"I love you." Turning to Maxwell, I take his hand and touch his mouth to blow her a kiss. "Say love you, Mimi."

"Mimi." Like my mom is of me, I couldn't be prouder of him.

We spend time together before I get him bathed and to bed. He's fast asleep, blessing me with an easy night. I'm exhausted and starving. I find a bowl in the fridge with chicken salad full to the brim. My mom's the best.

I settle in on the couch, turn on the TV for some background noise, and think about the day behind me. Noah is attractive, annoyingly so. But more than his looks, the unknown that he's brought into my life has me concerned.

I know I need to tell him about Maxwell, but the complications surrounding the issue are immense. He also brings out my insecurities. I'm alone. Could that hurt my case?

Who knows?

Maxwell deserves a father who's present, though. Someone who wants him, will love him, and will always do what's best for him. Is that Noah Westcott? I sure hope so because he's about to find out he's a father.

3

Olivia

THE JUDGMENT I've felt in the office on occasion and the dirty looks stabbing me in the back as I pass hit twice as hard today. As if it wasn't hard enough dealing with the jealousy of some perceived "easy ride" to middle management, on top of the bitterness I've tasted when I've overheard employees talking badly about me in the break room, or whatever it is that has others hating me so much, now I also have to contend with Noah Westcott.

The other stuff pales in comparison, so I hold my head up and keep walking.

I can't help but glance across the office and the rows of cubicles to Noah's closed door. I hate that disappointment saturates my better judgment. I need to keep in mind that getting to know him for the sake of Maxwell is not the same thing as getting to know him for the sake of professionalism, or even on a personal level. *Personal level?* What am I thinking? There doesn't need to be anything personal with that man.

I drop my bag off in my office and head right back out. I'm on a mission this morning and ready to tackle all the obstacles in my life. Rounding the corner, I head straight for my father's office. When I approach his assistant's desk, I ask, "Hi, Jennifer, is Mr. Bancroft available?"

Her expression falls. "You just missed him."

"Missed him?" I check the time on the gold watch he gave me for my high school graduation. "It's seven fifty-three in the morning."

Taking her glasses off, she stabs the arms into her hair that hangs loose today. I've always liked Jennifer. She has never treated me as spoiled or undeserving, and smiles when she sees me. Beats the scowls I'm sometimes on the receiving end of.

"It was an early start for him, but he had a breakfast meeting schedule this morning."

"With whom?" I glance down the hall when I see other employees arriving.

"Mr. Lowe, Mr. Lowe, and Mr. Westcott."

I tweak my neck from turning back so fast. Mr. Westcott . . . I try to contain my huff, but I see Jennifer laugh under her breath. "Yeah, with the Lowes back in the city and Mr. Westcott jumping right into the deep end, is it me, or does it feel a little—"

"Cutthroat? No," I say, staring out the window behind her as rage burns inside. "Not just you."

"I was going to say energized." A slight shrug of her shoulder partners with the cringe on her face.

"Yes, that's what I meant." I know she doesn't believe me, but I haven't even had coffee yet. As my acting skills won't be convincing, I decide not to dig this hole any deeper and end the embarrassing misery. "Will you let him know I came by to see him?"

"Of course." When I turn to walk away, she adds, "I know what you mean about cutthroat, Olivia."

I stop and turn back. "Yeah?"

"You're doing a good job. I know he doesn't tell you, but sometimes he tells me."

"Yeah?" Coming closer, I stop in front of her desk again.

She nods with a reassuring smile. "His meeting at eleven thirty is Brooklyn." While she studies the monitor in front of her, she adds, "Then his next meeting is at three o'clock in conference room one to close negotiations on a new client."

"What about between his meetings? Can you schedule me in for a thirty-minute slot?"

Pulling her glasses from her head, she returns them to the bridge of her nose and starts typing. She looks up from the monitor, and says, "Not today. Actually, there's nothing all week."

"How about twenty minutes?"

"I don't even have a ten-minute opening I can book. He told me explicitly not to add anything to his schedule for the next two months."

"Then how did Mr. Westcott get a breakfast with him?"

"Mr. Bancroft called the meeting."

My hopes fall. I hate that I still feel . . . anything when it comes to him. I should be used to the disappointment, especially after the situation with Chip imploded. Yet somehow, I'm still never fully prepared. Empathy reaches her eyes, or maybe it's sadness, pity even, which doesn't make me feel especially good though I know that's not her intention. "I'm sorry."

"It's not your fault." Pretending to blow it off like it doesn't matter, I smile. "Busy is good. That's what he always taught." Jennifer's one of the few who has supported my return to the office. After a year away, although I was working remotely, I came back to a staff that had conjured its own narrative about my disappearance.

Horrible things weren't said only to my back. A few people made sure I overheard their nasty gossip. That's when I realized I'd never win over some people. Doesn't matter what I do or how nice I am. Those efforts will be wasted on them.

The decision to protect my personal life has left me fighting the misconceptions they've developed ever since.

Lik e any proud mom, I wish I could have a framed photo sitting on my desk, but I keep my office clear because they don't deserve to see the best part of my life.

My mom tells me to ignore it. My father seems oblivious to the noise.

I'm stuck somewhere in the middle, wondering if I'm ever going to win not only their approval but also my father's.

I can't stand around here any longer, not even to make polite small talk. As much as it would be nice to have a water cooler conversation with her, it's best if I keep my distance from everyone and focus on my job instead. "Work is calling. Have a good day."

I can ignore the gossip, but the wrench that's been thrown not only into my working day but also my life can't be ignored. I will protect the things that matter most at all costs. *Maxwell is worth it.* I was hoping to get more insight into my month and, if I'm lucky, Noah. Guess I'll have to do the dirty work myself and start digging.

Settling in at my desk, I call Cassandra to check in. "Hello," she answers.

"Hi, how are you? How's Maxwell? All okay?"

"We're great. I'm about to take him to his baby gym class, then I was thinking about a picnic in the park."

Although it shouldn't, my heart hurts. She's living the life I can only dream of experiencing—spending the day with my baby. That's not a possibility, though. I need to provide for him and that means working.

"That sounds really nice. Thank you, Cassandra."

"Gosh, it almost feels criminal being paid for this job. Maxwell's the best baby. We have such a great time together."

I grin with pride and love for him. "He is. Well, you know the drill. If you need anything, call or text."

"I will. Hope your day goes well," she says just before hanging up.

I stare at the screensaver that pops up on the screen when we disconnect. It's Maxwell and me on my birthday. Just the two of us and a small cake to share. "Enough distractions." I smile, then angle toward my monitor to get to work.

Since I already know I'll have an email from Chip because, apparently, he's back in New York, I check to see if I'm right. I can't believe he's been back, what? A night? And he's having breakfast with the company owners and Noah. Chip loves a surprise when it benefits him, like never telling us whether he'll show up to work.

And people have a problem with me? I'm here working my ass off while he's off gallivanting across the Baja Peninsula, it appears from his expenses. I don't know how he always manages to convince his dad and mine that not only should they pay for his extravagant lifestyle but that, somehow, he's an asset they need to keep on the payroll.

And people have the nerve to say my role in accounts and finances is owed to nepotism. *Go figure.*

Just thinking about my ex and the other three together doesn't sit well, but when I specifically think of Chip and

Noah possibly becoming friends, my stomach churns. *What if . . .* oh God, no. *Stop.* Don't even think about them chumming up and becoming buddies or comparing notes.

Focus on work, Liv.

The moment Jennifer said Chip was back, I knew I'd have an email. I click open, and yep, there it is. So predictable. I'll have to brace my eyes because I know I'll do extensive eye-rolling over the next two hours. He tries to get the company to pay for every expense—personal or work—so I already know it will take me time to work through exactly what we'll reimburse and what we won't.

Two hours are lost weeding through this unhinged email of requests. It's not just the nerve of some of the expenses he's trying to get paid back for. It's the winky face and the line in the email that says, "Take care of this, muffin," that makes my blood boil.

By two in the afternoon, I have a major headache from staring at the screen all day, picking apart the numbers of the marketing team and how much they're spending. I shoot my dad an email short and to the point, which is how he likes it:

WHEN CAN *you meet to go over the marketing expenses and budgets for the next quarter?*

OLIVIA

I NEVER HEARD FROM HIM, but laughter filled the corridor at one point in the day, penetrating my door for a few hours. The merry band of best buddies had returned, but Noah's voice had traveled as if to torture me. There wasn't a chance in hell I would let him get to me, so I hunkered deeper into the numbers until Chip's entire team had an outlook and budget in place.

Three o'clock rolls around before I realize that I've lost track of time and haven't eaten today. I wouldn't have remembered at all if it weren't for my growling stomach.

I scan the two kitchens on opposing sides of the floor before deciding that Cheetos and a soda might not be the best choice to tide me over until dinner. But if I hurry downstairs, I can order a salad or maybe get soup from the deli next door before it closes.

Naturally, the elevator is slower than molasses. When it finally arrives, I squeeze on. Bonus to being last to fit in is that I'm first off as soon as the doors open in the lobby. 3:27. *Dammit.* I'm wearing the wrong shoes for a jog today.

I rush past the guards toward the street and cross to the next block.

Tugging the door open, I hear, "Unless you want a pimento hoagie with jalapeños and extra pickles, we've already put everything away. The pimento is on the house, though." The guy behind the counter drops the sandwich on the glass display. It lands like a brick.

I rub my stomach as if it will ease the hunger pangs. Since I'm not interested in spending the rest of the day with heartburn or in the bathroom, I reply, "Thanks, but I'll pass."

"You can have my salad." I felt it the moment I walked in, but thought it was hunger. It is. Just of a different kind.

The voice . . .

The soothing dulcet tone.

Energy sparking in the air.

I gave in to a whim once. I won't fall for him twice.

4

Olivia

I LOOK BACK over my shoulder to find Noah sitting at a table by the window. "I didn't realize anyone else was in here." I turn, feeling trapped between him, the door, and a quick getaway.

"You didn't find me so easy to ignore before." There's no offense written in his expression, though that surprises me since all he does is offend me personally. But then he cocks a brow, and that just sends my blood pressure through the roof.

Crossing my arms over my chest, I reply, "Everything doesn't have to be an innuendo back to that night in the Hamptons."

He chuckles to himself, his gaze locked on me like I might escape. It's tempting. "When I said *before*, I meant yesterday at work." He rests his arms on the table, leaning forward. "Glad to know you remember more than you tried to forget. So do I."

"Pfft." I try to play it off, but my annoyance with him has my eyes rolling again. "Is this what we're going to do every time we see each other?"

"Travel down memory lane?" He gives me a wink.

Ugh. "Talk about a night I can't imagine you remember much more than I do. Was it whiskey or scotch you were drinking that night?"

"Whiskey." He sits back again, amusement bright in his eyes as he stares into mine. It's a look that got him laid the night we met. That bonfire flickering in his eyes set my soul on fire for a few hours. I won't tell him that, but I look away from him now. I'd hate to fall prey once again.

He pushes a plastic bowl toward me. "It's not much, but it's yours if you're hungry."

"That's okay. Thanks." I walk to the door, and my stomach, being the traitor it is, growls loud enough that the tourists on Liberty Island could probably hear. When I grab the handle, the bell chimes above my head.

"It's okay to break bread with the enemy," he says to my back.

I glance at the salad, then at him again. "That's legit not a rule of war. Breaking bread brings people together."

"It's a salad, Liv. Take it or leave it, but I'm not waving a white flag for you."

"Olivia," I correct with an edge to my tone. The sharpness comes easily these days. I've tried to temper it, but after the hellscape I've been navigating over the past few months, it's felt more permanent as of late.

"It's a salad, *Olivia*, not a surrender on your part either." He pushes it a few inches closer to me.

Is this the battle I want to fight? *No.*

I let the door close and move to the table. Standing, he

signals to the chair across from him. "Would you like to join me?"

"No, I wouldn't like that," I reply softer. The words fall off my dull-edged tongue because I'm less sure of myself. I should take the opportunity to get to know him, but I can't. *Not yet.* I'm still trying to figure out how I might tell this man about Maxwell, so having a meal with him feels like it's too soon without a plan. I still take the salad since he's offering it, and I'm starving. "Thank you."

"You're welcome."

I can't help but notice how handsome and relaxed he is in the diffused light from the window, the world passing by outside giving him a little privacy in the middle of the busy workday. "Seems you're settling right into the office and the neighborhood."

"It sounds like there's a question in there." He shifts, glancing at the deli guys busy cleaning the floors. "The office, yes. I was hungry, so I took a walk and found this place. It's a good pastrami, Antonio," he calls out.

Antonio lifts his head with a wide grin. "Best in town, Noah. Tell your friends."

"Will do." The smile on Noah's face reminds me of that night on the beach. That smile tempts me to sit down and eat the salad with him. *What can I say?* It's a really great smile.

And that would be my cue to go. Taking a step toward the door again, I thumb over my shoulder. "I have hours of work left to finish before the end of the day." I hold the container up. "Thanks again."

"You're welcome." He stands, crumpling the sandwich paper and holding his drink to take a sip. "I need to get back as well."

Flashes of the gossip that would be created populate my

brain. That's not a situation I want to be in—us walking in together would just stir the already swirling pot, making us the hot new topic. "See you later." I rush out the door, not sure why I even hung around in the first place. I must be delirious. Clearly, I need food to cure me.

I hear the door chime behind me but keep my gaze ahead while walking. Unfortunately, I'm caught at the crosswalk and start admonishing myself for lingering at the deli. I could have been long gone, but instead . . . I'm stuck next to him.

Do I make small talk? No. Don't even look at him. *Keep your eyes forward, Liv.*

"Hello again," Noah says from beside me.

"Hi," I reply, gazing at the crosswalk sign ahead.

I see him rock back on his heels in my periphery, and then he comments, "This game would be easier to play if I understood your rigid rules."

My mouth falls open before I snap, "My rigid rules? Uh, no. I'm not taking the fall in your mind or otherwise. Asking to keep things professional isn't being rigid."

"You told me to quit in the best interest of the company. You're playing a game, Ms. Bancroft. I'm just simply asking for the rules to get a fair chance—"

"To win?" I turn to him, and my head falls back from the epic eye roll he's caused. Leveling my gaze on him, I ask, "Is that all you care about, *Mr.* Westcott?"

"You have made assumption after assumption about me since we saw each other in the conference room. I have no idea why you seem to have it out for me, so I thought it only fair to at least know the rules by which we're playing."

"Is everything a lighthearted game to you?" I shake my head. "It's not to me." Shoving the salad against his chest, I say, "I'd rather go hungry."

The crosswalk changes from stop to go, so I go. There's no point having a conversation in the middle of Manhattan for the whole world to hear. Because if there's one thing I know, I'm not a fool for his Mr. Nice Guy act.

"You're embarrassed because we've slept together. I get it."

I turn back so fast that I wobble on a heel. "I'm not embarrassed."

"Then what is it?"

"You. You existing, Noah, here in my world."

A horn causes me to jump, stumbling into his arms. I look up into those eyes that are even better when in proximity, the feel of his strong arms holding me in safety—Oh God, no! *I don't think so.* Not today. *Not ever!*

My breathing slows as I push away, our gazes unlatching as I turn to move from the entrance to the alley to the sidewalk again. I head for the doors, having no interest in discussing this with him or talking about anything with him. The enemy, I remind myself. He's the man who can take Maxwell from me.

"You're mad at me for existing?" The door is pulled open as soon as I reach it. Ugh. He wouldn't be so quick on his feet if he had to wear heels like me.

I enter the lobby, walking and talking. "You're welcome to exist, but why must it be in my space?" I flash my badge at the guard and head to the bank of elevators.

"I didn't know you worked at Bancroft & Lowe. I also had no idea you were a Bancroft before showing up yesterday. How would I? First names only. No strings attached. Remember, Liv? That was the deal we made."

Stopping for what feels like the hundredth time in the span of three minutes, I turn to him again. I'm glad the lobby is practically empty. I wouldn't want witnesses.

"What did you mean when you said *you get it*? What do you get?"

"I get that you never expected to see me again." He's not wrong. He leans in, but he's smooth enough to keep it slight enough for no one else to notice. "But here I am, sweetheart, so you'll need to learn to live with it. I have no intention of quitting."

The sound of his shoes bounces off the slick floors before I can swallow his words. "Intentions are empty without actions to back it."

His feet halt, and I see the flicker of his hand fisting. Does it feel good to know I've gotten to him? Why yes, yes, it does.

Noah starts walking again, not bothering to reply.

As my gaze travels past him, it's then that I realize he's going to ride up to the office with me, exactly what I'm looking to avoid. It's fine. I'll just let him catch the first available elevator. I walk to the bank and wait. Just the two of us with ten feet keeping us apart. I wish I could stand the silence, but I'm kind of bothered by his lack of response, and because I'm curious, I ask, "So you wouldn't have taken the job if you had known I worked here?"

He slowly turns to look at me over his shoulder. "Why do you think I took this job? To make your life hell? No, sorry, but this isn't about you, Olivia."

"Oh, now you remember my name." *Figures.*

"I remember more than your name, babe."

His smirk punctures the air, causing my body to riot against my sensible head. I definitely remember more than his name, too. That's the problem. I remember everything so vividly. I remember how he made me feel alive, wanted, sexy. I felt like a woman instead of a side piece, whole instead of underestimated.

If not careful, Noah Westcott is dangerous to my resolve.

Then he opens his mouth, and says, "You better get used to this mug because it's here to haunt you." And I have no problem remembering why we should never work together.

A scream rages through my veins, but I don't release it. I won't let him revel in my anger. "Screw you, Westcott."

"Already been there and done you, Bancroft, but thanks for the offer." The elevator that opens is right in front of him. Naturally. *Damn him.*

He waves me in. "You can take this one."

I don't hesitate. I pass him quickly and punch the button for the forty-sixth floor, thrilled to have an empty elevator to blow off steam before I reach the office. "Don't follow me upstairs."

"Don't act like I'm the stalker. You're the one who tracked me down at the deli." Those words leave his mouth just as the doors close, but I shove half my body out. "For your information, I did not stalk you at the deli. I missed lunch."

Feeling better, I stand back up and straighten my jacket before punching the button to get these torturously slow doors to close.

As if he's entertained, he wears a smug-ass smirk on his stupid face. "Sure. Whatever helps you sleep at night."

"I barely sleep at night, so stalking you won't help the situation." Oh my God, why am I blabbering to him? *Ignore him.*

Speaking of buttons, he's pushed every one of mine.

But when another man, a very attractive man around my age or maybe a few years older, well-groomed with his perfectly styled hair, clean-shaven face, and dark-gray suit that fits him to a T, steps on the elevator with me, I discover there actually are a few buttons left to push on Mr. Westcott as well.

With my eyes back on the jerk, I grin, knowing exactly how to end this. Just as the doors begin to close, I lick the corner of my lips, and ask the stranger, "Which floor are you going to?"

"Hold the elevator!"

Damn him.

5

Noah

THE GUY STICKS his hand between the doors to keep them from closing. His mistake is my gain. Although I have visions of destruction for the way he was looking at Liv, the fool gives me the pleasure of ruining her little game.

I step inside, grinning ear to ear. "Thanks, man."

"No problem."

Another roll of her eyes has me thinking she'll injure herself if I stick around much longer. While she's in the corner cursing my existence, I do a quick summary of this guy, noticing the baseball cufflinks. Jumping in to take advantage of the opportunity, I ask, "Mets or Yankees fan?"

He laughs like I've uncovered a secret obsession of his. Nah, I had summed up this joker the second I saw him. Some call it a talent of mine. I call it skill. Rubbing his jaw, he says, "Braves. Just moved from Atlanta."

"Oh yeah?"

"Got a job on the . . ." Not actually interested in what this guy has to say, I catch Liv holding her breath. I never have problems reading a woman, just like I did this guy, but she's been a challenge since our reunion. What I thought would be a good thing apparently is the worst thing to ever happen to her. Add in the stares that hold daggers along with her clear as fucking day words to my face, and I can't say she's been part of the Bancroft & Lowe welcome wagon.

I'm blind to the reasons the staff calls her the Ice Queen, but I get a taste from her lack of a warm reception.

She releases her breath as if her day is made as soon as he continues, "Thirtieth floor." I can't say I'm not relieved as well. The last thing I want is to watch some other guy come in and sweep her off her feet.

Wait, that sounds like I'm here for the job . . . I'm here to work, not the sweeping of Olivia Bancroft. We had a good night, but she's made it more than obvious that's the extent of it.

She's been nothing but a pain in my ass since I walked in.

Her threats aren't even veiled at this point.

And the way she grits her teeth around me makes me think she'll slap me with a dental invoice any minute now.

It would be wise to be as good with the one night as she is . . . But I don't know why I've wanted to dig a little deeper about her. There's more to her story than she's letting on.

"Congrats on the job." We shake hands. His grip isn't as firm as I expected. Or maybe mine is just a little firmer. I want to chuckle. "Noah Westcott."

"Halden Myers."

The elevator dings for his floor. "I just started on the forty-sixth. Guess we'll be seeing each other around." I angle to expose Liv to the conversation she's worked hard to avoid. "This is Olivia Bancroft."

Reluctantly, her hand goes up. "Hi," she replies.

"Hi." He smiles at her, and it's a little too friendly for my liking. "Guess I'll be seeing you around as well."

Okay, fucker, eyes off. Sticking my hand out, I hold the door open for him, making sure he gets the message. "This is your floor." Confusion embeds in his face as he searches for the highlighted number above the exit. Gut feeling—this isn't the first time he's been lost in an elevator. "This way," I add, pointing out.

"Ah. See you around."

As soon as he's out, I remove my hand and push the button to close it in a hurry. "Yeah, see ya." I re-situate myself with my back to her, knowing that drives her nuts.

When the doors close, she says, "You have a jealous streak."

I glance over my shoulder. It's not her self-satisfied tone that flames the fire inside me. It's the smug grin sitting firmly on her face.

Through her insistence, I quit wading through her moods in the past few hours. She didn't rattle me. But seeing the way this Halden Myers guy just checked her out like she's something to conquer did.

It was great sex. That's probably not something she wants to hear since the past seems to be forbidden to discuss with her, but who needs words when the memories live rent-free in your head?

I push the button in rapid-fire succession, not feeding into her ploy. Despite how hard she's trying, I won't let her get to me. The doors slide open in the nick of time. I hand her the salad and step off the elevator. "The only thing I have is a meeting to get to."

Her huff is heard as I cross the lobby, causing me to grin.

Audrina stands from behind the reception desk with a grin and a sway of her body. "Hi, Noah."

"Hey."

"Ms. Bancroft," she greets Liv right after, but the distaste shadows her tone. I'm not sure what that's about, but if Liv's treating everyone as she has me, then Audrina's reaction wouldn't be such a surprise.

I tap Leanna's desk as I pass by. "Ready?" Leanna has been an asset to me since she was assigned the new guy. Me. Working for the company for two years, she knows the ropes and has been teaching me how things operate around here. I'm not sure why she's assisting when it's obvious she excels at marketing because she's already tossing out ideas that have some weight to them. If things go well for me, I want Leanna on my team in a more prominent position. Just give me a month or two.

"Sure am." Grabbing her electronic notepad, she comes around her desk and follows me down the hall to Mr. Lowe's office. "Did you get the Torres email?"

"I did." I stop just before reaching his assistant's desk. Lowering my voice, I ask, "I'm coming in late to the situation. He wants to discuss his future with Bancroft & Lowe over dinner next week but won't give any details. Just that he wants a face-to-face with his new rep. What do you know?"

"He's difficult, but his wife is five times tougher. Not that she's unreasonable. She just won't accept anything but perfection. Creativity is lost in the cost of perfection."

"Did you just think of that?"

She grins. "Off the top of my head."

"It's a good lesson. Regarding the Torres's, it sounds like they're expecting guarantees we won't be able to give them. So am I being set up for failure?"

"Leslie wasn't a good fit for them or Bancroft & Lowe. She left them in a lurch when she quit, causing them to miss their second-quarter launch date. They're giving us another chance to accommodate the changes on our end but want a new game plan before they renew their contract."

"What happens if they don't renew?"

"They'll be suing for the one point five million they've invested over the past year and a half."

"No pressure."

Leanna laughs. "None at all." She connects with Mr. Lowe's assistant, the two of them whispering conspiratorially.

I give them privacy and turn just in time to catch eyes on Liv near the other end of the hall.

Despite our confrontation, her expression is neutral, masking her combativeness toward me. I have a hunch that hiding her genuine emotions is an area where she's quite skilled. Based on an old theory, she wouldn't bother with me if she didn't care. Underneath the spite, there's still a spark, and I know that pisses her off the most.

When she disappears behind a closed door, I return my attention to Leanna when she calls my name. She says, "Mr. Lowe can meet with us tomorrow at eleven. I don't have anything on your schedule for that time. Should I take it?"

"Yes, it will give us time to get a plan together before meeting with him. I won't be the guy who loses the Torres account. We'll come in strong and get their account renewed."

"I like the enthusiasm. We've been lacking that in the office." She sets the meeting, and then we spend the last hour of the day brainstorming because it's not just the Torres's I want to win over.

ONCE I REACH THE BAR, the tension building in my shoulders from the first two days of work begins to fade. I know it's not the work, though. My job has been easy and enjoyable.

I can't say the same about the five-foot-just-shy-of-my-shoulder woman throwing a wrench into every aspect of my workday. Liv's got some fine-ass nerve expecting me to quit to make her life easier. She seems to believe I'm only here for the opposite.

The last-minute text to meet my brothers for drinks is a welcome reprieve from that tension.

The pub is dark, pool tables and the bar giving light to the wood-paneled walls. Much like I do, Loch and Harbor stand out in a crowd, so they're easy to spot. "I'm late. I know." Holding my hands up in surrender, I stand at the edge of the pool table.

"Glad you could fit us in," Loch teases before I have a chance to shake his hand. Pulling me in, he ruffles my hair like I'm still eight years old.

"Fucker," I grumble, half teasing. *Half not.* I try to smooth my hair back into place.

"It's hair. You'll lose it soon enough anyway."

My brothers have given me a hard time since the day I was born. That comes with the territory of being the youngest of three. I have no problem serving it right back any chance I'm given.

Thank God the last to be born was a girl, though. I'd hate to be kicking ass from the middle. I leveled the field by matching Loch and Harbor's height, then growing taller than both. I'll take six-three, but I have a hunch they still won't let the "little" brother stuff go.

"Speak for yourself, old man." He's only six years older, but it's enough of an age gap to properly tease him. Otherwise, he gets an attitude like we're expected to respect our elders, aka him. He's thirty-one, not eighty.

Loch and I harden our stance at the end of the table, crossing our arms over our chests and watching Harbor line up the shot. He takes forever, so I finally ask, "You gonna hit that ball or just fondle it with your tip all night?"

Harbor cracks the balls, sending them flying and sinking two stripes into the pockets.

His eyes shift to mine as he stands proudly on the other side of the table. "It's been what? Two days of having a job, and you're already talking shit like you own the company?"

"All in due time, brother."

Shaking his head, he chalks the pool cue as he comes around. Holding his hand out, I slap mine against it. A solid handshake brings us together, chuckling. "How's the new job?"

"Good." Liv would probably be happy to debate that response because it seems she loves to argue about everything with me, even a salad, apparently. But otherwise, I haven't lied. "How long are you in town?"

"The team and I fly out on Sunday. I'm meeting with the commission again on Monday in Geneva."

"You're really going to do it?"

He grins. The spark in his eye tells me he's not only serious but also excited. He's come a long way from a few years ago, healing his life and building a multimillion-dollar business on the verge of billions. I would have been wise to follow in his footsteps, but million-dollar-plus custom cars weren't something I had much interest in school. How could I when so many hotties were running about campus? And baseball kept me busy.

He replies, "My business is cars. Owning a piece of a Formula One team is a natural progression."

"And cool as fuck," Loch adds.

Harbor chuckles again. "Definitely sick as fuck." He studies the table and then maneuvers around to take his next shot. "If this goes well, maybe one day I'll own an entire team." He angles lower, eyeing a ball, but looks up and asks, "But let's talk about you, little brother. Tell us the good, the bad, and the ugly about working at Bancroft & Lowe."

Settling down on a barstool, I reply, "I could pick it apart if I tried hard enough, but it's actually been really good."

"Did you get laid yet?"

"HR was quick to point out the no-dating policy. It's not something they enforce, but it's frowned upon. A relationship went south and ripped through the office in the aftermath."

Loch comes around, pulling a stool nearby to sit on. We both know Harbor will spend the next ten minutes setting up this shot. "What happened?"

"I have no idea. That's all they would say." When I first heard, I tried to piece the puzzle together, but there were no obvious pieces to connect. "I'm thinking those involved don't work there anymore."

Harbor looks up again. "Sounds like that's for the best." Dipping down again, he hits a ball but doesn't sink it. "Fuck. You're up, Loch."

Loch always gets to the point, even in a game of pool. Stepping up, he shoots before we can even smack-talk. To his credit, he sinks a solid. He dusts his pool cue and then asks, "Are we doing dinner tonight? I need to let Tuesday know."

Although there's the age gap between my brothers and me, we've grown closer as we've gotten older. Being in the "real world" now helps them see me more as an equal than just their tagalong kid brother. "I'm starving, so wrap it up and let's go for steaks."

He hits the next ball like he's lost interest already and is texting before he leaves the table. Tucking his phone in his pocket, he says, "She's ready for a baby. It kind of hit her out of nowhere, and now she talks about babies all the time and where she wants to put the nursery."

Harbor chuckles. "Did this happen to be after she spent the day with Lark a few weeks back?"

Sending our brother the evil eye, Loch replies, "Might have been."

"I'd apologize," Harbor says, sliding off to pat Loch's back, "but I wouldn't mind if you joined the club."

"You two are such suck-ups. You'll make Mom's dreams come true," I say with a grin. "But at least that will give me plenty of time before I have to settle down."

Loch's eyes shoot to the ceiling. "You just fucking graduated. No one wants you settling down. Dude, enjoy your twenties. The years go fast, and when you find a woman who tolerates you, make her your wife because we all know there aren't many out there who will." Whipping his gaze back to Harbor, he adds, "And I'm not sure about this club."

Harbor shrugs. "No one is, man. I know that Lark will be an amazing mother, and I'll do my damnedest to be the best dad I can."

I've always tried to keep to the lighter side of life, but it feels good to be trusted enough to join in on the heavier stuff. "We have good role models," I say.

Loch says, "I told Tuesday I wanted a family with her when I asked her to marry me. I never wanted that before her. Now, I'm beginning to see the bigger picture, and babies are the direction we're heading in."

"You guys are light-years ahead of me," I say, kids being

the furthest thing from my mind.

Loch laughs. "You're lucky you don't already have a baseball team."

"It's not luck. I'm careful . . ." I pop my shoulders and take another sip of beer. "Most of the time." Harbor cringes enough for me to see the disapproval taking over his face. Quick to hold my hands up, I say, "Save the lecture. I've learned my lesson."

He asks Loch, "Do we want details?"

"Definitely not," Loch replies.

I chuckle. "Don't worry. I'm not sharing any details." I have no idea why Liv comes to mind. I told myself to compartmentalize that situation, to let it go for tonight and leave it for tomorrow. Yet somehow, here she is, invading my brain with images of fucking her in the Hamptons, mingling with that glare of death she loves to shoot my way at work. Life isn't as black and white, good or bad, as she makes it out to be. Sometimes there are a lot of grays to wade through.

Complicated.

So fucking complicated.

Loch checks his phone once more. "Let's go eat."

"I'm ready, but Noah . . ." Harbor pulls me in to pat me on the back. "Congrats on the new job. We're proud of you."

Sappy fuckers.

"As an attorney, let me give you a little advice, though." Loch slips on the jacket to his suit and grins. "Keep your sex life out of the office. Don't become a liability to the company."

Getting him wound up is one of my favorite pastimes, and I still have the magic. "What exactly constitutes a liability?"

They both shoot me a look, but Harbor says, "Some things never change."

6
———

Olivia

"That's a lot of water."

I don't have to see Chip to feel nauseous. My body cringes spontaneously upon hearing his voice. It's so tempting to ignore my ex-boyfriend—the cheater of all cheats, womanizing, commitment-phobic, condescending misogynist—but since he's also the reigning heir to the Lowe part of Bancroft & Lowe, I usually try my best to be the bigger person. I can tell it's going to be a struggle today.

"Got the email you were back. Thanks for the warning." I stand from where I was filling my large cup at the water cooler and look over my shoulder.

Chip's eyes are glued to my backside, ogling my ass. "It's fuller." *Gloves are off.*

I spin to hide said ass from his disgusting gaze. "You're such an asshole."

His hands fly up in front of him like he's innocent. "Just noting your ass is bigger. I didn't say it was a bad thing."

He knows just how to get a reaction from me. I grip my

stainless cup tighter, my anger convincing me I might crush it. *Walk away, Liv. Walk . . . away.*

Heading for the door, I decide it's best not to say another word to him. Since our breakup two years ago, our interactions are usually kept to a minimum, and I've already broken my limit. Our blowout before I left that year had the rest of the office caught in the crossfire. I never want to lower myself to his level again. "It's mind-boggling how you never change. You still act like an entitled man-child."

"Why would I when I get everything I want?"

"I guess what I was really wondering is *how* you get away with it. I get that you have your daddy living vicariously through your conquests, enjoying the stories, and encouraging the philandering. I mean, we all know like father, like son. But I don't understand why any woman would ever put up with your shit."

"That's something you should ask yourself."

"I did. That's why I'm no longer subjected to it." I start walking, but the irritation he's caused makes me itchy for a comeback. Although I try to be the bigger person, I don't always succeed. I turn back on my favorite patent black heels, the ones that make me feel strong and, honestly, powerful by the height and stance they provide. "Talk about me, or any body part of mine again, and I'll be filing a report with HR for harassment."

"You wish I was still harassing you."

Stupid me. I forgot he always must get the last word in. If I stay, we'll keep going in circles, and since that's the definition of insanity, I leave.

Colliding into a wall of muscle, fine Italian wool, and silk, I bounce back, wobbling on my heels, dropping my cup, and losing my balance.

I'm caught so fast that my neck jerks back. "Gotcha."

Pulled forward, I'm set right on my feet again. Coming face-to-face with Noah at this early hour of the day is not something I was prepared for. Is my lipstick still fresh, my blouse still wrinkle-free, and my hair still styled how I like it?

Oh my God . . .

I scream inside.

Why do I care? I hate myself for being so easily baited by his stupidly handsome good looks. I'm usually better than this. Chip has thrown me off this morning.

I need to cure myself from ever making the same mistake I did with Noah in the Hamptons from happening again.

He says, "You seem to be making a habit of falling for me."

That will do it! I'm cured.

"Men," I snap, rolling my eyes. I bend over to pick up my cup, but we bonk heads. "Ow!" Rubbing my head, I look straight into the warmth of his brown eyes with green centers and a smile so genuine that I forget we're enemies for the briefest moment in time.

"You okay?" he asks.

"Fine," I whisper, redirecting my gaze to the cup in his hands. I stand when he does, at a loss for what to say or even how to react. I finally look up at him again. "Are you okay?"

He chuckles. "Yes, I'm fine." His breath is heavy as if he's struggling like I am to know what to do or say next.

"She's a walking disaster," Chip says under a heavy laugh when he passes us. "Best to avoid it if you can there, buddy." He pats Noah on the shoulder.

Shrugging him off, Noah replies, "I can handle her."

"You say that now, but you've been warned."

I don't know why the corners of my eyes fill with tears.

It's a nuisance, though. Taking the cup from him, I spin to rush away. "Thanks."

"No problem."

In the safety of my office, I lean against the back of the door to steady my breathing and swallow down my weakest feelings. No one can hurt me if I keep my emotions tucked deep inside.

I hit reset and move to my desk. A knock has me instantly annoyed. Can't I just have a minute to myself around here? "Come in."

Noah pokes his head in. "Busy?"

"Always." I turn my attention to my monitor and start typing a reply to an email. "What do you want?"

He walks in, closes the door, and stands there looking like a runway model in his incredibly flattering suit. Brighter than navy but still muted compared to royal, he's found the perfect shade of blue to complement his tan and hair on the lighter side of brown. He looks like he just got back from vacation, while I'm starting to feel as if I'll never see the likes of one again.

Damn him.

He shoves his hands in his pockets, and says, "I've been thinking about us."

"There is no us."

"In the office sense."

I stop and pivot my chair to face him. I'm having visions of déjà vu from, what, two days ago? I quirk a smile but try my best to wipe it away. "What about the office?"

"And us."

"Yes, Noah. And us." Sometimes it feels like he's lingering just to spend more time together. But being around marketing associates for years now, I know creatives can be long-winded with their entertaining stories and charismatic quips.

I'm tempted to snap my fingers, knowing there are never enough hours to finish my work. At least I have job security.

"Why don't we call a ceasefire and start over?"

"I'm listening." I rest back, liking what I'm hearing. "Go on."

He takes a seat without being invited. Just mentally noting because it doesn't upset me like it did on Monday. I'm actually calm . . . should I be worried?

Noah leans back, making himself comfortable, and not even the smirk bothers me today, even if it is only slight. "I don't want this tension with you. It's not good for either of us."

"I agree."

Resting his forearms on his legs, he asks, "What can I do to make this better between us or, at the very least, professionally cordial?"

"What do you suggest?" The opening to talk, the desire to tell him everything hits hard. I bite my lip, thinking it's best if I just listen for now and gain insight into this man.

"The past is the past, but—"

The door opens. Chip barges in, causing him to stand, and silences us as if we got busted making out. "Why are you being so bitchy, Livvie?" His eyes shift to Noah and then narrow before a fake smile punctures his face. "Sorry, man. Didn't know you had a meeting."

"You should be apologizing to Olivia. It's her office."

Chip looks back and forth between us several times, then lands on him and bursts out laughing like he heard a joke. Noah's not laughing. *I'm not.* Hitting Noah in jest on the chest, he says, "We should grab a beer sometime. I bet you can pull in the ladies."

"I don't need to pull. They come willingly." His even tone contains no emotion, not even arrogance, though he'd have a right to be that way. Look at him. He tells no lies when it comes to women. I came willingly a few times under his hand . . . tongue . . . and other heady body parts. Turning to me, Noah bows his head. "I apologize for the disruption. We can continue another time."

Now Chip has really pissed me off. It was going so well with Noah, too, which was a nice change of pace for us. "I think that's best under the circumstances."

"Maybe you can send that financial report over before then." He drops an alibi.

I pick it up. "Certainly. I'll send it by the end of the day."

"Olivia."

"Noah."

He looks at Chip when he passes him. "Chip," he says, subtly popping the p. It is a ridiculous name. If Noah only knew his full name was Chipper.

"We'll grab that beer." Chip points at him like they're buds, but Noah is already gone. *Well-played, sir. Well-played.*

I ask, "What do you want?"

"Why are you being such a bitch to me?"

I sigh because this exhausting topic has played out too many times before. "I'm not anything to you. You're just offended that I'm not stroking your ego or laughing at your male chauvinist jokes." I brush my fingers toward the door. "Run along and bother someone else, Chipper." Okay, I do go low sometimes . . . I really despise that he brings out this side of me.

Between the threat of Noah blindsiding Maxwell's and my life and Chip returning at the worst time, it's a lot.

He walks to the door, and his hyena laughter echoes off

the wall. "I knew you hadn't gotten over me. It's kind of sweet how you're holding on to our relationship."

The offense is impossible to keep from my face. I stand, him literally getting a rise out of me. "Leave."

"Settle dow—"

"Now!"

He looks over his shoulder for witnesses. Although I don't face the atrium of cubicles, and there's no office across from me, I know I'll be the one judged for losing my cool in this situation.

Smarter than he looks, he leaves. I move around my desk and close the door, this time locking it. Returning to my chair, I lean back and close my eyes.

Inhale.

Slowly exhale.

Inhale.

Breathe out.

Imagine a sunny day at the park with Maxwell.

My anger ceases to exist with such a happy image in my head. I open my eyes again, feeling much calmer.

"Okay. This is good. Chip is gone. Noah and I are talking. I'm alone. It's fine. All good."

A knock has me cursing the interruption. I don't think I can deal with Chip again. Please don't let it be him. "Yes?"

"It's me, Olivia," my father calls from the other side of the door. When the knob rattles, I jump to my feet and rush to unlock it. He looks at me like I'm crazed. Maybe I am after the start to this day. "Why is your door locked?"

"I wanted to focus on the quarterly reports today."

"Ah." He walks to the window behind my desk, then turns to sit on the sill. "Close the door."

That's not good . . .

Doing as I'm told, I close it and then stay there to stand

in my discomfort. After crossing his arms over his chest, he says, "Were you yelling at Chip?" The accusation stings, though I did yell.

Disappointment tugs his unruly eyebrows together. He let them go after my mom left him, and now I can't stop staring. "We've talked about this, Olivia. One of the conditions of returning to the office was not yelling at Chip. Lowe Sr. isn't in yet, but if he hears about this—"

"Then the office is gossiping again." How is this already so twisted? "Why is everyone allowed to talk about me as if I'm the wicked witch . . ." I throw my hand out in the direction of Chip's office down the hall. "But he skates by like the hero." Shaking my head, I sit in a chair near the door. "Do you even care why I yelled?"

"No." He stands and walks to the door. "I need you to be less reactionary and fall in line with expected behaviors."

"What behaviors are those exactly?"

"Less . . . emotional. Ever since you came back from working remotely, you've been . . ." He pauses as if he's hesitant to say it. It's not like my father not to speak his mind. For someone who's built a successful corporation on relationships, he's never seemed to understand the basics regarding his own daughter.

I stand, angling his way. "What have I been?"

He looks down, rubbing the bridge of his nose. When he looks at me, the words don't have to come from his mouth. They're seen clearly in his expression.

"A woman? I've been acting like a woman?"

"I didn't say that."

"No, you made me say it instead." I sit at my desk and turn to my monitor in order not to act on impulse and prove him right. "If you'll excuse me."

He opens the door. "I'll let you get to it. I have lunch

scheduled with Noah anyway. He's the injection of energy we've needed in this company. Have you spent any time with him?"

"Some."

"He's great, right?"

"Yes, Dad, he's great." Although I'm conflicted over the situation with Noah, it's not a lie.

A smile with pride shaping it shows up. "Speaking of, are you seeing anyone these days?"

We don't often broach my personal life since Chip and I broke up two years ago, but this question is thrown from left field. Dating? How in the heck would I have time for dating? He seems to always forget I have a baby at home. But maybe this is genuine interest in his daughter.

"Dating isn't something I'm interested in. I'm too busy with the bab—"

"There's more to life than work, Olivia."

Even though logically, I know it's on him, my heart aches, knowing I've never lived up to what he's expected, and the tradition continues with Maxwell. "I don't need to date to be happy. I have all that I need."

"That's good." He taps his watch. "Because if it weren't for the non-fraternization policy in place, I'd suggest you spend more time with Noah. He's a great catch." He leaves like that's the end of the conversation. It sounds more like Noah's the son he never had.

He wanted Chip and me to work out, but I also resented how much of a suck-up Chip was to my father. Dad claimed he saw right through him but still supported Chip after the breakup. I was just the mean one, the Ice Queen, and Chip was the innocent.

It makes me wonder if my dad would still side with Chip if he knew the truth.

Feeling every bit of my childhood insecurity, I rush to the door. "Hey, Dad?"

He turns around, and I think I see a smile in his eyes when he looks at me. "Yes?" I don't get my hopes up just yet. I've been burned before, which is one of the reasons I don't force him to have a relationship with Maxwell. I'm winning if I can spare my child the same pain I grew up with.

I shouldn't set myself up for disappointment, but I can't help but hold on to hope that one day we'll be close. "Do you think someone would be lucky to catch me?"

"Don't be ridiculous, Olivia. You're my daughter."

His daughter. Not because I'm good enough or even stand on my own, as a separate human being. He believes my value lies within him.

I nod, staring into his eyes, wanting to wither. *I don't. I won't.* I lift my chin and say, "Have a good lunch." I don't question why he's leaving at nine thirty in the morning to have lunch with Noah. It's really none of my business.

What I do know is that he didn't have even ten minutes for me all week, but has made room in his schedule for Noah to slide right in. For him, the great catch, he has time. For me, nothing until next week at the earliest.

Sounds about right.

7

Noah

ANGER COURSES THROUGH ME, my heart pounding in my chest as I pace my office. I strip my jacket off, hoping to cool the rage. It doesn't help.

I would have leveled that prick if we'd been anywhere other than in the office during my first week of work. *Bitchy? Laughing at her?* Chip is a real piece of work. I got a taste of his asshole behavior at lunch with the bosses the other day, but he's good at the masquerade. The fucking suck-up. His dad practically eats every word he feeds him as if he's God's gift.

It goes beyond pride. Mr. Lowe believes Chip walks on water. It's a damn boys club, and they're the only members.

Mr. Bancroft played along and laughed where he was supposed to, but he wasn't engaged in the conversation. He did better than I did. It may be my first week, but I won't blow smoke up that asshole's . . . asshole. That would go against how I was raised. I'd rather side with the genuine underdog than gain favor with the higher through lies.

Though I have no interest in Chip Lowe himself, one thing is clearly obvious after this morning's display between him and Liv. They used to date. Which honestly surprises me. Everything about Liv gives the opposite of Chip.

She's whip-smart, can hold her own in an argument, and independent. Chip is a spoiled and entitled toddler who needs to be put in time-out. What could she have possibly seen in him?

A soft rap on the door is followed by Leanna dipping her head into my office. "There's been a change. Mr. Bancroft and Mr. Lowe want to meet at Salisbury's. I added the lunch to your calendar but wanted to check with you before replying. Confirm?" As soon as the question is asked, she quirks her head. "What's wrong?"

"Nothing. You can confirm." At a standstill, I glance out the window. Lying is not something I favor. I've told my fair share, and I'll do it to get by, but I want to earn respect, not be known as untrustworthy.

She leans her shoulder against the wall just inside the door, crossing her arms, and sports an all-knowing grin. "Want to try again?"

Fuck it. I ask, "What does Chip do exactly—"

"Ah. Chip." She shuts the door behind her and comes to sit down.

"I get he's in marketing, but he doesn't—"

"Ever seem to work?" Tapping her nose, she adds, "Ding. Ding. Ding."

I return to my desk and sit across from her. "I came onboard to be part of a team, to build something greater than what's already been achieved."

"That's noble, Noah."

"I'm trying to be noble. I want to succeed. That means

making sure the company is profitable." Resting forward on the desk, I lower my voice. "Chip operates differently."

"He sure does."

"I've known plenty of guys like him. They'll stab you in the back to get credit for your work. Is that what I'm dealing with here?"

Her back is straight, and her gaze has shifted beside me as she appears to mull the answer she's comfortable sharing. When her eyes come to me, she replies, "I'm not one for gossip, but I wouldn't be upset if Chip were gone. For good. He makes everyone's life miserable."

"I'm sorry to hear that."

"I should clarify that he makes the women miserable." She leans back. "Let's just say he likes to be hands-on. Not with me, but some of the others. He talks down to us as if we're all here to work for him."

Hearing this doesn't help my blood pressure. We've only been working together for a few days, but we share a level of comfort as if it's been much longer. "I trust you, Leanna."

She smiles. "I trust you, too, Noah."

"Can I ask you something that's really none of my business and trust that it will stay between us?"

"Of course." Her body language is relaxed, her expression open.

Despite the lack of time we've spent together, my gut tells me she's an ally I can talk to. "HR went over the no-dating policy. They didn't go into detail but mentioned it was put into place in the past two years due to a situation."

She looks down at her lap, her fingers twisting along with her lips to the side. "Chip and Olivia." Her eyes plead with mine when she adds, "Don't let it get out I told you. I like Olivia, but she gets a bad rap around here. Some people love to stir up controversy to discount her hard work while letting Chip skate by on his last name alone."

I appreciate having my hunches verified, but I'm confused as to why she's so disliked by some. "Why is that?"

Ticking her fingers one by one, she replies, "Smart. Funny. Obviously beautiful. The boss's daughter. The blowout with Chip. Everything and anything." Leanna stands. "You should get going so you're not late for the lunch appointment. I'll call a car."

"Thank you." This newfound information regarding the Ice Queen fills in some of the blanks. It also might help me understand how to reach a truce with Liv since it sounds like she's taken the fall for other people's misdeeds. I grab my phone and say, "I'm ready to go."

I spend the next few hours with the company's name-sake. It's not a bad lunch or conversation. Something feels off with Lowe. Although I've now met him a few times this week, something hangs in the air between us—a slight intimidation tactic in his mannerisms. It doesn't work, so I let it go, but it's noted.

I've met a lot of characters over the years from professors who threaten to fail you if you question one thing that doesn't make sense to coaches who make you drop and give them push-ups because you're two minutes late to practice. I'm not threatened by him or his son, but there's no connection with them either.

Unlike his daughter, Mr. Bancroft is a breeze to read. Listens intently. Open to hearing ideas, even basic brainstorming. Easy to please because he likes me.

What I don't like is the way he treats his daughter. I'm not jumping into the middle of family history, but it's not all roses between them. That much is clear to everyone who works here.

So although I'm already forming opinions on each of them, I don't question their knowledge of business practices. They've built a solid company and work solely off referrals with a waiting list begging to become clients. I was hired to do a job, and I'll do that to the best of my ability.

When I return, I pass Leanna's desk, tapping it on my way to my office. "I take it the meeting went well?"

"Better than well. Come into my office and close the door behind you."

When she arrives, she sits down. "So what happened?"

"They've given me a lot of leeway to save this client, so let's figure out the best method to proceed. I'm thinking about dinner with the Torres's. They agreed to Friday night." Kicking back in my chair, I add, "Drinks, good food, and great company if I do say so myself." I turn back to her. "If I can get one hour of their time, I'll have them renewing the contract."

"Dinner is perfect." She jots down notes. "Wine them. Dine them. *Woo them.* I'm sure you'll have no trouble winning them over."

"I appreciate the vote of confidence." Leaning back in my chair, I stare out the window, hoping to solve this concern before it becomes a problem. "There's only one small issue."

"What's that?"

Glancing her way, I say, "I need the expenditures for every campaign, target, and medium utilized on their account. I know it's a lot to ask, but can you get me the files so I can brush up on their account?"

She looks up from her notes and nods. "Shouldn't be an issue. I can put in the request. It may take a day or two, though."

"We need to see where things have gone wrong by

connecting the creative to the finances. Mrs. Torres is all about the bottom line. I want to come to the table with explanations, not excuses. What are the chances I can get a peek at that file tonight?"

"It's a big job and after three. I doubt it can be compiled in that time. What do you need exactly?"

Anchoring myself in place, I reply, "An expert who not only understands the client's past spending but can get my concepts approved during dinner if I can get them to a yes." I swing my hand. "I'll close them in one quick swoop and land my first account." Giving myself a nod of confidence, I grin. "Technically, I'll be saving the account, but same thing."

"It will be a feather in your cap."

Just the way I like it. "And a great way to kick off your career."

She sets the e-pad on her lap, her excitement waning. "The only thing is the expert."

"Surely the company has someone who can handle this type of situation."

"They do." She chews the side of her cheek and looks down nervously. "I'm just not sure if this is something they'll do. You're talking about dinner, which is not during the workday hours. That's going to be considered a favor. You need to figure out what's in it for them."

The left side of my mouth rises, confused to the verbal dance around. "I'm pretty good at convincing people and a great team player. MVP status."

She laughs. "Yeah, but—"

"You're keeping me in suspense, Leanna. Just tell me who I need to invite to dinner, and I'll take care of the rest."

"Only one person currently handles the client's financials, and she never attends company events."

"Why not?"

Leanna shrugs. "I have no idea. People call her the Ice Queen."

"The Ice Queen." Dipping my head down, I rub my temples. Olivia Bancroft and I haven't reached a truce. For all I know, she's still the last person who wants to see me succeed. My sigh comes heavy. "Fuck."

"So you've heard about her? Have you two met outside of the conference room introduction?"

"Yeah," I start, well-aware that Liv and I are still on shaky ground, to say the least. Since we didn't get to finish our conversation, that might be in order before asking her for a favor. If it goes south, which it just might based on the past few days, I'm certain she'll be thrilled to serve me some humble pie in exchange for that file. "We've met all right."

"You got this, Noah," Leanna says with a laugh.

I throw a few air punches and then make my way down the hall. Cracking my knuckles, I do some light footwork before entering the ring aka Olivia Bancroft's office.

Does Olivia intimidate me?

Hell no.

Will she try?

Absolutely.

She just won't win. Not wanting to drag this out, I knock on the door five minutes before five. With it being the end of the day, I assume she'll respond quickly to get out of here on time. Of course, assumptions are a foolish man's last alibi for sacrificing facts in the hope of a favorable outcome.

"Come in," she replies.

Here goes nothing . . .

I open the door and am quick to close it behind me. She's always so worried about us being seen together that I figure my asking her out, even though it's strictly business, is not something she wants circulating around the office.

Not a word is spoken when my eyes meet hers. The formality of greetings doesn't exist. It's just the two of us standing here in a smaller office than mine, staring at each other.

She finally cracks, blinking her eyes. "What are you doing here?"

There's no anger like the other day or impatience like with Chip. She's shifted into neutral since this morning, which means I need to turn on cruise control and match her tone.

I went through so many intros in my head before landing on the perfect way to talk her into this favor, but now it eludes me. I never go blank or lose my cool under pressure, but something about Liv makes me feel much like a schoolboy with a crush on a cute girl.

Is it her eyes that draw me in? I wade into the shallows, hoping to reach her deeper waters. Or maybe it's the way her mouth always gives her thoughts away. A tug under her teeth or a smile that plays at the corners. It's the only part of her that I've had any success reading.

Her body is relaxed and sunken into the plush leather of her chair. Being at the end of the day, I have a feeling she's been stuck behind that desk all day.

"Noah?" Her head angles to the side as she waits for me to reply.

She's Eve in the Garden of Eden, tempting in her very being. She may want to forget, but I'm struggling to get that night out of my head.

The taste of her body when I licked her from navel to neck, a mild salt flavoring from the beach still remaining.

A silhouette of her nipples on display in the moonlight after I made her come.

And those eyes . . . the way she looked at me like we had a chance at more than one night?

How can I erase the best sex of my life?

I can't.

But I have to . . .

A loud snap has me returning to reality. "Did you come in here to stare at me?"

"No. That'd be weird."

"It would be." Her snark tilts her mouth sideways, and she raises an eyebrow. "Very weird."

I clear my throat, remembering my mission, and shift closer. Squeezing the back of the chair, I say, "We have a client ready to bail to another firm. We need to put our best efforts into saving the account."

"That sounds like why you were hired." Her eyes slide back to the monitor in front of her. "Anything else?"

Does she really believe we can find middle ground, or am I never getting anywhere with her? "I understand it's my job, but it involves you. Otherwise, I wouldn't be here."

I'm hit with a glare, and then her expression goes downhill from there. "How does this involve me?"

"The clients want all the financials with a full breakdown of expenses."

She starts typing. "Fine, give me the client's name, and I'll send it over."

"It's not that easy."

Laughing, she says, "Nothing with you ever is." With her elbow anchored to the desk, she rests her chin on a fist. "Go on."

"They want a presentation to back the campaign I'll be presenting. Accounting down to the penny."

Although her eyes widen, she nods. "Okay. I can do that if you can send the pitch over in the morning." She checks her watch and then stands and begins slipping her jacket on. "I can have it to you by lunchtime."

"Actually, they want you at the meeting."

She stills and then looks up from the bag she had set on the desk. "What do you mean?"

"We both need to be there. I represent the creative side of the marketing campaign, and you'll talk about the financial commitment."

"That's not really how things are done."

"You said it yourself. I was hired to take things in a new direction."

Planting her hand on her hip, she sighs. "When?"

The woman is anything but intimidating, but she puts on a solid show. I turn to leave, opening the door because so do I. "I'll see you Friday at seven o'clock."

"In the morning?" Turning back with a winning grin, I'm met with concern darkening her face. "If I must, but I'll need more advance notice from now on."

"No, Liv. Seven o'clock in the evening over dinner."

Her brows shoot straight up. "Dinner? Like you and me having dinner?" Shaking her head, she grabs her bag and comes toward me. "No way."

Standing in the doorway, I add, "With the clients."

"Noah," she cautions, stopping with not two feet between us. "I get that you want to win over the clients, but I can't make that work. I'll get you the files and even create an analysis for you to take. You can present it." Patting me on the arm like we're old buddies, she says, "You'll do great. Much better without me." With me in the way of her making a quick exit, she blinks several times. "I need to go."

I step aside, hoping she stays just a minute longer because as much as I'm glad her hate has tempered, a small exposure of faith has been revealed. She doesn't detest me as much as she portrays. I say, "I understand your hesitation, especially since it's a favor to me. It's a lot to ask of you to work late on a Friday night, but they were specific. These aren't clients I'm trying to sign. I'm trying to save the account that the previous guy screwed up."

"Chip and Leslie. The Torres account."

Figures it was his client. I knew I smelled a slimeball. "Yes. They weren't given what they were promised. I want to make that right, not only for myself but also for the company." Her stance has softened. Her eyes have lifted from the floor to meet mine. "Listen, I know we got off to a rocky start this week," I clarify because we couldn't keep our hands off each other the first time we met. "I'm sorry for upsetting you."

"Don't apologize on my account." Adjusting the bag on her shoulder, she takes a breath. The silence between us stretches so long that I hear her swallow just before she says, "It won't fix things."

"What needs fixing? I wasn't hired to make your life hell. I didn't take the job to get back at you—"

"What reason would you possibly have for getting back at me?" She crosses her arms over her chest. Her defenses are up when that's the last thing I want to do.

"Let's not delve into the minutia of the past when we have a pressing issue to resolve for the company." I step closer, wanting to reach out and pull her to me, like I did that night, kiss her until her lips swell from ecstasy and her body begs me for another round.

She stills, a deep breath filling her chest as her eyes stay trained on the wall outside her door. The emptiness of the space between us lengthens, and she starts walking. *Fuck.* I've blown it with her. *Twice now.*

Only gifting me the view of her back, she asks, "Where?"

"Buddakan."

"I'll need to dress up." Her head falls to the side as if the weight of the world hangs on her shoulders. Maybe it does. I wouldn't know what's going on with the ebbs and flows of her moods. That night in the Hamptons was fun to explore her differing sides, but we kept things physical more than discovering who we were on the inside.

Her reactions are impulsive, and her beauty is so incredibly distracting, but I don't take it personally. I need to stay focused on my career despite how much I'd love to kiss her again. "I need you, Liv."

She turns back, some of the concern lifted from her brow. No animosity is disrupting her fine features, but a look of determination bears down. She leaves, calling over her shoulder, "I'll see you there at seven."

8

Olivia

SETTING the bags on the counter, I don't bother emptying them yet. Instead, I wash my hands and cut through my bedroom to reach my bathroom. Maxwell sits in his stabilizing chair in the tub, immediately splashing with a loud squeal when he sees me. "Mama."

Cassandra and I share a smile before I kneel beside the tub. Reaching in, I tickle his tummy, causing an uproar of belly laughs. That sound shoots straight to my heart, filling it. "Hi, Maxwell."

I duck just as he sends water my way. Laughing, I say, "He loves to splash me."

She holds out her shirt and says, "You're not alone."

"Aw, hey," I start, getting up to sit on the edge of the tub instead. "Sorry I was late."

"It's only a few minutes. I don't mind if you need to run errands. I know it's much harder with Maxwell in tow."

"I appreciate you staying, but I'm going to pay you for your time."

Getting to her knees, she adjusts her jeans. "I won't say no."

"Good." Rubbing Maxwell's chunky little leg, I add, "I can take over."

"You sure?"

"Positive. I appreciate the extra help, but I enjoy my evenings with him." I glance over at her again. "He brings calm to the chaos for me."

"I can see that. He's been fed and is happy." With the towel in her hand, she moves closer to give it to me. "I've already washed him. He's just playing now."

She's more than I could have asked for. Cassandra has become a friend. Not but a few years younger than I am, she loves kids, and especially my son. We've spent holidays together, and she's dried my tears when life overwhelmed me as a new mother, and I was working again.

I've been there for her when she had a kitchen fire and no other place to live, gone through a breakup, and graduated from NYU. I say, "He loves the water."

She hands me the towel. "So much. I didn't have the heart to pull him out just yet, but he's ready whenever you are."

"Thanks for taking care of him." Holding the soft terry towel, I stand, not sure how to ask her about Friday without her thinking there's more to it. "How would you feel about staying late on a Friday night? I can pay overtime."

Her eyes slightly widen, but then she tries to calm her reaction. Nice try, but I already know what's coming next. She asks, "Is it a date?" I laugh when she continues, "Because you know I'll stay all night if you need a night out or a night in at his place." She's not lying. She's only mentioned that I should find a companion for a night or life a few hundred times or more. I've not been looking for either and don't intend to anytime soon.

Her giddiness gets the better of her, and she giggles. "Please tell me it's a date."

Maxwell is the one laughing now. I rub the top of his head, admiring this handsome kid. "She's funny, isn't she?"

"Fun," he says, but I think he's unaware of the fact he said an actual word. He's also quickly distracted by a rubber ducky floating in front of him.

It feels good to laugh. Unwrapping the towel, I set it aside, ready to plunk Maxwell in it. I glance at Cassandra. "It's a business dinner, not a date." Willing away that night in the Hamptons with Noah hasn't erased one memory despite my best efforts. A date would undo any progress I've made . . . *if I've made any at all.*

It's best to keep things in perspective—a professional dinner with clients.

Taking hold of Maxwell, I bring him against me. I don't care that he's soaking my shirt. I love holding him close.

"Well," she says, looking over the baby's shoulder. "Business or pleasure, I'm glad you're getting out. This Friday or next?"

"This Friday."

"I'm available. Next Friday, I'm going to the Hamptons for the weekend."

I burst out laughing as I settle on the edge of the bed. Maxwell squirms, wanting his freedom. Too soon for me, but for him, I set him down so he can stand on his own. "Be careful. The last time I went to the Hamptons for the weekend, I came back with this guy."

He drops to his knees and hurries across the floor toward my closet. He loves seeing himself in the mirror in there. I maneuver behind him, keeping enough distance for him to feel independent of me.

Cassandra looks down at her stomach before souring her face. "Yeah, I'm not sure what to say to that."

"Don't worry. Neither was I."

We're laughing as I get Maxwell dressed. We walk her to the door, and she waves before heading toward the elevator. "Thanks again. See you tomorrow."

When I close the door, I rub noses with my cutie. "Looks like it's you and me, kid." I carry him to his room and get comfortable on a gingham-covered chair and ottoman. The pale creams are serene, and the chair is comfy enough to put me to sleep many times since he was born.

The routine of reading him a book before bed is my favorite part of the day to spend with him. Other than that first-thing-in-the-morning grin he always sports for me.

My contagious yawn catches on, and I watch him yawn before he leans against my chest. I chose a shorter book because we're both too tired for something that will keep us up too long. I kiss his head before I start reading.

Not twenty minutes later, I'm laying him in his crib and tiptoeing out of the room.

Opening the fridge, I pull out a bowl of berries and then break off the end of a baguette to snack on. I'm too tired to make anything, much less even bother buttering the bread or grabbing the olive oil to dip. I'm not sure this will tide me over, but I'm too drained from the day.

I watch TV for a bit, hoping it takes my mind off things. So much from Chip to Noah to Friday night circles in my brain that even a sitcom can't win my attention. I almost roll my eyes, but my apartment is an eye-roll-free safe zone. This is where I come to recover from the straining all day.

A giggle erupts as I pad into the bedroom. I'd be an

Olympic Gold medal winner if it were a competition. It was my one rebellious act as a teenager. My dad hated it, so I leaned into it. I wasn't perfect, but damn near close to it. I never stepped out of line, but it still didn't matter. I could never live up to his expectations.

After slipping on my coziest pajamas, I take my time doing my skincare ritual. I don't always have the time for it, but it seems like a good idea to while away a few minutes before crawling into bed.

My phone buzzes on the counter, so I look down at the screen:

> Will the file have the breakdown of expenditures, including who approved the spend and who spent the money specifically? Or will it be an overall budget without details?

I get spam texts all the time, but this one is pretty dang specific and directed at me. I reply:

> Who is this?

The three dots roll and then a reply pops up:

> Noah.

In my surprise, I stare at the screen. His sudden ability to contact me takes me back to a time I used to pray to hear from him. He sure didn't bother then, so I try not to get worked up now. But really . . . where was this text two years ago? Not the one about the numbers but hearing from him. I'm getting worked up, so my fingers fly across the screen:

> How did you get my number?

His response comes just as swift:

> The company directory.

I didn't even know there was a directory. The serum I just dropped onto my face drips down my neck. Rubbing it in, I then glance back at the first message before I type again. Me:

> Why?

> Why what?

> Why do you want to know about the expenditure approvals and details?

> In their last email to me, the Torreses said that money was wasted. Some clients will consider money that doesn't recoup the spend a waste. Others might not know where their money went.

I'm not sure if I can allow myself to be impressed that he's working at this hour. It's not late, but it's hours after the workday ends.

> Are you at work?

> I'm out with a friend, and I was thinking about the details of this file.

> Date must not be going well if you're thinking about numbers and clients instead . . .

It's not a date. I'm having a drink with a friend.

Not sure what comes over me, but this conversation makes me laugh.

Is that what the kids are calling them these days? Friends? Are benefits involved?

There's no quick reply.

There aren't even the three dots like he's going to.

Did I cross a line?

I'd hate if someone made assumptions about me . . . well, they do already, and I hate it. I definitely crossed a line with him.

I rush to type:

That's none of my bus—

Are you jealous?

I read the message as soon as it pops up on the screen. Another follows:

Don't worry. This is not that kind of friend.
Not anymore.

I'm not sure if I'm more offended by the accusation of jealousy or that he had to tack on "not anymore" to the end. *Ugh.*

Huffing, I cross my arms over my chest, not sure why I'm bothered by either part. It's not like I'm attracted to the man. Just because he's hot and knows how to wear a suit doesn't mean I want to jump on his hard body and climb him like a monkey.

Oh good lord.

Do I . . . Do I want to climb Noah Westcott like Mt. Everest and mark him as my territory?

No.

It's not butterflies that start fluttering in my stomach. It's a tingling I feel between my legs just thinking about him naked under me, on top of me, the way he stretched me and filled me, leaving me empty afterward that has my head spinning.

A cry from the other room breaks through the fantasy . . .

I'm hit with reality, *my* reality to be exact. I exhale, trying to clear my head. I need to stop this. Noah Westcott was a one-time thing. *A vacation fling.* A rebound at best and a memory in the least. *That's it.*

I wait, listening, while my heart races through ragged breaths. No other sounds are heard. I glance at the monitor to see Maxwell sound asleep again. At least one of us can sleep.

Lying in bed, I can't seem to stop thinking about Noah. He may be the father of my baby, but there's absolutely no way the two of us will ever tango in the sheets again. I'm not sure why I feel . . . down . . . disheartened.

It happened once between us but didn't work out thanks to him. So I can't ever let that happen again. I won't set myself up for a second round of disappointment.

I need to end this part of our relationship and focus on telling him the truth about my son. The sooner, the better so we can move on, hopefully to a peaceful co-parent situation instead. I reply:

> I'll get you the details of the expenses tomorrow by close of business. Good night.

Another message doesn't come right away, though I feel

relieved by the way it ended. But then my mind starts into overdrive . . . Did he get the text or is he too caught up in his friend to notice? He bugs me after hours, then leaves me waiting on him. *Figures.*

What the hell?

I hate myself for worrying about this. *For thinking about him.*

I'm totally failing at forgetting about him.

Let it go. *You know he has.*

Frustrated, I call it a day. Who cares that it's only eight thirty-seven. I finish getting ready for bed and climb under the covers. I'd lost my sexual desires when I realized I have no one in my life to want. And since I don't plan to date anytime soon, I don't know why that tingling persists.

I'm left with only two things I can do:

1. Take matters into my own hands.
2. And try to forget that Noah was not only the last man to give me an orgasm but he also deftly did it four times that night.

LYING IN THE DARK, I slip my hand under the covers, succeeding on the first and epically failing with the second.

I may be unsuccessful at forgetting about him, but the one thing I won't fail at is protecting my heart and my son. *No matter what.*

9

Noah

"I NEED A WHITEBOARD."

Leanna says, "Added to the list. Where do you want it hung?"

I remove an awful piece of artwork from the wall. "This is printed, not even painted. Let's hang the board here instead."

Looking at the wall, she nods her approval. "I can have it in place this afternoon."

"Thank you. In the meantime, I'm still waiting on the exact details of this account, but something is off." I set the canvas outside my door and then close it again. "Between us, okay?"

Shoving her stylus into her bun, she says, "I'm always a vault, boss."

"I don't want anyone hearing a rogue theory that includes accusations toward the boss's so-called prodigy."

"Oh wow. This is about to get juicy."

I start laughing. "Not that juicy but it could get me fired

if I'm wrong. Hell, it might get me fired if I'm right." Stealing company funds is criminal. The accusation could be career-ending. Makes me question why I was given this account as my first with the company. Am I being set up?

I'm letting my thoughts run wild. If something dodgy is going on, they hired the wrong guy to cover it up.

Her mouth slacks, but she pulls the stylus from her hair. "Do I need to take notes?"

"No. And I'm not going into detail with you just in case I'm wrong. No point in both of us being fired."

She leans back in the chair and watches as I walk the length of the windows. "You're not giving me anything? Not even a hint?"

I grin. "Not yet." Sitting behind the desk, I click on my schedule. "And for now, I have a call. If you receive the file first, let me know as soon as we get it from Olivia."

"Yes, sir."

When she leaves, I pick up the phone and call my mom.

"So punctual these days," she teases. "I approve."

"Hi, Mom."

"Hi, Noah. How are you doing? How's the job? How's living in New York?"

"Better than expected. Going well." I can't see her, but if I could, I know she's smiling. "How are you and Dad?"

"Fine and dandy. Marina has a show tonight at the university."

Rocking back in the chair, I kick my feet up. "You should have told me. I might have been able to come down for a performance."

"It's a long drive."

"How many miles did you guys drive to come to my baseball games last year alone?"

"Too many to count."

"Exactly." I nod, smiling. My family has always been my biggest cheerleaders. I was approached by coaches in the minor leagues a couple of times over the past few years. I thought I'd go pro, but something changed last year.

A sprained ankle from sliding into home gave me six weeks to reevaluate. I was a star third baseman. *Fucking good.* I just realized that wasn't the life I wanted to lead.

My dreams changed after last summer in the Hamptons. I was over the partying, the women, the legacy I was trying to uphold.

I changed.

Looking around the office, it's nice, but I laugh. Would it have been better than a dugout or being on the road with the guys? It's not the biggest, but it's nice. I don't regret the path I chose, but I'm still working to find peace in my decision.

She says, "The show runs through Sunday night. You can stay here for the weekend if you want to go." I tick through my weekend plans and come up empty. Before I can say anything, she adds, "You know you don't have to. Marina doesn't expect you to be there."

"I know, but I want to be there."

"There's no pressure. She knows you support her, but let me know if you decide to come down, and I'll order tickets for you."

She always told me that I'll always be her baby no matter my age. I may not understand the whole parent role, but I know as the kid in the situation it's time I stand on my own. "You don't have to do that. I can order the tickets, Mom."

"All right," she concedes.

"Let's have dinner next time you're in the city."

"I'd like that, Noah. I'll be there in a few weeks. When I have my plan, I'll let you know what dates."

"Sounds good." I kick my feet down. "I need to grab lunch before the hour's up. Miss you, Mom."

"I miss you, too. I love you."

"Love you."

I tuck my phone in my pocket as I stroll out of my office. Leanna is gone from her desk on her lunch hour. I keep walking toward the break room but stop when I reach the door. Tight skirt, great ass, curves that extend from her torso to her chest, and long dark hair that falls in gentle waves over her shoulders. The shoes . . . *fuck me*. She knows how to get my attention.

"Were you staring at my ass?"

My eyes shoot to Liv's.

"Your shoes, actually." *Why lie?*

I drag my tongue across my bottom lip remembering how she tasted like sin in summer. *Fuck* . . . if I'm not careful around her, I'll be hard. And I don't want to give her the pleasure. She seems like the type to collect ammo to use against someone at the least opportune time for her victims.

The thing is, she doesn't appear mad.

Interesting.

Lifting one foot in the air behind her, she twists to take a look as if something is wrong with them. "Why?"

I'm not at a loss for words. I'm at a loss of words that won't get me fired on the spot. Do I really want to be searching for another job because the thought of her legs draped around my neck while wearing those shoes is something I'll get off to later? Or that I imagine her standing in those shoes at the edge of my desk, and she's naked, begging me to fuck her from behind?

Yeah, probably best if I don't mention those scenarios.

"You always wear really high heels, yet no one really sees them."

She sets her foot down, but glances at the shoes in front of her again. "I wear them for me. Nice shoes . . . high shoes make me feel stronger."

"Stronger is a fascinating choice of words." I walk to the beverage fridge and pull out a bottle of mineral water. With my eyes locked on hers again, I twist the cap off and start drinking.

She watches and licks the corners of her lips as if she's a parched woman returning from the desert. In a huff, she turns away to head for the exit. "I'm sure a therapist would have a field day with me."

"So could I?"

"What?" she asks, snapping back. She's fucking gorgeous, and I'm beginning to think she doesn't even realize it. *How?*

How is that possible? She must get hit on all the time.

Fuck it. I'm not going to lie. If she reports me, she reports me. If she doesn't . . . guess we'll see. "I could have a field day with you."

"You already did and look how that turned out."

"Abso-fucking-lutely fantastic from what I recall."

"Guess we recall two different events." The blow to my ego hits hard. She kicks up a heel and smirks at me. "And the memory is all you'll ever get."

"You sure about that, sweetheart?"

"Abso-fucking-lutely," she says with a wink, "sweetheart." She walks out, those fuck-her-over-my-desk-shoes tapping across the linoleum as she exits.

Resting against the counter, I watch her go because it's a great fucking view, but damn she's got a whip-smart mouth. My thoughts go south from there.

Audrina enters right after, smiling when she sees me. "Hey there. How's the first week?" And that's the end of my erection. But under the circumstances of me being at work and all, that's probably best.

No doubt Liv has left me in a state that will have me thinking about her all damn day, though. I reply, "It's going."

"Yeah, tell me about it." She grabs a bag from the fridge and then comes to stand close to me. Too close considering we're the only ones in here. "You happy it's the weekend? Any plans?"

"Looking forward to it. You?"

"There's a concert down at Little Island. You can go if you want." She casually shrugs as if it's nothing. "We can get drinks and hang out?"

I skirt around a small table with four chairs, making a move to get out the door without it being too obvious I'm hightailing it out of there. "Sounds fun, but I have a few commitments already." I turn to leave. "Have a good one."

"You, too."

I detour toward the elevator, hoping it arrives before she returns to the front desk. It's okay talking to Audrina, but I can tell there's an undertone of flirting. She isn't taking the hint that I'm not interested.

It opens, and I jump in.

Liv hops in just before the doors close again. I expect a look of disappointment, especially after the break room interaction. But she half smiles. HALF smiles at me. I'll take that half with full intention to win a full grin soon enough. "Where're you headed?"

Leaning against the railing, she holds it with her hands behind her. The smile is still in place. Maybe we do have a chance of calling a truce. "Fresh air. I'm really feeling . . ." Wobbling her head, she releases a breath that comes from deep in her chest and then fans her neck with her hand. "The heat today in the office."

"Anything I can do to make it better?"

I swear to God she gulps again and looks away as if she was busted staring. She wasn't. It felt like a normal exchange between us. Clearing her throat, she angles toward the doors. "No. No." She swallows again. Umm... What the hell is going on with her? "You've done enough."

"I've done enough? What have I done exactly?"

Her gaze lands on me again, and deep pink floods her cheeks this time. What the hell? "Are you okay?"

"I'm fine. Yeah," she says, fanning herself even though she's in a sleeveless shirt when she's usually all buttoned up in a suit. "Is it hot in here?"

I can't stop staring at her. "I'm good, but you're really flushed."

The doors open, and she practically runs toward the exit. "I need fresh air."

Leanna stands off to the side, staring at Liv. When I step off, she asks, "Is she okay?"

"I have no idea what's going on. Think I should check on her?"

With her attention back on Liv, she nods. "You might want to. I don't think I've ever seen her so animated." Turning to me, she says, "Good luck," and gets on the elevator.

"I'll need it."

I cross the lobby, watching Liv through the glass as she hurries down the sidewalk away from the building. When I reach the outside, my stomach tells me to go left to the deli. But since my mom is still on my mind, she'd give me a solid lecture about not checking on someone in need. Acting out of character, I'm certain Liv is someone in need.

Taking a right, it's easy to keep an eye on Liv up ahead. She's erratic, bopping and weaving through the throngs of people. Impressive in heels, especially considering she's tripped into me twice wearing them.

I cross the street and close the distance, purposely leaving ten feet or so between us. She detours into the park. I continue to follow her until she plops down on a bench, fanning herself wildly with her hands.

She dips her head back, soaking in the sunshine. A hint of sweat glistens along the curve of her neck, and I'm reminded again about the night we spent together. Strangely, I thought it had the potential to lead to more. Now I realize that was ludicrous to even consider. She might have enjoyed the physical connection we had, but otherwise, the woman detests me.

I never hesitate, but with her, I'd be wise to take this slow. "Liv?"

When she looks up, the sunshine fills her eyes, causing her to squint, but not so fast that I don't catch the myriad of colors—golds turning to greens and browns mingling. She's captivating without even trying.

It's hopeless to entertain feelings when it comes to Olivia Bancroft. It's best to abandon all thoughts of a potential reconciliation before I get burned twice.

Shielding her eyes from the sun, she asks, "What are you doing here, Noah? Did you follow me?"

Lying will get me nowhere. It's obvious I did, so I reply, "Yes. I wanted to make sure you were alright."

"I'll be fine. I just . . ." Her gaze pivots to a couple walking by and then back to me. Her shoulders fall as if she can finally breathe. "Thank you for checking on me."

"It was that or a double meat Italian sub."

She laughs, the grace of her hand covering her chest. "You chose me over double meat? I'm flattered, Westcott."

"Who says they're mutually exclusive?" It earns me a smile and a chuckle under her breath. *I'll take it.* Beats seeing her upset.

I nod to the path from where we came. "It's good to see you're fine. I'll leave you to it."

"Thanks again."

"You're welcome." I don't make it five feet before she says, "You can stay."

I turn back. "Something must really be wrong to warrant that kind of invitation. You sure you're feeling okay?"

She laughs again. "I'm feeling better now." Patting the bench beside her, she adds, "I think . . ." She searches the sky for her thoughts, and then looks at me again. Sincerity softens her gaze. "You're being very kind to someone who hasn't been the same to you."

I didn't see this coming . . . "That's how people react when threatened."

She says, "I appreciate the grace, but I am sorry."

I return to sit on the other end of the bench, not because I couldn't have sat closer but because I want her to be comfortable. "Thank you, but it's okay."

"It's not." Gentle laughter rocks her shoulders. She scans the park, her eyes eventually latching onto some guy rollerblading while a dog runs beside him. "We should talk."

A chuckle reverberates in my chest as her words strike a funny chord inside me. "Oh yeah? What do you want to talk about?" Watching the pigeons peck around on the sidewalk, I ask, "Do you want to talk about what happened back at the office?"

"Not really."

"Okay. Have you read any good books lately?"

Her laughter has me glancing over at her just enough to see a genuine and beautiful smile. "A few great board books."

"Yeah?" Now I chuckle, leaning forward to rest my arms on my legs. I tilt my head to look at her. "Do you have a favorite?"

"There's a truck book with an excavator in it. I've discovered I love to say excavator. Why is that word so fun to say?"

"Excavator." I grin, thrown off by the most unique response I've ever received. "It's a good word, but I didn't take you for the baby book type."

A quick shrug of her shoulders reminds me that she's younger than she lets on most days. Her job has sucked the vivaciousness she had when we first met right out of her. Seeing her relaxed in the sunshine and enjoying a few minutes in the park changes my outlook on her.

She stands and moves in front of me. "We only have a few minutes left of lunch. What do you say we go get your double-meat Italian before we run out of time?"

I stand, and we start walking, together this time. "Why does it sound so dirty when you call it a double-meat Italian?"

"Is there any other way to say it?" She cracks up. Whatever was getting to her earlier has faded away. It's not like two coworkers walking together; it feels more like friends on the same side.

Like she soaked in the sun, I take her in—her voice, the laughter, her eyes as she glances over at me, and the smile. . . the smile that makes me feel like maybe, just maybe, she doesn't hate me as much as I believed.

10

Olivia

"I SHOULD HAVE CHANGED into sneakers. These heels are killing my feet."

"I bet." Noah glances at my shoes, then directs his gaze ahead again. "They still look amazing on you." He stops in front of our building as if the compliment is part of our everyday conversation. Yesterday, I would have been annoyed. Today . . . not so much. *Is he growing on me?*

If I were to analyze the complicated feelings he brings out in me, I think it's that no one else in that office, even my father, would have checked on me. But Noah did. Without anything to gain, he put all my snide remarks aside and was there making sure I was okay.

I'm starting to believe I wanted to hate him to protect myself and Maxwell. It would be easier to be a mama bear in this difficult situation than to open the door and allow him to take my baby away from me.

Instead of lining my ducks up in a row to be prepared for a court battle, Noah appears to be the kind of guy I'd want

Maxwell to have in his life. At least from what I've witnessed so far.

So instead of focusing on the negatives of the situation, maybe it's time to acknowledge the positives.

He's not a stereotype.

Sure, he's drop-dead gorgeous with incredible eyes that make me want to strip off my clothes, but he's not another jock without a brain. He's clever and always asking questions to educate himself.

He smells so good. Do villains smell like the ocean on a sultry night? No.

Noah Westcott is an in-the-flesh, walking seduction.

His ambition goes beyond the job. He doesn't seem to want to settle based on all he accomplished in college. I might have peeked at his file . . . *judge away.*

Other than my mom, he's the only one to ask me how I'm doing. I can't remember the last time anyone asked me. It feels like Noah is always well aware of my moods and cares.

He asks, "Your feet are already hurting. Don't feel pressured to go to the deli."

Standing beside him, I just realized that I feel good around him. Something about him makes me feel safe and, more importantly, seen.

I look toward the deli one block down and then back at him. First, he comes to the park just to make sure I'm okay, and now, he's giving me an out to save my feet. His concern hits me sideways, right in the heart.

"I want to go with you. I'm a little hungry myself." I'm not hungry in the least after the big salad I tackled at lunch, but I'll take any reason to get to know him better.

He stares at me like he's seeing a different person. Two

lines dig between his brows as he studies my face. He does that a lot, stares at me. He did in the Hamptons as well.

Not in a creepy way, but more like he has a lot going on in that head of his. Maybe I misjudged him, pegging him as the knight in shining armor coming in to save the company. My father talked him up.

I'm getting a bitter aftertaste of jealousy.

Is that what it is?

My feelings are hurt because my dad never talked about me like that.

I nod in the direction of the deli, and we start walking together again. It's strange feeling comfortable in his presence, but I probably shouldn't be surprised since I was extremely comfortable with him naked once. My cheeks flame from the memories I used last night to help take the edge off that damn tingling he created inside me.

The traitor.

He knew what he was doing . . . God, did he know. *So good.*

"You need water?" he asks, pulling open the door for me.

"Water can't cure me."

"Huh?"

Oops. Didn't mean to say that out loud. Fortunately, Antonio calls out, "Hey, Noah! What can we get you two today? You gotta try the pastrami."

Noah chuckles. "How are you doing, Antonio?"

"I'm good. Buried elbow-deep in potato salad today. Got a catering job over at a pier later today. They're shooting a commercial for that real estate agent on some of the benches. Bigwig. Loves the potato salad and our homemade rye bread sandwiches."

"Sounds like a big job. Congrats."

"Thanks." Antonio comes to stand in front of me,

leaning his arms on the high cold case. "What are you thinking today?"

I don't want to insult the guy, so I'm not sure what to say. It smells good in here—fresh baked bread wafting through the air. I hold my hands up. "I didn't bring my wallet. I came to keep him company."

His arms go wide. "Noah, my man. You gonna let this pretty lady starve?"

"No. No," I say, shaking my head. "I'm not starving. It's okay."

Noah glances down at me out of the corner of his eye. "I'm happy to buy you lunch, Liv."

It's the first time I've heard that name from his lips and don't want to snap back at him. Oh God, I'm softening to him. He has always been quite charming. "Why do you call me Liv?"

"That's how you introduced yourself."

I grin. "I know I used that name in the Hamptons, but not many people call me that."

"Ah." He nods his head, looking back at the menu. "Let me guess, the honor is reserved for friends and family?"

"No. Most of them still call me Olivia."

Antonio grabs a hunk of meat and starts slicing. "I'm telling you, man, the pastrami is the only way to go."

"Sold," Noah replies. "I'll have the pastrami on—"

"Rye. Only rye, my friend."

"Rye it is, then." When Noah laughs, I admire how his smile is magnetic in the ease of the lines, his lips full enough to land a great kiss, and the slightest of his five o'clock shadow already appearing before one o'clock.

He nudges me. "What can I get you?"

I turn back and point at the chips. "The original kettle chips and a water, please."

"You got it," Antonio says, rushing to grab a bag from the clip on the rounder.

Taking the bottle of water and chips, he hands a cup to Noah and then gets busy behind the counter constructing the sandwich. I decide to sit at a table to let other customers who have walked in get closer to the counter.

With a cup full of soda, Noah sits next to me, resting his arms on the table. "Why'd you tell me to call you Liv?"

A small shrug keeps my shoulders light. It's that or the company, and I'm willing to bet that Noah plays a big part in creating the comfort level between us that I can't take credit for.

"Here you go, Noah," Antonio calls him to the counter. While he holds the sandwich out to him, it gives me a moment to realize how good it feels to be with Noah.

His calm, casual tone has no expectations. It's almost hard to look away from his naturally handsome face.

I saw how women eye him on the street and have heard a few people talk about him in ways that HR would get involved if they knew. But when I really look at him, I don't just see a great face and incredible body. I remember how he took care of me in the Hamptons—sexually, emotionally —checking in with me and making sure that it was more than physical, that I was okay and good in all ways.

Watching him pay, I bite my lip, taking in the strength of his profile—a bump on the bridge of his nose that only adds to how attractive he is, his jaw that cuts sharp underneath, shadowing his neck under the width, and the wave in his hair that reminds me of a breeze across the water of the bay. Until he catches me staring and smiles as he slides back into the chair beside me. "What's on your mind?"

I could be honest and talk about the tone he uses with me that eases my defenses or how his grin feels personal, like a secret that only we know. I don't, though. My emotions have been all over the place regarding him this week. Now that Chip is back in the mix making my life hell again, is it wrong to want to enjoy the peace Noah and I share? "You asked why I told you to call me Liv. For one night, I wanted to be someone else. You gave me that chance."

"Why'd you want to be someone else?"

"I'm not sure this story is meant to be told over pastrami." He grins, standing and picking up his soda. "Another time?"

Telling him about a failed relationship or how atypical it was for me to rebound with a one-night stand doesn't feel like a conversation I want to have, ever. I like who we are right now at this moment—*friends*—too much to ruin it. "Maybe another time."

"I hate to cut this short, but I need to get back."

"Me, too," I say, standing and scooting around the table toward the door. I don't. All I have is a bunch of numbers that don't change the pace of my day or anyone else's. "This demanding marketing associate insists on receiving some over-the-top detailed accounting file."

Chuckling, he holds the door open for me. "He sounds like a nightmare."

I laugh. "Totally, but . . ."

"But?" He stops on the sidewalk, curiosity getting the best of him. Cocking an eyebrow, he waits as if I'm about to say something monumental.

Not wanting to let him down, I reply, "Maybe I misjudged him."

"Ah." He sips his drink, his gaze lengthening the path back to our building. We start walking again, and he asks, "Maybe?"

"I did. Does effort to change my perception count for anything?"

Smirking, he gives me a wink. "Everything."

Riding the elevator together this time doesn't worry me. It never should have in the first place. I'll never please some of the other employees, the gossipers, the energy drainers, or the soul suckers.

Instead of making sure I never give them any ammo on me, I enjoy the conversation with Noah and walk off the elevator in a fit of laughter. "What happened during the next game?"

"The umpire had a decision to make. Expel me from the game because his daughter liked me or piss her off more."

"What did he do?"

He laughs. "I was thrown out, but the coach fought the call, and I was back in by the third inning. As for his daughter . . . um, yeah. That's a story for another time."

"Seems we have a few stories to share one day."

Audrina looks utterly annoyed with her crossed arms and puckered face. Her eyes stay on Noah, but when I look at him, he smiles at me. I don't know what possesses me, but I smile right back, not caring about anyone seeing or judging me for it.

It feels good to have that weight off my shoulders.

Just a few days ago, I thought Noah was here to ruin my life, but in less than an hour, he made me feel comfortable enough to lower my guard and give him a chance. I'm glad I did because I saw the real him, and I'm grateful for that opportunity.

We reach my office, and I stop outside my door. Noah stands in front of me, his gaze dipping to my mouth and then back to my eyes, lingering between blinks as if he has other things on his mind. Me, specifically.

If he only knew that I was starting to feel the same. That will be short-lived once I tell him he's a father. I can only imagine how much he'll hate me.

Today was good, a step closer to seeing the kind of man he is and telling him. But since we're in the office and surrounded by others, now is not the time to share the news.

Surprisingly, those same conditions exist, making it feel like the end of a first date—a little awkward, a lot of anticipation, and that moment. That moment, like now, when it's so tempting to close my eyes and kiss him again. Just once would be enough to satisfy my craving since I left the Hamptons, left the bed with him sleeping, and thought we'd have a second chance.

That chance never came . . . *until now.*

A throat clears, and we both step back. My shoulders hit my door, and the doorknob stabs my ass. Leanna smiles, sympathetic to the reality that she's definitely interrupting something.

It's in the air, the tension, that anticipation.

Instead of rushing to make excuses or apologize, I breathe it in, reveling in the connection I've only ever had with this man. I lick my lips and look down at the shoes that he admired earlier.

Leanna says, "Mr. Bancroft wants to see you."

Noah nods. "I'll be right there."

Reaching forward, she takes the drink and the sandwich. "I'll put this on your desk."

"Thank you."

She slowly turns and walks away, leaving us alone again.

My heart races, and I suddenly feel a little awkward, like other peoples' eyes might be on us, so I say, "I'm almost done with the Torres file."

"Good." Shoving his hands in his pockets, he clears his throat. "That's good. Thank you."

"You're welcome." When I swallow, his gaze grazes over my neck as if the sight of it alone could bring him to his knees. My breathing deepens as memories come racing back to me . . .

His lips kissing my inner thigh.

The tickle of his fingers against the back of my knee.

The scrape of his tongue against my clit . . .

Oh God. "I need to go," I say, scrambling to open my door. I'm absolutely certain that if I stand here another second, I'll combust before his very eyes.

"Bye, Liv."

"Bye." I shut the door behind me and toss the bag of chips on my desk. I rub the cold bottle across my neck and chest for relief from the fire burning inside me. "Good lord, that man."

Rushing to my desk, I sit down and quickly pull my phone from my purse. Holding the bottle to my cheek, hoping it can cool me off, I dial my mom. As soon as she answers, I say, "I'm in trouble."

"What's happening?" she replies in a panic.

I really shouldn't worry her like this. I giggle, though, through a silly grin. "Mom, he's nice."

"Who's nice, Olivia?"

Going against everything I had told myself to do, I instantly recognize the feeling coming over me. After setting the bottle on the desk, my shoulders sag in defeat. Emotionally, I'm right back there in the Hamptons with him again. "Noah."

11

Noah

Bancroft's fingers are steepled.

His eyes analyze me like I'm trying to sell him a used car.

I don't like the look on his face. It's one that captures hardened businessman and disdain equally.

He slaps his desktop and then grins. "You get one shot, Noah. Don't blow it."

"I appreciate the opportunity. I won't let you down, sir."

When I reach my office, Leanna jumps from her chair and follows me inside. Shutting the door behind her, she asks, "Well?"

"Fucking Chip Lowe. The jealous little rat bastard. He convinced Bancroft that I shouldn't be trusted to run this meeting with the Torres's."

"Oh no." She drops into a chair and watches as I wear a path into the carpet along the windows. "He's awful."

"He's a fucking asshole is what he is." Glaring out the window, I try to calm the anger raging inside me. Chip's smug smirk when he decided he'd act like a big guy and speak to Olivia like she was nothing to him. Jealousy from even the thought of Olivia moving on after him must eat him alive. I've tried to stay out of office drama. It's only my first week here, but Chip had to go and talk to her like shit. No way can I let that go. "He tried to be buddy-buddy with me the other day."

When I look back at her, Leanna's eyes are locked on the e-pad on her lap and she's shaking her head. Looking up again, she asks, "I take it that didn't go well?"

"I get along with almost everyone, including some assholes to everyone else I've known over the years. But this guy, the fucking weasel. I wasn't playing along with his little game because of how he was speaking to Liv like she's—"

"Liv?"

"Olivia."

"Ah. *Liv*. I see." She's not laying a judgment on me, but the all-knowing grin on Leanna's face has me realizing she caught that slip. Although we've become friends, my past with Liv is not something I can get into with her.

I continue, "So I guess he went to his dad to launch a complaint."

"So frustrating. Do you know what he said about you?"

"Something about me being more worried about hitting on women in the office than saving the account that he lost the company. Make it make sense."

"You can't, Noah. You're rational. He's not. He planted the seed to get you out of the picture, which means you threaten him. You need to watch your back."

Flexing my hands, I know myself well enough to be aware that my stubborn ass will always fight to get to the top. "The moment he opened his mouth, he started a war, Leanna. He's a chest-beating Neanderthal, challenging me as if he can compete."

"Don't be drawn into his nonsense, Noah. It's easy to get sucked into a bad situation, but he's the boss's son and will always use that leverage to take out his competitors."

"Too late. He set the stage for this battle when he said Olivia Bancroft was acting like a bitch. Fucking disrespectful, and it's bullshit to call her the problem. Now I'm on an account he fucked up, and he wants to know the details. I'm letting him back on again. So the war was waged when he came in treating everyone like they're beneath him, but I'll end it the next time he opens his fucking mouth."

Coming to stand near me, she keeps her eyes forward on the bustling city on the other side of the glass. She turns, keeping her chin down. "I've only known you a few days, but I knew instantly that you were a man of integrity. It's also your first job. Getting fired might not be the best idea."

I steady my breathing. "I guess I didn't realize that integrity and this job were mutually exclusive."

"Me either." Her soft smile matches her eyes. "But maybe we should have. It's called Bancroft & *Lowe*. Mr. Lowe will never do anything about Chip. He gets away with everything, and the office is left to pick up the pieces." She returns to the chair, leaving me with that nugget of reality to think about. "Your reaction is normal, but something tells me this isn't a normal situation."

Resting against the windowsill, I start weighing the repercussions if his behavior continues. And by repercussions, I mean punch his fucking face or if I'll be able to walk away twice. He's crossed me this time. I won't sit by and allow it again. "No, it's not. I can't control him or the lies he spreads. I can tell you now that I won't sacrifice my integrity to play along."

"I have no doubt, Noah." She shifts along with the

conversation. "So back to Mr. Bancroft. He's coming to the client's dinner?"

I stop pacing. "No, because I talked him out of it. I don't need another chef in the kitchen while I work."

"You and Olivia, then?" Her singsong tone has me turning back to find her eyes giving her away. I'd take the blame for that slip earlier, but I feel like me and Liv are both guilty. Although we weren't doing anything wrong, I had visions of pinning her against the wall and kissing her until her knees got weak, and we took it inside her office behind closed doors.

Fuck.

A fire ignites in my groin. I shift quickly and return to my desk to hide any evidence of my growing interest in Liv. Acting busy—shuffling papers around, arranging my phone and a pen just so, tapping on the keyboard to bring it to life —I try to keep any feelings I have for Liv under wraps. I make the mistake of glancing up at Leanna. She's taking in everything I do. I speak quickly. "Mr. and Mrs. Torres will be there."

I doubt she will fall for the evasive, albeit correct, answer. They will be there, but I can't say that I'm not looking forward to seeing Liv outside the office again.

Something about these walls sends hers soaring in defense. Like the sky outside, she becomes open to talking, sharing, even to me once we've left the premises.

"Nice try." Leaning in, Leanna lowers her voice like someone else might be listening. "What exactly did I walk in on earlier?"

I was watching how Liv's tongue dipped out to wet the corners of her lips, how her heart pulsed in the vein of her neck, and listening to how she swallows, not able to hide her reactions to me.

I'm not blind to how she physically responds to my proximity, but she appears to be completely unaware of my reactions to her.

I can't admit any of that to Leanna, though, so I reply, "You didn't walk in on anything. We were in the hall talking."

She gets up to leave. "Sure looked like something. And if it did to me, it did to others." Before she opens the door, she says, "Be careful, Noah. You already have Chip gunning for you. You don't need more trouble."

"Does this mean I'm your favorite boss ever?"

Bursting out laughing, she opens the door, and leaves. Quick to poke her head back in, she says, "Yes, but don't tell any of the others."

I kick back, grinning ear to ear. "Secret's safe with me."

With the rage tamed, I check emails to find that Liv sent the Torres file. I feel bad for making her do all this work when I see it's sixty pages long, small font, single-spaced. "Shit." It's going to take me all night just to read through it.

Figuring it's best to start now, I silence my calls and get to work.

———

Question . . .

I WAIT for Liv to reply to my text.

Answer . . .

She replies not a minute later, making me grin.

Thinking about texting her is fine, but I decide to call instead. It will be quicker that way. That I get to hear her voice is a bonus. The phone rings, and she answers right away. "Noah?"

"Hey. Hi. How are you?"

"Um. Fine. Why are you calling me?"

I shift. Not necessarily the greeting I hoped for, but she's not entirely closed to the idea of chatting by her tone, which has remained even. "This file shows Leslie worked the Torres account solo for six months prior to Chip being brought on board."

"Okay, so we're talking business?"

She actually sounds disappointed. I approve of her wanting more. Is this the way to her heart? Just call? "Would you prefer if I kept it personal?"

"No," she says, the response coming like a surprise attack. "This is fine. Um, yeah, Leslie worked the account from the dates I assigned in the file."

While I try to piece my thoughts together more coherently, I rub the bridge of my nose. It's a complicated issue that doesn't appear to have a simple answer. I squeeze my eyes closed to soothe the burning after staring at a screen all day and night, and then say, "Being new at Bancroft & Lowe, maybe I don't understand how expenses get approved because most of the money spent took place in the six months Chip was on the account." There's extended silence, so I ask, "Are you still there?"

"I'm here. I'm just confused."

"By?"

"When I was initially working on the file, I was only assigning names to the expenses already approved by my father based on the requests. I wasn't analyzing them. I can't approve anything our employees spend above ten-thousand dollars, so I wasn't investigating the client expenditures."

She sighs. "But I've also been distracted lately. Did you find an error?"

I'm close to laying my theory out for her, but I hesitate. She handles accounting expenses for associates and management. I expected the implications to ruffle her feathers, though that was the last thing I wanted because I know she's not in on a scam. I do think she could end up taking the fall, though, if she's not careful. "I didn't find any errors. I have questions that I need an expert to explain it to me."

"I don't have my computer open. Can it wait until we can meet about it during office hours?"

She does sound tired. It's not that late, but I'm sure staring at numbers all day is taxing. "Yes, but be warned, if you find me passed out on the desk, pour coffee into my IV. I should be right as rain after that." I start to close down my computer for the night, knowing it will be here waiting in the morning. I don't have to solve this mystery tonight.

She laughs, which has me pressing the phone to my ear a little more just to enjoy the sound. "You're still at the office?"

"I'm leaving soon."

"Yes, you should definitely do that. Get some rest, and we can look at it tomorrow."

"That's a good idea. I'm delirious at this point."

"Numbers do that to you. I should know." I chuckle. She says, "Have a good night, Noah."

I kind of hang on as if I can keep her voice closer for a bit longer. Though she's thawing when it comes to me hanging around the office and today felt like progress, I know I need to take things slow with her. I reply, "You, too."

As soon as we hang up, a text pops onto the screen and leaves me smiling:

Noah?

Why does it feel like we're whispering through typed text?

Yes?

Thank you for the water and chips today.

My thumbs zip across the screen:

Anytime.

Noah?

She has this way of making me feel invigorated and reenergized. She's become my third wind.

Yes, Liv?

Thank you for checking on me today. It meant a lot to me.

Not knowing what to say, I pause and read her text over several times. It would be simple to blow it off like anyone would have done it, but we both know she doesn't have allies in the office who care. I don't know why she puts up with that shit.

I text:

Always.

Good night.

Good night.

---

*I*T WAS A SHIT DAY.

I'm close to drinking a double before this dinner even begins. I don't think it's wise, and I keep hearing Loch judging me in my head. And though I know alcohol isn't the answer, I should have taken the edge off at home.

I work my way through the busy restaurant, passing the hostess without pause, and straight toward the bar area.

Holy fuck.

Olivia Bancroft is impossible to miss.

Looking like the bombshell she is, I run my gaze from her head to her toes, over her ruby lips and sultry eyes. The woman knows how to get my attention and every other man's in the restaurant. Per usual, she's clueless to the others taking her in, including me.

Red silk dress.

Matching red shoes.

A short black jacket draped over her shoulders while her arms remain free from the confines. Ruby-red lips perched on the edge of a wineglass. Her eyes dip closed as she takes a sip. She's beautiful and—I remind myself—off-limits.

That non-fraternization policy will do me in if she doesn't first.

"Hi," I mouth when she finds me coming toward her, too far to talk but not enough distance to keep our gazes from connecting. I see the quick once-over she gives me before lowering the wineglass to her side.

A fluttering of lashes is her tell, her gaze dipping away before it returns to me. The shape of her mouth forms a reply, and although I can't hear her, her greeting is warm.

I could study each reaction and assign it nothing less than she finds me attractive despite always trying to portray the opposite. I'm not sure I'm in the mood to hide my feelings. This may be a work-related dinner, but we are after hours. Surely, that gives some leeway to a policy that's probably legally unenforceable.

I note that I need to ask my attorney, aka eldest brother, when I see him next.

"You look beautiful," I say, reaching her. Though I want to slip my arm around her waist and pull her close, I restrain myself by putting my hands in my pockets instead.

Her gaze dips again to my neck before licking her lips. "Thank you. You look nice as well." Tilting to look around me, she rights herself again. "Where are the Torreses?"

"They're running late and told us to start without them."

"That's kind of hard to do since they're the reason we're here."

Brushing my fingertips across her wrist, I tell her I'll be back. Moving back through the crowd, I check in with the host, who leads us to our table. When we're alone, Liv takes a long drink of wine before she asks, "You got me out on a Friday night, Westcott. Now what?"

"You never go out?"

"No. Pretty much never these days."

A server interrupts to take our drink order. I ask, "I'm looking for a small batch barrel-aged bourbon. Do you have any recommendations?"

"I do," he replies, showing me the drinks menu and tapping the page. "I'd recommend this one. It's the one I drink."

"A double on the rocks. Thank you."

"Noah?" Liv's lips are parted as she stares at me.

Pointing at her almost empty glass, I add, "Another wine for the lady."

"Yes, sir." He disappears just as she scoffs.

"I wasn't asking for another glass of wine. You shouldn't be drinking a double before a work meeting."

A chuckle escapes. "You're literally drinking wine, and you're going to lecture me?" I'm lost how she doesn't see the hypocrisy.

"I was nervous . . ." She glances around the room, keeping me on pins and needles, but all she shares is an exasperated huff.

"You're not the first to have a drink to calm their nerves. And," I say, leaning closer, "we're in the social hours of the evening. It wouldn't be unheard of to have a drink during dinner with clients."

Her gaze lengthens, not seeming to set on one particular thing. She shakes her head. "I shouldn't have said anything. It was judgmental, and I didn't mean. I just . . ." God, her eyes are gorgeous, especially when they're staring into mine. "I don't care that you're having a double. Not to make excuses, but here's one from me: my ex used to get wasted at events, so it was a trigger for me, but you're not my ex."

There's no doubt in my mind that she's referring to Chip. "I'm not your ex," I say, keeping my voice low and intimate between us. I don't want her on edge. I want her to enjoy herself, especially if it's true that she never gets out.

"I'm sorry."

"Don't be. People have a way of fucking us up long after they're gone."

With her hands clasped in her lap, she nods. "You shouldn't always be so understanding, Noah."

"Will it make you feel better if I get mad? That kind of stuff doesn't get a rise out of me. Even barely knowing each other, you already know I'm nothing like Chip."

Her body bristles, her gaze falling.

The drinks are delivered, but I stop the server. "I'll pay for this, but do you mind making it a single?"

"I'll take care of it, sir."

Reaching over, she touches my arm as it rests on the table. "You don't have to do that."

"I know. I wanted to. I had a bad day, but liquor isn't going to fix it." My phone buzzes in my pocket. I pull it out to read a text from Mr. Torres. My thoughts start to race because we haven't gotten to the first course. If I tell her the news now, she'll leave, and selfishly, I don't want her to. I want her to stay.

"Is everything alright?"

I reread the message before replying to him. Tucking my phone back in my pocket, I lead with the truth. It's the only way to keep things on the right path with her. "The Torreses had an emergency in London. Their jet awaits their arrival, so our meeting is off the table tonight."

She sits forward with worry running through her expression. "Are you serious? What's going on?"

"He didn't go into detail. He'll contact me when he has a chance to reschedule."

"I hope they're okay." Troubling her lip, she shifts in the chair while looking around the restaurant.

"I think they're okay. They have an office in London, so I'm sure it's work-related."

Taking a breath that fills her chest, she gets comfortable again. "It really is a beautiful restaurant."

"It is." I don't want this chance with her to slip away, so I say, "What if we stay?"

"What if we have dinner together?" she says at the same time.

Laughing together releases some of the pent-up tension hanging in the air. This feels real, like I'm seeing the woman

I met on the beach in the Hamptons again. "Gotta love when fate intervenes."

She giggles, letting it trail off. "I didn't take you as a romantic, Westcott."

"There are a lot of things you don't know about me, Bancroft."

Her bare shoulders rise along with a devilish grin. The vixen. "We've got some time."

"We sure do."

12

Noah

"MY STOMACH HURTS from laughing so hard." With her arms wrapped around her middle, she laughs to herself. She finishes her wine and tilts her head so sweetly to the side to watch me. "Why do I feel like you have stories lined up and ready for any situation?"

"Guilty as charged."

"This comes so easy for you. You're entertaining and funny. You have a million stories to share. Attractive," she says with her first roll of the eyes this evening.

"So what you're saying is I'm the full package?"

A giggle bubbles up, and she leans back, the most relaxed I've seen her since the Hamptons, maybe even more than then. That night wasn't about this—talking, getting to know each other better, telling stories about dates gone wrong or most embarrassing moments. That night had a purpose, and I suppose I served it.

It doesn't feel like the time to ask why she never left me

her number or why she sneaked out of the house. It feels good just being here with her. There's no expectation of afterward, just dinner and great conversation.

"I'm not sure I'm one to ask."

"I'm teasing . . . kind of." I chuckle and finish my drink. We've had another round, but with our bellies full, it's been nice to let off steam from the week without the pressure of clients. "I owe my storytelling to my family. My brothers are older than me, and if I didn't come in with something to grab everyone's attention, it would be easy to get lost in the chatter."

"So you were a little brother fighting for his share of attention? Yep," she says, licking her lips. "I can see that." She rests her elbow on the table while her hand cups her chin. She's settled in, ready to spend a few more hours with me. "Are you close to your family?"

"We're a tight-knit crew. I imagine it could be intimidating for some to join in. Not because we're not welcoming. I have two great sisters-in-law who are a part of the family, but more that we're loud and a bit rambunctious, even now." I chuckle again. "I'm fortunate. I know that. My parents have been married forever—"

"Are they happy?"

The question hits me sideways. It's not one I've been asked before or something I've had to think about. My parents are just my parents and have always been there for us. "They are, always are," I say. "There have been mentions of my dad working too much in the past, long hours away from the family when I was younger, but that was something my brothers experienced, not me or my little sister."

"You have a sister, too?"

"Yeah, Marina." Like my brothers, I feel a sense of pride

when talking about her. For a few years, it was only the two of us since Loch and Harbor had already left the house. "She's two years younger than I am. We've always had a good relationship. Not that we don't get on each other's nerves because we do, but she's a good sister to have. I'm going home to see her in a play on Sunday."

She's invested; her interest hasn't waned, nor have her eyes left mine. "Pretty name. She's an actress?"

When I rest my arms on the table, we're much closer, with only a foot or so separating us. It's probably the wine or the whiskey that's given us this chance, but it feels good to be close to her, so I don't want to waste it. "Why don't we pause on the Westcotts? I want to hear about you."

We both sit back to make room when dessert is served. Liv's eyes widen like she's just fallen in love. "I could cry from pure joy just looking at this dessert."

"Maybe that's how it got its name Crying Chocolate." I eat a donut while she digs in. I'm not letting her off the hook, though. "Are you an only child?"

"I am. I guess one of me was enough of a handful."

"What's the wildest thing you ever did?"

"Sleeping with you." She takes her first bite and then closes her eyes to savor it. "Mm. So good."

That confession and her moaning in pleasure shoot straight to my dick. *Fuck me.* It was all going so well, too. How can I keep things casual when she's causing a riot inside me?

"Glad I could be of service, but that night—"

"Please, Noah. Don't take it away from me."

I'm caught off guard. She's made it clear that it was a night that should be forgotten since I showed last Monday. I run a hand through my hair, trying to find my way through the maze that's Olivia Bancroft. "I thought . . ." I look so lost in what to think or believe, how to feel about something more than a one-night stand in my memories. "I don't know what to say, Liv. You wanted me to quit. Why?"

"The night with you wasn't me." She sets her spoon down on the back end of a cringe. "It was me, but it was out of character. I wasn't thinking. I was acting on instinct. Doing whatever I wanted without thinking about the repercussions."

"I don't think so. I think that's who you really are. That's the issue. You don't have a lack of interesting stories. You aren't a one-dimensional ice queen. You're more than you let on. I have a feeling I'm the only one who's seen the real you."

Her breath collapses in her chest as something else overcomes her. Tears reflect the lights hanging nearby as she tilts her head back to keep them from falling. "I don't want to talk about this."

"I do."

I'm hit hard with a glare, but she seems to catch herself. The flash of anger softens as she leans closer to whisper, "We've had a good time. Let's not ruin—" Suddenly looking down at her purse tucked under her leg, she pulls it out and opens it. Her lips part as panic drifts across her expression.

When she looks up again, she says, "I need to go."

"What? Why?"

She sets her napkin on her chair when she stands. "I'm sorry, Noah." Grabbing her purse, she tucks it under her arm. "Put it on the card, and I'll send through the expense, approving it."

I stand, tossing my napkin to the table. "Is that what you think I'm concerned with? Expensing our dinner? You've got it all wrong, Liv—"

"Would you like the check, sir?" the server asks, standing between us.

Handing him a credit card, I say, "Yes, please close it."

"Was it to your liking?"

I finally turn to him. "It was very good. Thank you."

"I'll be right back." He rushes into the next room, leaving us alone again.

Liv comes closer, touching my arm like we're old friends. "It's not personal," she says. "My friend has food poisoning. I need to check on her."

"I'll order a car for you."

"It's okay. I'll catch a cab out front." She comes closer, our shoes bumping into each other's. "But I want you to know that I had a good time. I'm sorry I need to leave."

"I—"

"Here you are, sir." The server hands me my card and a pen. "Thank you for joining us for dinner tonight."

"You're welcome." I scribble my name, but it's too late. Liv has already left the table. Dammit.

I make it out to the street to find her standing at the curb with her arm up. "Liv?"

When she turns toward me, tears are sliding down her cheeks. Rushing to her, I take hold of her arm. "Why are you crying?"

"I . . ." A cab pulls to the curb. "I need to go."

Seeing her upset has my heart beating harder in my chest. I'll do anything to make her feel better, but how?

I pull the taxi door open and get in the back right after her.

"What are you doing, Noah?"

"I'm not letting you go alone." I shut the door with her still staring at me.

Opening her mouth twice, I can see her thoughts

warring in her eyes. Tugging the seat belt over her shoulder, she shares the address as she buckles in.

As the taxi starts weaving through traffic, I look over at her and ask, "Is your friend okay?"

Her gaze sticks to the window, but the sudden close of her eyes and fall of her head has me concerned. "Liv?"

She looks at me, her eyes taking me in like she's seeing me for the first time again. From fear to possibilities flashing through her expression, she's thoroughly confused me. "I need to tell you something, Noah." Her tone is as serious as her eyes when locked on me like a target. "Something I've told very few people, and I need you to promise me that you'll keep my secret."

"Okay."

"I need to hear you say it."

For a split second, I think she'll crack a smile and start laughing, but the tears are still in her eyes, and the intensity of her stare has me believing what she says. "I promise not to tell anyone."

Relief sinks in, her shoulders easing as she closes her eyes. I have no idea what to say or if I should be speaking at all. I think this is a conversation best left for her to lead. But the cab pulls in front of a building, causing her to lean over me to get a good look at it through my window. "This is me."

I pay and then get out, offering her a hand. With our palms pressed, a spark ignites between us. It's not sexual, but a connection that we're in this together. The taxi peels away, the rubber burning against the concrete.

We move from the smoke by starting for the door. She stops under the awning and glances between the door and me. "This could be the biggest mistake of my life."

"You can trust me, Liv." I take her hand and lead her to the door. "I swear on my life."

She stops just before we enter, her eyes pleading as she fists the sleeve of my jacket. "I'm not sure that's a promise you can keep." Her voice trembles as she tries to blink away tears. Her gaze hits my chest when she's unable to hold mine for any longer.

With her hand latched onto me, I hold her elbow and grasp her other wrist that hangs by her side. Her reaction to her friend being sick doesn't match the illness. "It's food poisoning. It's going to suck for twenty-four hours, but after that, she should be fine." I pull her into my arms for reassurance because I'm at a loss as to how to comfort her worries for her friend otherwise.

She comes so willingly that now *I'm* starting to be concerned. Where's the woman who bit my head off for even existing a few days ago, for disrupting her so-called perfect life, and the one who accused me of trying to ruin her career?

Something is deeply wrong. "Talk to me."

A sniffle has her vibrating against my chest, and then she whispers, "Please know I tried to tell you."

Stroking the back of her head, I ask, "Tell me what?"

When she pushes back, putting space between us, her cheeks are stained with red lines where her tears are falling. The hazel of her eyes is brighter with green under watery lashes. But the fear that crushes her pretty features concerns me most. I cup her face, breaking the streams on her cheeks with the pads of my thumbs. "I need you to tell me what's wrong, Liv. Please."

She takes hold of my hands and then leads me inside the lobby. "We need to get upstairs." Her breath shakes as much as her hands, but she walks with purpose. As soon as she punches the button to call the elevator, she looks up at me. "All I ask is that you allow me to explain."

What the fuck am I walking into? "Explain what?"

"You can hate me, but please don't hate Maxwell."

"Who's Maxwell?"

The elevator opens, and we step inside. She pushes the button for the twelfth floor, then takes a deep breath. "Maxwell is my son."

13

Noah

"YOU HAVE A SON?" I follow her down the hall as she rushes toward a door at the far end.

Without breaking pace, she replies, "Yes." Sticking the key in the lock, she hip butts it open and runs inside. "Cassandra?"

She disappears inside before I reach the door, so I let myself in, closing and locking it behind me. I wait a few seconds to be told where to sit or to make myself at home, but then decide she's busy taking care of her friend. This night has taken an unexpected turn. I'm not sure if it's for the better or worse, but I'm sure she won't leave me in suspense.

Speaking of suspense, who the fuck has she been with where she got pregnant? Have I read this situation with her all wrong? Is she dating someone? She dropped that bomb without further explanation, like I wouldn't have a million questions. Then again, maybe that's why she kept it a secret for so long.

Oh shit.

I just had the worst thought . . . Chip better not be the fucking father. That would be messed up. Okay, so I have a rough estimate of when they were dating, but I'd need to know the kid's age as well. As much as I'm ready to dive in like I'm on an expedition for the truth, I don't think I'm ready to think of another fucker hitting on her, much less anything else.

If she were mine, I wouldn't be having a secret romance. Nope. It would make headline news. Jealousy creeps through my veins, and if I ever met who she's hooking up with, let's just say I'm not in the mood to go to prison. I turn my attention toward the apartment. A mirror with hooks hangs by the entrance, a thin table rests against the wall, and a mix of kid shoes, pink sneakers, and heels litter the floor underneath them. I keep walking, but I can't get the fact that Liv is a mom out of my head. She dropped it like a bombshell, but I'm not sure why. And more importantly, why would I hate her or her kid? That makes no sense. What kind of monster does she think I am that I could hate a baby?

She doesn't know me well, but she doesn't need to worry about me getting along with her family. There's a lot of mystery to uncover, but not today.

This is not something I'm going to be able to figure out tonight, though. I'm taking the wins, the information she's willing to share with me, and calling it a victory.

Considering it's night and only a few lamps are on, the apartment feels wide open and fairly large by New York standards. It's on trend using modern style with a feminine softness of rounded corners instead of harsh edges.

The walls are light in color, not stark white, but a warmth that invites me forward into the larger space. Unexpected and the opposite of her ice queen title. I knew that because she's been giving me glimpses of the real her since we met, but it's good to see I was right about her. She's not as hard as she tries to convince everyone.

The furniture is not sparse, but every piece serves a purpose. It's serene in this room, with varying shades of beige, cream, and other neutrals. My mom would love it here. It's bright compared to the darker colors I chose for my apartment.

Crisp white quartz countertops and windows with shades pulled down finish off the brief tour. It's all money, that much I can tell. Between the building, the design of this place, and the location, it must have cost a fortune. She is a Bancroft, though, so I'm not entirely surprised.

Peeks of red, blue, and yellow are found in a basket in the corner of the room by the TV. The toys add the only hint other than the shoes by the door that a kid lives here.

"She's resting." Liv's voice reaches me before she comes into view. The sound of her padding down the short hall's wood floors has me turning toward her when she appears.

"That's good." When she enters the kitchen, I lean my palms on the cold stone countertop, and ask, "Does she need anything?"

"No. I think rest will help." The weight of concern she carried up here has gone, but now I'm left with a lot of questions I didn't have prior.

"You have a son?"

She pauses at the sink, her eyes lifting before she rinses her hands. She worries her lip, tugging on it, as her gaze falls again. "I do."

"Maxwell."

Her smile is as light as air, and her eyes brighten. "Yes, his name is Maxwell."

Liv is much more open with me. As for Olivia, she seems to be the one with all the secrets. "Why does it seem nobody knows?"

"Some know. My parents. Cassandra."

"Who's Cassandra?"

"My nanny and friend," she adds. "She takes care of him." Rattling her head with a little grin, she chuckles. "And me, if we're being honest. She's with him while I'm at work. She stayed tonight so I could go out."

Each response leads me to answers from another question lingering around my head. "That's why you don't go out. You have a child at home."

She nods and then exhales. The graceful lines from her neck to her arms soften, making me think these confessions have knotted her shoulders for years.

"Liv?" We both turn to see who I assume is Cassandra poking her head out of a bedroom. With her arm wrapped around her stomach, she says, "I need to get home."

"You can't," Liv says. "You're sick, and no way am I letting you take the subway. I'm happy to call a car, but I don't think it's safe for you to travel in this condition."

Cassandra walks slowly, making me think there's more going on than a case of upset stomach. She leans against the wall at the exit of the hall, her hand gripping the corner of the sheetrock. "I need to take care of my dog. He's probably out of food and water. My neighbor's not answering my texts or calls. I just need to get home."

Liv looks at me, not for answers but seemingly at a loss. I say, "Hi, I'm Noah."

She raises her hand, but a feeble wave is all that's managed. "You look dehydrated. Can I get you a glass of water?"

"It goes right through me." She laughs, but there's no humor. "I'm sure that's what you want to hear."

"It's okay. If I can help, I'm here and happy to."

"Thanks."

Liv says, "You need to stay. You can't travel in this condition."

"Bernie needs me."

Turning to me, Liv says, "Her Chihuahua is named Bernie."

"Great name."

She smiles, albeit briefly. "I can't leave Maxwell, so I'm not sure what to do here. Maybe . . ." Liv glances at me again. "Maybe I should feed Bernie."

"I want to be there. You know he's not good with others —*ugh*." She lurches forward, her arms tightening around her middle. Tears start to fall, and I see panic reach her eyes before she runs back down the hall.

Liv and I face each other at the same time. I say, "I could ride with her to make sure she's safe." As if we're planning a coup, I whisper, "But I'm not sure a complete stranger is going to give her comfort."

"I can't go because Maxwell is sleeping. I don't want to drag him all over New York."

"Liv?" Cassandra calls, her voice echoing down the hall.

Liv goes without hesitation, disappearing just as quickly.

I'm not sure what to do here other than offer to help how I can. I bide my time until she returns by walking to the window to check out her view. Rolling up a shade, I'm hit with a stunner of a cityscape. It's dark, but the city is wide awake.

"Noah?"

I whip around to see Liv coming toward me. "I need to ask a favor."

"Anything."

"We don't know each other well enough for me to ask this of you, but I do trust you."

"Trust is a good start to a relationship." The comment doesn't seem to faze her.

"I need to get Cassandra home and feed her dog. I'll make sure she's set up with what she needs tonight and then check on her again in the morning."

"How can I help?"

"I need you to stay here with Maxwell until I return." Her words flow faster as she continues, "He's a good little sleeper and shouldn't be any trouble. If he cries, you can wait a few minutes, and he'll usually fall back asleep again."

I'm still in the pit lane, and she's crossing the finish line. I need a sec to catch up to the obvious. "You want me to watch your baby?"

"Not really."

I balk at her honesty. It doesn't soften the blow, but at least I know she'll tell me the truth. A slight grin shuffles onto my face. "But I'm all you've got?"

"At this time of night? Yes." She takes a breath and then keeps whispering, "It will take about an hour."

I glance at the hallway before asking, "And he's down there sleeping?"

"Yes. Are you up for it? Please be honest with me."

This is a lot to process. First, Olivia Bancroft has a secret son. Second, she trusts me enough to share this part of her life. Third, she needs me. Despite leaving me that night in the Hamptons with no communication or even a goodbye, tonight healed some of those wounds that were left festering. The past is finally behind me. She needs me now, and there's no way in hell I'll let her down. "It will be fine."

Relief washes through her, and she moves in to give me a

hug. Catching herself just inches between us, she stops. Her breathing is heavy as she stares at my chest. But then she stops fighting whatever imaginary obstacle was thrown in her path. Throwing her arms around me, she rests her head on my chest.

It's tentative at first, though all I've wanted to do since seeing her again is rekindle what we left unfinished two years ago. I wrap my arms around her, dipping my nose to her head. The smell of fresh flowers—exotic and warm, if warm had a scent—fragrances her hair.

"I'm ready." We push apart, and Cassandra shuffles to the door. "I'm sorry," she says.

Liv runs her hands down the front of her dress. "I can't wear this. I need to change." She walks away without looking back at me. It gives me one last opportunity to admire how incredible she looks in red silk. "I'll be quick. I promise."

Cassandra and I are left standing across the apartment from each other. I tuck my hands in my pockets and rock back on my heels. "I'm sorry you're not feeling well."

"I'm sorry for ruining your date."

Liv would hate it if she heard it called a date. And though I wouldn't mind if it was after spending time with her tonight, I should be somewhat professional. "We work together."

Glancing down toward the hall and then to me, she says, "Do you have kids?"

First time I've been asked that. Welcome to adulthood, I suppose. "No."

"Kids are great, especially Maxwell."

"Yeah," I reply, making casual conversation.

"Liv's a great mom, too. Tonight was the first time she's been out in forever. I hate that I caused it to be cut short."

Although I'm not opposed to the idea, it wasn't a date. But for some reason, Cassandra seems pretty convinced it was. Now I'm wondering how that conversation played out.

She continues, "She likes to be home in time for the routines—dinner, bath, book, and putting him to bed. It's so sweet. I know she wishes she could be with him during the day. She's so dedicated to giving him the best life she can. I'm sure you see how hard she works since you're also in the office."

I thought she was falling back on Bancroft money. That she's working to earn it herself comes as a surprise. I look around the apartment again, seeing it in a new light this time. Does she pay for this herself?

Without using a trust fund to help buy my apartment, I wouldn't have it. Now I'm curious about Liv's situation, but it's not my place to talk to her about her finances. "We don't see each other at work much since we're in different departments, but I know she works hard."

I'm starting to think she's quizzing me for reasons other than passing the time. I think we're both wishing Liv would return. She asks, "Have you ever held a baby?"

I want to laugh, but I restrain myself. "My little sister."

I slip off my jacket and drape it on the back of a dining chair. It was a good momentary distraction, but then we're left in the quiet room again.

"Oh." Her face gains some color back when she smiles. "How old is she?"

"Twenty-three." I chuckle while rolling up my shirt-sleeves.

She moves to rest against the counter. "I'm too weak to laugh, but that's funny."

Seems laughter is good medicine. I'm out of jokes, but I share something personal to my family, "One of my brothers and his wife are pregnant with their first. First grandkid for my parents."

She nods. "I'm sure the baby will be spoiled with love."

"Yeah, we're all pretty excited."

Liv stops in her socks as if she's interrupted. "Excited about what?" Wearing fitted workout pants and an oversized NYU sweatshirt, she hustles to slip on her pink sneakers. I'm digging this new side of Liv that's been revealed. It's like a secret club that only members are privy to, and she gave me a golden invitation.

"My brother and his wife are having a baby." Liv's smile is instant. I continue, "First grandkid, so I was telling Cassandra how excited we all are to welcome a baby into the family."

Her expression falls, an overwhelming emotion I can't quite identify striking her face. I'm not sure what happened, but I've caused tears to fill her eyes. "Did I say something wrong?"

"No," she says, waving me off. "It's fine." With her head tilted, she wipes her eyes as if I can't see her visibly shaken. She then grabs her wallet from her purse as if nothing had happened. "You have my number."

"I do." I move closer, but she walks away. I can't take it personally since she's not even looked at me in the past two minutes to know. "I'm sorry."

She pauses and takes a stumbling breath. "I should get her home."

"We'll talk when you get back?"

"Sure," she replies as she walks out the door. "Call me if you or Maxwell need anything."

"I will—" The door closes before I finish speaking. "What the hell just happened?" Returning to the window, I drag a hand over my head while staring through the glass.

Just when I think Liv and I have made progress, we end up back where we started . . . and not the first time, but instead, we're stuck in that conference room with her shooting daggers.

The worst part is I have no idea how I screwed this up. Fucking hell.

I can't seem to win, but that won't keep me from trying.

———

I DRAG my arm over my head to block out the noise.

It doesn't work.

Ripped from a dream that Liv was starring in, *fully naked*, I might add, I rub my eyes before I can open them. The noise is . . . crying?

I open one eye and then the other, the burning real and causing me to clamp them closed and rub. When I reopen them, I don't recognize the ceiling or the couch where I'm lying. Why am I on—shit. I'm at Liv's.

Bolting upright, I grab my phone to see two missed texts from her:

> We're at the ER. It's her appendix.

The second reads:

> They're prepping her for surgery. I'm going to stay. I'll keep my phone on if you need me.

I hear more crying.
Maxwell.
Oh fuck.
I jump to my feet, still feeling out of sorts from my unin-

tended nap. The texts were from an hour ago, but I call out, "Liv?" just in case she came home and was letting me sleep.

Maxwell screams. Only little cries but he doesn't sound upset, which is a relief. I follow the sound to a closed door in the hallway, and slowly turn the knob to peek in. A giggle erupts in the dark before my eyes have time to adjust, and I'm met with eyes that reflect the little light I let in.

Standing at the crib's railing, he starts bouncing excitedly, his laughter getting the better of him. To say he's cute would be an understatement. He's freaking adorable with his big grin and wide-as-saucer eyes. "Hi there, big guy."

I'm greeted with a, "Hi," that slices the air, and he bounces again. I don't know what I was expecting. Maybe a five-year-old or a toddler. He's littler and younger. Leaning down so he can see me better, I say, "Hey, Maxwell. I'm Noah. Noah Westcott."

No clue why I'm introducing myself like he understands the formality of the act.

He raises his arms, and I think he wants me to pick him up. "I'm not sure that's a good idea. You're supposed to be sleeping, not playing."

In response, I catch a few "Blab blab blabs" and a "Mama."

"Your mom will be back soon." I debate what to do. He seems content, so maybe he just wanted some company. I scruff his hair and tickle under his chin. *He's cute.*

Round face, chubby legs, and a cowlick of brown hair that he'll be fighting the rest of his life. "I feel your pain, Max. I have a matching one." I tilt my head down just to show him. If blowing spit bubbles means he likes this game, then I'm winning at this babysitting gig.

"You need to sleep. Will you lie down?" He sits. "Nice party trick but keep going."

I can't see much from the crack of light sneaking in, but I don't think he's going back to sleep anytime soon. Cooing and grinning, he grips the bars of the crib and rattles them. "Strong kid." Leaning over, I ask, "Want to go night-night?"

Wide awake is an understatement.

What do I do?

"Hold him until he falls asleep again." Cassandra's advice comes to mind.

Since he's already pulled himself to his feet, I ask, "Are you going to go to bed or—"

His arms shoot into the air again.

It's my sign. I reach in and pick him up, pulling him against my chest. Our faces are close enough for me to see his eyes even better and for him to see mine. His tiny fingers rub over the scruff on my chin, and he grins. "Hey there," I say again, just to make him feel at home in my arms.

It's odd how at home I feel already holding him.

I move to the cushy chair and settle in. Rocking him in my arms comes to mind from movies and such that I've seen, but I think he's past that. Before I can arrange him, he lays his head on my chest under my chin. One hand holds me, and the other wanders as if it moves of its own accord.

Grinning, I take it and hold it in my hand. His eyes close without needing prompting. His breathing steadies, and he's fast asleep. With one hand, I pull my phone from my pocket and text Liv:

> Don't worry about us. Maxwell and I are doing fine.

14

Olivia

MY HEART STOPS BEATING . . .

And then it rolls across my chest like thunder.

I should feel panicked seeing Noah holding my baby. *But I don't.* My heart feels too big for my chest to contain, every beat magnified like someone's hooked an amp to it. I worry it's too loud for the quiet of a nursery, and I'll wake them up. I close the door so they can sleep a bit longer without the interruption of my blooming emotions getting in the way.

But I can't resist and peek inside again.

There, in the chair where I've rocked my baby to sleep through the past year, sleeps a giant of a man, and cradled in the nook of his arm is Maxwell. Both slumber like reflections of each other.

Maxwell's ninety-five percentile ranking in size, well, it's not from my side of his family. In appearance, from hair to eye color, Maxwell is his father's son.

I have such conflicting feelings, a hurricane of them swirling around my head. Is it okay to love the sight of them together? To hope that Maxwell could have the love of a supportive dad?

Our past has dictated every move we've made and each word exchanged since he walked into that conference room. Getting to know him has been a struggle of my own doing. I knew ... deep down, I already knew he was a good man. Not just from how he made love to me with care, but by putting my needs before his, and holding me in the aftermath like we could survive the next morning.

Leaving my number for him wasn't as hard as I thought, considering I was fresh off a breakup. It also wasn't done in a moment of weakness. I didn't expect to connect with anyone. It's not what I was looking for, but spending time with him changed something in my chemistry. He wasn't just a physical attraction; we were fireworks together in bed. It was more. He had me believing *we* were more than a one-night stand. I followed my heart and believed him.

After that, I blamed the alcohol for blurring my rationale. My relationship aside because that's another story altogether, I've come around to the idea that Noah not calling me isn't something I can hold against him. He has a right to play a role in Maxwell's life. Seeing them together now cements that in my heart.

It's only right he knows sooner rather than later.

I close the door as a wave of emotions barrel over me. Leaning against the wall, I drop my head in my hands just as the tears start to fall. The unknown is terrifying. I've imagined a million different scenarios, but I won't truly know how he'll react until I tell him.

The grief over losing time with my son to share him with someone else, the joy I'd carried in my heart when I realized how much this would mean to Maxwell to have a father who's there for him, and the mixture of being out at sea on a life raft that was never meant to weather the storm—yet I'm surviving—have me floating between the three in uncertainty.

Warm hands caress my shoulders, and Noah's arms envelop me. "It's okay, Liv." Tears transfer from my face to his chest as I breathe in the cologne lingering on his skin. He holds me to him. I don't fight it like I've been carelessly fighting him since he's been in the city. With the image of him holding Maxwell still in my head, I soak him in. "Why are you crying?" he whispers against the top of my head and then places a kiss there.

Do I deserve his kindness?

Not for how I've behaved so ruthlessly. Does it matter that I was protecting the most important thing in my life? Yes. Now that I've witnessed him act so caring toward my son and me, I know he'd never hold that against me.

But keeping Maxwell from him any longer might cause a ripple of anger that can't be repaired. I don't want that to happen to us, so it's in my hands to make sure it doesn't.

At this moment, I revel in the feel of having him around me again, holding me in a way that no one has in longer than I can remember prior to him in the Hamptons.

When I look up, our eyes meet, and though I know I shouldn't . . . I really should not kiss him, I'm overwhelmed with the need to be connected to him again. The desire to forget who I am, to feel like Liv again for a few hours takes over. I lift on my tiptoes and kiss Noah with reckless abandon.

And he kisses me right back with just as much passion as if he's been saving it for years like I have. His hand slides up my back and my shoulder to my neck, then he cups my cheek as the heat between us magnifies. When I pull back, only our lips lose the connection, but I still feel it deep within me.

I'm relieved to see his breathing picked up and that the look in his eyes is wild like mine. With him, I can savor this hunger unabashedly, not giving a damn what the world outside thinks of me.

He leans his head against me and closes his eyes. "Are you sure? Because—"

"I'm sure, Noah." I caress his face, and when he opens his eyes, I add, "I want to be with you so badly." There's a plea to my tone that I don't recognize. *Weak to him?* It's illogical to need him so much right now, but that's all I can think will make the world disappear before it falls apart again.

"Do you know how long I've waited to hear you say that, to want me like I spent so much time wanting you back, even if I could only have one more night?" He kisses me without hesitation and lifts me into his arms, preventing my spinning thoughts from taking over. As soon as my legs wrap around his middle, he turns, pushing open the door to my bedroom as if he lives here.

Setting me on the bed, he crawls on top of me, but I push my hands against his chest. "Wait."

He stops, his chest rising and deflating under the shirt that was crisp hours earlier. Like his hair, he's disheveled but so damn sexy. "What?"

"I've been sitting in a hospital and riding in cabs. I'm dirty and a mess."

He runs the pad of his thumb over the apple of my cheek with a small smile. His gaze wanders from my eyes to my mouth, my chin to my forehead, as if he's searching for something to back my claim. Leaning down, he kisses the scar above my right eyebrow. It's barely noticeable these days, but his lips are tender against my skin, making me feel loved.

Too soon for that word . . .

Too soon for love of that kind . . .

"You've never been more beautiful." Cared for. That's how I feel in his arms. Inhaling, he briefly closes his eyes before leaning his head against mine again. Excitement brightens his eyes. "But I'm liking this idea. What if we shower together?" Grabbing me by the hands, I'm pulled to my feet before I can back out. Not that I would. I've seen this man naked before. That image has run through my mind many times since, so I'm not upset about seeing him or feeling him all over again.

He says, "Let's get you clean." I go willingly. Holding my hand, he leads me into the bathroom and closes the door behind us.

"You afraid someone's going to walk in on us?"

He leans around me and locks it as if for good measure. "One day, you'll be glad you got in the habit. Ask me how I know."

I start to laugh. "I'm thinking that's a conversation for another time."

"Probably best."

Moving to the shower, I reach in and turn on the water to warm it up for us. I was never confident about sex before I met Noah. And although my body has changed from when he last saw me, I feel confident in his presence and kick off my shoes without a thought.

Maybe I shouldn't be jumping into sleeping with him again after the rough week we had. But tonight, that all changed. I saw him for the man he is instead of the monster who wants to take my baby away.

Or maybe it feels good to be wanted and treated like I

matter. Either way, I win in the end. I kiss him again as we keep stripping clothes from our bodies. There's something so incredibly magnetic about Noah Westcott that I don't mind skipping a few steps when it comes to him.

His pants drop, and just as he steps out of them, I press myself fully against him. Sliding my hands over the broad of his shoulders, I lift to kiss him again. His large hands covering my lower back make me ready to yield to his every desire. A squeeze of my ass has my insides clenching in desire.

But the way he tilts his head and nudges to get access to my neck has my nipples hard and my body turned on. Trailing kisses down my neck, he stops, his warm breath heating my skin, and then he travels back up to my mouth.

I'm backed toward the shower, taking two steps before I stop again. "I need to get something."

Trust is not only seen in his eyes. It's felt when Noah bends to kiss me. "You know where to find me. Be quick." A slap on the ass has me squealing—the burn and tingling a warning of what's to come—and has me moving quicker in anticipation.

I don't have alcohol or a pill failing to blame this time. I'm sober and well aware of the possible outcomes. I also know with Noah, I need double the protection.

Inside my closet, I kneel to dig through the bottom drawer of the left built-ins. Filled with old bikinis and sexy bras I no longer wear, I pull out a box of condoms and flip it over to check the expiration date. There hasn't been a need to use protection in years.

We'll use these in the nick of time with one month to spare. I grab all three from the package, detouring to the counter to drop two off on the way to the shower. My feet still as my breath catches when I see the reflection in the mirror.

Oh.

My.

God.

I spin around, gripping the counter's edge to keep me upright.

Noah's an attractive man, probably the most handsome I've ever laid eyes on, but I did not expect to get a front-row seat witnessing a god in the flesh wash himself under a downpour of water. With his eyes closed, his head tilted back, and his hands rubbing over his abs, no one could convince me that Noah Westcott is mortal.

It's impossible that he exists, much less walks among us.

My tummy tightens as my body awakens to the sight before me. To know he wants to be with me adds the cherry on top.

Scrubbing his hands over his head, he pushes the water from his hair, and it slides down his body. I bite my lip, ready to watch the show, but he looks up, and our eyes connect through the glass door. There's no smirk or arrogance found. *Only sincerity.*

I feel tipsy from the intoxicating look he's giving me, the come-hither stare that draws me to him. He opens the door, and asks, "You want to join me?"

"Do I ever." I enter, and the water coats my body. It's hot and beginning to steam inside the enclosure. I hold up the foil packet in front of me. And there's the smug grin I expected earlier.

Taking me by the hips, he sways me as he comes closer and kisses my neck. "I'm glad you're prepared. Protection was not something I thought to bring to a business dinner."

Dinner? It's a shock to the system to realize that was

tonight. So much has happened since then that it's hard to wrap my head around the hours that have disappeared. "You told me you were prepared for that meeting," I tease as the weight of his erection falls against my belly.

With a strong desire to please him, to turn him on so much that he loses control, I slip my hand between us and wrap it around his erection. I start with a slow stroke up and then down.

His eyelids dip closed, but then his gaze latches onto me. With one hand, he brings two fingers under my jaw and drags the tips across my skin until he reaches my mouth. Dipping them between my lips, he says, "Suck."

I close my eyes, then close my lips around him. Sucking on fingers has never been a fantasy of mine until now. My body is electric, with sexual energy flowing through me like a live wire. I take him deeper while I pick up the pace with my hand.

He slides his other hand beside mine, covering it and squeezing until I'm holding him so tight that it just might save my life if I fell . . . *fall for him*. Too late. I've already crossed that threshold.

Turnabout is fair play.

And he's getting his revenge in the most devilish of ways. The water pours over us, soaking our hair, my makeup running wild across my face. You'd never know it by how he stares at me like he's the lucky one.

That look empowers me, making me feel sexy.

It's an incredible feeling, like ecstasy.

Just as he reaches the apex between my legs, he swipes two fingers gently over my entrance and then back again. I open my eyes to find his fixed on mine, my reactions too visceral to restrain—weakened knees, my breathing heavier, and my mind blurring as I struggle to remember my name.

When he dips inside me, I suck harder until he rips his fingers away and replaces them with his mouth. Our tongues tangle as we set each other's worlds on fire. Our bodies become a frenzy of kisses and hands, nails digging into skin, and cold stone walls that send shivers down my spine.

He fucks me as I stroke him closer to the edge of his own orgasm.

On the verge of finding the bliss I haven't captured in so long, my body feels empty without him. He kisses me harder this time, an intention that's turned with intensity. As if it's too much, too much fire, too much heat, too much desire to keep feeding, he pushes himself away from me. His chest is heavy with the breaths he's releasing. Staring at me with the water raining down between us, he says, "You feel too good. I need to be inside you, Liv."

Liv . . .

He never saw the masquerade I was wearing. He just saw me. *Always me.*

"I want that, too."

Grabbing the packet, he rips it open and covers his erection. He slides his hands around my shoulders, kissing me, then spinning away from facing him. My hands are anchored to the wall when I feel the slick of his body against my back. "Watch your head."

I look at the stone tiles I have my palms pressed to just as I realize what he means. Shuffling, I brace as he positions himself at my entrance. He asks, "You ready?"

The slightest of nods barely escapes before he fills the emptiness inside me. "Oh God," I cry out, never wanting this fullness to vanish. My elbows loosen, but when he pulls out and thrusts again, I straighten, bracing myself for everything he's willing to give.

His groans twist my insides, his whispers of desire elicit goose bumps over my skin, and when he bites my shoulder, the pleasurable pain shoots to my core. I feel my body giving way, my knees weakening. He wraps himself around me and fucks like he has no other choice.

Erratic.

Intense.

Powerful.

Passionate.

It's fast. Hard. Dangerous as I take his unwavering thrusts that touch parts of myself I thought I buried long ago. He unearths every one of those emotions and memories. Unleashing the secrets that are the heart of me.

My head drops forward as my mind goes blank. The quakes of my body erupt around him as he pumps inside me, taking me like he'll never have another chance.

The sound of his release comes in a "fuck" that echoes off the tiles and sends my body to bend at his command again. Thrown into turmoil, I come a second time at the end of his. My fingers press so hard to the wall that I feel like I could crush it beneath my fingertips. "Noah." I suck in his name on a breath that catches in my throat as I'm dragged into the beautiful oblivion again.

I fall and fall until I'm caught in his arms and covered with kisses, bringing me back to life again. When our harsh breathing evens out, he turns me around and caresses my chin. "You're so beautiful it hurts."

I wrap my arms around his neck, kissing the corner of his jaw, then higher on the side of his mouth. His eyes look tired, as if he's been fighting his own tidal wave of emotion, and the exhaustion has caught up to him.

It's the sex.

But there's more to it than that. When it comes to the

complications of the two of us, we have so much to talk about when the time comes.

Touching his lips with my fingertip, I follow with a quick kiss, and then say, "It's almost four in the morning."

"It's the weekend, so we can sleep late."

"I've not had that luxury for a while."

I hate that I have butterflies, considering what we just did, but they're fluttering with nerves because I want to leave the past where it lives and focus on the second chance we've been given, so I ask, "Will you stay?"

15

Olivia

I SMILE, and when I do, he does as well. Smiles are contagious in the right situations, *like this one.*

He leans down to kiss me, his lips full and taking mine. When he pulls back, he licks his lips, and says, "I'd like that."

We're moving so fast that I don't know if we've had time to consider the repercussions. I'm still throwing caution to the wind.

With him, it's easy to forget the world outside.

In here, it feels safer in his arms.

My body feels weak, and my legs wobbly. "I'm so tired."

"I got you." His arms come around me, and the strength of our connection keeps me from slipping as we finish our shower. He asks, "Why were you crying?"

I had hoped to escape that line of questioning, but I should have known better. Noah would never leave someone in such disrepair. "It's been a long day, and I had a lot of emotions to deal with."

As we dry off, he keeps his eyes on me as if he knows I won't say anything to upset him. "You can talk to me." His tone remains as steady as his eyes. "Is it Cassandra?"

"I am worried about her. I hope she'll be okay."

"Is she not?"

"She is." After wrapping the towel around me, I tuck in the tail and then apply my moisturizer. Leaning against the counter next to me, Noah watches in a way that's not intrusive, but he might be taking mental notes. I continue with my routine because that look in his eyes makes me feel like a million bucks. "I stayed until she came out of surgery. They told me she did well."

"That's good." Moving behind me, he massages my shoulders, causing me to sag under the incredible feel of his hands. "Talk to me. What else is on your mind? Maybe you're hungry." He places a quick kiss on my neck and then another. "I can make a solid omelet depending on what's in the fridge. Or I can order you something?"

Our eyes meet in the reflection of the mirror. Leaning back, I have no doubt he'll catch me. Big arms swallow my frame as I'm sure he's struck with the vision of us together as a couple like I am. I fit so well with him as if I was built to fill the spaces of his frame. "That's not necessary. Thank you, though."

When he nods, a slight yawn tries to steal the show, but he fights it, reminding me of how Maxwell does the same. Turning around, I run my hands over his chest and upward until I wrap them around his neck. "I'm glad you're staying."

My body feels small in his hands as they run from my waist to my hips, repeating the path several times. "I'm glad you asked."

Cupping my face, he moves in to kiss me, this time deepening it. When we part, I stay lost in the beauty of our bond for a few seconds before I open my eyes again. "Hey you," he whispers. "Let's get you to bed."

I'm scooped into his arms and carried into the bedroom. "I need to check on Maxwell first." He detours out the door and sets me at the foot of the nursery. Seeming just as interested in peeking in, he stands behind me when I open the door. The gentle breeze of light that shines in is enough for me to see Maxwell sound asleep in his crib.

Noah's shadow engulfs mine, and for a moment, my mind can see him in that chair again, holding Maxwell like he is his own. He is already, and I just know in my soul that their bond runs deep.

I listen, needing to hear his breathing to feel comfortable enough to close the door. "He's good."

Taking Noah's hand, I bring it to my mouth and kiss it. Holding it there, I soak in the way he blended so easily into my night, my home, my life.

I'd like to think about what happens tomorrow, but that didn't go so well for me last time. Is it better to set my expectations aside and enjoy our time together?

The top of my head, my hair still wet from towel-drying it, is stroked, and then he leans over to kiss me there. We linger in the hall, both of us a little unsure about the next step, but maybe . . . maybe not each other this time around.

He pulls me into his arms, holding me where we started tonight. Noah whispers, "He was never upset. Max laughed a lot and then zonked out on my shoulder. I think he called me here to meet and hang out." A light chuckle appears to be caught in a memory. "It's like the trust was already there between us the second I opened the door."

"Noah?"

He tilts to see my eyes. Can he see how they're filling with tears? That telling me he and my son shared more than a few laughs and sleep, that they share blood and a resemblance, and even a name?

My body feels wrecked from the emotional overload, but I can't hold on to this secret any longer. Not just for Maxwell but also for Noah's sake. He needs to know Maxwell trusts Noah because he feels safe with him.

Rubbing his hand along my neck, he adds, "Let's get you to bed."

I'm too tired to carry this burden any longer. It's too complex to navigate my thoughts through the pros and cons of the situation. But really, it's just Noah being here, being himself, that has my heart bursting with joy to tell him. "I need to tell you something."

He holds my wrist and leads me back into the bedroom. "You can tell me anything," he replies as if it will be nothing more than small talk about the weather.

Pulling back the covers, he steps away just enough for me to crawl into bed first. He's quick to lie beside me and offer an open-arm invitation to snuggle against him. I do. I settle right in, thinking about how it would be nice to talk about the weather with someone, to make small talk over coffee, and to—What am I doing?

His being a father to Maxwell doesn't come as a package deal with me attached. I'm not opposed to the idea, but I'm not the priority. I still can't bring myself to regret what we did in the shower or how I'm lying with my arm draped over his chest like I do this every night. I savor this night, closing my eyes and letting the feel of his beating heart soothe me.

But my head is determined to ruin everything good in my life, to blow it up with guilt riddling through my heart until I tell him everything. How? How can I ruin what we're sharing? Using his words, it's so beautiful that it hurts.

My thoughts are suddenly in overdrive, my heart racing. I know why, but I'm not sure how to break this news to him or when. Is there ever a good time to have your life turned upside down? Once he's told, I can't take it back. Although I've realized he needs to know sooner rather than later, what if he's not prepared?

I swallow hard, knowing I'm being a fool. No one prepares for something like this. I wasn't, then went it alone for months before I told my mom. She became a shoulder to cry on, the only person I knew would help me through without judgment.

It sure wasn't my dad.

I think a part of him still believes this is Chip's baby. I think he wants to because otherwise he's facing a societal shift inside his belief system. Not only did his daughter have a one-night stand but she's having a stranger's baby. By choice. How would he explain that to his country club buddies out on the golf course or, worse, the office? He took it as a personal affront to what he was trying to accomplish.

So much resentment has built up inside me that I refuse to give him any more of my strength. I pray Noah will take the news better than my dad did. I think he will, and that alone comforts me to know I'm doing the right thing.

Despite the nerves on how to tell him, my mind is made up. My soul is settled on the subject. Noah's a good man and should know the truth.

His breathing is even but shallow, making me think he hasn't fallen asleep yet. "Are you awake?" I whisper, drawing figure eights on his chest.

"I'm awake." He sounds on the verge of sleep, but I grin in the dark, realizing he doesn't want me to know. He wants to be here for me. Warmth and a dreamworld of emotions swell in my chest.

I'm still unsure how to say this, so I tilt my head up, thinking I might find the right path when I look into his eyes. "Noah?"

A light chuckle rocks his body when he looks at me. "Yes, Liv?"

Like a Band-Aid, I need to rip it quick. "You know, you were the last one I was with." I leave the confession in the air and wait for a response with bated breath.

"I hope so. It was only twenty minutes ago."

"Even tired, you haven't lost your sense of humor."

"I'm certain nothing was funny about that bad joke. I'm blaming it on the hour." But then he says, "That was two years ago." Disbelief tinges his words. There's a pause, and I can tell he's inching closer to the truth by how his brow furrows, and the grin is gone. He glances at me, tightening his arm around me. "That's a long time."

God, he feels sorry for me. I could almost laugh, but I'm worried I'll end up in tears from the tension beginning to permeate the air. "Yes. It's been a while." I sit up, planting my hand on the bed to rest my weight. Making sure he's okay, I swallow my fear and go for it. "I want you to know . . . I *need* you to know—"

"What do you want me to know?" A lazy grin swims into place just as he tucks a few strands of my hair behind my ear. "You're so goddamn beautiful, babe."

Babe has me melting inside. Looking down at his chest makes it easier to accept his compliment. His eyes always give him away, and right now, they're determined to make me believe there's a possibility of so much more between us if we allow it to bloom.

It's addicting, feeding not only my ego but also my heart the one thing that keeps it beating. *Love.*

My cheeks flush, so I press a hand to my cheek to cool it down. It doesn't work. He's determined to kill me with a case of the swoons, but I have my own goals, and blurt, "Maxwell is fourteen months old."

A slight squint of his eyes releases, and he rubs my back. "Are you alright?"

"Fine. I just need you to hear what I'm saying."

"I hear you. No sex since the last time we were together, and Maxwell is fourteen months old. Got it. You seem stressed. Is there anything else on your mind?"

His fingers brush against my leg, and it's not lost on me that he's making all the right gestures to make me feel secure with him. I do. I feel safe with him.

"Yes." I lead him toward the truth, hoping he realizes I'm not losing touch with reality. I just need him to help me out here. I take a breath, and say, "Maxwell's middle name is Noah. *Maxwell Noah.*"

I expect him to react, but he doesn't, so that causes my mind to go into overdrive again. "What do you think?" I ask, a small shake to my voice.

"Think . . ." The thought trails off when his eyes leave mine, staring into the darkest part of the room before pivoting his gaze toward Maxwell's door. "You haven't been with anyone else." I barely hear him, but I hate that I've assigned alarm to his tone. Nothing indicates he is, but my heart throbs in my ears, and I might be hearing things. "Maxwell is . . . fourteen . . . nine months . . . *fuck.*"

He swings his legs to the floor and gets out of bed. I can't tell if he's mad or trying to calm himself down, but I'm worried. "Noah?"

He stills, his back facing me, but there's no response. His

head drops forward, and he drags his fingers through his hair. The only sound in the room is his deep breathing, especially because I don't feel like I can breathe at all.

I scramble to my knees, unsure how to help or even what to do, but I think I should get dressed. I go to him first, needing to know he's not mad. Reasoning through my brain that it's normal for him to need a minute or an hour or more to process this kind of major life news.

Feeling helpless, though, I touch his shoulder. My hand is left in the air when he drops out of my reach. Turning toward me, he says, "You told me not to hate you. You said that before telling me you're a mother." Maybe I preferred his back because when he angles toward me and I see the anger in his eyes, I shrink inside myself. "You told me not to hate Maxwell. It didn't make sense to me then, but now . . ."

He pinches the bridge of his nose and rubs his eyes. A hard swallow follows the minutest of headshakes. "What have you done, Liv?" His voice is calm, eerily so. I've lost the ability to speak, though. My throat is choked entirely under the intensity of his glare.

I look away, needing the reprieve. I didn't think telling him would be easy, but I never predicted anger being a part of it. The air stills, or maybe it's my heart breaking into pieces. Just as a tear slips down my face, I reply, "I can explain."

"I need you to explain." His chest rises and falls with quick breaths. The anger has burned out when I look up at him again. All I see now is confusion. "I need you to tell me the truth, Olivia."

Olivia.

The name alone from his mouth is a stab to my heart. My shoulders fall as my hopes crash along with it. The happy image of him and Maxwell, even the three of us potentially becoming something more than what we are now that I'd created in my head vanishes from the slip of his tongue.

I can't fight this battle once I realize I'm the enemy. I raise the white flag and surrender, lowering my armor and shield that protected us to lay bare at his feet everything that matters most to me. "Maxwell's your son."

16

Noah

"MAXWELL IS MY SON?"

The words don't make the least bit of sense, but when I say them out loud again, they fall into place. "Maxwell is my son."

Devastation tears Liv apart right before me, her tears falling as silent sobs wrack her naked body. I can't seem to make myself move to comfort her. All I can think about is the little boy in the next room.

As if I'd been drowning, I break the surface, suddenly feeling everything all at once—air in my lungs, the sound of a siren somehow reaching this building's floor, my eyes adjusted to the darkness of the room as if it's noon.

I go to the bathroom and begin pulling on my clothes. I don't care about wrinkles or that I'm tugging on clothes that were left in a pile on the floor. I just need to be ready.

For what?

A conversation with her?

To barge into that bedroom to wake up the baby? My baby.
Call my brothers, or talk to my mom?

I have no fucking clue what I'm supposed to do, but my thoughts are too muddled to think clearly. Before I button my shirt, I go to the sink and splash water on my face, hoping it wakes me from whatever this is—nightmare, daydream, requiem, celebration. "Fuck," I mutter as water drips from my chin.

I look up and see Liv in the mirror—her beauty, full defenses in place under crossed arms, and the vulnerability of fear hanging in her eyes. Clothed in a short robe, she leans against the doorframe, cautiously watching me. I grab the towel off the nearby bar and dry my face before tossing it on the counter and turning around.

She says, "I know you're angry." I hate hearing her voice shake, and then I see her hand doing the same.

"I'm not angry, Liv. I just need to sit with this before—"

"Before what? I need to know what you're thinking, Noah. Can't you understand that the silence or the blowup was my fear all along? But at least if you're yelling, I know where you stand."

That only leaves one place for me to reside in this situation—in the middle of the two. Keeping space between us, I lean against the counter. I'm a big guy. My voice can boom if I lose it, and I don't want to lose it with her. The last thing I'd want to do is to scare her. I lower my voice, trying my best to keep it even. "I'm not mad at you. I just need . . ." I rub my forehead, hoping to get clarity before speaking, but nothing in my past has prepared me for this. "It's taking everything inside me not to go into that room right now."

Looking at the floor between us, she closes her eyes, but when she looks up, the fear's subsiding, curiosity growing in her expression. "What would you do if you could go into his room?"

I glance at the door where she's standing, estimating the steps to the baby's room from here. "Hold him again. If I would have known . . ." A pain in my chest grows, resentment sneaking in and feeding the ache. I look away, not wanting to carry that burden, not wanting to assume I know the full story before she tells me. "I wouldn't have put him back in the crib. I would have held him all night if I could."

Her crying voids my pain. If I can't process my feelings, I can only imagine what she's going through. This isn't just about me. It's about all three of us in different ways.

Closing the space between us, I should probably ask before I take her into my arms, before closing my eyes and dipping my head against hers, before reassuring her that everything will be alright when I don't know if it will be. But I don't. I just do it. I do it because she's in pain, and although it's unlike mine, it's not less intense.

She's diminished in my arms as if the truth being put into the universe has stolen a part of her existence as well. When her arms come around me, her cries soften, though. It's a small positive at the base camp of the tumultuous mountain we're being forced to climb. I don't know the emotions that will be shed along the way, but I'll take the risk if we can get to the top with less weight dragging us down.

I whisper, "Tell me what you're feeling."

"Lost." Her arms squeeze me even tighter. "What happens next?"

Reaching around me, I take hold of her hands and bring them between us. I rub the softness of her skin, needing the connection as much as I assume she does. "We'll get through this. Nothing will happen to him." I don't even know what I'm saying. I just know that Maxwell is safe, and I intend to make sure he stays that way. "Don't be afraid."

She pushes back, her eyes searching mine as if she's lost a piece of herself and is desperate to find it again. "What would I have to be afraid of?"

"That's not what I meant."

"What did you mean, Noah?" She starts gathering my socks and jacket before I have time to address the question.

"Look at me, Liv."

"Don't you mean Olivia?" she snaps as if her name is a bad word all of a sudden, as if I've sworn it off as such.

"Don't do this."

Offense straightens her back right quick. "Don't do what?"

I go to her and take my shoes out of her hands. "I meant that I know he's safe in the current situation."

She cradles the rest of my stuff to her chest like a lifeline. "*Current* situation? I'm all he knows." Her voice tightens, her hands fisting the clothes to her body. "You're not coming in here to disrupt his life."

"I don't want that either."

"But I don't know what you're thinking. I don't know how to feel or . . . My world hinges on what you decide to do. What do you want, Noah? Tell me. *Please*. Please tell me."

"I can't. I just found out I'm his father, and you want me to make a life-altering decision on the spot. Here's one—I want to get to know him. I want him to know me as his dad." I hate that my voice rises, but I can't seem to control it any longer. "We need to calm down."

"Calm down?" Panic rises in her eyes, but her tone is clearer, firm in her stance. "I want you in his life, but I can't lose him. I won't. You can't have him."

If there was a button, she just pushed it. "I can't *have* him? He's my son. If I want to—"

Dropping the clothes, she walks into the bedroom, leaving me with the great proclamation I was ready to make hanging on the edge of my tongue. "Fuck." Yep, she knows just the buttons to push. I follow her into the bedroom, ready to hash this out tonight. Before I can get a word out, she points at the door. "I think it's best if you leave."

"Leave? What the hell are you talking about? Don't act like this—"

"It's not an act. You've crossed a line—"

"*I've* crossed a line?" I balk, tapping my leg. "Let's get something straight. The reason you are *all* that Maxwell knows is because I fucking didn't know about him. So I haven't crossed a line. I haven't even gotten close to it." She stands her ground when I get even closer to her. "I'll tell you one thing, though. You turn this into a fight, we'll fucking fight." I point toward his bedroom. "But you have no right to control how I react to finding out I have a child, a child that I've missed every day of his life for fourteen months until now."

I leave her in the bedroom, needing space to think, to pace, and to clear my head. Though it's tempting to leave altogether, I have a son to consider . . . *a son?* I have a child, a part of my soul in the other room. How can I leave and act like I don't know that? How can I leave him behind and walk out her door?

I can't.

I know I can't, but I may have no choice tonight.

This is her apartment. She has rightful custody of him. She's raised him. She's everything to him. I'm nothing to him but a guy who babysat for a few hours.

Dropping to the couch, I let go of my shoes, and my

head falls into my hands. My eyes water under the strain of the shock I'm in, the anger of being forced out before I have a say in the matter. "What the fuck?" I want to rage, to throw something, to punch a wall, to turn back time and get to be there for him before he was born. A tear escapes, which fucking angers me even more.

The couch dips beside me. I can't look. I don't want her to see me this way. I'm in no place to be rational or reasonable, to behave in some way that she deems respectable. I just need to sit here to process what the hell is happening.

Liv's hand covers the back of my neck, and she whispers, "I'm sorry." Her head falls forward to rest against my shoulder, and she says, "I didn't know your last name."

First names were enough. That was the deal we made.

I regretted it then. *I hate myself for it now.*

My anger felt justified when it was aimed at her. Now, I don't know how to feel other than numb. I lift my head and wrap my arm around her.

None of this makes sense, but we made a deal that we can't change the terms of now. So is it fair that I hold some resentment toward her? *I don't fucking know.*

The answer is likely no, but I know it won't fix the damage.

Angling toward her, I lift her chin until our eyes meet. Hers are red around the lids and puffy underneath. There's also not an ounce of hate to be found, despite how I just treated her. But I have a fucking stubborn side that won't let this go without getting some answers. "Tell me you tried."

Her eyes well with tears that gather in the corners. "I tried to find you, Noah. I swear I did. I went to the house and knocked on the door. I called and emailed every rental management property in the area to find out who rented it for the summer season. I was desperate to find you but didn't know how."

My heart thumps in my chest, watching her plead her case like she's on trial and about to be found guilty. I can't do this to her. She braved the world and brought my baby into it. She took care of him. He's healthy and happy. Could I ask for more than just wanting to be a part of his life? That alone would be fucking amazing.

I say, "I believe you." She sits up, those gathered tears falling. "It must have been difficult to go through alone."

Her mouth opens but then closes again as she stares at me in disbelief. "You believe me?"

"I'm not happy that I missed so much of his life. All of it until now, but I have no reason to believe you'd lie to me when you didn't have to tell me at all." I look at the time and realize the lack of real sleep is catching up with me. "I don't think this conversation can be constructive at this hour. There are a lot of details to go over and we're not in the right frame of mind to do the work we need to." I glance back at her, and add, "Biggest regret of my life is agreeing to no strings that night."

"More than strings attached." A halfhearted smile arises on her face. "Sorry. Too soon?" Her smile has lost its shine in the tension we're caught in. This night's been hard on both of us. "Honestly, I wouldn't have it any other way. He's the best thing to ever happen in my life."

I hear the raw emotion in her voice and look over at her. She's more beautiful than I've ever seen her. With her walls lowered, she sits in her vulnerability.

She wears her heart like an accessory on her sleeve instead of a shield over her chest. Beyond her sharing the truth, she's letting me in to see the real her. The beauty of her heart and her strength in telling me are the reasons I trust her.

No matter how reactionary I've been, I owe her a debt of gratitude. "Thank you. Thank you for choosing to raise my son, thinking you'd be alone in that role."

"*Our son*," she says without anger or bitterness. *She's not wrong.*

"*Our* son. Thank you for taking care of him, for loving him with your whole heart, but most of all, for protecting him because you've done a hell of a job."

Though her chin is raised, a tear falls on the far side of her face. "I didn't do it—"

"You didn't do it for me. I know. You did it in spite of my absence, though. And that's okay. He's here." I release her and stand, my focus on the bedroom where he sleeps. "He's here because of you." When she stands, I grasp her by the shoulders. "But you don't have to do it alone anymore."

Walking around the couch, I pace from the living room to the kitchen and back again, looping around. I'm able to start processing the reality of the situation. "I'm a dad." As much as that scares the shit out of me, I'm grinning like a fool. "Look, Liv. I don't want to upset you, but I don't want to be upset either. This is good news. I have a son." Throwing my hand out toward his room, I say, "I know things will be a fucking mess until we figure things out, but tonight, I just won the fucking lottery. I have a son."

I'm usually so good at keeping my emotions in check, but this is big, biggest thing to ever happen to me, and I just want to celebrate. "I have a son. Maxwell Noah. Damn, it's so good, Liv."

"What?" Her concern brings her attention back to me, her eyes wide like saucers. "What is it?"

"His name." I can't be trapped in by shades that hide the

view. I understand why she likes the privacy, but I roll one up to feel less closed in. I stare at the city, a cluster of buildings across from us with only a few lights dotting the windows at this hour. The sun will rise in the next few hours, but I start to wonder if it will reach us here. "You put Noah in there. For me."

"It's all I knew of his father that I could give him."

I return to her, standing just a foot between us. It's so tempting to hold her, but I'm having a hard time telling where we stand. It's not together. Not yet at least. And I'm not sure I can give her the reassurance she needs regarding custody. That's obviously her fear—that I'll take him away from her. It's natural to feel that way.

I won't, but I can't lie and tell her I don't want to be in his life. I do. Very much. But that will be part of a bigger conversation, a different mountain to climb on another day. "I always imagined being a part of naming my kid."

"I'm sorry."

"No, don't apologize. He has a great name." An image of my family flashes through my head. How am I going to break this to my family? Telling them is something I can't take lightly. "My family has this weird tradition with names."

"What is it?" she asks with the tears dried and the streaks fading. I appreciate her efforts. Without them, I wouldn't be here.

"We all have water names."

"Water names? What does that mean?"

Trust takes time, especially when it's ripped out from under you. I know she has trust issues, and so much more makes sense now, but I still sit, hoping she'll sit next to me. "They're bodies of water, or conversely, water-related. My parents' names are Delta and Port. When they were deciding on names, they got this crazy idea to continue with each of their names. Loch is the oldest. Harbor is the second born. I was a surprise, so they didn't have time to do more research and didn't love a lot of the other options."

She sits beside me, only a few inches left between us. "Noah. Noah's Ark."

I grin not only because she's joining the conversation, but because she's open to the exchange at all. She doesn't have to be. Trust. It only takes a seed planted to watch it grow. "Yep, that's who I was named after."

"Can I tell you a secret?"

"Did you have twins? Ow—" I'm whacked on the arm but still chuckle. "Bad joke?"

She starts to laugh, and when she smiles, it brightens the room. Maybe I'm imagining that, but I feel the warmth shining on me. "No twins, but Noah has always been one of my favorite names."

"Oh yeah?" Working through our past and future, we'll get there, but the reprieve is nice to have in the meantime.

She leans back, resting her head on the cushion. With her eyes redirected to the ceiling, she nods, but then she turns her gaze back on me, and asks, "I remember you telling me your sister's name is Marina. That's a lot of water names."

"It sure is."

"So that's a tradition you wanted to carry on?"

Shrugging, I then lie back next to her. "It's not something I was married to."

"But you would if you could?"

Rolling my head to face her, I reply, "Sure, but maybe less obvious. He has my name. There's not much more I can ask for." I reach out, stopping just shy of touching her leg to rest my hand between us. "I'm more than good."

"He has more than that."

She's grinning like she has another secret. I'm not sure if I should be curious or scared of what's coming next. "What do you mean?"

"Maxwell." Liv sits up, angling her knees toward me. When she slides her hand into mine and our fingers fold together, it feels a lot like we're making a new agreement. The details to be defined at a later date, I'm sure. "The name Maxwell wasn't just something I liked. I loved the meaning behind it. Strength and courage, which I knew my little guy would need in this world."

"I like that. Those are admirable traits to possess." I sit up and bring our hands to my mouth. Holding the back of her hand to my mouth, I kiss once and then again. "He has a good role model in you." She lifts enough to shift onto my lap. I bring her closer and hold her by the hips. "A lot is coming at us all at once, Liv. Together, we will weather it better than we can alone. Whatever happens, I can promise you that you don't need to be afraid of me hurting you or Maxwell. I only want what's best."

"I don't know that's a promise you can keep, Noah. Once you consult a lawyer—"

"I have no intention of contacting a lawyer. We can settle this between the two of us."

With her arms around me, she rests her head against the top of mine. "Thank you," she whispers in a staggered breath. Lifting, she caresses my face, then stares into my eyes. I can see the questions and feel her unease right now. We can't know what the future holds. Tears fill her eyes again when she stares into mine. The only way I know to calm this storm is to assure her that I'm not going anywhere. I lean in and kiss her, promising her everything I can at this moment.

"Great stream," she says. "That's what Maxwell means." I pull back, allowing what she just said to sink in. "I wasn't sure why I loved that part so much. It just spoke to me, but now I know. It was meant to be."

Under her kiss and living in those two words, my life just changed forever. "Great stream," I say. *My son.* Maxwell Noah.

17

Liv

THE SUN BREAKS through the cracks of the curtains like a spotlight shining in my eyes. I grumble, rolling over in hopes of finding sleep again. Then I open them again only to realize I'm alone in bed.

Hurt. *Disappointment.* My emotions run the gamut of betrayal.

Should I have expected it? *I didn't.* I didn't see it coming after how we ended our night. Noah and I talked for an hour before we decided he should stay and sleep here. What was I going to do? Kick him out? *No.* We were on good terms, understanding where the other one was coming from, and made a new agreement to keep things the same for now.

Whether it's right or wrong to have feelings when it comes to him, I wanted him to stay. I like his warmth. *Fine .. . I* roll my eyes at myself. I like *him.*

We didn't make love again, choosing to talk until we fell asleep. It was so late that I started thinking the sun would rise before we closed our eyes, but the moon kept us company, the dark remaining a bit longer.

I'm surprised to find him gone so early. I look at the clock on my nightstand. 9:13 a.m. A sigh escapes only a second before—*Oh my God!*

My heart starts racing when I realize I overslept. That's not something I've done in more than a year. I flip the covers off and jump to my feet. Grabbing my robe, I swing my arms into the sleeves as I rush toward Maxwell's room. I don't hear anything from inside, which exacerbates my anxiety. Opening the door, I'm not greeted with the usual squeal and happiness, clappy hands and bouncing when he sees me. My heart stops and drops to the pit of my stomach when I find the empty crib.

Noah.

I push off the doorframe and run into my bedroom to grab my phone. With the phone pressed to my ear, I listen to it ring as I pace the floor. "Hello?" he says as if all is well in the world. *Not mine.*

"Where is Maxwell?"

"He's okay." I swear to God he chuckles. "He's eating."

"What? No. No." Oh God, what is he feeding my baby? "What is he eating?"

"Well, he requested a strawberry frosted cake donut, a large Americano, and a Denver omelet. It's impressive. The kid can eat."

"No," I say unable to control my anger. I shove my hand high against the wall, ducking my head to say, "That's not what he eats. Cassandra makes his food."

He chuckles. "Not today." He freaking laughs again.

I'm about to blow a blood vessel. "Noah, stop him. He can't eat that."

"Why not?"

"Because he eats pureed cantaloupe with a dash of beets for fun coloring and extra nutrition, a soft homemade oat bar with brown sugar and cinnamon, and a sippy cup of milk on Saturday mornings. And when Cassandra has time, she gets the peaches fresh from the peach truck on certain weekends. He loves peaches."

"He looks to be loving donuts right now. Just sayin'."

Donuts? I pace the floor, trying to cool my anger, but it reaches my cheeks, setting them on fire. I rest the back of my hand on my forehead, trying not to think about the sugar coursing through Maxwell's veins. I could scream. *Damn him.* "Do you not understand? He'll be bouncing off the walls." God, I could rip Noah Westcott apart right now. I fist my hand, flex, fist, flex while squeezing my phone tightly in the other. "What have you done? Where have you taken him?"

"You're overreact—"

"Don't you dare say it." Knowing him the little I do, I bet it's sitting on the tip of his tongue. "Noah," I warn.

"Liv?"

He's infuriating.

Irredeemable.

Downright cruel for pulling this stunt. "You took him when I was sleeping."

"We're in the—"

"How do you think that made me feel? And dammit . . ." He knows exactly what he's doing. Well, he can push my buttons all he wants, but he won't win this round. "You can't just take him whenever and wherever you want, Noah." I move to the edge of the bed and sit to keep myself from flying off the handle. It's not working.

"Calm down, Liv."

"Nothing calms a woman down faster than being told to

calm down," I snap, sarcasm dripping from my lips. "Maxwell has a routine."

He huffs. He freaking dares to huff like I'm the one in the wrong. "I wanted to spend time with him. And believe it or not, I wanted to let you sleep in. I figured it's been a while. He's great. Eating like a champ. We're bonding. Maybe this can be a new routine. Spending time with me on Saturday mornings."

"No." Every word he says feels like another threat. I can't lose my baby. "He doesn't need a new routine. His routine is just fine."

"What do you mean no? Listen—"

"No, you listen to me." Bolting to my feet, I hold the phone in front of me as I stomp down the hall into the living room, ready to storm this city looking for my son. "Maxwell—"

"Maxwell what, Liv?" I look up from the phone to see Noah sitting at the dining table with Maxwell in front of him tucked in his high chair. My heart floods with a combination of relief and love for my son the second I lay eyes on him. Noah lowers the spoon and smiles. "Good morning, sunshine."

Maxwell looks over his shoulder. When he sees me, he squeals with joy and starts kicking his feet. "Mamamama."

As much as I love hearing him call my name, even in a funny way, rage grows for the man next to him. "Are you kidding me right now? You were here all along?" I take a few steps, but the lump in my throat hasn't cleared and my chest still feels full of congested emotions. "You scared the life out of me, Noah."

"I'm sorry." With a shrug, he cocks a grin. "I tried to tell you we were in the living room."

My hand rests on my chest as I take in the sight before

me, which is so unnatural to how most of my mornings begin. I try to calm down, but the upset is lingering. "I thought you took him."

Disappointment craters his expression and sinks his shoulders. "So you said."

Tears swell in my eyes, which I hate. I hate feeling in front of anyone, especially him. Vulnerable in ways that can make me shrink into myself if I'm not purposeful on stopping it from building.

Noah stands. "I'm really sorry, Liv." This time, his tone holds no laughter, and I hear the depth of regret instead. The effort he's making matters to me. I called him irredeemable, but he proves me wrong as I watch him sit with my son. Our son.

Does it fix it? *No.*

Does it make him redeemable? Probably . . . *definitely*. And it makes me swoon because he's taking responsibility. "I panicked when I saw Maxwell wasn't in his room. My mind went to the worst place possible." Now I need to redeem myself for the distress I brought on myself. "I'm sorry for assuming you would do that to me."

Noah watches me with a spoon for Maxwell in his hand. He lowers it along with his head. Scratching the back of his neck, he sighs. "I'm not sure what to say about that." When he looks up again, he adds, "I said it last night, but it bears repeating. I won't hurt you or Max. Not ever."

Maxwell waves his arms in the air, and another delightful giggle escapes. I toss the phone on the couch and move in to give him a kiss. *Maxwell, not Noah.* Although Noah does make it hard to resist him sometimes. Especially when he says things like he just did. And how he looks. *Like now.*

How does he look so damn good on so few hours of

sleep? His hair's a mess but in that sexy just rolled out of bed and then walking the runway and hanging out on a yacht in the South of France hair.

My train of thought disappears down the track, and I'm left drooling over the man I was just arguing with. Seeing him shirtless, sitting in his dress pants with bare feet. . . . I fan myself. "Is it warm in here?" I say, playing it off while his incredible abs are on display, along with that billion-dollar smile that weakens my knees.

He's stupidly handsome, and his deep, dulcet tones shoot straight to my—"Liv?"

"Yeah?" I dumbly stare at him like he didn't just catch me preoccupied with him in real time.

Typically, how I look in the morning is not something I concern myself with since I'm getting a sweet baby out of bed and feeding him, which almost always results in a mess on me. But mainly because it's just Maxwell and me here alone, and he loves me as I am.

I still pull the scrunchie from my hair and wrap it around my wrist as if I can look even 10 percent as good as he does when I get out of bed. My hair was still damp when I put it up, so it's wild with kinked curls and teased sections that patting with my hand has no real effect on taming.

Real sexy, I bet . . .

I cringe with a small eye roll, imagining he must be figuring out his exit plan after seeing me. Noah is probably used to waking up next to supermodels or women who have trained themselves to sleep on their backs to avoid having any wrinkles form during the night. That's not a skill I've acquired. It's one I've not even tried to achieve.

Touching my face, I can feel the line embedded in my skin from sleeping on top of a crumpled sheet. *Stop, Liv.* This is the last thing I should be thinking about right now.

First, this is not about us or how he makes me feel things that no other man ever has. Second, this is strictly about Maxwell and his safety.

Will Noah take care of him like I will?

The fear lingers, but it's beginning to dissipate as I look at them together. Noah is caring for him. I didn't ask him to. He's doing it on his own.

When I bend down to kiss Maxwell this time, my hair falls like a curtain over his face, tickling him and making him giggle. The sound brightens my heart, reminding me how fortunate I am to have this little guy in my life.

Needing caffeine, I move around Noah to go into the kitchen. "Coffee?" I offer, dragging my hand over his tanned shoulder as I pass. Selfishly, I want to connect with him physically as well as whatever else we're doing here, which looks a lot like playing house.

Should I be worried that we're falling into a family so easily? *Maybe.* Or maybe the energy I already expended turned out to be a false alarm that keeps my brain from working overtime now.

Noah scoops another bite from the container and tries to feed Maxwell, but he's not having it. I rub the top of Maxwell's head, and say, "He likes to try to feed himself."

"Ah." Noah hands the baby the spoon, which he promptly throws to the ground, and the little bowl bounces on the tray, spilling the food everywhere, including on Noah. With the red oats streaked across his chin and chest, his smirk disappears. "That didn't work out."

I could offer him a towel or get the supplies to clean, but he seems set on handling this himself. I grab a mug from the counter before starting the coffee machine. "You didn't really feed him donuts, right?"

When I turn around, he catches me—hands on my hips,

eyes locked on mine, a smirk that makes me wish it were Maxwell's naptime. God, that makes me feel like a horrible mother. It's just been so long since I felt desired by a man who appreciates curves not in all the "right" places. I've come to terms with fuller hips and a belly that's no longer flat. I've even come to appreciate those attributes because I got Maxwell out of the deal. But Noah is a real-life Adonis. To see him look at me like I'm about to be his breakfast, my entire body feels the heat of that stare.

He glances over his shoulder at a messy Maxwell who is perfectly content licking the bowl and then turns back to me. "Nope. No omelets either. Not even coffee, for that matter." He chuckles. "But he loves whatever that stuff is."

I want to laugh that he just got played by a fourteen-month-old. I'm doing something right. "Because it's dessert. A cherry crumble. I bet you let him choose."

"No wonder he picked that container. Smart kid."

I can't help but laugh. "He knew what he was doing." The smell of coffee wafts through the air as I wait for the machine to finish brewing. "What time did you get up?"

"When I heard Max. It was around seven fifteen."

"Seven fifteen? We didn't go to bed until after five." I find myself leaning in, our voices lowering to whispers between us. "You must be exhausted."

"I'm doing okay. You seemed like you needed the rest more than I did."

It's so hard to keep my hands to myself when he's near, so I don't. Sliding my palms over his shoulders. I say, "You got a little something all over you." I can't stop myself from laughing.

"Oh yeah?"

I grin. "Yeah."

"What should we do about it?"

Maxwell screams, causing Noah and I to part like our parents just walked in on us. Noah goes to him without hesitation. As much as I find that wholly endearing, this Mama needs some attention too. I giggle but pour myself a cup of coffee, hoping this will help me focus on the situation at hand instead of how many hours we have until naptime because nine thirty is way too soon for a nap . . . or for us to have some grown-up time together.

Adulting is hard sometimes. *Holy wow!* Like now.

With Maxwell anchored in Noah's arms, I set down the mug before I drop it. A new fantasy has been unlocked—*the hot dad*. Good lord, this man!

While I stand there like the sight of him does not impregnate me, he tilts his head and laughs. "Eyes up here, babe." My gaze shoots up to see Noah's smug face, cheek to cheek with my favorite little face of all time. "I'm going to get us cleaned up." Popping his bicep for me, he adds, "But don't worry. I'll make sure to take care of you later today."

"Promise?"

He winks. "I guaran-fucking-tee it."

And I'm dead.

A pile of swooning mush of emotions is all that remains where I once existed. There's no way in heaven I'm going to survive co-parenting with this man if all he's going to make me want to do is throw caution to the wind every time we're together.

Taking a sip of coffee, I lean back on the counter, watching him walk away, and grinning like a fool because I'm okay with this arrangement. Technically, more than okay.

Here's to Daddy Westcott.

18

Noah

"It's all fun and games until you shit on yourself. Take it from me, kid, it's no fun after that." After dumping the dirty diaper into the bin, I tuck the tabs of the new diaper into the top of it. Max sits up, and it falls open again.

I didn't know I needed a masters in engineering to work this thing. He's a wiggler, but I look at the tabs once more. "Lie down for me, buddy." How hard can this be to figure out? I don't want to have to google this, but hm . . . Ah! I press down the front and pull the tabs around securing them.

Max has a new lease on life now that he's clean. "I get it," I tell him.

One diaper down and I'm not looking forward to more. I'll ask Liv how the potty training is going and see if I can help onboard him quicker to the concept. I wash my hands in the attached bathroom and then open the door, letting this little beast free to roam through the apartment. And by free, he crawls some and then uses the wall to remain upright as he works his way into the other bedroom. "Mama," he calls for her. It's really stinkin' cute.

We find her sitting in a chair putting on makeup. Maxwell holds his arms and seems to be having an entire conversation with her that only the two of them understand. It's an unexpected side of Liv that no one else gets to see. There's no way they'd call her the Ice Queen if they did.

Her eyes connect with mine in the mirror as she holds him in her lap. If only the office could see us now, sharing lingering glances, kisses that lasted long after the connection was broken. I wish they knew her like I do, but they won't bother to look behind the rumors to the truth right in front of them.

If I had never met her, I might have done the same. Sure, she has a great body and face, but who she is as a person matters. She gave me her trust last night when she didn't have to. Glancing at Max, I acknowledge she gave me more than I could have asked for.

She says, "I talked to a nurse earlier."

"How's Cassandra?"

"It sounded like she's doing well. She wasn't awake to talk to me, but I thought I would go visit."

"Want some company?"

Her smile is so painfully genuine that my heart aches. "I'd love some." Turning to Maxwell, she asks, "You want to go on an adventure with Mama?"

His arm swings out, and he points at me. "Dada."

Liv's mouth falls open as she stares at me. "When did he learn that?"

"I don't know." Raising my hands in surrender, I say, "I'm innocent." Sitting on the side of the tub, I start laughing. "My side of the story is that I introduced myself as Noah, his daddy. When I picked him up out of his crib, he said Dada."

"What's his side of the story?"

"He knew who I was the moment he met me?"

A broad smile takes ownership of her lips, and she turns back to him. "Who's my super smart son?" Tapping his nose, she adds, "You are."

I slip my phone out to sneak a photo of them. The way he looks at her like she's his whole world . . . It reminds me of how much I've missed. I push that down because it doesn't matter. I can't change the past. I can only embrace the present.

The present is stunning in her bra, towel wrapped around her waist hanging down, bare feet, and little makeup on. Her hair is in a clip. I'm sure she'd have something to say, most likely of the snarky variety, if I tell her she's gorgeous. So I keep my mouth shut for now. Admiring this incredible woman who created the most amazing human I've ever seen.

I look at Max, feet dangling, a head of wisps in disarray, and wearing only a T-shirt and diaper. The two of them together look like the kind of morning I want to wake up to more often. Not just more often. Every day. Forever. *They* are my forever.

They're home and so comfortable in being themselves that I almost feel like an intruder to their shared moment. *Hate that.*

Snapping one more photo, I catch her eyes on me. "What are you doing?" There's nothing but a smile built into the question.

"I don't want to forget this."

She hugs him and kisses Max's head. "Will you send it to me?"

"Of course."

Setting him down, she comes to me and settles on my

lap. With her arms draped so casually around my neck, she says, "You've been busy this morning, but I wanted to check in with you. A lot happened last night." She glances at Max. "How are you doing?"

"I'm good." I wouldn't tell her otherwise. No need to add to her worries. I still need time to think about this outside of the situation, but for now, I didn't lie.

I let my eyes trail down her body from the neck to her breasts before a finger pulls my attention back up. "Eyes up here, sweetheart."

Chuckling, I readjust her so she's more stable on my legs. "They're gorgeous to stare into."

"Back at ya." She looks down, and her words are reluctant. The smile has faltered as do her shoulders when I finally get her gaze shining on me again. "You're taking everything in such stride. It's a lot. Life changing. Do you want to share your thoughts? What is your heart telling you?"

"I don't know. I'm not overthinking this. I've just been going off instinct."

A gentle smile rolls across her face, the corners of her eyes softening. Dragging a finger over my chin, she leans in to kiss me before resting her forehead against mine. "You're amazing, Noah. You've . . ." She takes a calming breath. "You stepped right up, but what happens next?"

"Maybe," I say, pulling back to see her eyes again. "Maybe we don't define it just yet. I'm his dad, and I want to be whatever that entails, but otherwise—"

"But otherwise, you and I should wait."

"I didn't say that. Is that what you want?"

"No. I just feel like I've dropped you into this world without your permission, and you think you need all the answers to move forward, have the perfect plan in place, and know how this should play out. You don't. *We* don't. Do we?" She licks her lips and then says, "This wasn't a trap—"

"Is that what you're worried about? You're worried that I think this was a ploy to get me to what? Stay? Hang around? Date?" A humorless chuckle escapes me as I rub her leg. "Do you really think I'd fall for a scheme so easily?"

"I don't want you to think I'm trapping you into a life you didn't ask for."

"I haven't had time to process everything. Time is a luxury I've been given, but you weren't." I tread carefully not wanting to open boxes I'm not prepared to unpack. "Listen, Liv. We have time to figure this out. But I need you to hear me. For Max, I'm here because he's my son and I care about him. For you, I'm here because I want to be. But if you get tired of me invading your space, I can head home."

"Maybe that's what I'm worried about. I don't want you to leave." I reach up and caress her face, rubbing my thumb over her soft skin. Her body is sheltering in itself. I don't want that. I want her to be the bold woman I know she is. "And that scares me, too. I've put you in an impossible situation."

I tilt up to kiss her. I kiss her again and then again, tasting her confessions that she was brave enough to share. "It's not impossible if I'm being given the option. I want to stay."

Her smile returns. "You do?"

"Yeah, I do." Tightening my hold on her hips, I straighten my back. "What if we spend the weekend together? We'll go see Cassandra and then grab some lunch—"

"Take Maxwell to the park?"

"Absolutely. Whatever we want. We can stop by my apartment on the way to the hospital. I can take a shower and then grab a bag for the night. Dinner in and whatever we decide to do after that?"

"I know what I want to do." Honestly, it doesn't matter what she says next. I'd never deny this incredible woman a request. "Do you think . . ." She drops her head into her hand and laughs. "God, this is so embarrassing."

"What?" I ask, rubbing her hips, egging her on. She's so fucking sexy. "Tell me."

She looks back at Max sitting on the floor, playing with a hairbrush, and then leans in conspiratorially to whisper, "Have you ever . . ." Biting her lip, she glances to make sure Max isn't listening before pressing her lips to my ear. "Watched *Sons of Anarchy*?"

"The motorcycle show?" She's nodding so much that I reach up to put the back of my hand on her forehead. "Are you feeling alright? Having a fever dream?"

She's downright giggly. "What the hell am I missing?"

"Nothing," she says, struggling to hide her grin. "It's just . . . I know it's not for everyone. I wouldn't even typically watch a show like that. It's violent, and there's lots of . . ."

"Motorcycles?"

"I was going to say guns." She laughs again. "But motorcycles too. Anyway, it's okay if you're not into it. I can watch it by myself some other time."

I set her on her feet and stand. Kissing her once and then twice, I say, "If you want to binge a show, we will goddamn watch any show you want." I kiss her. "Let's get dressed and head to my place to start this adventure so we can get back here to binge to your heart's desire."

"Give me about fifteen minutes. Do you think you could get Maxwell dressed?"

"I can," I reply, feeling confident after the victory I had with the diaper. I bend down. "Max?"

He looks up and then says, "Dada."

Pride fills my entire being. *That's my kid!* I glance at Liv, who's rolling her eyes. "I swear I did not teach him to say that."

She bends over the counter and dabs makeup on her face. "I'm letting you off the hook on that one only because it's kind of cute. But let's discuss the Max part of this equation." Bouncing a sponge off her face, she says, "I've always called him Maxwell because that's his name."

"But everyone needs a nickname. Well, Noah is about the only version of my name, but take you, for example. You're Olivia by day and Liv by night."

"First of all, everyone calls me Olivia except for a few people, so it's not like it's that common for me. Second of all, why do you make Liv sound so naughty?"

Waggling my eyebrows, I smirk. "Kind of is since sex was the purpose of the night you introduced yourself."

"Shh." Her finger flies to her lips, and she nods her head toward Max.

I chuckle. "I think we've got some time before he understands what I just said. Speaking of, Liv, you haven't corrected me once in the past couple of days."

Dusting her face with powder, she stops and looks at me in the mirror. "I was tired of fighting it. You're a stubborn man, Westcott."

I come up behind and smack her ass, the towel muffling the sound. "I'm not that stubborn. I just knew deep down that I brought out a side of you that you haven't been in touch with in a while."

She turns around, her arms looping my neck. Leaning back, she admires my face as she licks her lips, looking at mine. I'm getting hard, which is easy to do around her. She's not subtle when she brushes her middle against mine, instigating this erection that I definitely cannot hide. "You see me, but I also see you, Noah Westcott. You're the hotshot in the office, the playboy after hours, a last name that comes with prestige and a first steeped in family tradition. The golden boy, the all-American hero. You're all those things, but I've seen beneath the surface." Running two fingers along my lips, she seems mesmerized by them before kissing me.

"What do you see when you look at me, babe?"

"You're the only one who bothers to ask how I am, the only one who came to the park to check on me despite how I treated you prior. You listen, *really listen* to people, not just the words, but you observe who they are as a person." She tilts her head to the side, and says, "You make everyone around you feel special. Like they're one of a kind, and every word they say matters."

"You are special."

"To you, and that's more than I can ask for. So thank you for being exactly who you are."

I'm a bit of a cocky ass sometimes, but she's good with the compliments. My ego is fed, and I'm left grinning like a fool for her. "So I can call him Max?"

"Yes. You're his dad, so if you want to call him a nickname, that's your right."

"Promise to tell me the truth?" When she nods, I smirk. "How do you really feel about being called Liv?"

"Truth?"

"Full truth."

"I hated that I liked hearing you call me that name."

The day feels easy, the hours short when I'm with her. I don't want to weigh the morning down by making her uncomfortable, but I want to know so much about her. "Why'd you hate it?"

"Because the memories of the Hamptons always came with it." Pushing me away, she adds, "Now go. Go before this gets too deep."

"Going. Going." Bending down, I pick up Max and head for the door. "Fifteen minutes?"

"Twenty at the most." She starts adding pink to her cheeks.

"Hey, Liv?" When she looks at me in the mirror, I say, "You're beautiful." I tickle Max under his chin. "Right, Max? Your mom is beautiful."

Grabbing a tissue, she wipes the corners of her eyes. "Why'd you have to make me cry?" She laughs, but it mixes with another sniffle.

"Sorry." As much as I want to stay with her, to spend this kind of time with her without the pressures of the outside world or other obligations sneaking in, I close the door to let her get ready.

In Max's room, I find a onesie with cars on it. "Do you like cars, buddy? *Vroom. Vroom.*"

He laughs. "Ca."

"Close enough, buddy." I kneel to dig through a bucket on the bottom shelf of a bookcase full of cars. When I find one I like, I hand it to him to keep him occupied while I get him dressed. The red Ferrari immediately goes to his mouth. "You have good taste." I chuckle at the bad joke, even if he doesn't. That might have been my first dad joke. "Cars are for driving not eating." I move his hand from his mouth, then work on getting this outfit over his head.

His head pops through just as Liv comes in. Grabbing a large bag from a hook, she sets it on the floor by the door. "I can take over so you can get ready."

"That was quick. You sure?"

"Yeah. I'm ready." She spins. "How do I look?"

The casual outfit is better than the workout pants and sweatshirt simply because of my selfish tendencies. I can see more of her. The jeans fit her body, hugging her curves and ending above her ankle. The sleeveless pink tee is loose but knotted at her waist, showing a sliver of her stomach and the great curves at her waist to hips. It's tempting to want to touch her there and then go lower. With a hoodie in hand that she carried in, she ties it around her waist, looking like a daydream. "You look great."

With a giggle, she flips her foot into the air behind her to show off the white sneakers. "New shoes."

"Nice sneaks."

"Thanks." She leans in to help me put this wiggle worm's arms through the holes. Pulling the rest of the onesie down, she snaps it between his legs and then helps him stand by holding his hands like the pro she is. "Voilà. Ready?"

"I'm ready."

In the hall, she opens a closet and pulls out a stroller. "I already packed his bag. Can you help me get him in the stroller, though?" She pops it, and it's ready to go.

Picking Max up, I settle him in, pulling the straps over his shoulders and buckle him up. "You're all snug in there."

When I'm walking away to get my shirt and shoes on, she takes the bag and pushes it into the bottom basket. I can hear her talking to him about his water and if he's happy to be going outside.

It reminds me that she's been doing this alone the whole time and is good at it. I don't have any training as a parent. I'm fumbling through diapers and onesies. I stepped up this morning like a babysitter, thinking I was the hero for letting her sleep a little longer. *What the fuck?*

"Anything I can do?" I ask, buttoning my shirt. It's a

disaster—cherry crumble-stained and wrinkled—but I'll wear it like a rite of passage. It has my kid's artwork, after all.

When I rejoin them in the hallway, her eyes widen when she sees me and takes an unabashed once-over. "Wow."

"Charmer," I tease.

"No, I mean it. There's so much I can say about you as a person, but I just really want to tell you how much I appreciate your ass in those pants."

I give her a spin to take it all in. But then I catch her hand and bring her to me. "I want you to know something."

"What is it?"

Running my hand from the side of her neck to the back of it, I pull her to me, and whisper, "You're a wow to me, too. No one turns me on like you do. So you finding me attractive —physically and otherwise? Just know the feeling is mutual." I bring her in and kiss her with purpose, making sure she has no doubt that she's the only one I fantasize about.

19

Liv

NOAH'S APARTMENT is nothing like I expected.

I could say the same about him.

I thought he would live in a studio apartment with a mixture of black and browns, leather couch and laminate cabinets barely holding together. Despite his last name, I imagined a twenty-five-year-old recent grad school graduate would be living his best bachelor pad life. That's not what this is. I mean, he's got leather barstools, but now I'm questioning if all recent Beacon University graduates live like this because this is not a typical first New York apartment rental. This is an apartment that someone in upper management or even a celebrity would own.

"This is yours?" I ask dumbly because I'm just in awe. *It's stunning.*

Leaving the stroller at the entrance, I pull the baby out and set him on his feet to walk beside me. I attempt to keep my astonishment in check.

"Yes." He even looks pleased with it. *How could he not be?* This apartment is a showstopper.

Situated on the west side of a Tribeca building, he has big windows, sunset views, warm wood floors, exposed brick, and I swear the walls feel like suede. "Is this suede?" I lower my hand and grab Maxwell's before he has a chance to sticky-print after he ate an orange.

"No," Noah replies, heading down a long corridor. My hall isn't even long enough to call a corridor. "It's wallpaper that feels like it, though. It's unique?"

"Very."

"Make yourselves at home." He leaves Maxwell and me to explore on our own. Looking down at my little guy, I whisper, "He means me. You don't need to put your fingers on everything."

He's grinning and giggles before he pulls away from me and teeters over to the couch. I do a quick survey. It's not entirely childproof, but why would it be? Maxwell's probably the first child to step foot into this apartment.

I also begin to explore, getting caught up in the details. Purposeful design, like the x-frame chairs in the living room and the modern barstools tucked under the large island, feel like they're custom to the space. The size of the place is the most surprising aspect. It's not quite double the size of mine, but it definitely has impressive square footage.

Noah comes in pulling a T-shirt down over his head. "Can I get you anything to drink?"

"No, we're good." I move around the chairs and sit on the couch that I'm certain actually is suede. That means I need to be careful with Maxwell. One spit up and this fabric is a goner. "Can I ask you something personal?"

"You can ask me anything." He sits in a chair closest to me and puts on his sneakers.

"I thought Bancroft & Lowe was your first job after graduate school?"

"It is. Why?" Guess he picks up on my nonverbal cues of gawking at the apartment because he asks, "Ah, you're wondering about the apartment?"

"Yeah. It's beautiful. *Big.* Expensive neighborhood and I can imagine the unit costs more than a few pretty pennies."

Resting his arms on his knees, he sits forward. "Truth?"

"Full truth," I reply, smiling as our earlier time comes to mind.

I appreciate that he didn't take insult to my nosiness. It's New York, though. Everyone talks real estate and money here, so maybe he's already used to it. "I used a trust fund to pay it down, and my salary covers the remaining mortgage."

Although it makes me feel weird about my own situation and certain trust funds that I've not been given access to, I'm not going to judge him for using his resources. I took an offer I couldn't afford to refuse to buy mine. It's not something I've shared with anyone, but this feels like we're in it together. "My mom helped me secure my apartment."

"Oh yeah?" He's nodding without a lick of judgment on his face.

"Money she got in the divorce. She told me I'm a worthwhile investment." Hearing myself say that out loud makes me feel even stronger. "I can't afford that apartment on my salary, so her support—financial and emotional—changed our lives."

His eyes search mine, and he takes a deep breath. "I wish I could have been there for you and Max."

He just says the best things. His words instantly wipe away the negatives of the past. "I know you mean that." Reaching over, I rest my hand on his knee. "Thank you."

Covering my hand, he replies, "Thank *you*."

We sit a second in the sounds of Max babbling as he crawls toward the window, but then I say, "Tell me about this place."

He already seems to know that I'm better with the distractions sometimes than sitting in the heavier topics and is quick to reply, "It's a great building, but the apartment was really in disrepair. I got it at a discount." I love the smile that he got away with finding a deal. Most men in this city would never want someone to know they didn't pay top dollar as they sip their expensive liquor out of decanters in the finest restaurants. Noah is real with himself and with everyone who meets him. You know what you're getting because he's on the level.

His eyes follow Max as he continues, "Once we got in here to evaluate, most of the damage was surface. Fixed it and worked with an incredible designer and her assistant to bring it together."

"Which design firm?"

Chuckling, he says, "My mom and sister." He pats his knees before getting up. "Want a tour?"

"Yes, please."

He takes Maxwell into his arms like he's been doing this all along. That's something I've noticed. He's adapted to the news so well, too well. It makes me wonder if he understands the scope of what it means to be Maxwell's father.

Of course, I could come up with assumptions, but I have a feeling that Noah will want to be a part of every step. Many things are within my control, but this is not one of them anymore, and I'm okay with that.

He guides me through the space—kitchen, dining, bar area, which granted, he's twenty-five and single so a bar makes sense, office, guest bedroom, and then he finally opens the last door at the end of the corridor. Angels aren't singing. It's quite the opposite.

I think this is where sin comes to life. "Oh wow, Noah." I walk into the bedroom. "It's stunning."

Sexy and soulful. *Like the man.*

A gorgeous walnut wood-framed bed. King sized. Doesn't surprise me. The walls are the prettiest shade of deep brown bordering on black. It's rich and comforting, like Noah's arms wrapped around me at midnight. The heavy drapery matching the paint color has me thinking you wouldn't know if it were day or night when they're closed. Muted gold accents the room and a plush rug is tucked partly under the bed but would keep the feet cozy when walking around barefoot.

I say, "Your room is the opposite of mine in color palettes, but I really love it. Warm and inviting. Homey but high end." I go to sit on the bed and decide to lie instead. "I bet it's so cozy in here in the winter."

"Guess I'll find out in a few months."

He sets Maxwell down who immediately pulls at the bedding and brings a pillow to fall like a rockslide. "Sorry."

He picks up the pillow and tosses it on the bed. "It's okay. It's his home too."

The sharp stab of reality has me taking a breath, holding in any initial negative reaction I might have. I close my eyes and let myself feel what I need to feel to help move past the moment. I open my eyes and stare at the ceiling. "Yeah, I guess it is."

While he starts packing a bag, I lie there thinking about how hard it's going to be to drop off my son and leave him here. He climbs onto the bed next to me, and our eyes meet when we turn to look at each other. His hand slides over to take hold of mine.

The stillness.
The comfort.
The peace.

It's not a small feat, but he manages to settle my racing heart merely by his proximity. We stare into each other's eyes, not needing to say anything to fill the space. It's filled with spinning thoughts and shared breaths.

He pushes over to kiss me.

Like every other time we're together in this way, he manages to share the fire that burns inside him with me, igniting more complicated feelings. It was never no-strings attached with him. Now I realize that was not a possibility. The desire to attach myself to him in ways that could be called stringy surges through my veins.

When it comes to us, it's getting harder to separate fact from fiction because he has me believing in the fairy-tale ending. But that's not who we are, not at our cores. We aren't that naive. Things haven't gone according to society's expectations, but they've worked out how the universe planned.

I need to be careful . . .

We've had fun for the past twenty-four hours. Noah gave me grace and jumped feet first into a life I've kept secret. He's been here for us, fully showing up when I told him the truth. But come Monday, he has his own life again. A life that only includes Maxwell. Noah isn't mine and doesn't owe me anything, so where does that leave me?

I roll over to move closer to him, wanting to make the most of the time we do share. His hand slides over my cheekbone and weaves into my hair. Holding me still, he kisses me with intention and pressure, and then slows, ceasing altogether.

He pulls back, though the tips of our noses are so close

that our breaths still mingle. "What's on your mind?" he asks.

I let my gaze drop between us because it's so much easier to stare at his shirt than look into his eyes. There's too much truth to discover in his irises, and I just want to play house with him for a bit longer. "What's not on my mind?"

When we hear, "Dada. Mama," our eyes flit back to each other because we know it's time to go. I lift, not any happier than he is about ending this so early, but we don't need any little witnesses to the confusion of our relationship.

He asks, "Should we get going?"

"We probably should." *For many reasons.* What do I want from him? I could lie here all day and still not understand our relationship. But asking anything feels like too much, especially based on the past week.

I've been leaving pieces of myself wherever he is in hopes of him finding them. It felt too good in his arms, and though he's right about needing to go, I wouldn't have minded a moment to collect myself. Not needing to drag this out.

Sure, we've had sex. We've kissed when it probably wasn't in our best interest.

There is no *us* in this equation.

I push myself up and scoop Maxwell into my arms before leaving the room. It's too comfortable in here—the colors, the fabrics, the large bed, but mostly Noah. He's jostled the configuration of my chemistry and left me out of sorts for two years now.

The only thing I'm certain of is that I don't have a right to stake a claim, so I must free him to be my son's dad. It's a lot to take on, but I'll carry the burden of unrequited sentiments.

I set Maxwell in the stroller, rolling him back and forth

until Noah arrives. He shoves a backpack in the bottom of the carrier and then opens the door for us. Our conversation has stilted, but I don't mind the quiet time to think. We ride down the elevator, and when we cut through the lobby, I say, "Thank you for bringing us here." I look around. "It's good to see where you live."

"Of course. I like having you here."

"You do?"

"You and Max." Walking into the sunshine, he stops on the sidewalk and slips his sunglasses on. Black Ray-Bans. I wouldn't expect less. He's the guy who makes old-school style look cool again. "It's fun to share this side of my life with you."

The tree-lined street reminds me more of Brooklyn than this part of the city. We stroll slowly, my guard still down around him. The bubble of trust we've created follows us down the street. "My father wanted a male heir to carry on his name and legacy. He never wanted a daughter." We cross the street, and he asks if he can push Maxwell. He's been nothing but one hundred percent committed to Maxwell since he found out. He's a lucky little boy to have Noah.

Noah looks at me when I stop talking. "You okay?"

"Yeah," I say, not realizing I had just been standing there. "I grew up in the shadows of his shattered dreams. Was he cruel to me? No, not in a sense that would stand out to anybody. I just knew I could never live up to his expectations." A humorless laugh releases without permission. "The gall of him to treat me horrible is not something I've ever been able to wrap my head around."

"Your job as his daughter isn't to wrap your head around the ways he's failed you. That's on him."

That hits a raw part of my heart, a stab wound my dad inflicted when I was born that's never healed. I touch the scar above my eyebrow. It's a small reminder of how hard I've tried for him. "I got this when I was fourteen. I was on a sailing crew. My father loves sailing, so I spent all summer working this massive sailboat that had once raced in the America's Cup back when there was less technology involved. It lost, but it was a beautiful sailboat." We stop at a light. I look both ways when the light changes, and we resume our journey.

I continue, "It was windy, which is great for sailing, but it got intense fast. Some kids lost control of their stations. The mast came fast and with no warning. It punted me right off that boat."

"It hit you in the head?"

"It hit me so hard that I was knocked unconscious."

"In the water?"

Not a story I like to revisit, but it did make me realize that I'm stronger than I thought. "I woke up gasping for air in the middle of the ocean. The captain had jumped in and reached me just after I came to. He put his life on the line for me and didn't think twice about diving in. He didn't even have time to put on a life jacket." I lead the stroller to the inside of the sidewalk and stop. I haven't thought about this in so long, but now it's clear. "That man saved me, but all I remember is wondering if my dad would have done the same."

I'm not crying. My heart doesn't hurt anymore. As a mother, though, it makes me angry. No child should ever have a revelation like that regarding a parent. Bending down to hold Maxwell's hand, I kiss his fingers, then his head.

When I stand back up, Noah embraces me. Not entirely since he keeps one hand on the stroller. And that's how he's already a better father than I had. I hug him fully, wanting him to know how much I appreciate him stepping in without hesitation to be there for his son.

That matters.

More than he'll ever understand.

But Maxwell will, so that's all I can wish for.

20

Noah

I CAN'T STOP STARING.

Liv even reached over and whacked my arm, telling me to stop on the way to the hospital. All in good fun, of course, but she hates attention. That much I've learned. I always wondered how she was so oblivious to the attention she receives.

She's not. She's ignoring it.

She drops breadcrumbs of information for me to gather as insight into her life. I devour each tidbit, craving everything she gives me and hoping she shares the full loaf one day.

When we arrive at the hospital, I can't help but notice we look every bit the little family. I grin at our reflection in the windows while approaching the doors. My brothers and I joked around about me not having kids anytime soon. I stood firm that I had no interest in kids at this juncture. Starting my own family seemed like a foreign concept. *Why wouldn't it be?*

I'm barely out of grad school and haven't dated anyone seriously in years. The woman at the counter might be to blame for that. Things changed fast. Now look at me, bouncing my own kid on my knee in a hospital waiting room.

I've been successful at keeping the future at bay, but thinking about how I just saw my brothers the other night is a swift kick of reality.

I'm a dad. *A parent.*

I scrub a hand over my face. What am I going to tell them and the rest of my family? *How? When?*

I haven't even processed this fact yet, much less how we move forward from here. When I go home tomorrow, do I go home alone? I don't have a nursery or anyone to take care of him while I'm at work. If I leave him at her apartment, how do I move on with life like this didn't happen? Or do we work to find a middle ground?

I didn't picture having a family dropped onto my lap. Literally. But now I can't imagine what it would be like without them there, without me being a part of their daily lives. How do I live life without seeing my son every day?

Fuck. I scrub a hand over my face. We have so little time to figure things out, and I don't know where to start.

Drool coats my hand, bringing my gaze back to my little guy. Doesn't matter what the adult world demands of me, I smile because Max has done a one-eighty to my perspective. "It will work out, right, Max?"

"Dada."

"Yeah, I'm your dada." I grab a wipe from the bag while Liv gets an update on Cassandra. She returns with a smile I read as good news, squats next to the stroller, and pulls out a rubber ring. After clipping it to his sleeve, she hands it to him. "He's teething."

"He's a happy chap for teething."

"He's happy with you."

I kiss his head. His hair is soft, and his smell wakes parts of myself I didn't know existed. I see the world differently. It happened in the blink of an eye. The dangers lurk from a plug to a creeper standing at the corner eyeing Max when we're out of the apartment. I see everything in a new way, and it revolves around this kid and the need to protect him at all costs. I wrap both my arms around him. "I'll always be here for you, buddy."

So many thoughts crowd my mind that I can't think straight. My heart thumps in my chest just staring at her because she's done the same to me but has awoken different emotions. *Again.*

I thought I was over her, but I was hiding from the truth. She couldn't push me away this week because I didn't want her to. I've been holding on to hope since I laid eyes on her in that conference room.

Fate brought us together again, but a second chance is up to us.

God, I sound like Marina. She's going to have a fucking field day with this situation.

Liv picks Max up and cuddles him to her side. Their bond means she gets to take these things, like holding him, for granted. "They're going to let Max and me visit Cassandra. I hate to have you just sitting here."

"It's okay. I don't mind." Standing, I tuck my hands in my pockets. "I can do some work." It's been less than twenty-four hours, but work seems like a million years ago.

"There's a coffee shop around the corner. Would you rather meet there instead of hanging around a hospital?"

"Sure. Want me to take the stroller?" She sets Max in it just as I ask the question.

"No, it's okay. I'll use it."

She slips on the hoodie and makes sure he's settled before pushing off. Looking back, she says, "I'll see you in a little while."

I don't know what happens. Nothing makes sense to me. I'm running off instinct instead of logic. I go to her, caressing the side of her neck as she looks into my eyes. We share a silent exchange that tells me she's as lost in the circumstance as I am.

But we have each other, and that elicits a smile made just for me. I kiss her, savoring the gentle pressure, and let her go. "See you later."

Despite the way we appear to the outside world, we're not a family in the traditional sense. I'm his dad, but what am I to her? The father of her child. A coworker? A one-night stand that turned into two?

What is she to me? Is she my endgame? Emptiness washes through me as I watch them walk away. Do I want her to be? I find myself standing there and staring down the hall where they've long disappeared. Judging by how I feel without her, she just might be.

Exhaling, I turn and leave the hospital.

It's a short walk to the other end of the block to find the coffee shop, but that's not what draws me in. It's the toy store beside it. A bell rings above my head when I enter. The colorful wonderland of toys has bookcases packed beyond their brims and overflowing shelves of odds and ends. Even the floor has toys all over, kids giggling as they run the short aisles at the back as their parents chase them.

"Welcome." The girl's smile is wider than the Grand Canyon, her blue hair and purple dress with green tights fit in with the vibrant environment. She hands me a lollipop and asks, "How can we spark your imagination?"

I hold the lollipop over my shoulder. "Just saw the store and came in."

"Fantastic! Let's get you some toys. What do you like to play with?"

The words alone send my mind to the gutter and have me wondering if Liv has any toys she'd like to play with . . . in front of me, of course. Wrong type of toy store. *Focus, Westcott.* "Um, I don't know?"

"Are you buying for yourself or someone special in your life?"

The obvious answer is Max, but Liv is more than his mother. The lights of who she's becoming to me already shine brighter. "I have two people who are special to me."

"I love that. If you share a little about each of them, I can steer you in the right direction."

Looking around, I go with Max. "I have a son. He's fourteen months old."

"That's sweet. Do you have a photo?"

A photo. The only one I have is of Liv holding Max in the bathroom. Since she's only in her bra, it's best if I don't share that one publicly. Failure hits fast. "I don't."

"That's okay. What does he like to play with?"

"Um." I scan the aisle nearby and exhale, feeling like an embarrassment of a father. "I just found out."

Her eyes widen, but she keeps on smiling. Should I have confessed that secret? Probably not, but I don't want to live in lies. She says, "That's some pretty awesome news."

"It is." My ego doesn't feel so wounded, so I ask, "I like cars. Do kids his age like cars?"

"Kids his age *love* cars." Without an ounce of judgment, she turns on her white Doc Martens and says, "Follow me." She leads me down an aisle and then cuts over to another. "This whole section is age-appropriate toys. Have a look around and let me know if I can help you with that other someone special."

"Thanks."

I bend to look at the wooden ones, but they're not that interesting. I mean, if I'm getting a car, it should be something real I can share with him. Max had a whole bucket of them, so I should contribute to the collection.

A car catches my eye. The miniature Aston Martin is bigger than his other cars but small enough for him to hold in his hands. Safe for a kid who puts everything in his mouth. I get one in blue and another in silver that matches mine.

I stand back up and cruise a few aisles, thinking about Liv and what she might like. Or maybe I'm way off track, and she'd prefer flowers?

Unlike the salesgirl who fits in with her surroundings, I have no sense of my place in Liv's life.

She likes salad, sexy-as-fuck shoes, and apparently, *Sons of Anarchy* is a secret she's been keeping, but otherwise, I have no clue what she likes. I scratch the back of my neck and study the store. Standing in front of the stuffed animals, I think about her apartment. It's clean and neutral. Like, there's not a lot of clutter. None at all, actually.

I grab a lobster and head toward the register, figuring Max will probably like it if she hates it. Or I'll keep it if they don't.

The salesgirl grins, looking at my hands. "What treasures did you find?"

"Cars for my little guy and a stuffed lobster for my . . ." Friend? Baby mama? This is so fucking confusing. "Friend."

"I think your friend and son will love these. Would you like me to gift wrap them?"

"Yes, please."

She takes the supplies and taps on the register. "I'll wrap them extra special."

"Thank you."

A few minutes later, I go to the coffee shop with my bag of presents and sit with an espresso at a table near the window. Scrolling emails does nothing to take my mind off Liv and Max. I even attempt to reply to a few, but my head is not in it. A few days ago, I was riding high on a new job, making friends at the office, enjoying life in the city, and discovered a money scheme by one of the owners' sons.

I don't care about any of that now.

Resting forward on the table, I rub the bridge of my nose. How is it possible for a week to feel like a year? I'm sure it's the lack of sleep, but will rest give me the clarity to know how to handle all this?

I have people I can talk to, but I already know what they'll say. From my parents to my sister to my brothers, it won't be about right or wrong. They don't lay guilt on without a reason. They'd tell me to forget about what others think and follow our hearts. All that matters is what Liv and I decide is best for Max and for us.

I sip the espresso, wanting to feel normal, to feel like any part of my old self again. I'm still free to do as I please when I want to. I can date . . . I'm not an angel, but I never claimed to be. My sex life came to a grinding halt after that night in the Hamptons because I was hung up on her. It took time to get back on that horse, but I have a contact list full of names I can call any day or night.

None of that's appealing anymore.

The truth rears its head. My thoughts are no longer jumbled. Rubbing my temple, I've come to terms with the fact that my life will never be how it was before last night.

The thing is, I'm not interested in merging two lives. The only thing I want is to be a family with them.

A text from Liv brightens my idle phone.

Be there shortly.

I pick it up but don't reply yet. Looking out the window, I notice the gray of the skyscrapers, the black exhaust from a passing cab, and the dirt on the streets, and I know things didn't play out how they were supposed to. In an ideal world, I would have been there to celebrate the pregnancy, Maxwell's birth, his first birthday, and his life. But I didn't get that chance.

It doesn't matter what happened, though, because I can't get that time back, no matter how much I wish for it. What matters moving forward is how I can stay in their lives without turning this into a legal spectacle. She doesn't want that either, so at least we're on the same page.

I scrub my forehead while staring at the screen. It's been a good morning. I don't want to ruin the rest of the day. I have a lot to figure out and need to know how long I'll be forced to keep her secrets. I want to tell my family. I want to tell the world about us. My feelings are set, but I don't know where Liv stands regarding us and the idea of being a family.

A knock on the glass has me jumping in my seat. "Fuck me." I'm hit with a glare. Eyeing the woman at the next table, I say, "Sorry."

Turning back to them, Liv's waving Max's hand, and they're both laughing. God, if only I could see this every day, I'd keep her secrets forever. Standing, I point at the door and say, "I'll come outside." Even though I know she can't hear me, I down my drink and set the cup on the counter on my way out.

"Hey," she says, so happy to see me that she's beaming. "Cassandra is doing well, and her parents are staying at her place to take care of her dog."

"That's good news."

"Yeah, it is." Her eyes dip to the bag. "What's that?"

I thought I'd give this to her later but now seems like a good time. "I got you something."

"You did?" Her shoulders round as her expression softens.

"I did." Should I be this proud of a lobster? I'm probably setting her up for disappointment if she's going off my grin that matches hers. Guess we'll see.

I give her the present, and I take Max, both of us winning in the exchange. "Hi, Max."

Max reaches for the brightly colored paper and white bow. "Don't worry, bud, I have goodies for you too."

Liv pulls the bow off and says, "I never really liked surprises, but I have to admit I'm excited about this one." Her sing-song voice has Max mesmerized. She tickles his tummy, receiving the biggest giggle in return. "Are you happy to see Dad—" Her eyes dart to mine as if she's done something wrong and is afraid of the repercussions.

We still, but I'm not sure why. "It's okay."

She turns back to Max. "Are you happy to see Daddy?"

Reaching out for me, Max says, "Dada." *Most amazing kid ever.*

"He's the smartest kid ever." My eyes return to Liv. "Am I allowed to say that?"

The question has her doing a double take. She laughs. "Of course. He's yours."

Mine.

He's mine.

I'm his daddy.

God, it strikes me every time. I'm a lucky fucking bastard.

I hold him to my chest as his fingers run mindlessly along my prickly chin. His eyes look into mine, and I tell him, "You're so smart, Max."

The paper is ripped, but Liv stops to stare at us. "He was born with deep blue eyes. Around seven or eight months, though, they started changing. I always thought they resembled mine, but seeing you two together, it's obvious where he gets the coloring from."

I hadn't said anything to her, not shared my concerns regarding the sudden change in my life, in her life as well. But somehow, she knew. She knew that I needed to hear I'm a part of something bigger than myself, making me realize that it's not just the two of them. *It's the three of us.*

Max and I look at each other again and grin. She says, "Like father, like son."

Like father, like son.

That hits deep, causing my heart to swell.

I have so many questions that need an answer and so many details to figure out, but right now, holding my son and spending time with Liv, I realize there's no rush. We're good as is, and it will only get better.

"You got me a lobster?" She sets the paper down in the stroller and holds the stuffed animal to her chest. "It's really cute."

"I wanted something to remember when we met. A lobster was the closest thing I could find that reminded me of the Hamptons."

"Well, we do have Max." She laughs. I do when I realize yep, we have this memory for the rest of our lives. "But I love this lobster. I love it because you thought of me when you saw it." She leans up and kisses me. Max grabs the lobster, but she's okay sharing. "Seems we both love it."

"I'm glad."

Taking hold of the stroller, she asks, "Are you ready?"

I lean over and give her another kiss. Just because I want to.

Her eyebrow arches as she licks the corner of her lips. "What was that for?"

"For him. For you. For us." I signal toward the corner. "I'm ready."

21

Noah

"I DON'T THINK I've gone to bed before ten o'clock since I was in middle school," I say, fighting a yawn.

The afternoon flew by with lunch and then a nap for Max. He opened his present but was more interested in the box and paper than the cars. Harbor won't be impressed since his career revolves around high-end custom cars. But I have no doubt that when Max actually knows what a car is, it's something he can bond with not only me but also his uncle.

Now that he's settled in bed for the night and we've binged four episodes of *Sons of Anarchy*, I'm fighting sleep. It was busy all morning and kept going once we got home.

Home . . .

The word catches on the end of my tongue. *Huh.* I'm not sure what to do with that. I'm sure it's just a turn of phrase that came without great meaning. It's probably best if I ignore the inner alarms sounding in my head. What good are the alarms when they tell me to move forward instead of away? Maybe I should listen rather than disregard.

I hold Liv a little tighter as we lie on the couch together. She yawns. "Welcome to parenthood. I'm in a constant state of exhaustion."

That yawn is my gateway. I go for it. "Since we're both kind of tired, do you want to—"

"Go to sleep?" She turns in my arms, seemingly wide awake now. This is not what I was going for. Well, the awake part works but not the sleep.

"Since it's Saturday night, I was kind of thinking we'd go into the bedroom." *Hint.*

As if that doesn't compute, she stares at me with her brows pushed together. "And sleep? Is that what you're suggesting?"

I blink and then narrow my eyes. "Um, no. That's not what I'm suggesting."

She laughs lightly against my chest. "My brain is too tired to riddle through this maze, Noah. You'll have to spell it out for me."

With our legs tangled together, my dick struggles to find enough room between us. "Do I *really* need to spell it out? I think it's kind of obvious."

"So I feel." A wink and smirk are given in return. I really fucking love this side of her. "It's that easy, huh?"

"All it takes is you, Ms. Bancroft, and I'm a lost cause."

Like the wind came in and swept her off her feet, her body slacks on the edge of the couch. Fortunately, I'd never let her fall. At least not to the floor. She leans in to kiss me. "You're not lost. You're right where you're supposed to be."

She deserves more than a kiss for saying that and for making me a part of their lives. But that's what I have to give her, so I kiss her with passion, running my fingers along the back of her neck so she knows that I'm not only grateful but I want her so fucking badly when I get that first taste of her. "So the bedroom?"

Releasing a jagged breath, she nods. "The bedroom."

We waste no time grinding together as soon as we're on the mattress. *Tongues tangling. Hands frenzied.* She tugs at my shirt and pulls hard. "That's my neck," I say, laughing through the burn she just caused along the base of my neck. "Just in case you forgot, my head is still attached."

"Oh sorry." She bends to kiss the spot that stings, not bothering to hide her laughter. Scrunching her nose, she fails at restraining her smirk. "It would be easier if you remove your shirt."

I push up, grabbing the back of my collar, and yank it off. The lights from the city shine bright enough for us to see everything and each other. So giving her a show might be fun. I start on my jeans, and turnabout is fair play. "Let me see those great tits of yours."

"Noah," she says, her mouth hanging open.

She feigns offense, but I don't think she means it. We're about to find out. "Is that the line? Did I cross it?"

"Not complaining." Scrambling to her knees, she tugs her shirt over her head. "Just shocked that I liked hearing that so much." Her bra falls to the floor, and she starts on her jeans on her own accord. *Someone's horny.*

We'd both be found guilty by a jury. Those dangerous curves, the tits that are a soft handful, the blush of her nipples peaking for me. "I can't wait to be inside you."

"Where?"

That mouth . . . Fuck me, that mouth. I raise an eyebrow at this cocky little vixen. *So fucking sexy.* "Do you want to play?"

Anchored up on her elbows, she brazenly takes my body

in. I rub over my dick a couple of times, drawing her eyes to the prize. She replies, "I'm game."

Her striking confidence is a major turn-on. "You'll have me coming before I get back on the bed."

Her laughter filters through the air as her gaze continues to roam freely over my body. "Would that be so bad?"

I move onto the bed again, sliding in next to her. "Yes. To my ego." I roll to start peppering her neck with kisses.

A shallow moan catches her off guard, but she still reaches between us. Her hand embraces my erection, and she smarts, "Your ego is as big as ever."

So. Fucking. Sexy. "You say the sweetest things."

She bursts out laughing. I love that we can have fun in and out of the bedroom. She says, "Making me laugh is the way to my heart."

Lowering my hand over her stomach and between her legs, I say, "I have other goals in mind, but tonight, it's not your heart I'm after."

Happiness still shapes the corners of her eyes, though her smile is only slight. "Oh yeah?" She rolls on top of me, pressing her hands to my chest while straddling my cock. Leaning down, she kisses me and whispers against my lips, "What are you after, Mr. Westcott?"

I exhale when her words shoot straight to my dick. She knows exactly how to play this game. "What am I going to do with you?"

Lifting enough to look into my eyes, she grins, knowing just how to play me. "Whatever you desire."

Fuck me. "You know what I want? I want to feel you, your body wrapped around mine, the heat scorching from our connection, and to see the look on your face when you come." Holding her harder against my dick, I grind against her pussy. "I also want to come inside you."

Resting her head against mine, she closes her eyes and inhales. "I love that you tell me exactly how you feel and what you want." With a quick tilt of her head, our eyes find each other again. "But on that last part, you mean with protection, right?"

I chuckle. "Yes. Be right back." I lift her and set her beside me. Padding through the apartment with an erection isn't my idea of fun, but one kid is enough for now. I grab my backpack left by the front door and start back. Sifting through the bag, I pull out a box of condoms and set them on the nightstand. "Figured we should stock up since we're making this a regular thing."

Propped up on one elbow, she giggles. "Open the drawer."

When I tug it open, two large boxes fill one-half of the drawer. Glancing at her, I ask, "Got big plans?"

"I sure do."

You wouldn't know there's been an interruption when I climb back in bed. Our lips find each other as our bodies cling together. I run my hand over her stomach and then knead her breasts. A moan escapes her chest, encouraging me for more. I won't disappoint.

I'm so hard for this woman. Stopping, I rip a packet open and put the condom on. Moving into place, I find her legs spread wide and ready to welcome me. I not only like the view but also how her legs wrap around me, holding me to her like she can't wait another second, which has me pushing in without warning.

Her back arches, and a harsh breath follows. I kiss her and fuck, thrust and pull, her nails scraping down my back as she kisses me in return. I deepen it—the kiss and the fuck until her moans are uttered words in the form of *faster, harder,* and *oh my God.* The sound of our bodies fills the air, slick against each other as we push and pull, take and give.

I lick her jaw and then take her earlobe between my teeth with a gentle tug. "I want you back on top of me." It's so much at once, feeling, touching, hearing, smelling, and not enough. I want more. I want all of her, inside and out. I force myself away, lying on my back and tucking my hands behind my head long enough to catch my breath and slow my thoughts so I can enjoy myself instead of feeding the devil inside me.

She comes without a breath escaping before we're reconnected, sinking down on me as if she owns my cock. Her possessive nature only makes me harder. With her palms flattened to my chest, the leverage gives her the upper hand. Rocking back and forth on top of me, she keeps her gaze fixated on mine as a smile widens. "You sure do look smug, Mr. Westcott."

"I have a gorgeous woman fucking me. What's not to be smug about?"

She rolls her eyes, then leans back to anchor her hands on my legs. With her tits out, she rolls her hips, and her expression goes from challenging with a cocked eyebrow to a point of ecstasy that drops her mouth open and has her lids closing.

The tips of her hair brush over my legs as I take hold of her hips and help her along. Running one hand across the suppleness of her thighs, I dip my fingers between her legs and slide down between her slick, soft folds to find her clit.

After a moan and the swirl of her hips, she increases the pressure against my fingertips. Her eyes are barely open, but I see them set on mine. She bites her bottom lip as her body begins to pursue her orgasm.

"I'm close." Her breathing picks up when I rub her sweet bud quicker. "It's so much. So good. Keep going." Each word releases a desperate breath, and soon, she's leaning forward again, taking what she needs to get off on me.

Releasing her hip, I gather her hair in my fist as I sit up. I'm still fucking her, still rubbing that juicy little clit. Breathless and struggling to hang on, she falls into her orgasm when I pull her head back by her hair, opening that mouth and throat. So damn tempting to fill it, but I won't keep her from coming first. "You going to come for me, baby?"

Her eyes are still closed, her breathing erratic as she bounces, chasing her relief. "Yes. God yes."

I lick the column of her neck, tasting the salt and sweat of her skin before clamping my lips on the side and kissing, nipping, sucking, and falling under her spell.

"Oh God, yes," she cries out in a fury while being pulled to the abyss. Her body quakes around me as her body rushes her release.

I push.

I push.

I thrust to catch up, to find the darkness and then myself again. I'm buried to the hilt and still fucking until I finally reach the precipice. Nails scrape against my skin, but there's no pain. The ache I was hunting drowns in my release.

She falls forward, her bare and glistening body my temple and salvation.

I push, and she takes until the trembling stops, and my body is depleted. We're so wrapped around each other, wrapped *in* each other that I don't want this to end. When my breathing finally evens, she says, "You're going to be in so much trouble if you gave me a hickey."

A release of a different nature welcomes me back. A kind

welcome after the heat of the other. Inspecting her neck, I rub my fingers over the bruising skin. "When you say trouble..."

"Noah!"

22

Liv

HEATED SKIN.

Hard muscles.

Heartbeats steady in his chest.

Waking up to Noah has its perks. I've never felt safer, more cared for, and lov—I shouldn't think about that five-letter word. It's too soon for feelings that hold that much weight in the world, much less my heart.

The sun shines across his chest, and I don't blame the light one bit for wanting to touch him. *I do too.* I kiss his shoulder, not wanting to wake him before I slip out of bed. Pulling on a T-shirt, I grab a pair of cheekies to wear before sneaking out of the closet to go to the kitchen, careful to quietly close the door to the bedroom behind me.

I slept like a baby after our activities last night. This morning, my body is loose like I had a great massage, though my thighs let me know that muscles that haven't been used in years are still there. All the kinks have been worked out, and I'm ready to tackle the day. Though kinks are relative this morning. Last night was a different story.

There's no embarrassment with Noah. I can do whatever feels good, and he's all about it. That has me thinking that I might want to try new things with him. It's a little early for the tingling below my stomach. Coffee is needed first, and then maybe I'll wake him up.

While the coffee brews, I click the remote to raise the shades and let the sunlight brighten my place. I sit on a dining chair and kick my feet up on the windowsill, taking in the city. It's an incredible view, but Noah's apartment is still on my mind. I've always appreciated my place, but it's exhilarating to think about a new perspective here and there. I'm jumping a few steps ahead, but what if we were more than just co-parenting?

It's silly to even consider a relationship at this stage. Maxwell needs to come first. Always. But this contentment I'm experiencing, the happiness that fills my bones is welcomed with open arms. It's been a long time since I've felt so good, and Noah is a part of the reason. Maxwell is the love of my life, but maybe my heart has started making room for someone else.

It's early, but I text my mom:

I told Noah he's Maxwell's father.

My mom has always been an early-bird riser, so I'm not shocked when my phone rings. I answer, "Good morning."

"Good morning to you. How are you? How did the conversation go? How did he react?"

I glance back toward the bedrooms as if I'll wake them. Whispering, I reply, "I'm so happy, Mom."

"This is great news. What happened?" She doesn't sound

suspicious, though her question tilts it in that direction. She's been my rock my entire life, and I want to tell her everything, but some things about Noah and I should remain between us.

"There's so much to discuss and figure out, but seeing him with Maxwell . . ." I grip the phone tighter, holding it closer to my mouth. "He's a natural, and Maxwell already adores him."

"Olivia, that makes my heart so happy to hear. What a relief to have a dream reaction from him."

"It is a relief. As much as I tried to prepare myself for the worst, he did the opposite and stepped in for Maxwell *and* for me." I take a breath. "It's so good. But is it too good to be true? I'm so happy that I almost can't trust my own instincts." I lower my feet, a new fear hijacking my happiness. Happiness has never lasted, so when will the other shoe drop?

I'm overthinking this. What happens tomorrow happens tomorrow. Today, I need to stay in the moment and enjoy each day. *Trust your gut, Liv.*

"The hardest part is over. You know his response to the situation. From here, the two of you will decide how to move forward."

Standing, I walk to the window and stare out—a quiet home behind me and the early morning sounds of the city waking up outside. "Mom?"

"I'm here," she whispers as if we're surrounded by eavesdroppers. She lives alone, so I glance behind me once more to make sure I still am.

The coast is clear. "Am I being too trusting? Should I be worried?"

"If you trust Noah, it's because he's proven you can. I think you're worried about the unknown, which is natural."

There's a pause, and then she says, "You told him the truth. You told him because you knew it would be best for Maxwell. Focus on that. How it plays out with custody is currently out of your hands."

Is it out of my hands?

I have no doubt she'll hire the best lawyers if this ends up in a court battle, but I really hope it doesn't.

"I have a confession." Really, I'm just bursting at the seams to tell someone.

"What is it?"

"I slept with him." I'm met with silence.

"Oh." Another pause sucks the air out of the conversation. "Well, once won't do any—"

"A couple of times." I wobble my head back and forth. "And a few other acts that would fall under the same categories."

"Oh, um . . . Alright." She's flustered and stumbling through her thoughts. Out loud. I wasn't trying to shock her. I need advice. "Hmm."

"I'm telling you because I need to share it with someone, Mom. If it's too much . . ."

"No, it's not too much. It's not something I want to think about either, but you're a woman with needs that should be met. That's where your father struggled."

"I hate to be mean, but I don't think I can handle a conversation about you and Dad having sex."

"That was the problem. We weren't having sex."

La la la la la.

It's tempting to plug my ears, though I know I'm in the wrong. I'm a grown woman who should be able to talk about these things. It's just so weird when it comes to my own parents.

She says, "This isn't something I want to relive. Just

know that I understand. You're twenty-seven. You should have an active sex life, Olivia."

The woman is gorgeous and funny, endearing and wise beyond her years. I can't imagine life without her, but I also want her to find happiness as well. "So should you, Mom."

"Oh, I do," she replies. *Was that a giggle?*

"You do? I thought—"

"I don't need a husband or even a boyfriend, for that matter. I don't even need a human to have an active sex life—"

"Mom." I shake my head, needing not to have these images populating my mind.

"I'm just saying that some great products are on the market these days."

Wait, what? Did she just say . . . oh God. "Okay. I got it."

"I can send you one of my favorites."

"I'm good." Noticing a pigeon on a window ledge across the street, I'm glad for the distraction from this conversation and the other reason is because the coffee's ready and I need to down a cup. "I've got all that covered."

"And I have a few regulars on speed dial."

"A few? *Mom . . .*"

"Sorry, TMI. Let's get back to you and Noah."

I almost feel bad for cutting her off, but damn, this is a lot to process about your sweet, innocent mom. Apparently, she's not so innocent, and I'm kind of proud of her.

Returning to the chair, I wrap my hands around the hot cup. My thoughts are all over the place. As much as it's been interesting and eye-opening to talk to my mom so openly about our love and lack of love lives, my worries are always nipping at my happiness. "I'm worried that . . ." I want to harness my feelings and turn them into words with meaning. I struggle under the halo of last night and the warmth that's come over me when I think of Noah. But taking a breath, I then ask, "What if he's being nice to—"

"You just told me you're happy. Happy, Olivia," she reminds me. "You can worry about this to the point of pushing him away, but don't ignore how he makes you feel. Your intuition matters."

"What if my intuition is wrong about Noah?"

"Honey, you can run a million what-ifs around your head, but until you two talk, it won't do you any good."

I know that's true, but it won't change anything until I get answers. I don't want to be blindsided. We need to get this settled. "I don't want to lose Maxwell."

"You won't, but you may have to offer Maxwell the opportunity to get to know his father alone."

Maxwell spending time with Noah means I'd be alone as well. I'd miss him so much that my heart aches simply from the thought. "I hate the idea of the alone part."

"Let's not get caught up in guessing and focus on what's real." I nod, though she can't see me. "What are you and Maxwell doing today?"

It's a good transition to get me out of my head. My mom knows me too well. "He's still sleeping, but no official plans."

"I could come over and spend some time with my grand-baby. That might give you and Noah a chance to talk privately and sort out some details before going into the week ahead."

Have I mentioned she's the best? *She is.* Who needs a dad when you have a Trudy? "Thank you. Let me talk to him when he gets up, and I'll let you know."

"He stayed over? Oh my, dear daughter." She sighs, but I can almost hear her joy. "You both are moving fast."

"Having a kid together pretty much sealed that fate."

She laughs. "I guess it did. Well, my little Maxie is just

the sweetest boy. I can come over, or you can drop him off at mine. Just let me know in a little while."

"I will, and thank you."

"Good morning." *Deep and sultry.* Noah's voice carries across the room and caresses me just before his arms do. Kissing the side of my head, he applies a gentle pressure to give him better access. So I do because when I close my eyes, this is what I imagine heaven to feel like.

"Gotta run," I say, getting sucked into his world. *Happily.* "By—"

I leave the phone on the sill and turn to face him, wrapping my arms loosely around his neck and staring into the hazel of his eyes. The gold is brighter in the diffused morning light. A lazy grin slides into place as his hands hold my waist and then slide lower to my ass. He gives a good squeeze and asks, "Why are you up so early?"

"Couldn't sleep."

Staring into my eyes, he then kisses me, long and lingering. When our lips part, our heads rest against each other's. I close my eyes and take a deep breath, inhaling him. He could get a girl drunk off his heady scent, an addicting mixture of masculinity, the beach, and a heavy dose of sexy.

And the way he holds me with intention. The palms of his hands grasping me like I'll slip away if he doesn't, the strength of his arms around me, making me feel safe, so safe.

I caress his cheek, the tips of my fingers scratched as I run them over his unshaven face—the pricks of scruff, the smoothness of his skin, the edge that drops off his jaw, and the fullness of his lips.

My breathing picks up from the proximity, my body awakening. I kiss him, rubbing myself shamelessly against him. I don't want any misunderstanding of what my intentions are. I'm weak to this man and need him to know exactly how I feel. It's not just physical. It's a chemical reaction I have to this man. It's an emotional connection that has me acting outside of myself.

I hold him even tighter. "You make me feel so much, Noah. So much of everything."

Nuzzling behind my ear, he whispers, "You say that as if you've given up." The warmth of his breath sends goose bumps across my skin.

"Not given up. Giving in. I realize I don't want to fight whatever this is between us." I don't tell him that my emotions have been blossoming because it's easier to hide behind the physical attraction instead.

Leaning back to look me in the eyes, he studies my eyes as if he might catch a lie hiding inside. "We definitely shouldn't be fighting. How lucky are we that we get to be together how we like and see fit? We can toss out the past and leave the future to worry about another day. We can live in the here and now and enjoy the present."

He chuckles. "What time does Maxwell wake up?"

I glance at the clock on the stove. "Thirty minutes tops."

"Challenge accepted."

"There's no challenge. Wait, that came out wrong . . ." And then I realize it didn't. I'm good with it if I'm called easy for wanting this man. Seeing him bare-chested and with only underwear on has me ready to tackle him with my tongue and other body parts.

"You sure about that?" He cocks an eyebrow and lands a smirk that causes my insides to twist in tingles. He kisses my neck while walking me backward toward the window. "Please sit." There's no room for argument, and it was not a question.

I sit because I'm not opposed to taking commands when

he's looking at me like I'm about to be his breakfast. With a finger under my chin, he lifts until our eyes lock on each other's, and whispers, "Can you be a good girl and keep quiet?"

"I can try," I reply with a smirk.

He kisses me, but the pressure is different. It's heavy and loaded with intent. "If you stay quiet for me, I'll make you come so hard you won't be able to walk without remembering how my mouth fucked so good." He tilts his head, staring me in the eyes. "How does that sound?"

"I want that."

He kneels before me. "Me too." Spreading my knees apart, he runs his hands over the outside of my thighs and then dips to kiss me as if he were kissing my mouth.

The tips of his fingers slide under the cotton of my cheekies, and then he pinches the fabric to pull it down. I lift enough to assist, but he drags them all the way down and frees one ankle and then the other. Just when I think he'll toss them over his shoulder, he doesn't. He brings the fabric to his nose and closes his eyes as he inhales instead.

As I lick my lips, he has me craving him the same way. I watch in rapt fascination when he opens his eyes. "You smell incredible. Just as I remember, and I can't fucking wait to taste you again."

I should be embarrassed for how wet I am from his words, for causing that look in his eyes, enjoying that face, and for savoring the feel of his fingers as they dip under the T-shirt and slip between my lower lips, taking ownership.

Nope, I've not an ounce of shame.

Instead, the back of my head hits the glass just as my hands leverage against the wood frame of the window. When he ducks under the hem of my shirt, he places one leg and then the other over his shoulders. Tucking his hands under my ass, he angles me lower, and his tongue slides across my clit. The sharp ends of his scruff scratch my skin, and the sound of the world just outside the glass plays like music in my ears. With every sense awakened, he sucks and licks, fucks with his tongue, and then soothes when I squirm.

I scratch the wood, letting him lap at me, holding me still on the windowsill, humming to the sound of my moans getting louder. "Oh God." I hold his head, fisting his hair, knowing I'm never letting go. "Feels so good, Noah."

He kisses my clit, and two fingers enter me, pull out, and thrust again. And then a finger escapes, sliding between my butt cheeks. "So fucking sexy."

My eyes fly open, my breathing erratic. I stare at him with my mouth hanging wide open but don't say a word. I think they've been stolen from my tongue. With his fingers pumping in and out of me, he looks up with a glistening chin. *Why does this turn me on even more?*

With one hand, he reaches under my shirt and squeezes a breast. When he pinches my nipple, my entire body jolts, back arching to his will. "Ah," I say, but it seems enough to encourage him for more.

"How do you like that, baby?"

I don't know up from down, much less the words to respond with any coherency. When he enters me again, I scoot forward, gripping his shoulders. "I, I . . ." Then he retreats, allowing me to catch my breath.

With his fingers still in my entrance, he lifts and kisses me with a chuckle. "It's okay. I'm just seeing what you like."

My breathing still jags in my chest, but I grin, relief rolling through me. "I didn't dislike it. I just . . ." With his thumb on my pulsing center, rubbing the sweetest of repeated circles, I lose my train of thought and start riding his hand.

The build is fast, so I chase my release, not giving a damn about anything else. "Oh God, yes. So close."

His pace quickens, and his relentless attentions topple me. I grab and push, gyrate, and fuck his fingers until I can no longer hang on. Falling back to the glass hitting my back, I throw everything I am into getting off.

I'm consumed so fast that I'm spinning without thought, traveling on instinct into the fireworks as they burst behind my lids. "Noah—"

My mouth is covered, and my moans swallowed. Our tongues dance under the fire burning between us. When my body calms, I open my eyes to see him staring at me with reverence shining in his eyes. "You're beautiful, Liv. So beautiful."

It's not the words that choke me up, though I'm touched by them. It's that look that turned from hunger to satisfied to adoration that inspires me to lean forward, slink down on my knees in front of him, and hug him. Tearing up, I tuck my head into the crook of his neck, and whisper, "I don't deserve you."

"Hey." He leans back so our gazes connect and cups my cheeks. "There's no deserving or undeserving. I'm here because I want to be. I'm here because of you. I'm here because you trusted me, and it pleases me to please you." Leaning in, he kisses me and my insecurities away.

"Thank you."

"My pleasure. Literally." Chuckling, he stands and helps me to my feet. My legs are unstable, but he grabs my underwear and holds me as I step back into them. He wins my heart when a kiss is placed along my legs as he slides them into place.

His palms are hot against my skin, and his lips are warm, but when he dips his tongue out just to lick a spot on my inner thigh, the air-conditioning cools in contrast.

I wasn't wrong earlier. I've never felt like this about anyone, but I recognize the feeling.

When he pulls back, he wipes his bottom lip, and then with the same thumb, he wipes mine. With a hand planted above my head, he stays there, leaning in, and then asks, "Want to go to a play with me tonight?"

23

Noah

PEEKING into his room just after seven thirty, I couldn't wait for Max to wake up.

His eyes are open, and he pushes himself to his feet with a big grin as if he's been waiting on me for hours to save him. "Dada."

"Hey, buddy," I say, picking him up and hugging him to me. "Let's get you cleaned up."

I change his diaper and rock him back and forth against my chest. His room is peaceful, the hour still early enough for him to relax in my arms.

"I don't remember when I was your age, Max, but I remember my mom coming to get me in the mornings when I was a little older." It's only one core memory, but I remember how it made me feel. "I was old enough to walk and run, to tell my mom what I needed, but I didn't need to. She already knew. She'd hold me in her arms when it was just the two of us. I never felt so safe, content to leave the day to start without us."

A comforted smile crosses my mouth as I stare at my little guy. "I want that with you, buddy." Blowing his lips, Max babbles and sits up, wiping his eyes. I whisper, "Good morning."

"Sun," he replies, pointing toward the window.

"Yeah, sun." The word rolls around my mind and on my tongue.

I open the shade, and we stare out the window together. Leaning in, I kiss the side of his head, realizing the significance. "Son." He glances at me, but then returns his attention back out the window. "It's a nice view, kid, but one day, I'll get to take you to my hometown. It's called Beacon. Can you say Beacon?"

"Be."

"Close enough." I hold him in place on my lap as he looks uninterested. I'm not going to let that deter me. "Beacon is a little drive but not too far. You can meet my mom and dad, my brothers, and my sister. Your aunt Marina will love spending time with you." Tickling his tummy, I ask, "Would you like that, Max? I know I would."

We sit in the chair, and I hold him upright while he bounces on my legs. He hasn't had breakfast, so I know our time is limited before hunger strikes. He's like his mom that way, from what I'm gathering. Half a smirk consumes my face.

And then Max mimics me.

He's not all his mom in characteristics. "I think we got another lady-killer on our hands."

His leg goes straight out, and he pushes away. "You want down?"

"Dow." Dow. He's so close to saying new words. I don't know what he's supposed to say at his age, but I'm impressed. I set him on his feet. He holds on, but soon enough, he's toddling away.

I won't claim I'm not sleep-deprived. I am. But seeing him trying to leave . . . leave me hits me in the feels, making my chest ache. I'm unsure if it's that or the harsh reality that I'm returning to my apartment today.

Without Max.

Without Liv.

Without my heart still intact.

Fuck.

It's probably best if I don't dwell on the inevitable. I scoop him up and bring him into the living room. Liv's attention is captivated by the sight of him, and she's already heading straight for him with her arms open wide. "Good morning, Maxwell."

As I watch her hug him, the love she has for him on full display makes one thing certain. I could never harm him by keeping them apart for long, even if it hurt me. I must be strong for the sake of my son and for both of them.

She smiles when she opens her eyes. Her expression is soft and gentle in nature but also genuine. I understand this on a deeper level now, and I've only known him since Friday night. Max is mine. I still can't seem to wrap my head around that fact. It feels too big to comprehend in such a short time.

I embrace them, dipping my head and placing a kiss on both of their heads. Liv doesn't fight it. She leans in, wrapping her free arm around my back. Max is a wiggler, but I wouldn't expect anything less. I always had trouble sitting still as well, but he doesn't understand the gravity of the situation either. We'll always make sure to shield him from our troubles.

Stepping away, needing the space to start a gradual separation—physically and emotionally—I ask, "I can feed him if you have something you need to—"

"I don't have anything to do."

"Oh." I nod, realizing distance won't make my heart stop beating. Losing them will. "Okay. Well . . ." I shove my hands in my pockets. I watch as she sets him in his high chair and moves around the kitchen. I'm not sure what I'm supposed to be doing. "Am I in the way?"

"No," she replies, coming so close to me that it's tempting to kiss her while I can. "You're not in the way, Noah." She takes my hand and leads me into the kitchen with her. "After feeding him, we can be as busy or lazy as we want. It's Sunday." The way she includes me, as if that's the only natural assumption, shifts my mood to a better space. She stops suddenly. "I almost forgot. My mom is going to watch Maxwell for me tonight." Looking up from the dish she's preparing him, she waggles her eyebrows. Wonder where she got that move. I chuckle. "She said she can take him for the night."

I've not met her mother, but she sounds like an important part of Liv's and Max's lives. "What are you thinking?"

"I think we should take her up on the offer. It's a long drive to the play, but we wouldn't have to worry about returning by a certain time."

She sets a plate of food in front of the little man and then turns to me, where I've sat across the table from her. Maybe it's the lighting or the sun shining in her eyes, but it looks a lot like excitement highlighting her eyes. The green is brighter, but the gold glimmers.

Her hair's in a mess on top of her head, and she's wearing no makeup, but she doesn't need it. Still wearing the T-shirt from this morning, she's added a pair of shorts. She's fucking stunning, making my heart hurt.

"She has a full nursery setup," she starts. "And is on the Upper Westside."

"Sounds like there's a question for me in there."

"Since we're driving a long way tonight and it will be late, I was thinking," she says, her fingers fidgeting just at the edge of the table. "Maybe you could stay here again tonight? With me?" I don't have time for a breath, much less a reply, when she adds, "You can say no. We both have work in the morn—"

"Yes."

She searches my eyes as if she didn't hear me. "Yes, you'll stay?"

I nod, not keeping her in suspense. "I'll stay."

"Even if Maxwell's not here?"

I reach over and rest my hand on the table in front of her, palm side up. Looking between my hand and my face, she slips her hand into mine with the sweetest smile. "Even if he's not here. I want to stay with you."

Her fingers lie flat against my hand, and we look at them. Hers are so much smaller, but the feelings this connection evokes is bigger than the two combined. When a banana slice slaps against the skin of her neck, causing her to flinch, and then slowly peels back and falls to the floor, I don't see anger come over her. She laughs.

Quick to straighten her face, she pulls her hand away and angles back toward him. "Do we throw food, Maxwell?"

He's nodding like a little terror high on sugar.

"No," she says, "we don't throw food."

His head bops around on his neck as if he's just discovered he can move it. She covers both his hands in hers, stilling him, and repeats the question as calmly as the first time. "Maxwell?"

Looking at me, he says, "Dada."

"You're on your own, kid." I stay quiet to let her handle it because she's the expert.

She asks, "Are you going to eat the food, Maxwell, or throw the food? If you're going to throw it, I'll put it away until you're ready to eat."

"Foo," he calls out.

The tension from her expression softens, and she smiles at him. "Okay, food."

When she turns back to me, I ask, "How did you learn to do that? I have no idea how to discipline or even talk to him."

"You're doing great. He loves when you talk to him. For me, I try to give him choices to let him make the decision on how to proceed. Sometimes it works out. He did great just then. He let me know what he wants to do." On the tail end of a roll of laughter, she adds, "Sometimes he throws the entire plate."

"You make it look easy, but I know it's not." Getting this insight stirs emotions I'm unfamiliar with. Unsettled, I stand, crossing my arms over my chest, and stare out a window. With so much on my mind, I think about my mom and how she would have been the first I told under normal circumstances. I turn back to her. "I want to tell my family."

Her smile wipes free from her face. "Tell them what?"

"Tell them about Max. I . . ." I drop my arms back to my sides, hoping this doesn't upset her. I might be wishing too much, but we'll work together better if we're in agreement on most issues. "I would have never kept this from them if I'd known." Coming closer, I stop, keeping space so she doesn't feel trapped. That's the last thing I'd want her to be, much less feel. "Since I know, I can't keep him a secret. I don't want to."

Liv stands, takes a step toward the kitchen, and then

stops. Her back faces me, and I know she's fighting her instincts to react. One of her hands balls at her hip, and her head drops down. She moves into the kitchen and opens a cabinet that hides most of the view of her from me. "I understand, but maybe we should—"

"Your mom knows. She's gotten to be a part of his life since before he was born."

She stills, but I see her chest fill and slowly exhale. Gripping the counter in front of her, she replies, "Please understand that I had no one but my mom."

"I do, but my mom—"

The abrupt swing of the cabinet door closing stops me from speaking. There's no satisfying slam since they're soft-closure doors, but the effect still ripples from ten feet away. I'm hit with her tear-filled eyes, her parted lips as if she can't take in enough air, and a slight bend to her spine as she rests her weight on the countertop.

I should go to her, reassure her like I've been doing, like I've done, but I can't. My feet won't move until I get every word out. "They're already going to be disappointed that they missed so much of his life and the celebration beforehand—baby showers, gender reveals, the health of both of you. Don't ask me to keep him a secret, Liv, because I can't. My family doesn't lie to each other."

Her back springs straight. "It's not a lie, Noah," she says, just above a whisper as if Max won't hear a thing even though he's sitting between us. Maybe that's how it's going to be. Max being the only thing bridging us together. "I just—"

"You just what?"

"I need time."

"Time for what? You've had time." I move around Max and into the kitchen. She stays where she is, but her arms are now crossed over her chest. I'm not putting her on the defense, though I know she won't believe me. That's not something I can change. This is a tough topic. "I need to be honest about how I'm feeling. My mom will be thrilled to meet him but devastated over the time she's lost being in his life."

Stepping closer, I continue, "Imagine how much more love he'll have in his life. I have three siblings, my parents, and my sisters-in-law." I close the gap, reaching out to unwind her tightly wound arms. Holding her hands, I kiss each one and then bend to look into her eyes. "You're Max's mom, so no matter what happens, you'll always be a part of the family."

She crashes into me, her head on my chest and her arms wrapping around my midsection. The lightest sound of sniffling is heard as I cover her in an embrace. "I don't know what being part of a family means. It's always just been my mom and me, and Cassandra more recently. That's been enough. To know there's more . . ." She looks up, resting her chin on my chest. "I don't think I could have wished for a better man to be Maxwell's father than one who not only accepts him without conditions but accepts me as well. So I'm at a loss of what to say. Thank you? It's not enough."

"It's not necessary. You've given me a son. I will never be able to repay you." I rub her back and kiss the top of her head. "I want us to have a good relationship. That means we're always honest with each other. Even when it's hard."

"Even when it's hard." Her voice cracks at the end. She nods again and takes a step back. "Do you want to tell them tonight when you're in Beacon?"

"We won't be there long enough to open the topic up for discussion. Let's focus on enjoying the evening. I also want to support my sister. But how do you feel about me telling them at another time?"

Taking my hand, she folds our fingers together and smiles. "It's scary for me—the unknown—but it's exciting for you and Maxwell. I think I've already overstepped the issue. I don't get to control who you tell or when. I just ask that this is kept out of the office."

"I can do that." Pulling her to me, I slide my other hand around her lower back while staring into the windows of her beautiful eyes. "I have another question."

"Okay."

"When do I get to tell everyone in that office how fucking amazing you taste?"

She laughs, the playfulness returning as she whacks me in the arm. "Tomorrow if you're looking to get us fired." *Sexy smart-ass.*

"Different topic. I need to head to my apartment." I look back at Max and then to her again. "But it feels wrong to leave you guys."

She sighs, looking down again. "I know what you mean. Are we rushing things?"

I'm not sure, but at least we're doing it together. "We're going at our own pace."

24

Liv

I ALMOST ASKED Noah to come with me to drop Maxwell at my mom's. I don't know why I didn't, other than I've had so much happen in the past forty-eight hours that I really don't want to do the introduction dance today.

It's just easier and quicker if I go alone while he heads to his place. Though I did give him a key just in case he was done before I was and arrived at my apartment before I did.

In the cab, I let my mind wander. Life throws me curveballs, but I've never been a better catcher than I have this weekend. Sure, I have momentary lapses, letting fear get the best of me, but they're short-lived, and Noah's been right there to reassure me. Nothing is how I predicted it would be with him, and having that weight of guilt off my conscience is glorious. He knows what I've kept a secret from part of my world.

My mom remarked that I have a glow about me. That was followed by a "use protection" talk. I opened a can of worms this morning on our call. Now she won't stop talking about sex. *What have I done?* I shake my head but also laugh.

That conversation has me thinking about the future. Do I want more kids? Do I want more kids with Noah? We have a solid month's supply of condoms in the nightstand drawer, but will we be together to use them?

Although I know it's too soon to think about a relationship, I can't say I don't want more kids. Giving Max . . . oh wow. Noah's rubbing off on me. Giving Maxwell a sibling is something I wouldn't mind doing. I don't have any brothers or sisters, and it would have been nice to have that built into my life.

But it's the way Noah's supported me and Maxwell since the moment he found out that has opened me to possibilities I didn't know existed before Friday night.

Walking into the lobby of my building, I add his name to my guest list, giving him twenty-four seven access to stop by or come over anytime. As Maxwell's father, he should have that right. As my . . . I'm not sure what he is. I think he'd flip out if I called him a coworker at this point. He's clearly more than that. He's more than Maxwell's father as well. I'm just not sure what he is in my life.

Yet.

I'm feeling optimistic, but the *yet* lingers up to my floor. I don't know if we're going out as friends tonight or if it's a date. Either way, I'm hoping it will help us determine more of our role in each other's lives.

Form-fitting black dress.

Heels that will turn a certain someone's head.

I see how Noah eyes my legs and lower. He appreciates the effort I make to wear gorgeously made shoes. But I have a feeling he would like to appreciate them in the bedroom. I need to fulfill that fantasy and wear nothing but my sexiest heels.

When my hair is styled and my makeup is done, I stand in front of the mirror. I'm overdressed for three thirty in the afternoon, but with a long drive ahead, I figure my makeup will lighten over the hours and my hair will relax, hopefully making it perfect by the time we arrive. I should probably wear something more comfortable in the car, but the last thing I want to do is change clothes in a gas station bathroom.

So this is it. And I feel amazing.

Resting my hand on the bed, I lift my foot and slip on one platform heel. "You're a gorgeous woman, Liv, but wow. You're breathtaking tonight." His dulcet tones warm me through like a sip of whiskey. When I turn back, I see Noah standing in the doorway admiring me.

I drop down on the foot without a heel to catch my balance before lifting that leg again to stand like a flamingo. My cheeks still heat, and putting on my shoe is a good distraction. "I see the key came in handy."

"It did." He comes toward me with a confident swagger to his steps. Dressed in all black, from the dress pants to the button-up and even the large watch wrapped around his wrist, he's drool-worthy.

Not a hair is out of place despite the concerted effort to make it look like he might have rolled out of bed looking like that. He didn't shave, and I'm not one bit upset remembering how that jaw scraped deliciously along my inner thighs this morning.

I wobble while trying to balance, but he's quick and supports me by the arm. "Gotcha," he says, chuckling. "Here, sit and let me put your shoe on."

Moving to the edge of the bed, he kneels and holds me

by the ankle, running the tips of his finger along the arch of my foot before retracing with kisses. Goose bumps strike like wildfire across my skin, making me wonder if I should convince him to spend the night in instead.

He says, "You make me want to skip the play."

I laugh out loud. "I was just thinking the same, but I think we should go for your sister."

"I know you're right, but I might need a few minutes to get past this erection."

With his eyes focused on the task of slipping the heel onto my foot, he replies, "You're incredibly sexy."

It's a victory—small in nature—but a compliment from him is always a win. And I think I have him figured out. He is solidly into the whole sex kitten look.

After slipping the other shoe onto my foot, he stands and then helps me to my feet, bringing me into his arms. It's a slow dance—holding hands, eyes fixed on each other, light touches of knees bumping, sly smiles, and the giddy that's building in my tummy. *This is a date.* A real one.

"I love spending time with Max, but I've been looking forward to spending time with you all day." We bring our heads together and continue to sway before he adds, "But unfortunately, we do need to leave. I have a car waiting downstairs."

"I wondered how we were getting to Beacon. It's quite the drive."

He leads me into the living room. "It's not too bad, but it's all about the adventure tonight." Our hands fall from each other's, and he picks up a bouquet from the counter. Standing in front of me with a wild mixture of varying shades of purple and mixed greenery, he hands them to me. "These made me think of you."

"You brought me flowers?" I take them, smelling them

twice, then hold them to my chest. "They're so pretty, Noah. Thank you." I kiss him, hoping to make him feel as good as he's made me feel the past couple of days.

The phone in his pocket vibrates against my belly. The interruption is probably for the best, though admittedly, I'm still completely open to the idea of a last-minute change in plans.

He pulls it out and glances at the screen. With a disappointed sigh, he says, "We really need to go."

"Let me grab my clutch." I hurry into the bedroom and grab my phone from where it was charging. I peek down at the nightstand drawer. *Should I bring a condom?*

Honestly, the man makes me do crazy things. *Obviously.* It won't be unwise to prepare for anything. I grab the condom and tuck it in my purse before walking back out to the flowers in a pitcher of water on the counter and Noah Westcott looking gorgeous with his arm out waiting for me.

And seeing him looking this amazing is exactly why I packed protection.

We may have done things a little out of order, but this is what dream dates are made of, and I intend to enjoy every minute of it. I take his arm, and we leave together. He locks the door and waggles his brows. "Thanks for the key."

Standing at the elevator, I poke him in the chest with a teasing laugh. "Don't make me regret it."

Catching my finger, he brings the tip to his lips and kisses it. "Never."

A driver waits at the curb in front of a black Suburban. When we reach the SUV, I lift my leg, but there's no way without hiking my skirt that I'll be able to get into the back seat. "This skirt is too tight for large steps."

When the second attempt fails, I start to hike it up, but he says, "Wait."

Scooping me into his arms, he sets me on the leather seat. "My hero," I say, laughing. "Adventure indeed." When we're tucked inside, I reach across the gap between the two seats. He grasps my hand just as the Suburban weaves into the lane. "Thank you."

"No worries." His grin is gentler, but there's a lofty hope hanging in his eyes. Somehow, I have a feeling it's a reflection of mine.

"Not just for helping me into the SUV." My heart starts racing. I take a breath and exhale. "For tonight, for this weekend, the past two nights, the mornings, and for being you."

"Me? Hmm." His gaze dashes away as if the words need mulling over. When he looks at me again, at our hands joined in the middle of us, he says, "You've been treated less than by the men in your life. I won't do that to you. Not ever, Liv."

I almost fill the space with a reply, but one's not needed. I hold my tongue and take in his promise. I'm not sure if I'll always have butterflies with him, but it feels good to be excited about someone in my life. I welcome the change.

Just as I ease in for the long ride ahead, the SUV turns off the main highway. "Where are we going?"

His gaze distances over my shoulder, and he points out the window. "There."

When I turn, we're traveling along a row of helicopters. Jerking my eyes back to him, I ask, "We're taking a helicopter?"

"Figured that would be more fun and a lot faster than sitting in a car for four hours each way."

I stare in disbelief at the sight before me. The black and gold helicopters are large, a vision of luxury even on the outside. "How long will it take us to get there?"

"Around an hour."

Still holding hands, I rest my head back and smile. "You didn't need a helicopter to charm me, Westcott. You were doing just fine all on your own."

"If this can charm a Bancroft, I'm doing something right."

If only life had been how he sees it in his rose-colored glasses. I had food and clothes; the necessities of survival were covered. But I would trade my fancy uniforms, the car I got when I turned sixteen, and even my pride for my dad's love.

Now I'm glad I didn't. No child should ever have to beg to be cared for.

The SUV stops, and Noah comes around to help me land on my feet. I grab my clutch in one hand. Noah holds my other tightly in his and leads me to the helicopter. We meet the small crew and prepare to board.

I hike my skirt just enough to bend my knees, sparing my knight in all black the burden of carrying me again.

Beige leather captain's seats that recline, a charcuterie platter on a small table between us, and champagne on ice. There's only enough room for the large chairs and table, so the attendant pops the champagne, fills our glasses, and then shows us where the other drinks are stowed away. The stairs are tucked in when she steps off, and the pilot asks if we're ready.

Noah glances at me. "I'm ready. How about you?"

The question sounds loaded with possibilities. I answer honestly, "I'm ready if you are."

He kisses my hand. "I've been ready for more than two years, baby."

25

Liv

"Don't be so surprised," I say, adjusting my headphones over my ears. "Not everyone's been on a helicopter before."

"Your last name is on a prominent building in the New York skyline. Guess I figured some perks came along with that."

Angling my hips toward him, I add, "You know that my father and I aren't close. I'm the disappointment he didn't ask for yada yada. He didn't take me on business trips or vacations. My mom would travel with me during breaks from school. It was just the two of us unless we were needed for a photo-op." I roll my eyes. "A family always looks better for promotional purposes or to land a big deal." I put up with so much, and where did it get me? Well, technically, in a helicopter with Noah. I guess it all hasn't been so bad.

I continue by asking, "Want to hear the cherry on top of my childhood?"

"I'm starting to wonder if I do or not. It makes me fucking rage how he's treated you."

"Buckle up for this one." Should I be sharing every dirty family secret? With Noah, I won't sacrifice myself to protect my father anymore. "He took credit for every one of my accomplishments."

"What?" I appreciate that he takes offense on my behalf. "What the hell do you mean?"

"When I graduated salutatorian, he reminded me that second place is the first loser. When his buddies told *him* congratulations at my graduation party, he said he guided me every step of the way. When I got into NYU, he told me NYU was no Yale, which is his alma mater. He was so disappointed that he could barely look at me. Later, I overheard him telling his cigar buddies that he chose NYU to expose me to new experiences. They clapped him on the back for it." I drop my head back on the seat and roll my neck to face him again. "I could go on, but it's truly exhausting."

"I can only imagine." He's still staring at me like I'm a wounded animal he's found on the side of the road. I hate seeing pity shape his handsome face, but I feel better for unloading.

"I'm not telling you so you feel sorry for me. I'm telling you so you understand that although I carry the Bancroft name, it's always been on borrowed time. It's like the lease will run out eventually, but I just don't know when."

"I grew up with money. Not helicopters. That's all Harbor's doing in the past couple of years. Our house was happy for the most part. We've had our trials and wins. As long as we had each other, we could get through anything. But a big family has different personalities to contend with. I can't say I've had a hard life because I haven't. But as a family, we've faced a few demons."

"How are things now?"

Grinning, he replies, "I think with my brothers settling

down, a serenity has come over the family." He looks down at his shined shoes. "They put my parents through hell, and in response, that made it easy on Marina and me. My parents realized they wanted to slow down and enjoy time with their family."

My chuckle barely contains any humor. "So what you're saying is there might be hope for my father?"

He exhales a long breath. "I don't have the answer to that. I know there should be. On the other hand, I'm starting to be in the fuck-him camp." He adjusts the headphones and asks, "How does he feel about Max?"

"You mean because he's the male heir my father supposedly always wanted?" I shake my head and look out the window at the beauty of the wooded land below. In the distance is a large lake, but I turn back to Noah, finding him much more interesting. "One day, he'll try to step into Maxwell's life and take that accomplishment away from me as well."

"Over my dead body." The venom in his voice leaves me breathless, not in fear but some other emotion I'm unfamiliar with.

My chest feels fuller, my heart thunders, and a lightheadedness spins my head. *Oh my God . . . No . . . can't be.* Is this what love feels like?

Am I in love?

I know I'm in lust with this man but love as well? The pilot tells us to prepare for landing.

It's too late. I've already fallen.

Oh no. It's true. I'm in love with Noah Westcott. Will it be possible to keep ignoring the feelings blooming inside? I must. I have no other choice. This weekend has been amazing, even more so that Max has his father in his life. My relationship with Noah has been nothing less than incredible, but am I pushing this too far?

The last thing I want to be is clingy.

God, how embarrassing would that be? I'm sure women fall at his feet on the regular. Do I really want to be that needy?

No.

But why'd he have to go sounding all growly and protective over our son? Does he realize what that does to the ladies? To me, specifically?

The helipad is situated in the middle of a grassy field surrounded by trees on two sides, a large home with a pool, and another building that appears to be a smaller house. Is he kidding me with this? "That's quite the property," I say with my eyes fixed on the stunning home. Bancroft holds weight in New York society, but damn, I wish I was a Westcott about now. Wait . . . what?

I need to get my head out of the clouds.

He says, "That's my parents' home."

Glancing back at him, I ask, "That's where you grew up?"

"Yes. It was great exploring the woods, fishing at the lake, swimming all day on the weekends, tasting freedom in a way that some will never experience. We were allowed to run wild out here since there were no immediate neighbors."

Seeing him smile as he looks out the window, there's a distance in his eyes, not a longing but maybe memories springing to life. He has me wondering about the son we share and the life he wants for him. "Is that where you want Maxwell to grow up?"

Stretching his arm out, he angles toward me, rubbing my leg. "I want him to grow up with us present in his life. That matters more than the location."

A lump in my throat has me nodding, though I cover his hand with mine in a show of solidarity when I'm unable to speak. I'm not sure why I'm so emotional. I would love for Maxwell to experience a place like this. As Noah said, to run wild without regard to concrete surroundings or people hurrying to get elsewhere.

I can already feel time slowing down just as we land. "He'd love it here," I say, finally able to speak.

"What about you? Would you like to spend some time here?"

"It's a beautiful place, Noah. I'm not sure how I fit into this life."

Gently squeezing my leg, he says, "You're Max's mom and the mother of my child. You're always welcome here."

Noah hasn't asked a thing of me since the moment he found out about our son. He's been supportive and kinder than I probably deserve. He's not made any threats except when we pushed each other to the brink the other night. And that warning came with no threat of taking Maxwell away from me. Not once.

Dammit. It's so clear now. I'm in love with this man. And I love being welcome here because of my relation to our son, but I want to be welcome here for my relationship with Noah as well.

I'm so screwed.

What am I going to do?

We set the headphones down, and Noah helps me out of the helicopter. But looking ahead at the large grassy field we're expected to cross, I say, "There's no way these heels will make it across this lawn without sinking."

I reach down to take them off, but he says, "I'll carry you." The man is insatiable with this hero ego of his. I'd tease, but I also find him incredibly sexy. *Balance, baby.*

Lifting me in his arms, he starts across the vast area, holding me like I'm light as air. To say he's given an ego boost for that would be an understatement. We both win.

With my arm hanging around his neck, I say, "The Westcotts are rich-rich." I'm joking . . . kind of. *Not at all.* They're loaded. It's the quiet kind of wealth—not flashy and pretentious but the kind where they have a helicopter but choose to do their own laundry. That's not the kind of wealth I grew up around.

He chuckles. "My brother Harbor put in the helipad last year. We're all busy, but it allows us to pop in more often. Since I haven't been gone long, it's the first time I've used it on my own traveling from Manhattan. It was a nice ride."

I can't even contain my awe, though I try. "Really nice."

Setting me on my feet poolside, he says, "And then we can return home tonight. It's a win." I straighten my dress, not realizing he's waiting on me until I look up again. With his hand out in offer, I take it, and we start walking together. "Ready to meet my parents?"

"What?"

He's chuckling. "It'll be okay. They're going to love you."

I tug him to a stop. When he turns back, I say, "What are you going to tell them?"

"The truth."

Trying to keep my eyes in their sockets is becoming a struggle. "The truth about Maxwell? I thought—"

"The truth about us."

"Us?"

He turns toward me, taking my other hand to hold as well. "This weekend has been one of the best of my life. I don't know what the future holds, but I'd like to introduce you as someone special in my life, someone who I'm seeing more than just tonight. How do you feel about that? What are your thoughts?"

"I . . ." I stare into his earnest eyes and hear the sincerity in his words. To know he feels the same as I do . . . well, maybe not the love part, but to know he feels that this is something special means so much to me. I lean in, close my eyes, and kiss him. When our lips part and our eyes open, I whisper, "I feel the same as you do."

He smiles, and it's the sweetest one I've seen. He kisses me again and says, "I like hearing that." We continue to walk with our hands gripping a little tighter. "I still think we need to wait on telling them about Max. It kills me inside to keep Max a secret, but a rushed conversation about it during intermission isn't the way it should be revealed."

"I agree, and as we mentioned, tonight is about your sister. Her final performance."

His grin couldn't be more genuine as he brushes my hair from my shoulder. "I'm jumping in feet first. If I'm going too fast for you, let me know, okay? We can slow down. Whatever you're comfortable with."

Swooning not only from the way he looks at me like I matter but also that he cares about my feelings has me ready to dive into the deep end with him. "I'm comfortable with this pace."

"We're on a steep learning curve here. You up for the climb?"

I've not felt this relaxed in so long. That's one of the most remarkable things I've noticed about being in his presence. It's more than easy; it's comforting. "I've already packed my carabiners."

His eyebrows shoot up. "You climb for real?"

Bursting out laughing, I shake my head. "No. I've just watched a lot of documentaries." We start walking toward the house again. "Did I tell you that I'm really into sports documentaries?"

"First, you're bingeing motorcycle gang series, and now sports documentaries? You are a fascinating woman, Liv Bancroft."

Nudging him with my elbow, I laugh. "Right back at you, Noah Westcott. Except the woman part. You're most definitely all man."

"Thanks for the compliment." He opens the door, and we enter the kitchen. I didn't expect to have such a large house feel cozy inside, but this one manages it.

A note next to a bouquet draws him to the island. I'm given a chance to look around. The house is still grand, but it's warm and inviting like every space is lived in.

"I have the tickets, and the flowers I ordered for my sister arrived."

I turn back. "It's a beautiful home."

"Thanks." He comes closer with hope returning to his eyes. "We're having a family gathering back here in two weeks. A cookout, end of summer type get-together. Took us weeks to find a weekend that worked for everyone. My sister is wrapping her play, and my brothers have their schedules. Their wives are busy with their careers. A billion emails were exchanged before we narrowed it down, but we managed to. Would you and Max like to come? That would be a good time to introduce you both to everyone."

I hate that his expression hinges on my answer. It shouldn't be like that for him, as Maxwell's dad. I step closer, resting my hands on the counter next to his. "Would it be easier if it were only you and Maxwell?"

Coming closer, he slides his hands around my waist, holding me to him. "Easier for whom?"

"For your family to have that time to adjust, time with

him with me out of the way." I wrap my arms around his neck but direct my gaze to his chest. "I don't want to ruin Maxwell's or their experience."

"What are you talking about? Look at me, Liv. You don't have to worry about them not accepting him. They are going to flip the fuck out from shock, but they will love him from the moment they meet. Trust me, his family just got huge."

"Sounds like a dream for him."

Slipping his hand around the back of my neck, he brings me for a kiss to my forehead. "For us, too. I also want you to meet them." Taking a step back, he adds, "You don't have to answer right now. The invitation stands."

"Yeah?" The hope in his eyes has spread, invading my veins.

"Yeah." He looks around. "I actually thought they might be here, but it's too quiet, so I guess they're out." He doesn't miss an opportunity and kisses me again.

Just as I get lost in this man, a throat clearing has us pushing apart. Startled, I look behind me. "Sorry for interrupting. I didn't know anyone was here."

The man begins to leave, but Noah says, "It's okay, Dad."

Dad?

And this is how I die.

26

Liv

My cup of humiliation runneth over.

Noah's dad walking in on us not only kissing but witnessing me shamelessly rubbing against his son might be the most embarrassing moment of my life. Is burying my head and pretending that didn't just happen a possibility?

Ugh.

It doesn't appear to be an option since Noah takes my hand, and despite my feet being full of concrete, he manages to turn us together like we're a two-for-one deal and then has the gall to introduce me like I'm not dying inside. "This is Liv Bancroft."

My hand pops up like I'm back in school. "Hi."

The man smiles, letting it reach his eyes. They're kind like Noah's—no judgment found in his thoughtful expression and matching smile. He's dressed in jeans and a pullover sweater with a crew neck tee underneath, and nothing about him is pompous.

My gaze dots across his face, studying his features and

build, hair, and eye color. He's the grandfather to my son, who might look like him one day, so my curiosity is running wild. The longer I look at him, the more I see Noah altogether.

Noah glances at me. "This is Port Westcott. My dad."

Collecting myself and remembering my manners, I move forward with an outstretched hand. "It's nice to meet you, Mr. Westcott."

Taking my hand between both of his, he replies, "It's very nice to meet you, Ms. Bancroft. I apologize for startling you."

It's easy to see where Noah gets his looks, not just similarities, but his father is handsome as well. "No, it's okay. This is your home, and it's beautiful."

"Thank you." He shoves his hands in his pockets. "But I can't take any credit. I'll make sure to tell my wife."

"And please," I add, "you can call me Liv."

Noah and his dad embrace. His dad says, "How's it going in the real world?"

"It's going." Noah's eyes connect with mine over his dad's shoulder. After they clap each other on the back, he asks, "How's semi-retirement?"

They release, and his dad laughs. "It's going." His dad walks around the counter. "I'm still not used to a helicopter landing on the property. I didn't pay for it, so I'm not complaining since I've seen both your brothers more in the past few months than I have combined in the years prior. Your mom flew to the city last Wednesday to spend the day with Lark and Tuesday, so it's getting some use."

"I'm thinking I should come for a game soon. If I get tickets to the Yankees, you want to go?"

Noah comes to my side and rubs my lower back. "That'd be good."

Bending down, he pulls out a bottle of white wine and two beers. "You have all that space; I could stay with you."

Noah doesn't bristle, but he stills his hand. There's a noticeable pause that ushers in a wave of discomfort. Max. I hate that Noah can't tell him. Their bond is obvious, so this must be impossible for him to hold this information inside. "Yeah, sure."

His dad's eyes narrow, and a humorless chuckle follows. "You don't sound so sure." Glancing at me and then back to his son, he adds, "I can stay with Loch or Harbor if it's not a convenient time for—"

"I'm sure. You're always welcome, Dad."

He twists the top off a beer bottle, and then says, "If you're not in a hurry to get to the play, we can have a drink together."

I look at Noah. He looks at me, and says, "We have time for a quick one."

Port asks, "Wine, beer, liquor, water? I even have tea and coffee." He holds up the bottle. "I've got a great white out of New Zealand."

"Tempting," I reply, resting my middle against the marble. "You twisted my arm. I love a light white in the summer."

"And since you're not driving," Port says, looking out the window at the helicopter. "I like her already."

"Since I am driving downtown, I'll have water."

As if he can't be more perfect, he proves me wrong again. Max will never be safer than when he's with us—separately or together. I'm confident about that.

We toast and take a sip. I like how casual this is—us just hanging around the kitchen island. "How did you meet my son, Liv?"

I practically spit my wine. I look at Noah, who fails to

keep a straight face. My heart races as I thumb through every possible excuse I can use. "We work together," I reply, thinking it's the safest route to go. Instead of telling him I met his son on a beach at night and decided on a whim to sleep with the stranger because I thought he was hot and was the rebound I needed at the time, knowing full well there wasn't any sleeping happening in that bed.

Yes, a lie is better. *For now.*

I take two gulps, then turn to Noah. "Where's the restroom?"

"I'll show you." He's chuckling under his breath as he walks me through the living room and toward the large entrance to the home. "You did good."

"Gee, thanks." I roll my eyes. "Ever hear of saving someone?"

"Honestly, I was blank as well. Well, my mind wasn't blank, but sharing what I was thinking about wouldn't have gone over well."

Too intrigued to let this opportunity pass me by, I stop, and whisper, "What were you thinking?"

"Having sex with you against that balcony door. The moonlight trailing in and the sounds of your coming mixing with the crash of the waves on the shore."

Did it just get twenty degrees hotter in here? I pluck the front of my shirt to try to cool myself, but now remembering that time in the Hamptons, I don't stand a chance. "It *was* pretty fantastic." As I look at the door tucked under the staircase, my mind wanders into the territory of possibilities. No, don't even suggest it, Liv.

As if I'm not utterly hot and bothered in front of him, he asks, "Would you like me to wait for you?"

I should not offer to have sex with him in this bathroom behind me. That would be frowned upon in polite society.

But lately, polite society is the last thing I care about. His dad is just around the corner, though, sooo . . . "I'm okay. Go spend time with your dad. I'll be quick."

Leaning down to kiss my cheek, he leaves the sweetest of impressions on my skin before moving to my ear. "You don't know how many times I've thought about every second and every position we shared that night. We should do that night all over again."

I drag a finger lazily down his face, turning so my mouth touches the corner of his. "Rent the house, and I'll be there."

He quiets, then straightens to his full height. With his brow furrowed, he asks, "Rent? That's my family's house." He sighs, rubbing a hand down his face. "You said you tried to find me by going back to the house and calling the local rental management companies." He falls back against the wall.

"Most of the houses around there . . ."

"Yeah, I get it. They rent them out for the summer. We don't because we use ours." He taps his head against the wall behind him, and a look of devastation comes over him. "Fuck." Pulling me against him, he holds me tight.

I rest my head on his shoulder and wrap my arms around him. He kisses my head and then says, "To see all the pieces lined up but none of them matching the time-lines of our lives leaves us with a bunch of missed connections."

Closing my eyes, I need to feel the full strength of his embrace. "You're not mad at me?"

"I'm mad at myself."

"Why?"

"For not getting your number, for not asking for your last name, for not being awake when you had to leave so I could tell you goodbye."

"I feel the same. I regret not trying harder." I lean back, gently rubbing his cheek and coaxing a smile out of him. "But I did leave my number."

His smile falls. "What do you mean?" he asks so genuinely that I'm taken aback a bit.

"What do you mean 'what do I mean'? I left my number. You just never called me."

Noah seems to comprehend my words but stares at me like I grew a third eye. "I didn't get your number."

"Well," I say with a pop of my shoulders, "I left it."

Standing upright, he shifts me back from him. Still holding my hips, though, he asks, "Where did you leave it?"

"On the dresser. You watched me write it out. We even joked about it."

"I don't know what you're talking about, Liv." His tone has turned, the playfulness disappeared.

I don't like this line of questioning and take another step back, feeling defensive. "What do you want me to say? I left my number on the dresser with your stuff. Your wallet, even your phone was right there."

"Why didn't I get it then?"

Crossing my arms over my chest, I reply, "I have no idea, but I left it for you."

"You're being serious right now, aren't you?"

I stare at him, so confused. "Why would I lie about this?"

"I'm not saying you are, Liv." He comes closer but is careful with his hands. Reaching out, he almost touches me but retreats again. "I'm just surprised to hear this. I would have called you if I'd had your number."

"Well, you did."

"I didn't get it." As if the world becomes clearer, he says, "That's why you were mad at me. That's why you hated me when you saw me in that conference room. You thought I didn't call you. You didn't realize that night with you was the best night of my life. Fuck, Liv. I'm sorry. I'm sorry you had to live the past few years thinking I didn't care." I lower my arms, hoping he gets the hint. He does and moves in again. Brushing the tips of his fingers through my hair, he says, "I can't explain what happened to your number, but if I'd had it, I would have called you that day to tell you what an amazing night I had and make plans to see you again."

The love in his words pumps through my heart like blood. "You didn't even know where I was from."

"Wouldn't have mattered." Slipping his arm around my waist, he closes the gap between our bodies. "I would have traveled to see you."

"Yeah?"

"Yeah."

I kiss him. Who cares about what could have been when it's happening right now? "No time like the present to make it right."

A wry grin slides onto his face, lifting the right side of his mouth. "There's no time like the present." Cupping my face, he kisses me with a thousand apologies hanging on his lips and the intentions I remember so well from that night.

But we both know it's not the time or place, and our lips part and bodies separate. He reaches back to scratch his neck, something I've witnessed him do multiple times. I think it's a tic he's developed when perplexed or uneasy. I take his arm and hold his hand. "We'll add this to our list of things to talk about, but for tonight, let's enjoy the evening."

"I agree." He nods. "I should get back."

As soon as I use the bathroom, I wash my hands and touch up my makeup. Since I went with smokier eyes, I chose a soft neutral pink close to the shade of my lips to draw his eyes to kiss instead of messing up. It worked as my kiss-swollen lips can attest.

Not wanting to waste any time, I hurry back, walking on cloud nine because of this day.

"Liv," Port says when I round the corner and see them. "I was telling my son he should take the convertible because it's a nice night. This gentleman doesn't want to mess your hair up."

He sure has no problem messing it up when it involves sex. *Rawr.* "He can mess it up."

Noah freezes with the glass of water to his lips. His dad doesn't catch the double entendre, but I have a feeling he doesn't want to. "See? Take the Jag. It needs to get out and about."

"You don't take it when you take Mom out?"

He starts laughing. "She doesn't like to mess her hair up."

I take another sip of wine but then start laughing. Covering my mouth, I don't want to spill it. I swallow. "Like father, like son."

Noah wraps his arm around his dad's shoulders. "Couldn't have a better role model."

"Don't go too far, kid. I've heard all about your reputation."

"And on that note," Noah says, "it's time to go."

We're all laughing again, but Noah pushes his glass forward. "So it seems you have your choice. Convertible or my car?"

"You have a car?"

"I do. I left it here when I moved to the city."

"Mm." I raise my eyebrows. "Now I'm curious. Your car, please."

He reaches into a cabinet and pulls a key fob from a hook. "You ready, babe?"

Our eyes connect the second the name slips out of his mouth. There's not an apology to be found, but I can tell by his look that he's waiting to see how I react.

"I'm ready, sweet cheeks." My lips wriggle, but I do my best to restrain them.

Noah fails at restraining his, though. Holding out his hand for me, I take it and am pulled to his side. He kisses my temple, not hiding anything from his father. I've never felt so good as I do in his arms for the world to see.

With his glass in hand, Port walks around the island. "I'm late for a call to my beautiful daughter."

"I'm surprised you're not going to the play," Noah says. "And where's Mom?"

His dad suddenly grins, but it's so devious. He's up to no good. "Um . . . We were banned three nights ago. Apparently, buying tickets to every show is frowned upon by the star herself." He chuckles. "But I always get a video chat in before curtain call."

"And Mom?"

"Not all of us listen." Stopping in the doorway, he says, "It was a pleasure to meet you, Liv."

I expected something parent-like to be said to Noah and me, maybe even demanding respect. That's what I'm used to with my father, but that's not what Port did. He just opened his arms and welcomed me into his life. The gravity of that isn't lost on me, and I get a bit choked up. "You, too, sir."

"Port, please."

I nod. "Port."

As soon as we're alone, Noah says, "You survived meeting my dad."

"He was just as amazing as I expected from knowing you."

"You would have never said that a week ago." Leaning down to kiss me, soft and slow, he whispers, "Look at us now."

With a wide grin, I reply, "Yes, look at us."

He grabs the flowers and the tickets before we walk outside to the six-car garage. When he opens the door, he glances at me, and asks, "Ready to meet my mom?"

27

Noah

"YOU FAILED to mention the drive would be this beautiful," Liv says, staring out the window. "The view from the helicopter was pretty, but this feels magical. Tall walls of ivy-colored bricks separated by forests and some of these mansions set back from the road are incredible. There's so much land out here."

Showing her my world and where I came from means more to me than just a casual date. That's not what Liv is to me. She's important not only as Max's mother but also as someone I connected with more deeply than only physically. I shouldn't dwell on it when I have no idea what happened, but knowing now that she left her number and wanted me to call her has been pivotal. Things were already coming together prior to discovering that information, but after, a switch flipped in my brain.

No, nothing about this relationship is casual. I'll take it slow for her, but I'm already all in.

Glancing over at her, I say, "I took it for granted for years.

In the past year I was here, I started to see it through the perspective of moving away, and that's when I started to appreciate it again. Time away or, in my case, the looming threat of moving, kicked my sense of appreciation into gear."

She rubs the dash in front of her. "This area is pretty, but are you going to mention the car?" I've been keeping my hands on the steering wheel, but I've been missing this car. "What is it?"

I can't stop from smiling. "I've missed it. I got it not too long ago."

"Even though you don't need a car in the city?"

Gripping the leather, I missed the feeling of flying without wings, the feel of the tires hugging the pavement, and the sanctuary of escaping inside here while the rest of the world remains outside. "An Aston Martin DB11," I say with pride. "I bought it when I cashed out my trust fund to buy the apartment. But you're right, I don't need it in the city, so I keep it here."

"Why'd you buy it?"

"Because I'm twenty-five and have impulsive tendencies."

She cracks up laughing. "Is that what the kids are calling it these days?"

"It's what I'm calling it. Was it a smart investment? Ask me in fifty years when it sells for ten times what I paid. In the meantime, I'll enjoy driving it every chance I get."

"I didn't know you were a car enthusiast." She looks out the window, but when she angles toward me, she says, "We have so much to learn about each other."

"That's half the fun."

"What's the other half consist of?"

I reach across the console and rest my hand on her leg.

"For us, I think it will be learning to navigate these new waters."

"And here I thought you were going to say sex."

"Seems I've created a monster."

She rests her hand on mine and drags it a little higher. If I'm not mistaken, she wants my hand under the skirt of her dress instead of on top. If I go where we both want me to, the car might end in an accident. There's plenty of time to act reckless once we return to the city tonight. "I wish I could deny that allegation, but I can't."

I will never grow tired of hearing her happiness. It's something I couldn't imagine I'd be sharing with her not long ago, but here we are, dating in all senses of the meaning. Sure, I didn't make it official, but we're both on board. Hell, she's even met my dad, and more family shortly.

To say arriving at the university theater is the worst timing ever is not nearing how I actually wish we had taken a detour to the lake. A little making out. A lot of other activities to follow . . . It would have been a good time, and my sister would have been none the wiser since I'm surprising her.

But since that option is not on the table, I pull up to the valet stand.

Once inside, we get drinks. She sticks with wine, and I go with a bottle of water. The drive back to the house at night is tricky, with few lights illuminating the roads in the middle of the country. At one time, I drove that road under the influence without a second thought, but now, I'm not willing to risk our lives. A sign of maturity? About time.

We make our way down the aisle. Liv slides down the row to our seats, and I follow. She stops to greet her neighbor before sitting down.

I hear the neighbor reply and momentarily freeze.

"Mom?" I sit forward to come face-to-face with her while Liv rests back.

"Noah." My mom pops from her seat.

I stand and hug her. "Hey, Mom, how are you doing?"

"Much better now that I'm seeing you." My mom has always had a way of making her kids all feel like they're special. I can only hope I can make my kids feel the same. Kids ... Max. Guilt riddles my conscience. I didn't tell my dad, and now as I look at my mom, I realize how wrong it is to keep him a secret.

I can't just throw this information out there like it doesn't matter. They should meet him or at least have time to process when I do tell them.

My knee bumps Liv's, and I sit back down. "Mom, I want you to meet Liv Bancroft."

She's hugged before she has a chance to shoot out her hand. "It's so nice to meet you, Liv. I'm Delta Westcott, Noah's mom," my mom says with such pride as she looks back and forth between the two of us.

"It's very nice to meet you, too—" The lights go down, cutting Liv off. She whispers, "We'll talk during intermission."

"Yes." My mom starts clapping as the curtain goes up as if this is the first time she's seeing the play. Some kids do a lot of wrong in their parents' eyes, but not my mom. Her kids hung the moon that she dances under every night.

We join in the applause as the first actors take the stage.

By the time intermission rolls around, the three of us get in line for another round of drinks. My mom says, "It's always good to see my son, but what a treat that I get to meet one of his friends."

The "one of" stands out to me, but I know she doesn't mean anything by it, so I hope Liv also lets it slide. We step to the side with our drinks and talk. Liv looks so beautiful that taking my eyes off her is hard. Fingers snap in front of my face, though, so I turn to my mom. "Yes?"

"Liv was telling me that you work together."

"We do." A few seconds late in returning to my senses, I add, "Well, we met a few years ago but reconnected when I joined the company."

Liv clears her throat, and when I catch her eyes, she doesn't appear amused. *Shit.* We didn't tell my dad the same story. When a guy bumps into me, I lean toward Liv, and whisper, "It's okay."

I'm not sure if it's my words or the wine that eases her worries, but the straight of her back loosens her posture.

My mom says, "I've met your mother. Trudy is just a dream to work with on a project. So kind and lovely."

"Thank you," Liv says, smiling. "She said the same about you."

"My daughters-in-law are in the city, and both are very active in philanthropy. Maybe we can have a ladies' lunch the next time I'm in town?"

"Sounds wonderful. Noah has my number."

The chimes echo through the theater, so we make our way back to our seats. The play begins promptly on time. I'm sucked in by the acting, especially when my sister says her big soliloquy before falling to the floor in a heap for the reaper to collect.

The social commentary in the storyline lands the ending like an Olympic gold medalist and earns the actors a ten-minute standing ovation.

Liv leans over. "Your sister was amazing."

"She was." I'm happy for Marina. Broadway is not the same as being Beacon's shining star, but I have no doubt she'll achieve her dreams. And we'll be right there supporting her every step of the way.

Once the theater clears, we head backstage. My mom knocks on her dressing room door. "It's us, Marina."

"Come in."

Delta opens the door and goes straight in for a hug. "So proud of you. It was another incredible performance."

"Again, Mom?" Marina rolls her eyes over her mom's shoulder, causing Liv and me to laugh. "I thought you and Dad had plans."

"We did, but I couldn't miss your last performance here at the university." She stands back, taking her daughter in. "I'll miss seeing you every night once you're in New York."

"You're the best, Mom, but I'm glad Dad isn't here, or I would have been a teary mess the entire performance."

She finally looks at me in that bothersome little sister way she honed years ago and playfully shoves me. "Why didn't you tell me you were coming? I saw you in the audience and forgot my line, you jerk."

I chuckle, giving her the flowers and then a good hug. "No one noticed."

When she eyes my mom, my mom says, "I only noticed because I know all of your lines."

Marina face-palms herself. Laughing, she looks up, her eyes set on Liv. "She's done this my whole life." My sister's long hair is crimped from being in a wig, and her makeup is over the top for the stage, but she's beaming as she smells the flowers. "Thank you for these. Are you going to introduce me, Noah?"

"Hi, I'm Liv. You were simply amazing in the play. That wake scene had me tearing up."

"Oh," my sister says, her hand covering her chest. "That's

so sweet. Thank you. I'm Marina." She moves in for a hug. "It's so nice to meet you."

"You, too."

Marina gives me a wink of approval. I chuckle and find myself rolling my eyes. All of them are rubbing off on me now. My sister says, "You're very beautiful, Liv. How did my brother get so lucky?"

She turns to look at him to catch me shaking my head. I laugh, but say, "You don't have to answer that."

"Phew." She's still laughing. "That's definitely a story for another time."

My mom moves in to give my sister another hug. "I need to get home, but you were so wonderful, honey. Congrats on the show." She turns her attention to me. "I'll see you in a couple of weeks?"

"Yes, I'll be there." *With Liv and Max, my son.* I'd love to tell her everything but bite my tongue. Taking Liv's hand, I hold it.

Marina doesn't miss the gesture. "Are you guys staying, or do you need to get back to the city?"

"Unfortunately, we do need to get going."

She gives me another hug. "It means a lot that you came out to see me."

"Wouldn't have missed it."

To Liv, she says, "Hopefully, we'll see each other soon. I'd love to chat with you."

"I'd like that too," Liv replies.

"Bye, sis. Love you."

She walks out the door with us. Glancing over my shoulder, I smirk. I get a matching one in return. Her laughter fills the corridor. "Love you, too, big brother."

I move my hand to Liv's lower back, opening the stage

door for her to exit. She walks outside and then stops to let me catch up. "Your family can't be real."

Chuckling, I ask, "Why is that?"

"They're so nice."

They are. "I miss seeing them."

"I would too if they were my family." I hold her close, knowing that as much as she enjoyed meeting my family, it's a stark reminder of her own. I hear great things about her mom, but yeah, her dad is toxic.

Learning so much about how he's treated her has me wondering how to dance around him at the office. If I don't, I'll end up confronting him in defense of her, which will not play out well for us.

On the drive back to the house, Liv says, "You're right."

"I'm right about a lot of things." I rest my hand on her leg. "But what specifically this time?"

"I support you telling your family about Maxwell at the get-together."

The date had been thrown out as a contender, but that she's giving me her full support has me wanting to stare in shock. Since I'm driving, I only glance over. "What makes you say that?"

"Max deserves to meet his family. And because they're more than anyone could wish for, they should be given the opportunity to meet your incredible son and he the chance to know them."

"You're sure?"

"Positive."

When I park the car, I dip over and steal a kiss. "Thank you."

"You don't need to thank me, Noah. We just need to give Max all the love he deserves."

"I will." It's tempting to tell her the same, but she also

deserves to have confessions of the heart shared when the time is right.

We ride the high of this great day on the helicopter. There's a buzz in the air between us. I'm not sure if it's because we know we still have the night ahead for just the two of us. Our hands stay bonded together the entire flight. With a little time ahead of us before we land, she asks, "Tell me something no one else knows about you."

I mull over the question and look at her. Her eyes are eager, and her smile brighter than the stars above us. I don't want to disappoint her, but I also don't want to share anything about past relationships. Liv doesn't need to compete with my vivid past. Like her smile, she shines above all others. "I don't generally keep secrets."

"You must have something."

Should I just tell and not hold back? I could spend thirty seconds convincing myself not to jump in feet first, but that didn't serve me well the last time we were together.

"Hey," I say, resting my forearms on my knees. Angling her way, I hold a hand over my headphones, making sure technology doesn't fuck this up for me. I don't know what comes over me. My chest feels tighter, but somehow, I feel freer. It's fucked up to be so twisted over someone and think it's better off kept to yourself. "I like you, Liv."

Her expression holds as she stares at me. I start to doubt if she even heard me. "You like me?" She repeats the words without the meaning I intended.

"Yeah. I like you a lot. I like spending time with you, and I don't know." I shrug. It came before I could stop it, but I wish I hadn't injected the note of frivolousness into the conversation. "I like you . . . more than like."

Sweating emotional bullets, I want to look out the

window and pretend I didn't just expose myself. Before I can, she says, "I like you, too, Noah. A lot."

I get out of my seat to kiss her. When a little turbulence rattles the helicopter, I say, "Promise to make it up to you."

"You don't have to make anything up. That kiss was perfect. Now buckle in. I'd rather have us all land safely in one piece."

"I agree." I chuckle and buckle up again. I feel different than expected. I don't feel worried or panicked. I'm happy and content. For many reasons, it's been a long time since I've been in a relationship. But now I think it's because I was always waiting for this second chance with her. I ask, "How about you? Any secrets you want to share?"

"I got one." Her laughter intrigues me. "Remember how I told you my father was disappointed I didn't get into his alma mater?"

"Yeah, I remember." I remember he treated her like shit for it.

"I chose NYU over every other school I got accepted to. That includes Yale."

"You got into Yale?" She nods, and then a smile creeps across her mouth. "Holy shit, Bancroft. You're wilder than I thought."

"You haven't seen anything yet."

"Is that a threat or a promise?"

A smirk owns her face, pupils are dilated, and her target in sight owns me, and I know exactly how we're spending the next few hours. "A little of both."

The vixen.

28

Noah

I DON'T KNOW why I like that Liv rebelled against her dad, but that little truth bomb she dropped about rejecting Yale made my night. It was a solid "fuck you" to him, which I approve.

I'm still grinning from the memory when I bend down and kiss her head. She turns suddenly, wrapping me in her arms and opening her eyes bright with the new day shining in. "You forgot to say goodbye."

"I was letting you sleep."

"I don't want to sleep when you're leaving. I want to see you strut your stuff toward the door, look back, give me a wink, and then tell me how pretty you think I am."

"That sounds like more than a goodbye."

She grins, speeding up my heartbeats just from looking at her. "Is it so wrong not to want the weekend to end?"

I kiss her quickly, hoping I don't start getting hard, though that may be asking the impossible since my dick is wide awake now. We fucked twice. Once in the kitchen on the island and then in bed. After that, we slowed it down and made love in the bathtub full of bubbles. The woman is insatiable. Thank God she found someone who feels the same about her.

When her smile falters, I sit on the edge of the mattress and push her hair back from her face. Naked. Not a stitch of makeup. Hair just messy enough to take credit for creating that havoc last night. But it's her eyes and that smile, the way she looks at me like she's still on vacation from life—gratified, recharged, like she's not only ready to take me on but the whole fucking world. *Liv is magnificent.*

She's irresistible. I return to steal another kiss from her because fuck it. What's another minute at this point? She's worth skipping a Monday morning workout for. "I want to see you and Max tonight. I want to see you both every night."

"That's quite the commitment. You sure you're ready for that?" There's no accusation in her tone. As she brushes her palm lightly over my cheek, genuine concern for my well-being is all that is heard.

"I was ready years ago. We lost so much time. I'm just catching up."

"Lost years don't matter, Noah. Only what we do with the time ahead."

The physical attraction is there between us. No denying that. But it's her, the woman who has fought for every spot she's gotten, moved mountains to raise a child on her own and give him the best life possible, and her heart, how she's opened it for me to walk in that door has me hoping I'm the one she was waiting for as well.

Running the back of my hand under her chin, I ask, "Are we doing this?"

"Are we deciding to be together? I am. How about you?"

"I'm in." We kiss again before I try to push up.

Her arms don't loosen. She knows how to make a guy feel good. Too good, which is about to cause an issue with me making it to work on time. "This is crazy, wild. We're just doing this, acting on our feelings instead—"

"Instead of trying to rationalize our way out of it. Look, Liv, this weekend has been an extension of the night in the Hamptons. But it's not only the sex that's fantastic. It's sitting watching TV or laughing over stories at dinner. Buying Max a toy or holding him while he sleeps on my chest. It's seeing you loving our son, and then you allowing me to do the same. There's a bunch of big unknowns, but I know for sure that I want to be with the two of you."

"It's a risk we're taking, but I don't want to lose another two years either." She lifts to kiss me. "Let's do this."

"Let's be together, all in."

"All in. But I have a question."

"Ask away." I grin still staring down at her. "How is this going to work in the office?"

Her arms release me, and I sit up. "I need to think about it. Knowing what has really happened versus what I had been told. There's a vast discrepancy in how I'm treated compared to how you've been treated. I've only witnessed the inner workings of Bancroft & Lowe for a week, and it's not a place I see myself long term. But it's you I'm concerned about. What are your thoughts?"

"I appreciate that, but I've been there eleven years. It's aggravating but easy work that pays me decently. I can't afford to walk out and definitely can't afford to be fired. Dating a co-worker is a violation in the employee handbook."

I stand. "I need to get going so I have time to shower and

get dressed before I'm late. I think we carry on like we have been, and we'll discuss it tonight."

She nods. "Sounds like a plan."

Kissing her once more, I walk to the door. "I sure like having plans with you, babe."

Sitting up, she tilts her head, her long hair hanging around the bare skin of her shoulders, and her eyes set on mine. My breath halts in my chest just looking at her. I'm one lucky bastard. I say, "I . . ." The words come easy, but I stop them from being said. Too soon.

Seemingly sensing my turmoil, she says, "I'll see you in a few hours acting like—"

"You hate me. It's probably best. *For now.*"

Soft laughter fills the air. "Act? Who said I was acting?"

I chuckle because at this hour, I'm not at my best. "It's four forty-five in the morning. I have no witty comeback for you." I kiss her because now that I can, I'll take the opportunity every chance I get. "I have to run. See you soon."

"Still no goodbye, huh?"

"Nope. See you later, pretty girl." I force myself out the door because I'm already so caught up in her that if I stay a second longer, I'll be buried deep inside her. *Again.*

———

A KNOCK PULLS my eyes to the open door of my office. Leanna walks in. "You're here early."

"I didn't get any work done over the weekend."

"What are you working on?"

I lean back in the chair, rotating toward her. "The Torres's file."

"Oh," she says, her expression lifting in remembrance while she sits across from me. "I should have checked in, but

I got stuck out on Staten Island helping my sister move over the weekend. How did the dinner go?"

My memories go into overdrive thinking about how that dinner was the reason I was leaving her apartment this morning.

The way the wine glistened on Liv's lips after she took a sip.

Her head tilted back in belly laughter when I told her about dates gone wrong in the past.

Her eyes reflected the dim lighting but were brighter when she looked into mine.

We dropped our guards and never looked back. The brush of our hands on the top of the table. An exchanged look that we both knew we were about to cross a professional line.

More than what happened at that dinner, I have a son. I look at Leanna, wishing I could tell her and the rest of the world about Max and how he and Liv have imprinted on my soul. I don't take it lightly, but it's bigger than anything I've felt before.

The moment to celebrate was stolen when I found out, and tonight, we're figuring out how I can have him and his mom in my life full time, if that's even a possibility.

I grab my Mont Blanc and fidget, spinning the pen to open and close over and over again. I can't tell anyone about Max or Liv, not my family, so not Leanna either. "It went well."

Running my hand over my hair, I feel my chest tighten. I'm caught in the "lying by omission" rule my parents taught me was wrong. I rub the bridge of my nose and then blurt, "The Torres's canceled when we were already there."

When I look up, Leanna's staring at me. "So you left?"

"No, since we were already seated, we stayed."

Her grin spreads like wildfire across her face. "That's interesting."

"It actually was. We had a good time." I'm not going into sordid details, but I won't downplay it either.

"That's good, and it gave you time to go over the financials like you wanted but without the audience of the clients." When I turn my gaze to the windows, she says, "You talked about the hunch you had, right?"

Hm. What to say? I glance back at her before moving my attention to the monitor. "Not exactly. We kind of just enjoyed our time. The food was really fantastic, too."

"I feel like more than the food was fantastic."

It's a lighthearted conversation thus far, but we're circling the truth of what really happened between Liv and me, and it hits a little too close for comfort. "Don't jump to conclusions."

"So you didn't sleep with her?" She gasps, covering her mouth as her spine straightens in the chair. "Oh my God, I'm sorry. I shouldn't have said that. I don't know why—" She sucks in a breath as horror streaks across her face. Standing, she rushes toward the door. "I'm so sorry."

"It's okay." *Fuck me, though* ... I stand. "Leanna, stop."

I see her torso fill with a breath before releasing and turning back to me. She's shaking her head, and shame fills her expression. "That was so wrong. My apologies, Noah."

"Come back," I say, gesturing to the chair. "It's okay, Leanna."

She takes a few hesitant steps and then sits again.

"We're friends." I sit down again with a weary grin. *Fuck my hair.* I run my fingers through it and then rub the back of my neck. "Although it's not the most comfortable of topics of conversation, I'm not mad you asked. But if you don't mind, I don't want to bring my personal life into the office yet." This sounds incriminating, especially since I feel we're building a relationship that would share the good things that happen in our lives. "What I mean is we had a nice dinner and got to know each other better." I choose to leave out the fact that I'm falling for Liv, *fell*, and that we share a son. "Liv's actually quite funny, lighter than when she's in the office."

Leanna's concern softens and then disappears altogether. "I appreciate your understanding. I consider us friends as well, and I guess that just slipped out. It was rude, though, and inappropriate to ask in the office. Next time, I'll ask when we're at happy hour."

I chuckle. "Sure."

Alcohol is like truth serum, so I set a mental reminder never to go to happy hour with Leanna.

Things cool from the heated topic, and I'm happy to change this subject. Although I'm still reluctant to involve her. I probably shouldn't. "I have some questions about this file. Will you check Ms. Bancroft's schedule to see if she has availability this morning?"

"Fifteen minutes? An hour?"

"Um . . ." I look out the window. I could easily spend my day taking up hers, but she may not appreciate that. "Fifteen should be fine."

Leanna stands again. "Anything else for today?"

"Try to reach Mr. and Mrs. Torres to see when they'll be back in the States or if they'd like to have a conference call in the office for our next meeting?"

"Will do."

When Leanna gets up to leave, I ask, "How'd the move go?"

"Hot, but we got it done."

"That's good."

She nods. "Thanks for asking."

A few minutes later, she calls to tell me I'm on Liv's schedule in an hour. Something to look forward to.

I head to the kitchen to grab another cup of coffee. The caffeine of one cup wasn't strong enough to fight my fatigue this morning. When I walk in, I'm greeted with curves I haven't stopped thinking about, long hair with a gentle wave hanging over one shoulder, and eyes that hold a new secret —one we share. "Seems my timing is perfect."

"I'd say so." Liv finishes filling her coffee mug. Lowering the carafe, she asks, "How are you, Mr. Westcott?"

"I'm doing well. And you, Ms. Bancroft?"

"How am I doing?" She taps a stir stick against her lips. *The tease.* "I'm doing amazing."

"Amazing, huh?"

"So good." She walks toward the door. "Oh, Mr. Westcott?"

I struggle to keep my gaze on her more professional attributes. "Yes, Ms. Bancroft?"

"I got a notification about our meeting." Taking the stick between her lips, she sucks the coffee right off before tossing it in the trash on her way out. "I'll see you in an hour."

I watch her go, enjoying every sway of those full hips. "Can't wait," I reply, already knowing there's no way I'll be able to act like a professional around her.

Fuck me.

29

Noah

DREAD SETS IN LIKE QUICKSAND, slowly engulfing the integrity I held on to like a trophy. I know it's right to tell Liv everything, but something's niggling at the back of my mind that it's too soon, too dangerous, too careless to involve her at this stage.

She's an ally to everything I stand for, but she's also the boss's daughter. My son is his grandchild. If I march into Mr. Bancroft's office with accusations, I'll be fired. Starting a war with the Lowes and her father will make her susceptible to the charges I'll be waging against them.

If they go down, they'll drag her with him. They might even let her take the fall altogether. She did as she was told and had no reason to question her father's involvement in laundering the money. So it would be easy to frame her. She's in accounting. Did she miss what I found? Yes, but after hearing the stories about her father, I know what she was doing—accepting him at face value.

She questions his morals, his love for her, and even his

role in her life. But when it comes to business, he's considered an upstanding member of society. He's won awards and works with established and wealthy clients from all over the world. There was no reason to question his ethics.

As I stare at the numbers, the money that's been paid, a million in the past year, to a subsidiary that traces back to Chipper Lowe, I'm thinking exposing this information, which was right in front of everyone's eyes, is best kept under wraps for a while. I need to consult a lawyer before confronting the bosses.

There's also a matter of making sure Liv is safe. The only way I know to do that is by keeping her out of the details.

I pull up my schedule and cancel the meeting with her this morning.

My phone rings . . . my *personal* phone, her name flashing on the screen. "Hello?" I shouldn't be grinning, but she brings it out in me.

"Why did you cancel our meeting?"

"It's been put on the back burner, so I don't need to meet anymore."

"Couldn't you have kept the meeting, though?" A wisp of hope threads her tone.

I'm not usually this slow, but I finally catch on to what she's implying. Kicking my feet up on my desk, I stare out into the yonder of the cityscape, enjoying every moment of hearing her voice. "Do you still want to meet, Ms. Bancroft?"

"I was looking forward to it, so if you're not busy . . ."

"Since both of our schedules are free, I could fill your time slot if that will make you feel better."

"It would." Not a second of hesitation. The woman's not holding back. I approve.

Dropping my feet to the floor, I say, "Be right there."

I swing my door open, making eye contact with Leanna. She says, "I saw you canceled the meet—"

"It's back on. Please block out the next hour."

I'm already one desk closer to Liv when Leanna asks, "Do you want me to take notes?"

I wave my hand over my shoulder. "No need. I'll handle this alone." I round the corner, saying hello to one of the other assistants who passes me with a smile and greeting and then a guy from design before I round the next corner. My pace picks up until I'm standing outside her office and knocking.

"Come in."

I'm coming in alright. I open the door and close it behind me. Our eyes catch just as the sound of the lock snaps it into place. "Hello."

She smiles. "Hello. Please, have a seat.'

I come around the desk and lift her out of the chair. Sitting down, I set her on my lap. A giggle escapes as she wraps her arms around me. "Why did you cancel our meeting?"

"I had something come up." I probably didn't need to cock my eyebrow, but it went up on its own.

"Oh my," she says, teasing . . . er, I mean wiggling on top of me. "You sure did. How can I help you with that?"

"Should we brainstorm some ideas?"

"No." She gets to her feet and says, "I know just how to handle the situation."

When she begins to kneel before me, I try to stop her descent. "Hey. You don't have to do that. We're just messing around."

She lands on her knees, then reaches back to take off her shoes. Placing her hands on my legs, she slides them higher. "I know. I want to."

I tried . . .

Resting back, I watch her gaze, following the slow glide of her hands over my dress pants. Her pace remains the same when she reaches my belt, savoring every part of the process.

She lifts as she unzips, and says, "I've never done anything like this."

"I'm not saying I don't want to watch you fuck me with your mouth." I sit up, stroking the side of her head and then lift her chin. "I'm just wondering why now?"

"Because I'm tired of following the rules. They don't get me anywhere anyway. Because this connection we share has me wanting to please you. Maybe that makes me sound weak, but I feel strong in my desire for you. And because I want to live life on my terms. Lift."

I lift, and she yanks my pants down. *Holy fuck.* She demands my boxer briefs next. I oblige. I'm happy to give her what she wants.

Her hands stack on top of each other, wrapped around my dick. There's plenty of length left for her mouth to take ownership of, and she does. Without pause, her tongue sweeps across the head and then dips to lick around the edge.

Gripping my thighs, Liv possesses the brazen nerve to look me straight in the eyes before going all the way down. My eyes close, my head dropping back against the white leather. A wave of heat crashes over me as I sink into the pleasure of what she's doing to me.

What the fuck am I doing?

I open my eyes, wanting, *needing*, to watch her take me like she's never had anything so delectable in her mouth before. Grabbing hold of my erection with one hand, she strokes the base while her mouth takes my head repeatedly.

When her hair cascades around her and lands on my legs, I shift it over her shoulders to lock this image into my memories. "So good, babe. Can you go deeper?"

She covers half of me, her teeth scraping lightly as she retreats before going deeper each time as if it were a challenge she intends to beat. A moan escapes, the vibration of air causing my dick to twitch. But the way her hips thrust tempt me to take her over this desk.

My body tenses as my head rolls back, my orgasm striking before I have a choice. Grabbing her head, I still her as I pump in and out of her mouth, my release colliding with her throat. "Oh fuck."

The intensity of the high drops me back in reality, and I take a breath. I open my eyes to find her still consuming all of me. I rub her cheeks with my thumbs as she slides off and then dabs the corner of her lips with the tip of her ring finger.

The shine to her eyes causes me to ask, "Are you okay?"

A gentle smile plays on her mouth as she nods. "I'm good. How was that?"

My eyes narrow as confusion takes hold of me. "What do you mean how was it? It was the best fucking orgasm of my life." Leaning forward, I lift her from under her arms and situate her on my lap. "That's the fastest I think I've ever come." I kiss her swollen lips and hold my head against hers. "Incredible. That's how it was for me."

Although she closes her eyes, I keep mine open to watch as her smile grows, and then whisper, "You're incredible." Kissing her again, I savor the pillow plushness of her lips, soak in the heat of her tongue, and fall deeper into my feelings for her. Pulling back, I watch her eyes open, and I swear I see love written in the pupils of her eyes. It's intoxicating, like she is.

I swallow the words I want to say, knowing damn well this isn't the time for confessions of that sort. Hearing I love you after a blow job doesn't lend itself to romance.

Oh fuck ...

That's the first time in my life the words entered my head outside of a mere reference. She's also the first woman I've ever had the desire, much less the inclination to even say them.

"What are you smiling about?" she asks.

Her eyes shine only for me this time. "I'm happy." I've never spoken truer words in my life.

She scoots off my lap and straightens her skirt. "I should say so—"

"No."

"No?" She raises an eyebrow.

I stand, pulling my underwear and pants up. As I zip, I come face-to-face with her. "Don't get me wrong. I meant it when I said that was incredible, but when I said I'm happy, it's because I have you in my life. I'm not a guy who needs to be in a relationship. I've never been one to pretend to get laid. When I was with a woman, the cards were on the table." I caress her jaw, lifting just a hint, and run the pad of my thumb over her bottom lip. "I vowed not to hurt you. I also won't lie unless it's to protect you. It's not a sex act that makes me feel this way. So when I tell you I'm happy, what I mean is you make me happy. You and Max make me happy."

Her lips part, but I move in and kiss her until pink floods her cheeks. Leaving her breathless, I tuck in the tails of my shirt and then buckle my belt. She touches her lips and then rests her hand over her heart. "I've never had feelings like this for anyone. You make me happy, Noah. And I know you make Max feel the same."

"That's what matters, right? We can be happy together,

Liv. I want that with you." But to cover my bases, I add, "And more blow jobs because those make me happy as well."

Laughing, she holds the desk as she puts her shoes back on. "Duly noted." Her gaze reaches mine again, and she adds, "And same when you pleasure me." She lifts to kiss my cheek but grins when she drops back on the heels of her shoes. "How's your schedule looking tomorrow?"

"I'm free."

"Same time?"

"Same place." I give her a wink.

As soon as I open the door, though, she says, "Noah?" I look back. "Don't lie to me to protect me. I would rather handle the truth than sort through deceit. Okay?"

The lie about the money scheme comes to mind, but I still nod. "Okay."

As soon as I near my office, I tell Leanna, "Block off ten o'clock for meetings with Ms. Bancroft the rest of the week in the scheduler, please."

"Will do."

I open my door and go in, but before it closes, she's behind me. "Noah?"

Sitting down, I angle toward my computer. "Yes?" She doesn't say anything, so I look up. "What's up?"

Swirling her finger at her face, she closes the door behind her and then whispers, "You have lipstick on your chin."

Oh shit.

I drop my head down like it's possible to hide it at this point. "We're friends," she says, "remember?"

Lifting my gaze back to hers, I say, "Friends."

She smiles. "I have a mirror if you need it."

"I'd appreciate that."

Working with the woman I've fantasized about for years,

the goddess mother of my child, and the person who capti-vates my mind and soul, will be harder than I thought. It'll be impossible to stay focused, knowing she's across the office from me.

Good thing I'm up for the job!

30

Liv

"He'll be here any minute. Are you sure you want to stay?"

"I'm sure."

Why am I so unsure, then? Pacing the living room with Max on my hip, I try to settle my chaotic thoughts. I love my mom, but it makes me nervous to introduce new people or elements into my relationship with Noah, especially when we're figuring out how this all works tonight.

A knock has me stopping and looking toward the door. Not sure how long I do this, but it's apparently long enough for my mom to ask, "Do you want me to answer it?"

"No." I start walking. "I'll get it."

I open the door to find a shit-eating grin fixed on Noah's face. It's like he got a blow job at work or something . . . I roll my eyes just as he pulls us toward him and gives me a big kiss before he turns to Max, and says, "How's my big boy?"

Max . . . the nickname has grown on me so much that now I use the names interchangeably. He babbles, "Ca," as he bounces off my hip and right into his daddy's arms.

"Why didn't you use your key?" I ask.

"Because I wouldn't have been able to kiss you like I did."

"I don't know." I waggle my brows. "Try me next time."

"Oh, I will."

I turn, but he catches my hand and spins me back to him, looping his arm around my lower back. "How's this, pretty girl?" I am definitely giving him more blowies if this is what I get in return. A giggle bubbles up. Oh my God, I'm hopeless when it comes to this man.

I might have to take the key back if this is how I'll be greeted.

"You must be Noah," my mom's voice travels the short hallway.

My body is left cold as Noah adjusts Max in his arms, and then stands straight as can be when he sees her. "Hello. Yes, ma'am."

"Ma'am?" I eye him sideways. "When did you turn into a Southern gentleman?"

"I'm always a gentleman, Ms. Bancroft."

"The baby in your arms would say otherwise," I tease, enjoying this man squirming for the first time in his life. "By the way, this is my mom, Trudy Bancroft. Mimi to Maxwell. Mom, this is Noah—"

Max shouts, "Me."

My mom holds her arms out for him as she speaks in baby talk. "Good boy, Maxie. Yes, I'm Mimi."

Noah hands him over, but he appears reluctant. It's good his papa bear instincts have kicked in, but it's my mom, and he'll always be safe with her.

My mom says, "Come in."

"Yes, sorry," I say, taking him by the hand and moving him inside so I can close the door. "Come in. Come in."

With my mom in the living room, Noah and I have the corner of the hall as cover. I smile just looking at him. Mouthing, I say, "She wanted to meet you."

His grip tightens around my hand, and he starts walking, taking me right along with him. "Hello, I'm Noah Westcott." He releases my hand to shake hers. "I've heard a lot about you."

"Same." She studies his face and then glances at Maxwell. "I can see the resemblance."

Noah smiles with pride. "I think it's pretty even split between us. Liv's eyes—"

"Your eyes," I say.

"You think?" he says, looking at Max again.

Nudging his arm, I reply, "I know, silly."

"I see so much of you in him."

"You do?"

"Yeah, your nose. The shape of the eyes and your earlobes." Instantly reaching for my lobes, I feel them. He adds, "Yours are detached. Mine are somewhere caught between the two."

My mom looks at the two of us and then at Max. "That's so interesting. I never noticed." She comes around the couch, and says, "If you guys want to talk, I can take Max into the other room."

Max is all smiles and drooling. He has the best attitude for someone growing teeth like it's his business. As cute as he is, I look at Noah, wondering if we should just hop into the conversation we've put off for too long. "It would give us a few minutes before getting into the nitty gritty stuff."

Noah reaches for him. "Do you mind if I hold him?"

"You don't have to ask," she says. "He's your child."

Noah takes him, wrapping his big arms around my little

guy. Dipping his head beside Maxwell's, he whispers, "I love you so much."

My eyes meet my mom's eyes where tears have welled in the corners. She reaches over and gives my hand a little squeeze, now understanding why I'm already crazy about this man.

"He is," he says with a smile, still staring into Max's eyes. My heart aches, and it's hard to swallow around the lump in my throat. This is more than I hoped for and better than I thought possible. Remembering how I banged on that door in the Hamptons, called so many places trying to find answers . . . it was with a glimmer of hope I held deep inside me that Noah would want to be in my baby's life.

And here he is, showing up daily to play his part. I take a staggering breath, overcome with emotion.

Noah reaches over and touches the side of my hand. "You alright?"

"Perfect."

I'm given a satisfied grin before he turns to my mom. "I appreciate the offer, but I'd really like to spend some time with him before he goes to bed."

My mom rubs Max's back. "That's the sweetest." Turning to me, she says, "I will see myself out then."

"Thank you for the help, Mom."

"Of course, anytime." Tickling Max, she adds, "Good night, Maxie." She smiles at Noah. "Nice to meet you."

He replies, "It was really nice to meet you, Mrs. Bancroft."

She heads for the door. "You can call me Trudy or Mimi, but not Mrs. Bancroft."

He laughs. "Understood, Mimi."

Her own laughter fills the hallway as she walks to the door. "He's a keeper, Olivia." I know she doesn't mean to imply that I get to have him as part of some package deal since he's Max's father, but I still smile and glance at Noah.

Chuckling, he says, "She's not wrong."

We're starting to feel like we're a team—not only with us and our deepening relationship but also with our families coming together. Turning toward him, I wrap my arms around him and look up. "No, she's not."

He rubs my back. "You know how I feel about you and Max already, but it bears repeating. You're the best things to ever come into my life."

I could swoon, and my knees are already weakening on impact, but I stand taller this time, not fading away but toe-to-toe with him. "You are the best thing to come into our lives, Noah Westcott. And I'll always be grateful you're so hot."

Victory! He rolls his eyes. I'm quick to continue, "Because if you weren't, we wouldn't have this little guy."

"Nice save, Bancroft."

"I try. Anyway, it's not like you were just hooking up with any old hag. Right?"

"If this is a 'fishing for compliments' expedition, let me reassure you. You're not a hag, babe, and to prove it was raw physical attraction, your intellect was the last thing I cared about the night we met."

"Geez, thanks."

Chuckling, he adds, "Works both ways, sweetheart." He sets Max down to run around and then plants himself on the back of the couch, grinning like a Cheshire cat. "What won you over once we reconnected in the office?"

"Your ass." I laugh as I'm tugged in between his legs. "And your heart. Your arms. Your smile. Your eyes that told me I was more than a one-night stand."

Rubbing the outside of my thighs, he asks, "How'd they tell you that?"

"The first time you laid eyes on me, you were genuinely happy to see me again."

"It's true, I was." He cups the bottom of my ass. "And you couldn't have been more the opposite."

I brush the tips of my fingers through the hair above his ears. "I thought you didn't call me on purpose. I thought that night was all in my head—how good it was. The physical connection was obvious, but I felt something deeper with you from the moment we met. I'm sorry for treating you so badly."

"I don't need an apology. It's in the past." He stands, his hands gliding up my arms and stopping on my shoulders to rub. "Like I said today, I'm happy. I feel it in my soul, and that's because of you and Max."

"Me too," I start, "But we need to have that conversation and work out the details. Since it's Max's bedtime, should we do that first?"

"You relax. I got this." He scoops Max into his arms and sends him into a fit of giggles right before disappearing into Max's room.

I bide my time by getting a glass of water and thinking about what we should cover and what can be left for another day. I know we won't solve every problem, but knowing where each of us stands will help.

I hear Max's door open thirty minutes later, and then Noah appears. I ask, "How'd it go? I didn't hear any crying."

"No, he was good. We read a book, and he was ready for bed. Went down with no problem."

He probably thinks that's how it always is. Poor guy. He's going to have a rude awakening. I laugh to myself.

Sitting next to me on the couch, he says, "I've been

thinking about it. I don't want to shake up his world. I just want to be a part of it."

I couldn't have found a better partner. "An equal part of it. You and he both deserve that."

"I'd like that. What kind of arrangement works best for him and you?"

Noah always puts himself last in the equation. And although I appreciate him always thinking of me, I don't want him to feel like a backup parent, so I say the words I never expected to come from my mouth. I won't be the one to deny him this opportunity, the same one I've had all along. "As much as it will pain me, just being honest, as a parent, I think he should stay with you sometimes. You two deserve time to build your bond even stronger. I want him to know we're both in his corner, and he has two parents equally invested in his life and well-being."

So much weighs down his expression. I didn't expect to be celebrating, but I thought this would make him happy. He runs his hand through his hair and sighs. "I want my son to have a full-time dad, and I find myself thinking about him all the time, worrying, and wanting to be around him any spare time I have. I meant it when I said I didn't want to fight you over custody. I won't put either of you through that, so thank you for trusting me with his care and giving me the time we need together."

"It's the right thing to do."

"Maybe, but it's also the harder thing to offer."

Moving into the kitchen, I pull a glass from the cabinet, thinking wine might be nice to ease some of the tension I've been holding on to while waiting to have this conversation. "I've been thinking that you'll need help on the days you're at work or if you have something unexpected come up. If I'm unavailable, we need someone in place."

"I don't know how to go about that."

"Cassandra returns in two weeks. She works full time for me. If I cut her hours in half, she'll have to find another job."

He comes into the kitchen. "I could hire her, then Max would have the person he's used to and likes."

"That's what I was thinking. He's close to her, and they have a great bond. Whiskey or beer?"

"Whiskey."

I pull the glass down and add ice, how he likes it, before pouring two fingers. After filling my glass with wine, I say, "Before he comes over, you'll need to put together a nursery and child-proof your apartment."

"I'll take care of that, but I have a question for you."

Taking a sip, I then set the glass on the counter and spin the stem between my fingers. "You're keeping me in suspense. What is it?"

"What do I have to do to convince you to come over too?"

I can kiss him all night for that, but I resist knowing where kissing him leads. Instead, I reply, "Just ask."

Noah did ask.

Once the nursery was set up a few days later, and the apartment was child-proofed, he asked us both to come for our first sleepover. And somehow, from that time, whether it be at my place or his, spending every night together was all that mattered anymore.

31

Noah

"No helicopter this time?" Liv shifts on the seat next to me in the back of the SUV, slipping across the slick leather surface toward me. "And when I say that it's because it was an incredible experience."

It's only two weeks later, but this trip is very different, so I hired a driver to take us to Beacon for the family get-together, thinking it would allow time to talk if our nerves began to spiral. I've not traveled with Max. I'm not even sure if he's been on a road trip or what he needs. Liv packed a bag not asking for a thing, no help, or for me to bring anything over when I texted her about what I need to do to prepare.

Maybe I'm the only one feeling anxious.

It's not every day you tell your family you're a father. Not going to be, but already and currently are. I love my family, but I don't know what to expect. "No helicopter. My brothers are flying in together, and I didn't want to introduce you and

Max on the tarmac." I glance at Max who's been sleeping soundly in his car seat for the past hour of the trip.

"That makes sense." She brushes the back of her fingers along my neck. "How are you?"

"I'm good," I answer too quickly. Tugging at the collar of my T-shirt, I realize I'm starting to sweat. I reach forward and turn the air on higher. "It's hot in here, right?"

Zipping her hoodie to her neck, she says, "I'm freezing."

I can't help a half-hearted grin from arriving. I need to lasso in my concerns before they get out of hand. "Sorry. I hired a driver so I could relax today, and enjoy, have some drinks if I want." I'm close to pouring a shot now just to calm my nerves. I don't. "But the reality of what's about to happen is hitting."

"It's a big day. I get it, babe. You don't need to explain." Her calm voice and steady hands mean she's holding it together better than I am.

"Sure is."

With her eyes still on me, she says, "It's a long drive. You didn't want to stay overnight?"

"We don't have a setup for Max." I take her hand, and our fingers fold together on the seat between us. "It added another layer of planning that I didn't want to burden you with. My mom would have been more than happy to set something up, but—"

"You were afraid of her reaction?"

"No," I reply, shaking my head. "She's going to love him. Getting her help would have meant telling her over the phone. That's not how I want to do this."

Staring at our connection, she asks, "You're walking in with a toddler. Have you thought about what you're going to say?"

"No." I redirect my gaze out the window. It's easier for

my thoughts to quieten when I'm staring at the clouds or getting lost in the greenery of the trees. Turning back to her, I say, "I'm not selling them on an idea, so I didn't rehearse this. I'll speak from the heart. Max deserves that much."

"I'M NERVOUS." I know she's a worrier—maybe that comes with being a mother, or perhaps she was always more type A —but I've been impressed by how she's handled this. Now I know she didn't want to worry me. I don't want her fighting this alone, though. I want to be the one she leans on, someone she can always trust with her deepest concerns.

"We're in this together." I move our hands to rest on top of my leg. "I know telling you not to worry is easier said than done, but you've met half my family already and they love you."

"I still have two brothers and two sisters-in-law to impress." She holds her phone up to see her reflection. "How do I look?"

"Prettiest girl I've ever seen." Maybe it's natural not to believe someone who loves you, thinking they're going to say that out of obligation. It's what I truly believe she is inside and out, so I refuse to let any negative thoughts of self-worth touch her. "Liv?"

She angles her head to catch a look at herself in a new way on the screen. "Huh?"

"Liv, I want you to look at me."

Glancing, she does a double take and then lowers the phone as her brows pinch together. "What is it?"

"You don't have to impress anyone. You're my girlfriend, so that's all they need to know."

The phone is forgotten on the seat beside her. "I'm your girlfriend?" It's not anger or curiosity I hear in her tone. It's something else entirely that I can't put my finger on. Did I just fuck up?

Scratching the back of my neck, I reply, "Why do you make it sound weird like that?"

Her knee bumps against mine and stays. I like the way we're usually touching in some form, even when we don't realize it like she doesn't now. "You've never called me that before."

"Well, we're not really in situations where we talk about our relationship to others. Our families know, but otherwise, we're living in secrecy."

"I'm sorry about work—"

"I understand the need for privacy at the office. I feel the same. But I'm ready to share us, as a couple, with the world outside of there." I rest my head back and grin. "Today is a safe place to show what we mean to each other. Not only as Max's parents but as a couple choosing to be together. I'll understand if this is too fast or if you're not ready—"

"I'm ready," she answers without a doubt found in her eyes.

I touch her fingertips, wanting to kiss each one, but I look at her again. "We're together all the time, but maybe we've skipped a step or two."

I've been fine with the parts of the ride that have been silent, the small talk, and now the heavier topics, but I prefer her laughter, like now. "Or four."

"Yes, or more," I say, chuckling. Bringing her hand to my mouth, I kiss it. "I owe you so much, but I've been doing this all wrong. Let's back up just a bit. Liv, will you be my girlfriend?"

"I do . . ." she says ardently, light from outside catching in her eyes. Embarrassment takes hold, though, and her gaze and smile quickly start to fall. When she looks back up, her smile is smaller. I love all of her, but it hurts to see her shrink in any way. "I mean I will."

Kissing her again, I linger against her lips, and whisper, "I do, too." Because of the time we've spent together, I'm not scared to say that two-word phrase. Life has never been better than the time I've had with them. That's something I won't ever hide, especially from her.

The driver announces, "We're almost there."

I look out the window. Since I've lived here my entire life, I recognize every mile marker, crooked tree, and know exactly where I am based on the surroundings. "We have about ten minutes. Should we wake Max?"

Sliding out of my hold, she moves to tend to him. "Probably, or he'll be grumpy on arrival. I'm sure no one wants a screaming kid at their party."

There's nothing I can add. She's the expert and knows best when it comes to him. I just wish I could help with more. "What can I do?"

She's woken him with kisses and whispers. When he opens his eyes, fear is laden inside. His cries pierce our ears as she tries to soothe him. "Can you hand me a sippy cup from the cooler?" I get it quick. "Thanks," she says, giving it to him. He takes it from her hands and then promptly throws it. The moment it hits her jaw, she flinches and covers the area with her hand. "No, Maxwell!"

He's turning red in the face, oblivious to the pain he's caused her, as his pitch goes up two octaves. I grab an ice pack from the small cooler on the floorboard and come around her, holding it to her injury. "Hold this on it, and let's switch places." I climb over and let her slip across the seat. Grabbing the cup he threw, I move next to Max. "Do you want this?"

Screaming once, he releases his anger before he begins

to calm down. He stares at me, but I can't give him the usual smile I have for him. Not when he's choosing violence against his mom. He tries a cute smile and clapping hands, but I'm not budging this time. He won't be rewarded for that behavior. "You don't hit Mommy, Max. That's a no-no."

I don't know how my parents stayed calm with all we put them through, but this is tough. Caught between anger Liv got hurt and guilt for being firm with him, I don't like this feeling. I glance back at Liv. "Are you okay?"

"He really got me, but I'll be okay." Her eyes have reddened around the rims, but she's not crying. She's the strongest person I know, and she proves it over and again.

When I turn back to Max, I ask, "Are you going to drink or throw your cup?"

"Cup," he says, patting his lap. "Cup. Cup."

"Okay." I hand him his cup, and he starts chugging it like he's the thirstiest person on earth. "Why's he acting like we're the bad guys here?"

I feel her hand rub my shoulder as she rests back. "Some days it's a no-win, but that's not today." I look at her over my shoulder. "You did great, Noah. You're a natural."

"Then why do I feel like I failed?"

"You can be riding high, feel your kid is taken care of and healthy. Some days, I feel like I finally have this mom job under control. The next day, you get a sippy cup to the jaw. That's parenting for you."

That she's managing to smile gives me some relief.

And then we pull up to the gate to my parents' property, and I'm right back where I was earlier with nerves.

I tell the driver to take it slow, which gives us a few minutes to cruise the driveway through the property and for us to all prepare mentally for what's about to come. I have him stop in the front of the house. That will give us a few extra minutes before we go around the back, where everyone has gathered.

Liv puts the ice pack in the cooler, and asks, "How is it?"

"Red from the cold, but hopefully that keeps the bruising to a minimum."

Despite all that went down, she looks at Max as if she can't summon the anger to be mad at him. He stretches his hand out for her and wiggles his fingers. She pretends to bite them, sending him into a fit of giggles with the bonus of milk running down his chin.

We clean him when he appears to be done with his cup. Liv touches up her makeup while I change his diaper and his outfit. Now we're standing on the driveway. I have Max in my arms, and I'm holding her hand. Not wanting to arrive empty-handed, she's carrying a bag full of flowers and a strawberry pie she bought from a bakery.

I look at her, and she looks at me, and we start walking.

32

Noah

I FIND myself not only holding Liv's hand tighter but also holding Max protectively to my chest. He's awake now but still resting his head on my shoulder.

Liv looks as pretty as a summer day in her pale blue dress. Not needing a lot to look naturally beautiful, her style shines in her small gold earrings and beige flat-soled sandals.

Max's head pops up as soon as we round the corner to the back of the house, stopping in our tracks. The hustle of movement—Harbor and Lark sitting at the table under the umbrella with my mom and dad, Marina with her big sunglasses floating in the pool on a giant pink flamingo raft practicing her future role as a movie star, and Loch and Tuesday at the small buffet table near the kitchen—halts the instant they see us.

"This was a mistake," Liv whispers under her breath.

To keep her from running, I hold her hand firmly in

mine. No way is she leaving me to face this alone. I say, "Hi, guys."

Max giggles. "Ca." I turn back to see the cars lined up behind me at the garage.

"Good boy," I say, looking into his eyes. "Cars."

Most are wearing sunglasses, but my dad squints, his eyes shifting from me to the child in my arms. "Glad you're here, Noah," my mom says, pushing the chair out to come greet us.

When the world shifts back on its axis, I hear birds singing in the trees in the distance, the wind gently blowing against my skin, and my family returning to whatever they were doing prior to our arrival.

"Hi, Noah," Loch shouts, clearly more interested in food.

Marina waves like she's the Queen of England. It reminds me of when she was elected homecoming queen back in high school on a float in a parade and at university riding around the football field in a convertible. I think it's gone to her head. "Hey, guys."

Lark stands, and Harbor's right behind her, along with my dad. Although my dad wears a polo and shorts, my brother and sister-in-law are dripping in wet bathing suits, fresh from the pool.

Liv and I walk closer to the action just as my mom beelines for Max. "Who is this little guy?"

Oh shit. Do I just say it or at least get us into the party first. I glance at Liv. Every muscle in her face tells me not to do it, her hand squeezing mine like she's trying to kill me, and then I hear her whisper, "Not yet."

"This is Max."

"Oh my goodness," she says, glancing back at my dad over her shoulder. "He makes my heart squeeze. Come see,

Port." With her hand over her chest, she coos at him. "I would have had twenty kids if I could have."

Liv smiles, and asks, "How'd you decide on four?"

"Because kids are expensive," my dad responds, chuckling. He goes right in to tickle Max's belly, and then turns to Liv. "I didn't know you had a son."

The tension slips from her shoulders, and she eases up on my hand. Beaming with joy, she replies, "Yep. Here he is." This is the good stuff, the feel-good, pride-from-the-inside-out moments parents have in life. I feel the same, but I can't let it shine just yet.

My mom lifts to hug me with one arm and then moves around to embrace Liv. "He's so handsome." She can't take her eyes off him. I know why, but I'm not sure how to tell them that he's also my child. Maybe I should have rehearsed this after all. "He reminds me so much of my boys. He's a twin of Harbor at that age."

An eye roll threatens, but I control myself. "Harbor, pfft." Okay, so I slip . . . *sue me*. "Don't insult Max like that."

She playfully pinches my arm. "Now. Now. All my kids were beautiful babies, like Max."

I catch Liv's eyes on me, a knowing exchange shared between us.

Lark comes up wrapped in a towel, and embraces my free side. "Hey, Noah, how are you?"

"I should be asking you. How are you feeling?"

Rubbing her beach towel-wrapped pregnant belly, she smiles. As a doctor who is a recovering workaholic, she's managed to dwindle her hours to part-time in preparation for the baby and staying home. It shows. She looks rested and happy. Glowing, as they say. There's also a lightness to her eyes when she looks at Max. "You know what I think?"

She better not say Harbor, but I bite anyway. "What do you think?" I ask, angling Max for her to get a good look.

Reaching out her finger, Max takes it, eliciting her smile to bloom even brighter. "I think he looks just like Noah." Her eyes briefly meet mine.

Having an ally is good, but I wonder if she knows the truth. Women's intuition or doctor's expertise? I nudge her gently. "Is that your professional opinion?"

"It is." She moves to meet Liv as I shift over so introductions can begin for Liv and Max.

My mom gets us drinks while we settle in and then offers to play with Max in the grass away from the pool, telling us to relax and enjoy a few minutes off-duty. Liv sits with the others at the table, but I remain standing, watching my mom talk to him. You'd think they were having full-blown conversations by how animated they are with each other and the pockets of laughter that reach my ears.

Taking out my phone, I snap a few photos. It's not just something I know she'll love, but something I want to have as a keepsake of when she first met my son, her first grandchild.

Not that it matters that I am the first, and ultimate champion, in any kind of brotherly love competition for producing the first grandkid, or anything like that . . .

I rub Liv's shoulder, and her hand covers mine.

Sitting across from us, my dad says, "I didn't make the connection until after you left, Liv. Bancroft & Lowe. You're Lawrence Bancroft's daughter."

"Yes." She doesn't elaborate, leaving much room for interpretation, and then sips a glass of white sangria. I know her father is the last thing she wants to talk about, but she asks, "Do you know him?"

"We've met. A few years back. Booming marketing

business."

She glances at me. "He hires only the best."

Tuesday twists her hair onto her head, securing it, and then leans forward, her eyes connecting with mine. "Did you know your brothers had a running bet on you breaking the dating policy?"

I chuckle. "I have no doubt."

"They're truly terrible," she jokes with Liv. "Prepare for a lot of sibling rivalry." Touching Liv's arm, she whispers, "Not to scare you off. They're also the most loving family. Loyal and wonderful people."

Liv glances at me but angles her way like she's hanging out with a friend. Wouldn't that be something if they had that bond? She tells Tuesday, "I'm learning that. Everyone's been so welcoming and accepting of me, and now Maxwell."

I ask, "Which brother of mine had my back and bet the policy wouldn't be broken?" Glancing at Liv, I add, "I have a bit of a reputation."

Laughter erupts around the table. Loch asks, "A bit? Massive understatement. He's violated Westcott Law's policy and doesn't even work there."

Leveling him with a glare, I reply, "You're going to scare off my girlfriend." I glance at her. "It's all rumors. You know how people like to gossip."

She takes my hand and pulls me closer as she turns in her chair. "Your past doesn't scare me." My sweet woman adds, "As for reputations, coming from someone who has one herself, they're usually built on more than rumors." With a shrug, she laughs. "The ice queen didn't happen overnight, you know. It was honed with precision." Leaning down, I kiss her cheek. She holds me there, catching my eyes. "Let me guess. Playboy? That doesn't sound so far-fetched, babe."

Everyone is smiling. I didn't hold back during introductions and proudly proclaimed her as my girlfriend. It's freeing being able to touch, to kiss, to enjoy our relationship in the wide open. "I haven't been a playboy in a long time."

She looks at my dad. "What do you think? You mentioned his reputation last time I was here. Tell me the truth, Port. Was he trouble growing up?"

My dad is quick to raise his hands in surrender. "I'm staying out of this."

Marina sits in the chair next to Liv with a plate of snacks. Pushing her fluffy pink cover-up from getting in her food, they start talking. I'm glad they're bonding, but I'm also happy to have the heat off me, even if briefly.

"Excuse me," I say just before walking to join my mom and Max on the lawn. I shake my head but chuckle when I hear Marina talking about the "Noah Effect" to Liv. Walking backward, I call, "Don't believe her, babe. It's all an urban myth."

Marina is already laughing. It's a harmless theory of hers, so I don't worry myself that Liv is now hearing it. But I know I'll be asked about it later.

Turning, I move to sit down near my mom. She says, "He's precious." Max is holding her finger and happily teetering around her on the uneven ground. "He's strong."

"When did I start walking?"

She thinks for a minute. I know it's a long time ago, and she has a slew of kids' milestones to go through, but then she says, "Right around fourteen months. You were probably at this same marker as Max."

"How about Loch?"

She laughs, playfully slapping my leg. "We're not doing that. Just know that everyone does things in their own time."

Like telling her that I'm his father and hoping she

understands the reasons behind the delay. Max comes to me, all smiles and pure joy. I'll do anything to protect that, understanding more of what being a father means every day.

Flopping in my lap, he rolls to his back and kicks his feet into the air. I play with his toes and then pretend to bite one, making the sounds that get him laughing the most.

"I didn't know Liv had a child."

When I look up, her eyes are cautious, her sunny mood shadowed by overcast clouds. "I didn't feel that was something that needed to be thrown out there in the short time we had together at the play."

Max has relaxed on my lap, resting his head on my leg. I start stroking his head, his hair full of static from the grass. "Remember how my hair used to stand on end from dragging my feet?"

She laughs, resting back on her hands. "I remember you coming home covered in mud. You had been building forts out in the woods, trying to keep up with your brothers."

"We'd jump in the creek at the back of the eastern portion," I say, pointing toward the helipad. "By the time we reached the grass, I think we were covered with dirt from more than a mile."

"Did you have a good childhood, Noah?"

Our eyes stare into each other's, and I was unaware until now that she had thoughts that didn't match her sunnier disposition. I suddenly see her in a new light—good or bad —more human. I reach over and rub her back. "The best, Mom."

"Good."

The wiggle worm on my lap taps his feet against my chest. "Dada dadadada."

The heat of my mom's stare draws my attention back to

her. She knows.

Her hand wraps around my wrist, stilling me. "Noah." It's not a question nor a command, but it sends my heart thundering in my chest. I don't say a word, but I swear she can hear my heart pounding.

My mind freezes. Instead of filling in the blanks, I let her get whatever it is off her chest. "Noah," she whispers as if my name is all she can say. Her gaze darts over my shoulder at the others, but I can't read what she's thinking when it returns to me. She takes a deep breath with her hand on her chest, and when she releases it, she says, "This is your child."

"Mom," I start, my hand covering hers that's holding on to me like I'm going to fall from a cliff if she doesn't. Max rolls into the grass and decides to make a run for it across the lawn. And by run, I mean he toddles and is not getting anywhere fast. "I can explain."

Her eyelids fall, and she sucks in a deep breath. "Noah . . ."

I still can't read her mind or how she's feeling. Is she in shock? "It's okay, Mom. This is a good thing. I'm good. He's good."

When her eyes fly open again, tears fall down her cheeks. She drops her head into her hands. I rush to comfort her while still keeping an eye on Max. "It's okay, Mom. I promise."

Raising her chin, she laughs through the tears. "Of course, he's a good thing. Oh, Noah." She throws her arms around me, hugging me tighter than I think she ever has. "What a blessing."

My dad and the others rush over. "What's going on? Is your mom okay?"

Liv scoops Max into her arms and plants him on her hip.

Keeping distance from us, she watches as the whole crew comes over to make sure my mom's alright. My girl may not be afraid of dating a reformed playboy, but she protects her son.

My mom bawls her eyes out on my shoulder as I try to comfort her at the same time. "She's okay." I don't want everyone else to worry. Looking at Liv, I add, "She's happy."

"They're happy tears," my mom says, pushing up and rushing to Liv. As my mom cups Liv's face, I can hear her saying, "Thank you. What a gift you've given us."

The stoicism Liv's held on to for what I believe is years to safeguard Max crumbles under my mom's instant acceptance. Liv breaks down in tears, dropping her head on my mom's shoulder. Tuesday quickly takes Max and starts playing with him. She's so good with kids, but I know she's allowing everyone time to figure out what's going on to keep him from getting scared.

Lark laughs behind me. "I won that bet."

Harbor chuckles, and then I hear a smack on the lips. "I don't know how you knew." Resolved in his defeat, he adds, "You win. I lose. We get salad on our pizza next time."

"It's not salad, it's arugula, and it's healthy for us."

"It doesn't belong on pizza."

"It does next time because I won."

I shake my head because these are the kinds of quarrels I dream of having with Liv one day—entertaining and fun.

Harbor's hand comes down on my shoulder, and he says, "Congrats, you competitive little fucker."

Chuckling, I turn, pretending to sucker punch him. He flinches, and that's all I need to know. I still rule this roost. But then we embrace, the tone turning sincere. It's a momentous occasion. "You made me an uncle, kid."

"Guilty as charged."

Loch says, "What the fuck is going on?"

Harbor shoulders him and then pulls him back. "The short version is that you're an uncle, and Max, right over there playing with your wife, is your nephew."

"What?" Loch asks. "I'm going to need the long version."

They start walking toward Max and Tuesday, and I hear Harbor reply, "I'll fill you in."

I start for my girlfriend, whose eyes are filled with tears, love, and so much emotion that she can't hold it in and is crying again. Lark beats me to her, embracing her like a sister. There's a lot to be said for an only child to be welcomed and supported by such a large family. But this is what we do. One by one, they each go to her and then to me, bringing us all together as a family.

I'm drawn in by the moment, my soul captivated by hers, needing to be with her.

My whole being is filled with the love I have for her and Max as I hold her in my arms. I kiss where she was hit earlier by the cup, glad there's no bruising and then on that scar on her eyebrow, proud of her for surviving.

It's then, with her head on my shoulder, that I know even though I'm not the first guy Liv's fallen for, I will be the last. I vow right then and there that I will be everything she ever needs.

My dad is already holding Max when he comes to us. "Did you forget to tell me something, son?"

"Oh my God." Marina throws her arms out. "Is anyone going to fill the rest of us in?"

Harbor cups the side of his mouth, and replies, "Noah has a kid who looks just like me. Lucky fellow."

At least Liv thinks that's funny. My mom shrugs. "I'm sorry, Noah. If it makes you feel better, I have confused the two of you in baby photos before."

"No," I tease with a grin, "that doesn't make me feel better."

"What?" Marina's eyes shoot to mine. "When?"

Liv wipes under her eyes after a roll of laughter. "It's true. Noah is Maxwell's father."

"Huh?" Sliding her sunglasses to her head, she looks more confused than before. "How? You guys just started dating."

I say, "We actually connected a few years back and—"

"I don't remember you dating anyone back then."

My brow heavies. "Okay, we don't need to get into the dirty details—"

"*Ohhh,*" my sister hums. "It was a one-night stand."

Loch says, "The kid is right there. Max can hear you."

When Marina comes closer, I lower my voice. "He was not planned, if that's what you're getting at."

"Oh." This time, I see her cringe. "I didn't mean—"

"It's okay," Liv says, stopping her from having to explain. "I appreciate the honesty. I hope you understand that although we weren't dating when we met in the Hamptons, we were drawn to each other. I like to think that destiny played a hand in bringing us back together."

Marina happily sighs. "I love that. You know what else I love?" She smiles and throws her arms around both of us. "I'm an aunt." She laughs and then runs over to Max. Sitting next to him in the grass, I can hear her introducing herself. "We're going to have the best time ever, little man."

If I would have known having a girlfriend was so good, I would have done this years ago. And being a dad is pretty fucking spectacular.

I kiss Liv, wiping away a stray tear that escaped. "So . . ."

She smiles. "So . . ."

"How do you feel?"

"I couldn't have asked for a better reaction. Max and I are so fortunate to have you and your family in our lives." Caressing my face, she looks into my eyes. I've never seen her happier than she is right here. I want to give this to her, always. "How are you?"

"I'm . . ." I think, needing more than a few seconds to encapsulate these emotions. "Their response and reception, like you said, couldn't have gone better." We both look at everyone that matters to me enjoying our son's company. We're truly in this together.

The laughter that floated in the breeze and the joy that lingered all afternoon follows us long after we leave. In the back of the SUV, with a couple hours behind us and a few more ahead, Liv angles her shoulder under my arm, resting against me while facing Max in his car seat. Holding his hand, she says, "He's the best parts of us." She glances up at me as if I would argue that fact.

Today was a lot to take in. I'm still riding the high that we're a family. Not just my siblings and parents but Liv, Max, and me. We're a little unit that will always have each other's back and best interest at heart. "He is." I kiss the top of her head, holding her to me. "Today was a good day."

She nods against me, her eyes dipping closed. It doesn't take long until she's under a spell of sleep. I look out the window and then back at her and Max sleeping beside me in the back of this SUV. I hope he knows that I'll always take care of them.

I settle in, my body relaxed after the long day. I don't mind the quiet in the back seat, being left with my thoughts and the peaceful sight of my family around me.

I'm discovering there's a new form of bliss.

This is it.

33

Liv

ONE MONTH LATER...

"I THINK we should move in together."

I stop towel-drying my hair and stare at Noah in the mirror. "Move in together?" I ask stupidly, my mind struggling to wrap around the words he just flung out of the blue. I twist the towel around my hair on my head. "I'm not even wearing a bra, Noah."

He chuckles. How in the world is me standing naked with nothing but a towel the optimal time to ask me such a question, especially while he's fully dressed in a tailored navy-blue pinstripe suit and looks like he walked out of a magazine? How is this fair? Or neutral territory? Or make sense to anyone but him?

It doesn't need to make sense to me because it did to him. *He's such a romantic.*

"I've been thinking about this all night," he says, "for the past month even. I want the three of us living together."

"We practically do now."

"Practically is not the same thing as sharing an address. We live apart and bring our stuff back and forth." He takes hold of my waist, but his gaze grazes over my body, specifically my breasts. I've discovered that my breasts are his Achilles' heel. I wield the power with care, though.

Sliding my hand down the front of his suit jacket, I pick a piece of lint from the lapel. "Having this conversation on a Monday morning before caffeine is a lot to take in."

He lifts my chin until we make eye contact again. "I'll buy you a new coffeemaker, the best on the market. I want our stuff under the same roof."

"You're bribing me with fancy coffee?"

The corner of his mouth slips upward on the right side as he chuckles under his breath. "I am. My shame knows no bounds."

"I'm the opposite. I have all the boundaries holding me here." I'd laugh, but there's too much truth in that confession. I can't make a rash decision, though my heart hasn't led me wrong yet when it comes to him. "There's a lot to consider. Pro: Lugging Max's and my belongings between the two places is a real drag. Con: I like my apartment."

"Pro: You love my apartment and the amenities."

"Those are nice, especially the dry cleaning and the pool. Max loves the pool."

"Another pro," he says, checking it off in the air.

"Con: Both are in great neighborhoods with easy access to restaurants, groceries, and parks."

"How are those cons?"

"It's two pros, not cons. One in each column." I try to

tally the pros and cons, but I've lost track. "Wait, where are we with pros for mine?"

Chuckling, he replies, "We were doing pros and cons of moving in together, not which apartment, but I like where your head is."

"I knew I wasn't awake enough for this." Tilting my head, I ask, "Should we start over?"

"No, let's keep going and see where we land."

"Financially, your apartment is worth more than mine. If we sell it, you'll make a profit. If we move in there, it gains more value over time, but I have no stake in it."

Pulling me fully into his arms, he says, "That's just it. I don't want mine and yours. I want ours. Together."

"Mine is owned by my mom." I don't know why I feel less for admitting that. She got a huge settlement from the divorce and still owns company shares. She gave me the apartment for Max and me to live in, and I cover the mortgage. There's no shame in that.

He's looking at me, and I can tell his thoughts are plentiful. Finally, he says, "What would happen to it if you moved out?"

"I don't know. Maybe she'd sell it, but that leaves me no safety net."

"I understand that you want to be secure in your surroundings, in your investments, and to build your assets. Are you building it in your current situation?"

I know my mom will sign over the apartment one day. We've meant to do that for a while now but haven't gotten around to it. So I answer truthfully, "No."

Rubbing my shoulders, he says, "I never want you to feel beholden to me. If you're with me, it's because you want to be. I don't have the answer for you. This is a decision you need to make. But one thing I won't strip away is your independence and safety. I like your apartment, but there's nowhere to grow from here. I have an office space and two other bedrooms outside of the primary. I bought this to serve my life for years to come. If you move in with me, you won't need to pay me a dime. If you want to build your financial portfolio, that's your money to do with as you please."

"I wouldn't want to live for free. That means it's your apartment, and I'm just moving in. I want a stake in my home."

Kneading my breasts, he smirks. "We can negotiate. I'm open to hearing your terms." I knew he wouldn't be able to resist them for long.

"Why are you offering me anything I want?"

"I'm a changed man because of you. I don't want to shuffle our stuff back and forth anymore. I want to be with you all the time. I want to settle down."

Although we're very much settled these days, hearing him voice a future with me in such an important way has me lifting on my toes to kiss him. When I drop down, I say, "You didn't have to change for me."

"Sure I did. I want to be the man you deserve to have in your life, and I'm willing to earn my way each day as long as I don't lose you."

The steam from the shower has long since dissipated. I know I'm melting because of his words, though, and not the heat that remains. I lean against him, my cheek brushing against the fine material as he holds me. "I don't want to lose you either."

When I met him, I slept with this man out of pure selfish desire. That turned out to be the best decision I've ever made.

Even in this love that I feel for him, I laugh. "I feel a little underdressed for that kind of declaration."

He chuckles. "You have a really nice ass, babe."

I realize he's staring in the mirror. Pushing him away, I laugh. Taking the towel from my head, I wrap it around me, wanting to finish this conversation despite the lack of caffeine in my system. I ask, "Do you really want to move in together, or do you just feel like that's what we're supposed to do?"

"I don't give a flying fuck about rules when it comes to relationships. We should always do what feels right for us. Fuck all the other stuff." He checks his watch and sighs. "I need to go, but there's no rush to answer." Cupping my cheek, he says, "Think about it, and we'll talk when you're ready." He kisses my temple and heads to the door. "I'll see you at our usual ten o'clock?"

"Wouldn't miss it."

After giving me a quick wink, he leaves.

I'm not left guessing where he stands or how he feels about me. He not only tells me openly, but he shows me every day. Thinking about how amazing he is with Max has my heart so full that it feels as though it might burst. I thought this kind of happiness was only found in fairy tales, but it's become my real life. All because of that man. And he thinks I need time to figure things out. *I don't.*

I already know exactly what I want to do and what's best for Max. I start running. Swinging open the front door, I hurry out and call his name, hoping to catch him before he gets on the elevator. "Noah?"

The elevator doors close, and my heart sinks just a little. I shrug it off because I can tell him during our daily scheduled appointment at the office. I laugh to myself, knowing full well we never get any work done during those meetings.

When I turn around, my mouth falls open. *Oh no.* I rush to the apartment door and turn the knob, praying it didn't close all the way and lock me out. Shaking it, I stupidly kick it in a failed attempt to bust it open. I know it's Fort Knox, though, because I had the locking devices installed on it. "Dammit."

Of course, this is the day Cassandra took Max for an early sing-along at the children's museum. With Noah still on the elevator, he's my only hope. I tighten the towel around me and head for the stairs. Twelve flights. I can only hope that I catch him before he reaches the street, and I don't get a foot fungus from this stairwell. *Ew.*

I might also be hoping he gets stuck on every floor. I keep running, but even downhill, this is a bitch of a work-out. By the time I reach the third floor, my thigh muscles begin to shake. When I push through the lobby door on the first floor, every muscle in my body is on fire.

Twelve damn floors but I made it. I call out before I even reach the other side of the elevator, "Noah?" My dirty feet slapping against the marble floors, I race toward the exit to the street.

There's no one, no one but me in the lobby. "Dammit," I say, angry with myself for running into the hall like an idiot without a key. I bend forward, resting my hands on my knees to catch my breath.

I'm stuck and need a new plan since the desk attendant isn't anywhere to be found. Like this isn't embarrassing or anything, I could wait for someone to come off the elevator and ask to use their phone. I have no choice, but my head is still dropped in humiliation. "I can't believe I'll have to do this."

I right myself, so glad this tuck of the towel seems to want to stay in place. But just in case, I hold it for my walk of shame. When I turn around, I'm greeted by hazel eyes and a smile that I know like the back of my hand.

"Forget something?" Noah holds up a key.

I don't care that I feel like a fool and probably look like one too, with my sweating body and red cheeks, my hair a mess, and that I'm only dressed in a towel in public. I run and jump into his open arms and wrap my legs around him. Our lips collide along with our bodies. But when we part, he's the only thing I see and the only one for me. "I don't need time to think about it. I already know that I want us to move in with you."

His smile wins my heart all over again. "You sure?"

"Never been more so in my life. I want us to be together all the time."

The ding of the elevator has him moving us off to the side and trying to cover me, but the sudden shift tugs on my towel, forcing it to the floor. "Ack!" I practically climb into this man, using his suit as my shield and hiding myself the best I can. "Please tell me no one—"

"Be still."

I hear the clomp of shoes across the stone floors, then the door opening, letting the sounds of the city invade before it closes and goes quiet again.

"Close call, but he couldn't see anything." Noah bends down and grabs the towel. "You're lucky it's before morning rush hour." He's wrapping the towel around me as we shuffle back to the elevator.

"I'm lucky for more reasons than that." I punch the button since his hands are full of me at the moment. "What took you so long anyway if no one was on the elevator with you?"

"I heard you call my name, so I got off on the next floor and ran up the stairs."

I huff. "We must have just missed each other."

"If it matters, and it always does, you made excellent time." I start laughing as he kisses my head. He holds me so tight that I don't even care if someone sees me half-naked.

I have this man's love, and I know I can trust him with my life. I still have to laugh at myself. "What floor are you on again? Just in case I decide to try to beat my own record."

"I'm hoping next time will include clothes. I'm too fucking jealous to handle guys seeing my girl."

"Your girl, huh?"

"Yep," he says proudly. The doors open, and we let a few people off before stepping onto the elevator. As soon as we're alone again, he says, "And I've been yours since the moment we met."

The elevator opens back on my floor, and he unlocks my apartment. While I stand inside the doorway, he remains outside. This reminds me of when we were first dating. It's not so long ago that I can't forget that there's been nothing expected about our chosen path. "I've loved every minute with you since."

"I love you." I may have had my breath stolen away by that confession, but I've never seen him look so determined. "I love you, Liv. I've loved you all along."

"I still haven't had caffeine." He grins, comfortable in his stance to rush me in mine. "Screw it." I throw my arms around him. "Who needs caffeine when I have you? I love you so much, Noah. I've loved you since the day I stopped hating you."

He bursts out laughing. "What more could I ask for?" He kisses me with the passion of a thousand boyfriends, and I'm here for it. *And spending my future with him.*

34

Noah

Two months later . . .

"Hey, Mom." I close the door to my apartment. "I didn't know you were coming over."

"Hope you don't mind. I was in the city and stopped by to see my grandbaby." Max has a soft spot for my mom. He's a perfect angel for her. She jokes that he knows she can't deal with much, so he goes easy on her. Whatever it is, it's working for them. Their relationship has grown by leaps and bounds. The kid loves his Nana.

Even when I squat down to say hi, he's running to her. "Nana."

I laugh. "How fast they forget us."

She pushes up to greet me with a hug. "Liv's not feeling well. I ordered some soup. If I had known sooner, I would have made it for her."

"I'm sure she appreciates it."

"She hasn't eaten yet. I checked on her about thirty minutes ago, but she was going to lie down. I didn't want to disturb her again. I stayed so she could rest, and the perk is that I get to spend more time with my Max."

Glancing toward the bedroom, I ask, "Do you mind staying with him a little longer?"

"Take your time. Max has been fed, and I already bathed him. I'm in no hurry. I'm staying with Lark and Harbor for the rest of the week. We're on baby watch."

"Yeah, she's due, right?" I slide my jacket down my arms and leave it draped over a chair, anxious to get to Liv. Rolling up my sleeves, I make my way back to the bedroom and peek inside. The room is dark, matching the day outside.

I worked late but wouldn't have stayed if I knew she was home sick. Keeping my voice low, I say, "Liv?"

"Noah, you're home." The sound of the sheets shuffling is heard through the dark. "I would have gotten up."

"No, stay, babe." I cross the room and sit on the edge of the mattress. My eyes finally adjust, and I see her eyes looking into mine.

She says, "You shouldn't be this close to me. I'm sick."

"Don't worry about me. I'll be okay." Stroking her hair back, I stop and feel her forehead for a temperature. She's not hot. She's not cold or clammy. "How do you feel? What's wrong?"

"I don't know. I got chills and lost color in my face at work. Then I was sweating. No amount of caffeine this morning could get me moving. I felt like I was fighting something all morning, so I came home to lie down. Cassandra was here, and then your mom stopped by."

"I saw her." I glance at the nightstand to see a cup of water barely touched and half a bottle of a sports drink. The electrolytes are good, but I'm not sure the sugar will make her feel better.

"Are they okay?"

"She's fine. They're having a good time playing." I run the back of my hand along her cheekbone. "She ordered soup. You think you can eat?"

She sighs out loud, her eyes closing as she rolls to her back. "I'm not hungry, but it might make me feel better."

I stand. "If you can eat, you should, to gain your strength back." I get the remote and turn on the large screen across the room. "How about you have a night in here, try to eat, rest, and watch movies? You can recover, and I'll take care of everything else."

"You make it sound like you don't do that already." A halfhearted smile appears on her pretty face. Forcing herself upright, she leans against the headboard and reaches for the glass of water. "I think it's just a bug, but I shouldn't be around you guys."

"I'm sorry you're not feeling well. Let me take care of you." Heading for the door, I wait to open it. "I'll bring the soup. Tonight, you just need to heal and rest. Deal?"

"Deal."

"Noah?"

With my hand wrapped around the doorknob, I turn back. "Yes?"

"I miss you guys already."

I grin, understanding completely. We spend every evening together. We sleep together each night. We make love in the middle of the night. But it's her arms around me that I'll miss the most. She's a bed hog and never leaves me much space to spread out. If we're talking percentage of mattress to body mass, I'm getting screwed out of my share. I happily give her all the room she wants because I'm the guy who gets to wake up to this beauty every morning. "Me too, but if you need anything, anything at all, I'll be right out there. Just call, and I'll be here for you."

"I love you."

"I love you, too."

When I return to the living room, my mom carries a sleepy Max with half-closed eyes. "I think you wore him out."

"He wore me out," she replies, laughing quietly. "How is she?"

Washing my hands, I reply, "She doesn't have a temperature, but she thinks she has a bug."

"Oh, that's not good. What can I do? I can stay and take care of Max or be here for Liv."

I know she means well. After drying my hands, I press them to the counter because I'm also very aware that my dad let her run the household and deal with us kids most of the time. Unless we majorly fucked up, of course, and then he stepped in. I love my dad, but I want to be more present, not just there for the fun or bad times. I want to take an active role in my family. Max and Liv are my family. I want to be here for them through everything.

"It's okay, Mom. I can take care of them."

"Who's taking care of you? You look tired, Noah."

"It's called work for a reason." I hate that she might think I'm being short. "It's just different than I expected. Not as rewarding. I'd rather have more than a few minutes with Max, but that's all I've been getting lately."

"I know it's hard on you." She comes to me. Dragging hair off to the side from my forehead, she says, "I watched your dad burn out. It took a long time to recover. And even though he was doing it for his family, we would have preferred time with him."

"Yeah. I hear you." I look at my baby in her arms. He's almost outgrown them. "Liv takes care of me."

Glancing up at me, she doesn't say anything. She doesn't have to. Knowing I'm being loved is enough.

She hands Max over almost reluctantly. I smile, watching her admire my son. I couldn't have asked for more. Resituated in my arms, he's almost asleep when he rests against me. "Want me to call you a car?"

"I'm good. I'll catch a cab out front." Caressing my cheek, she says, "You're a good partner and father, Noah. They're lucky to have you."

"No, it's not luck. We make the effort to be there for each other every day and every night."

Her eyes begin to glisten, so I wrap an arm around her and bring her in to kiss her cheek. "I was lucky to have such a great role model."

Dabbing the corner of her eyes, she says, "I'll make sure to tell your father." Her laughter follows her toward the door.

"You brought the jokes."

After picking up her purse, she turns back. "He's a good man, too, but I'll be bragging about the role model compliment for weeks. Love you, honey."

Chuckling, I reply, "Love you." I lock the door behind her, then walk slowly toward Max's bedroom. His night-light is already on in the corner, so I kiss his head when I slip inside and set him gently in his crib. "Love you, buddy."

He's out for the night, so I leave his room and return to the kitchen to heat the soup. It smells good, causing my stomach to growl. I'll figure out what I'm going to eat when I have time. When I enter the bedroom with the bowl of soup, I notice she's watching *Sons of Anarchy* again. "You cheating on me with Jax Teller?"

"Do you believe in hall passes?" She sure looks eager and wide awake all of a sudden for someone who's sick. She readjusts on the bed before I hand the bowl to her. "My stomach just growled."

"For Jax or the soup?"

"Can't it be for both?"

Although she's not laughing at all, I say, "I see your sense of humor is intact." I watch her take a sip of the broth.

She hums and does a little wiggle. "It's good. Thank you."

"You're welcome." I go into the closet to pull some shorts out of the drawer. With them in hand, I add, "Max is in bed. I'm going to set up camp in the living room."

"Not the guest room?"

"I'm going to watch TV and wind down."

She clears her throat. "I really appreciate how you take care of us, Noah. I hate being a bother."

"You're never a bother. I just want you better." I'm about to close the door to the bedroom, but stop to add, "I don't believe in hall passes. Nothing about me could handle the thought of you with someone else."

"I'm not running at full capacity. So why do you have to be so swoony tonight and take me down so easy?" I recognize the up-to-no-good grin sitting on her face. "And for the record, I don't need a hall pass since I have you."

"Not even for Jax Teller?"

"Not for Jax Teller or Charlie Hunnam. They don't hold a candle to you or that great ass of yours, Noah Westcott."

I balk with laughter, returning to hold my hand to her head. "You sure you don't have a fever?"

"I'm already feeling better because of you."

Popping my collar, I say, "You sure know how to make a guy feel good about himself."

"I'll promise to make you feel even better when I'm well again."

I give her a wink, thinking it's best if I don't kiss her right now since she's sick. "I'm holding you to that. Both the well and the better parts."

This time, when I leave the room, I'm wearing the goofiest grin. I scratch the back of my neck and shake my head because the woman makes me smile even while not feeling her best.

I find a take-out container tucked in the refrigerator from the same restaurant the soup came from with grilled chicken, green beans, and potatoes. It's not a big meal, but it will do. I'm just grateful my mom ordered something for me because I'm too tired to mess with figuring out what to eat after the weeks of long days I've had.

More than three months into this job, I finally convinced Mr. and Mrs. Torres to give us another chance. While I heat the meal in the microwave, I think about the details of the payments made when they worked with Chip, the long hours digging through their original contract to make sure we did the opposite. While the original contract was light on expectations, the new one sets the milestones. The lack of transparency in their first agreement set them up to be taken advantage of. It also meant that no one with a title other than owner would ever see the payments since they're the ones who approve expenses at that level.

I had legal create an entirely new contract after that because I don't want any hidden agendas if I'm involved. Despite being the talk of the office for the work I've put in and for making the bosses happy, I still have a sinking feeling in my gut.

Sitting on the couch, I turn on a sports channel and lean back. Kicking up my feet on the coffee table, I start eating.

I'm too tired and hungry to even change out of my work clothes. At least I took off my shoes.

Since nothing good is on, and I can't stop thinking about Liv in the other room, I stand to get undressed, drop my underwear, and pull on a pair of shorts. I pad down the hall and listen at the door, wondering how she's doing and wanting to climb into bed with her. The couch doesn't have her comfort, the softness of her thighs, or the sweet mewls she sometimes makes in the night.

I sneak in to check on Liv once more, but she's fallen asleep. In a quick sweep of the room, I brush my teeth, turn off the TV, and collect the bowl on the way out the door. I've never been the neatest, but I've learned how the state of the kitchen is left at night sometimes contributes to Liv's mood in the morning. I take the time to straighten and clean the dishes before settling back in horizontally on the couch.

My mom was right for telling me to go with the custom couch, one that fits my build and is great for lounging around. It's coming in handy as a bed tonight. Although I have a spare bedroom set up, I can't hear her as well from in there because of the air-conditioning.

Turning off the TV, I prefer the quiet and listening for my son if he calls me or my wif—*girlfriend* needs anything. Even in the sky of the city, a hum sneaks in from the outside. It's not like in the country where silence becomes a friend you rely on. Here, there's always a bit of noise to contend with.

I've gotten used to it, but I'm not sure which I prefer anymore. I guess it depends where Liv and Max reside. I choose them. That's why I don't concern myself with the Freudian slip I just made. That and my mind is too tired to fight what my subconscious is trying to tell me. My lids grow too heavy to hold open as my body sinks into the couch cushions. I release the day, allowing my mind the reprieve to give in to sleep.

I see her in my dreams—soft curls flowing down her back and thin straps falling off her shoulder, kissable red lips calling me to her and heels that make her legs appear to go on for miles. She's a fantasy that's fooling me into thinking she was real.

I'm straddled, and pressure is applied to my chest as she slides herself over my dick several times, taking what she wants to make herself feel good while arousing me from dreaming. My name brushes past my ears on the breath of whispers that feel so real. "Noah. Noo*oah*."

I groan wanting to stay here, to be with my girl.

"*Noah* . . . hey there."

Heated skin and full tits. Hips that widen from below the waist. Nails scrape across my skin and wet kisses on my chest. I fight against the onslaught of a new day, not wanting to wake up.

The world rushes in when I hear, "Babe?"

I open one lid and then the other, finding Liv on top of me and hovering over my face. "Hey." My fingers dig into her bare ass on instinct, but it still takes my mind a moment to catch up. *Home. Living room. Couch. Liv sick*. Alarms ring in my head, waking me up. "What are you doing out here? Are you okay?"

She smiles. "I feel so much better, but I missed you." Her hands cover my chest and run over my biceps. Dipping down to kiss my jaw, she goes lower, and whispers, "I want you."

"You have me, baby," I reply, trying to shake the final haze of grogginess from my brain. Running my fingers over her back, I close my eyes, enjoying being woken up this way. It's my favorite way to wake up, in fact.

"No, I *want* you." She lifts her head while rubbing her pussy against my erection. Her lids falter, and she bites her lip. A moan slips out, and her head dips down. As if she can't bear it any longer, she says, "I need to feel you inside me. I need the connection, the fullness. I need *you*, babe."

Holding her by the hips, I sit up, kissing her behind the ear and then peppering them across her shoulder. Our physical attraction was a string attaching us together when we met. We've never denied our chemistry. The emotional bond has only grown since that first time. Like her, I often need one connection or the other, but mostly, all of her because the superficial is more incredible because of how I feel about her. I lie back. "I'm always here for you."

Honied heat engulfs me as she slides down, consuming me to the hilt. A pause has her steadying her breath as it deepens while she acclimates. I will never grow tired of how we fit together.

She begins to rock, taking her sweet time. I don't mind the slow pace. It matches the hour, giving me time to soak her in, to appreciate the feel of her soft skin and the perfection of her tits bouncing before me. That mouth, though, has me reaching up to fill it with my fingers. "Suck."

Her lips wrap around them and close, her tongue gliding to wet them. I pull out, keeping my eyes on her while I reach between us and rub them against her silken clit. I want to watch the buildup, feel the tightening of her body, and witness her peak as she falls apart on top of me.

Her moan teases my orgasm, summoning it to the surface, and my body tenses while chasing the heaven she creates.

"Noah." My name falls from the edge of her tongue as her body tremors around me.

I'm sent spiraling into my release along with her.

Holding her hips, I fuck until my body collapses beneath her. It's so tempting to claim her in other ways, to make us legal on paper as well. I restrain the words from slipping out, knowing they're better reserved for another day.

She lies on top of me and closes her eyes. The doodles from her fingers are drawings of figure eights. When her breath evens, I kiss her head and close my eyes, wanting to stay like this forever. She whispers, "I love you."

I thought I was dreaming, but she's real, and she's mine. Liv's my dream come true, and whatever was in that soup, I'm ordering it for her again. "I love you, too."

35

Liv

As soon as the car pulls up to the curb, I kiss Noah and give Max a smooch. He's all smiles for me this morning. The change in routine must be exciting for him. "So you'll drop him off at Cassandra's? Or you're meeting her at the vet?"

"Her apartment. She said she'll be back home by then. She just couldn't make it across town in time for me to get to work at a reasonable hour."

"Are they—"

"They're going to the park, and she'll bring him back to our place. Don't worry. I've asked all the questions. I've got it covered, babe. Go before you're late to the meeting."

"Okay. Okay." I force myself out of the vehicle but stand with the door open. After leaving sick last week, I don't want to be late for the Monday morning meeting. Noah is always given more leeway since he's in marketing, has a penis, and isn't related to one of the owners of the company.

Go him!

He's got the trifecta for earning my father's respect. I roll my eyes but then realize I'm off in my head instead of appreciating my amazing life here. "Thank you for taking him."

"No problem at all."

"I love you guys."

Noah stretches across Max's car seat, reaching for me. Our hands connect, and he says, "I love you so much, Liv."

It's always too easy to get caught up in him. I need to go, though, or I'll be late, and I don't want to hear a snide comment from my dad in front of everyone. Or privately, for that matter.

Wearing his words like armor to protect me from the outside world, I step away from the car and close the door. I stay there, waving as they drive away.

When I turn around, my dad is standing there. Staring at me.

My breath catches in my throat. My palms begin to sweat. His silence is unnerving. His unflinching glare has me wanting to do anything to make him blink to break the anger in his face. "I can ex—"

He turns away and enters the building, leaving me on the sidewalk.

"Dad?" I run after him, swinging the door that he didn't leave open for me.

The lobby bustles at rush hour, people cutting between us as I hurry after him. I bump into another lady and duck to the left before a delivery guy sideswipes me.

I see him ahead, stepping into an elevator, so I race and hop in before the doors close. It's packed, and he's at the back while I'm stuck in the front. The music plays too softly above our heads. I swear that everybody in the elevator can hear my heart pounding.

In the reflection of the metal doors, I see my dad leaning his head against the back wall. His eyes are closed, and although he's skilled at holding his neutral expression, he can't seem to hide his distress.

It's the most human I think I've ever seen him.

The doors open, and I step out to let a grouping of others off on the fifth floor before getting back on. Glancing at the buttons, we have two more stops before we reach ours. This time, when I look in the reflection, I'm hit with his disappointment. He doesn't blink, leaving no room to misinterpret his feelings.

I look away, tilting my head to ease the knot forming at the base of my neck. The doors open, and I step out again until another three people have exited.

One more floor before we're alone.

My mind rolls through a million excuses I can tell him, including apologies said right afterward. But those won't work. I won't lie anymore. Max and Noah deserve more. They always have, but I was too scared to lose my dad . . .

Dad? It's all wrong when placed as a representation of my father.

He's never been my dad, not like Noah is to Max. I smile, remembering how Noah chased him like a goblin through the apartment last night and how our home came to life with laughter echoing through it. I relish how my fight-or-flight response is gone when we're holding hands and walking through the park. Max sits tall on his shoulders, wearing his aviator sunglasses, and Noah wraps his other hand around his son's back.

I'm unable to hide my grin when I think back to the naughty bath Noah and I took last night that was anything but clean.

The elevator dings at the next stop, and the doors slide open for the last time. Other people's presence will no longer restrain my father's temper, so I'm not sure what will happen, but I'm done caring. It's too much of a burden to carry any longer.

This time, I step to the opposite side of my father, and the last two people leave. I don't beg for his attention or for him to speak to me when the doors close. I know he'll never give me that upper hand. It will be on his terms and only his in the end.

The end? Is that what this is?

Caught in a silent standoff, I don't even look at him. I'm twenty-seven, but he still treats me like I'm ten. How sad that my memories with him only contain bad times.

The elevator alerts us to our floor just before the doors open. He storms forward, making me flinch backward, and grits through his teeth, "My office. Now."

He's already through the main doors before I brush down my skirt and step off the elevator. Exhaling, I take one step. Two. Just keep moving. As if my day can't get worse, Audrina sings, "Someone's in trouble." Her cackling belongs in a Halloween movie, not the office.

I make a mistake when I look up. She adds, "Maybe he's come to his senses." Her eyes flashing with joy over my demise sends my blood pressure to outer space.

"You're a horrible person, Audrina." I walk to the door, knowing I should have never given her an ounce of my attention.

She stands, her sharp claws tapping against the reception desk. "You're pathetic, Olivia."

My feet stop without my permission, but running on adrenaline, I've never seen my situation clearer than I did downstairs. I have been living my best life outside the office for months and my worst in the confines of these walls for years. "You're right."

"I'm right?" She laughs again as she flops back in her chair, and mutters, "So pathetic."

"I've been pathetic for putting up with my father's, Chip's, and your insults, and the bitterness of this office for too long. God, way too long. But no more. If you think you have won, like you've finally run me off, you haven't. You and I both know whether I'm here or working elsewhere, my happiness is limitless while your lot in life is set."

She huffs, crossing her arms over her chest. "What are you talking about?"

"Let's get into it, shall we? Let's lay the cards on the table." I lean against the tall counter, overlooking her seated below. "You thought sleeping with Chip would lead to a life of luxury. Did he offer the world to you in bed and then ignore you afterward? That's his MO, Audrina, and you fell for it."

"You realize he chose me over you?"

"To fuck. *Nothing more. I* was offered the ring, the life, the future that was never attainable by you. You know why? Because he doesn't love anyone but himself. He's a user. He used me, and he used you. Instead of becoming allies, or friends even, you chose his side and made me the enemy. You've bashed me for years to anyone who would listen. Why is that?"

She remains speechless. By how her mouth hangs open and her breath is coming heavy, I think I hit a nerve. I say, "I know why. It was easier to hate me than yourself for falling for his lies." I don't feel better after all these years of imagining this takedown. I feel worse. *How did I end up here?* Arguing with another woman about something that doesn't even matter to me anymore?

This is not who I am. It's not who I want to be.

Audrina's still silent as if she never knew the truth. I look to the side, wondering what I thought victory would be like. *Not this.*

"He told me you were cheating on him." When I look at her, she says, "He told me your relationship was nothing more than a business arrangement. And I believed him because that was the only way I could look at myself in the mirror for what I had done to another woman."

There's so much pain wrapped in her words and filling her eyes that I can only think to say, "I'm sorry. I'm sorry for how he treated you. You didn't deserve to be a victim of his lies."

She stands on unsteady legs, holding the counter for support. With tears rushing the corners of her eyes, she takes a breath before shaking her head. "I didn't deserve to be lied to, but you didn't deserve that either. You didn't cheat, did you?"

"No." I lean forward. "But you know what? I didn't love him either. I would have never called it a business arrangement, but I think this company played a big part in it. I think we were trying to please our fathers, but we only hurt ourselves and each other." Reaching forward, I offer her my hand.

She takes it, and that brings a small smile back to her face. It's funny how pretty she is when she's not full of hatred. Her shoulders have softened along with the corners of her eyes. "What do you say we start over?"

I nod, and reply, "I'd like that."

"Yeah?" Hope lifts her features.

"Definitely." When we release each other, I add, "Not sure how long I'll be working here, though."

"We always have outside of work."

"True." I glance at my watch. "You should get going to

the meeting. I've been summoned to my father's office. I suspect I'll be fired."

"Oh," she says, opening the door for me. "What'd you do? Break a rule?"

I laugh, and the feeling is so freeing from the tension long held between us. I walk into the office and turn around, walking backward. "Rules were meant to be broken."

She's smiling when I turn back to go to my father's office. I don't know what's come over me, but I guess it's time to face my problems head-on. I couldn't have asked for a better outcome with Audrina. We should have had it out years ago. We could have been friends this whole time.

I round the corner and see his assistant at her desk. "Hi, Jennifer. I've been summoned." I can't not laugh. I'm high on life right now, and whatever happens next, happens. So be it. When the time comes, I'll deal with the fallout.

Lowering her voice, she says, "He wants you in the conference room." The warning in her tone is captured, but the concern wrangling her expression is what incites fear.

She's usually in the meetings, so that means he had her stay just to lead me to the slaughter. Not that Jennifer would do anything to hurt me. She's just doing as she's told. But no matter how I look at this demand from him, it doesn't look good for me. On top of it, he wants witnesses.

Just breathe, Liv.

"Thank you." I walk back down the hall and drop my purse off in my office, thinking I need to have my hands free. I don't know why. It's not like I'm getting in a fistfight or anything. I feel more lithe and ready to go, though.

When I push through the conference room door, my eyes land on my dad. Chip is perched to his right, where I usually sit, looking proud as a peacock. The weight of stares falls on me when my dad says, "Stand there, Olivia."

The door swings closed, and by the looks of it, there's nowhere for me to go anyway. It just bugs me that standing here equals obedience. I shift a few feet to the left. I'd shift farther, but then I'd be standing in front of others.

The room is silent until my father stands. "What happens when someone breaks the rules?" Quiet murmuring rumbles through the room. His eyes return to me. "Olivia?"

"I don't know, *Mr.* Bancroft. What happens to them because I've never seen anything happen to anyone other than me."

"Explain."

Why are we even playing this game? I'm his daughter, his only child, and he's willing to throw away the last shred of a relationship we have left? For what? To impress his employees with his domineering show of force? Narcissism?

I've spent my entire life trying to please him. He's not going to change. But I will. "You didn't promote me because I broke up with Chipper for cheating on me." I glance at Chip, whose smile tightens into a line.

"I broke up with you," he snaps.

"Technically, you begged me to take you back, and when I said I needed time away from you to think, you told me you didn't want to see me anymore." I eye him, not giving an inch. "I was a fool for even considering that maybe there was a possibility we could work out. I'm not that naive anymore. We were never good. We were terrible together. All of it. Just terrible. And you know how I know?"

I look around the room at the jaws gaping open, the pride in the women's eyes, and then my father, who looks . . . neutral. No emotion at all.

My gaze pivots to land in friendly territory. *Leanna.*

As Noah's assistant, she's become a friend to him. I know

we have kept our personal lives private, but her boundless support of Noah has helped him so much. So if I trusted one person in this office, it's her.

"I've found love. Real love. Soul deep, it hurts to be apart, love."

Leanna's face glows with her smile reaching her eyes. She knows.

With the room stunned in silence, I look back at Chip to say, "I'm not telling you this to get a dig in or to hurt you. I'm telling you because I deserved happiness when you gave me none. I deserved honesty when you chose to be deceitful. I deserved my dad to believe me instead of taking your side. You marketed yourself perfectly and got all the accolades, including my father's love. But I won in the end because I found true love." I take a breath and tell my father, "When my life was falling apart, you made a new employee handbook and added a policy that I've now violated. But you know what? I don't care. I'm tired of living my life in shame that you cast upon me. I should have never hidden what matters most to me to keep your reputation from being stained. I have a son."

An audible gasp fills the room, but I don't let it stop me. There's no stopping me now, anyway. It's too late, so I might as well walk out of here, placing the disgrace square on his shoulders where it should have been all along.

It had become so easy to separate my professional life from my personal life. So shame never followed me anywhere. It wasn't something I felt over having a one-night stand or having a kid on my own. So I guess he tried to place it on me, but it didn't stick after all. It just took me a while to realize it.

Since I've been dying to share the news since before he was born, I continue, "My son is seventeen months old and is the light of my life. He's my heart, and for you to deny your grandson the love he's owed unconditionally makes you the bad guy." I shrug. "I guess you always were, though."

"What a speech," my father says, sarcasm dripping from his words. "You've made our lives a spectacle, humiliating yourself and me. You've attacked others while pretending to be the victim. So tell me, *Ms.* Bancroft, as you sully *my* surname in the mud, what do you want from me?"

Want? Wanted is more like it.

I have a mom who fought this demon to be in my life, a man who has shown me the definition of fatherhood and is a true partner to me. And Max. I have a son whose sunshine cleared away the clouds of damage that my own father had inflicted. So I don't want anything from him anymore, especially not his approval. "Nothing," I reply.

I take a breath knowing that's not all I want to say.

This is it . . .

"I quit."

36

Noah

THIRTY MINUTES EARLIER . . .

WE'VE BEEN LIVING in a bubble of bliss.

But everyone knows that bubbles aren't meant to last. *They always burst.*

Cassandra's vet running behind threw us out of our routine. Liv's and my mornings have been full of rushing around to throw Max's bag together and call a car to transport us across town in rush-hour traffic. Taking him to her place last minute was not in the game plan when I woke up.

It won't do me any good to stress about what I can't control. We both know that everyone in the office will judge her before me, so I'm glad she made it almost on time.

When I hop back in the car, I pull out my phone as soon as we leave the curb to text her:

The package has been delivered.

Laughing, I wait for her reply to basically tell me how hilarious I am and pepper me with compliments about how entertaining that text was. Okay, she doesn't give compliments out like candy. She doles them out when there's truth in them. It's one of the things I love most about her—her honesty. I thought it was funny, though.

The three dots don't show up.

Although I know the meeting has started by now, I check the time anyway. She sits next to her father. When I entered that conference room on my first day of work, I thought it was a position of power. *It's not.* It's her father's way of exerting control over her. He makes her sit while he praises everyone else, and he never has to look her in the eyes to see the pain he's caused.

Fucker.

I scroll through my emails to make the most of my time and find the new Torres contract sitting in my inbox. I grin, ready to wrap negotiations and get started on their campaign. The car jolts to a stop, causing me to look up. Bumper-to-bumper traffic. *Fuck.* "How bad is the traffic ahead?"

The driver looks at me in the rearview mirror. "There's an accident blocking all lanes."

"Any way we can detour?"

"You mean us and every other New Yorker with some place to be at eight thirty in the morning?" Despite the chaos this morning, I'm in a decent mood, but I'm not sure it's good enough to appreciate his sarcasm.

"Yeah, maybe worth a try," I reply, certain I won't make the end of the meeting, even if we do find another way around this mess.

He laughs, not bothering to reply. Since we're not

moving at all anymore, I drop it altogether, but I do send another text to Liv:

> Stuck in traffic. Be there when I can.
> Love you.

And then send the same to Leanna to keep her in the loop, leaving off the love part, of course. Even though Liv might be too busy to respond, I expect Leanna to. When she doesn't, I start to wonder what's going on. That's not like her.

I lean over to look out the windshield once more. We're still not moving, spiking my body temperature. I'm not letting irritation win, so I start reading through the contract to distract myself. At least I can claim I was working. Two pages in and I spot the first issue. Within the first four pages, I've highlighted three problems, issues that will backfire on me if I sign these.

In the three months I've worked at Bancroft & Lowe, this account is the only one with endless red flags. *Why is that?* My only theory remains that this was Leslie's account before Chip was added to it. Leslie left six months later. She was called a spy and rumored to be working for the competition. I'm starting to believe those rumors are lies, and Chip's the culprit behind this sabotage.

Look what rumors have done to Liv's career at Bancroft & Lowe. Did they do the same to Leslie's?

I google Leslie's name, then read the most recent articles and work my way back to the time when she left. She went to the competition all right. The timeline aligns with what I heard. As for secretly working for them, that story doesn't appear to match on the surface. She was a star at Bancroft & Lowe and managed their biggest accounts along with Mr. Bancroft. *So what went wrong?*

I'm not sure I should be doing this, but I find her

number online and call. I'm sent straight to voicemail. I leave a message, "Hi, my name is Noah Westcott. I work for Bancroft & Lowe. I'm hoping you can help answer some questions I have regarding an account for Torres Manufacturing. You were running the account, successfully from what I've seen, and then were partnered with Chip Lowe. There are some holes I'm trying to fill. Since I was assigned the client, the NDA no longer stands. I'd appreciate a call back if you'd be willing to talk confidentially. Thank you."

Although I'd wish I could have spoken to her, I'm also not naive enough to think she'd be open to telling me anything negative. I'm sure she's washed her hands of Bancroft & Lowe and doesn't want to stir up old ghosts.

I've successfully put off the inevitable, but it's time for me to figure out my next step. I make the call to my attorney, who specializes in corporate law.

"Do you need bail money?" Loch asks without so much as a hello. It's like we're brothers or something. *Ha!* He clearly knows me well.

"It's Monday morning. Why would I need bail money?"

"It was Monday morning the last time as well." My brother's coming in strong with the jokes today.

"That was a joke."

"What do you mean it was a joke? I wired you a thousand dollars."

"Oops, about that—"

"Fucking hell, Noah." His puff of breath fills the phone, and I can imagine he's rubbing his temple to ease the headache I'm bringing on.

"Don't worry, I'll pay you back with interest." We've been moving slowly, but I look out the windshield again as if things are different from that angle. Unfortunately, they're not.

"I have a better idea." I like the turnaround in his tone. He says, "Tuesday really wants a baby."

"Sorry, I'm already in a committed relationship, so I can't give your wife a baby."

"Real funny, asshole. Hear me laughing." *Spoiler alert:* I did not, *in fact*, hear him laughing. I still chuckle because that was damn funny. "She wants to babysit Max."

"As far as paybacks go, I don't think she understands how babysitting works. Usually the *parents* pay the person to watch their kid. Not the reverse."

"Forget about the bail money, Noah. Will you let her spend time with Max? She wants a baby, so maybe that will help until she gets pregnant."

Loch has always been the most uptight of my siblings. He says it's because he had to be the responsible one. He's probably right. But this also provides a lot of opportunities to fuck with him. "Babysitting doesn't actually produce a baby of your own." *God, I love teasing him.* "Did Dad never go over the birds and bees with you?"

"I'm hanging up the phone."

I'd almost forgotten why I called him. "Wait. Loch?"

"I'm busy."

"I think I was hired to take the fall in a money laundering scheme."

I hear him sigh heavily, but being the awesome older brother he is, he calls out, "Leisa, reschedule my next call." There's a pause, but then he says to me, "We have five minutes. Did you do anything illegal?"

"No."

"Good," he replies, his tone turning firm. I imagine it's the same one he uses in court—all business and no fun. "Send me one thousand dollars electronically. That payment will establish the attorney-client relationship,

S.L. SCOTT

and you can pay the rest of the retainer when we hang up."

I send the money, listing what it's for to document everything. "It's done."

"Received. Okay, listen to me. Everything you tell me from this point on is protected by attorney-client privilege. What dirt do they have on you?"

"None. Dirty business belongs in the bedroom, not the boardroom." Some progress is finally being made with traffic moving again, but not enough to celebrate.

"If found guilty, a money laundering conviction can lead to substantial prison time."

"Are we talking country club prison or doing hard time?"

"This is serious, Noah. Manhattan district attorneys don't fuck around with their charges. Not that I can't beat them, but it's always better not to end up with the charges in the first place."

I hear what he's saying, but levity is necessary when I probably should have quit as soon as I found out. Now, I'm mixed up in this mess. "Look, I've known about this for months, but I didn't quite have all the pieces."

"Now you do?"

"No, but I have enough to see what's happening."

"Who else knows? Liv? She's in accounting. Does she know, or can she be implicated?"

This isn't my world, but I'm starting to realize that the associations alone can destroy our lives. *Fucking hell.* "They've circumvented her on these expenses. Her father approved them, but her name is on there as well because she has to enter them into the system."

"That's not good."

Max and I can't lose her. I won't let her take the fall. I'll do anything necessary to keep my family together.

He says, "I need to know what I'm dealing with. Is your name on any of the documents?"

"My name is clean, but I'm expected to sign the contracts I just received. That's why I called you."

"Don't sign anything. And if you have proof, you need to send electronic copies to yourself through email. It's free protection. That provides a date and time stamp if they go in and alter the documents. Though an x-ray audit can find all the traces of changes made to prove they were doing a cover-up. Your documents add to the evidence." His sobering tone should worry me, but I know I haven't done anything to contribute to wrongdoing in this case. "Do you plan to blow the whistle?"

"Do I have a choice?"

"You have a choice. Between right and wrong, saving yourself the trouble and moving on, or even ignoring, though I wouldn't advise the last one."

"So you're saying I don't?"

"I can't legally advise you on that aspect as it could blow back on me. An anonymous tip could always be left, a file leaked. Dad is almost retired, but I imagine he'd keep things legally off the record if you want his advice."

"And you can't?"

"I have a career ahead of me, a law firm to run, and a family to take care of. As your brother, what I can say is that you don't owe anybody anything. You can walk today and let it come out another way. Unfortunately, you could also be dragged back into this mess years from now. How the law views what you should report is not the same thing as telling you to go live life without reporting a crime."

"So I'm fucked?"

"No. You didn't do anything." There's an extended pause before he says, "But Liv needs an attorney. Today."

I scrub my hand over my face. "I've kept her out of the details to spare her from this shit." I'm mad at myself for even hinting at an issue with her. It may have been earlier on in discovery, but that could infer she was aware.

"If her name is on there, they'll go after her."

"We have to protect her, Loch."

"Let's get her representation and on record with her knowledge. I'll take her case if she chooses to work with me. The best thing we can do is get ahead of this. That means she becomes the whistleblower."

Fuck me.

"I appreciate the help," I reply, dropping my head back. "I'll have her contact you."

To make things official with my brother, I pay the full retainer he charges, and he tells me exactly what to do when I walk into the office.

Little did I know what I was walking into . . .

37

Noah

Audrina looks up from her desk with an earpiece in place. "Good morning, Noah."

"Morning." She's not someone I generally spare time to spend on because I know she's behind a lot of the nasty behavior toward Liv the past few years.

"I'm getting reports that the meeting is quite eventful this morning."

I stop and look back. "Eventful how?"

"The Bancrofts have declared war on each other." Her phone rings. She raises a finger, but before she answers it, she adds, "I'm rooting for Olivia to win. Mr. Bancroft is an asshole."

Rooting for Liv? *What the fuck?*

Whatever Mr. Bancroft did, it must be bad if she's on Liv's side. This just made things a whole lot more complicated. I push through the door and rush to the conference room. No yelling is heard upon approach. That's a good sign. But when I open the door, I hear my girl say, "I quit you, and I quit Bancroft & Lowe. Forever."

Liv and I see each other at the same time, a million words exchanged without a single one said. I have no idea what happened in the past hour since I dropped her off at the curb, but holy shit. *She just quit.* I'm sorry to have missed what led to this turn of events, but the pride I feel is extensive.

Her father says, "What's the agenda for today? Where's Jennifer?" He looks around, carrying on like his daughter hasn't spoken and ignoring me as if I'm not here at all.

Shit. I run my hand through my hair. "I'm late," I say, only sorry I wasn't here sooner in support of my girlfriend. "Traffic jam this morning."

Chip sits forward. "I made it on time."

Mr. Bancroft says, "This meeting is over. I'll speak to you privately in my office, Mr. Westcott."

People are running for the door to get out. Now my curiosity has piqued to what transpired over the past hour. I turn to Liv, and ask, "What'd I miss?"

"Uh." She laughs once, but there's no humor found in it. "My father was finally honest with me."

"In front of everyone?"

"I went down in flames." I move closer to her, and she says, "But I gave the soliloquy of my life before burning the bridge entirely."

I'm struggling to read how she's feeling inside based on her bewildered eyes. "Tell me what happened."

"I'll share with you later." She moves to grip the back of a chair that was abandoned. "I think I need to sit."

"Nice try, muffin top," Chip says, coming around to poke her in the side. What the fuck? He starts laughing. *AT* her . .
.

I punch him in the face, sending his ass to the floor. "Touch her again, jackface, and you won't be walking."

"What the—Fuck, you broke my jaw." He stares at me in disbelief, wiggling his jaw back and forth, obviously not broken. "You're going down, Westcott."

"It's not broken if you're still yapping, dumb fuck." Liv comes to me, grabbing hold of my hand and not giving a fuck who sees us anymore. Since we're blowing it all up anyway, I might as well light another match . . . "It's all in good fun, right, Chipper?"

God, it feels good to throw that asshole's words back in his face. I start for the door with Liv tucked under my arm. "Let's get you out of here."

"How's your hand?" From the sound of her voice, the shock has worn off, which is good. We can focus on getting her out of here.

I flex my hand several times. They're stiff, but my fingers still work. "Nothing to worry about."

Double stepping to keep pace with me, she asks, "What are we doing? Where are we going?"

I open the door to her office and pull her in, quickly shutting it behind us and locking it. "Grab whatever you want to keep as fast as you can."

"He's not going to throw me out."

"Yes, they will want us out as soon as possible." I rush to her desk and activate the screen. "I promise to explain everything, but we don't have time now." Pulling the chair out for her, I say, "Send everything you've ever worked on to the cloud."

"Huh? And who's they?"

"Please, Liv. Just do it. Okay?"

She sits down and starts typing. "My cloud or the company cloud?"

"Do you have access to yours?"

"Yeah. I work at home sometimes, so I pull from my cloud."

"Yes," I say, grinning. "That's good. Send it all to your cloud."

She's typing while I grab a box of copy paper and dump it on the floor. I take her diploma off the wall and the knick-knacks on the console behind her. She spins toward me and says, "Done. Now what?"

"Grab your stuff, and then I want you out of here. Go straight home and download everything from the cloud that you just uploaded to your laptop. Okay?"

"Okay?" She gets up, scrambling to go through the drawers and cabinets.

"I have business to handle with your father."

"What's happening, Noah?"

I shake my head. It's not something I can answer other than I'm not returning to this office either. Until this plays out, I don't know the repercussions of what will happen. I kiss her and then turn, but then turn around and kiss her again, cupping her face, and loving her through gentle stroking and our unbreakable connection. "I love you, babe," I say, hoping she feels only that and not the fear beginning to fill her eyes.

"I love you."

"Two minutes and I want you out of here."

I leave her there, closing the door behind me, and go around the pit of cubicles to get to my office. Leanna stands. "Noah, what's going—"

"I'm sorry. Not now."

I rush to my desk and send everything I have on the Torres's account through multiple emails to my personal account. The files are huge, so I stare, waiting until they show "sent."

Leanna knocks and then walks in. "What can I do?"

My gaze shoots straight to her. "Nothing. I don't want you involved."

"Okay," she says without hesitation. "That sounds bad, so I'll stick to what you missed in the meeting. You and Liv are a couple, and Liv has a child."

"She said all that?"

"She didn't name you, but she didn't have to for me. I knew. As for the child, wow. My mind is blown, but it makes sense. She left for that year. She was having to hide from these office piranhas. I feel terrible that I wasn't there for her. That I couldn't help in some way."

"Sent." I stand and start pulling out stuff from the drawers. I didn't have much so I'm not worried about leaving most of this crap behind. A card from my parents, my Mont Blanc pen, and not much else. Standing, I say, "You don't need to feel badly. Here's the truth. I'm in love with her. We live together, and we're raising our—"

"Olivia!"

Bancroft's voice explodes in the distance, traveling through the open door. I throw the stuff on the desk and run toward the sound.

I blink, not understanding what I'm seeing; Cassandra holding Max in her arms, the stroller behind her. Liv yanks her arm from her father's grip, dropping the box, and rushing toward them. As the entire office bears witness to this catastrophe in the making, everyone standing like witnesses to a car wreck, I run.

Liv's cheeks are streaked with red lines from crying, she takes our son and hugs him to her. Max sees me over her shoulder and holds out his arms. "Dada."

Time stood still.

And then collides us back to reality.

Audrina is the first to speak. "Dada?"

"Are you fucking kidding me with this?" Chip asks, "Is that my kid?"

Breathe. Just breathe ...

Liv and Max are my priority, the ones I need to protect. When I reach them, I slide my hand around her lower back and kiss her forehead. "I'll get your stuff. Take him and meet me downstairs."

The silence around us is profound.

The heat of stares is like a spotlight set on fire.

I lift Max from her arms, hugging him to me and giving him a kiss. He's not scared, which is good, considering the circumstances surrounding us. "Hey, buddy," I whisper.

Smiling like his day has been made, he touches my face and blows raspberries against my cheek. "Dada, Dada."

The light shines through my clouded view, my son reminding me of what really matters. I set him in the stroller and strap him in securely. "I love you."

I look up at Cassandra, who is pale and her eyes distraught as she scans the room. She's chanting, "I'm so sorry."

Liv reaches out to touch her shoulder. "You didn't know."

I reply, "It's okay, Cassandra."

She nods and reaches for the stroller, but Liv smiles. "I've got him." Leaning toward me, she lifts and gives me a kiss. "I'll see you downstairs."

Chip comes toward us. "Wait, if that's my kid—"

The palm of my hand keeps him from progressing. "He's not your kid. He's mine."

Yanking himself away, he goes to stand next to Bancroft and crosses his arms over his chest. "How's he your kid? You just met her a few months ago."

I'm not going to justify jack shit to this guy. Neither Liv nor I owe him a damn fucking thing.

Her father, on the other hand . . . "You dating my daughter doesn't give you the right to make claims over my grandson, the grandchild who carries *my* last name."

"You're right," I start. "Dating your daughter doesn't give me that right." I temper what I want to say because again, they aren't owed any part of our lives—past or present. *But in my defense . . .* "Fathering her child does."

"What are you talking about, Westcott? And you better choose your words wisely."

Liv's framed diploma shattered on the floor brings things into perspective. Bending down, I gather the things that fell from the box and stand up again. "You've wasted so many chances to be in that amazing woman's life. You'll never be given that opportunity again. And I hope you got a good fucking look at our son because it will be over my dead body that you ever see him again." I start to leave but then turn back once more. I flip my middle finger right the fuck up, holding it steady in front of his face, and say, "Consider this my two weeks' notice."

I see Leanna across the room, giving her a slight lift of my hand from the box as a goodbye as I leave. Audrina holds the door open for me, and I say, "Thanks."

"Good luck to you and Liv."

"Thanks."

Liv, Max, and Cassandra are standing in the lobby. Liv smiles when she sees me, weakened by the toll the morning has taken, and then shrugs. "So much for fast getaways." The elevator chimes, signaling its arrival. She laughs. "Figures."

We load on, and as the doors close, she sees the box. "Thanks for getting that." There's not much in it, but she's eyeing the items. "That's all I have after eleven years of working here."

"Stuff doesn't matter," I say. "It's the experience. The right to look back and know that this place brought us together again."

Coming to stand next to me, she leans her head on my shoulder and releases a breath. "I have no job, no money, no father."

I reach over and hold her against me. Kissing her head, I keep my mouth close to her. "You have Max. You have me—"

"And me," Cassandra says, raising a hand.

I catch Liv in the reflection smiling. She reaches out, and Cassandra takes her hand. "Thank you. You have us, too." Their hands fall apart after a few seconds of needed reassurance.

Liv's eyes find mine in the mirrored doors, and she asks, "How will we survive?"

I turn her chin and angle so we're looking at each other. Anchoring the box under one arm, I touch her scarred eyebrow with my free hand. I run the tip of my finger across it several times and leave a kiss there. "You've been left adrift at sea before, and you survived. You'll survive this, too. *We* will. *Together this time.*"

The elevator dings, opening onto a lower floor. A guy I recognize steps into the elevator, all big teeth and bigger grin. "Hey, remember me. Halden Myers? Olivia, right?"

Fuck me.

This guy again.

He snaps his fingers and points at me. "And Noah."

"Yep," I reply, not in the mood for this. "Look, buddy, when we met—"

"Halden. Nice to meet you," he says to Cassandra.

She perks up. "Cassandra Simons."

With my arm still around Liv, I decide to shut my mouth and let this play out.

By the time we reach the sidewalk, they've exchanged numbers and set up a date. Guess he's not so bad after all.

After ordering an SUV to take us home, Cassandra says, "I really am sorry about coming here." She digs a phone out of her backpack. "I found Liv's phone in Max's bag and thought you might need it." She hands the phone to Liv.

That would explain her not replying to my texts, though I think other reasons would have stopped her even if she'd had it in that meeting.

Liv says, "Thank you. And as for coming there, you didn't know not to because I never told you how . . . how messy my work-life situation was. I didn't want to involve other people unnecessarily."

The SUV pulls to the curb, and we load inside. On the way back to the apartment, they talk while I text Loch everything that just happened.

He texts my entire family's group:

Westcott FM statim.

"Noah?" I look at Liv, and she asks, "Are we going to be okay?"

I reach over, cradling her knee in the palm of my hand. "We're going to be fine. I promise."

"Isn't stat short for statim in Latin?"

Loch's code is our family's secret phrase. It's to the point without being too obvious. If you know, you know, though. Glancing back at the text, I reply, "Yes."

She's searching my eyes, and asks, "What does FM stand for?"

"Family meeting."

"You're meeting your family?"

I give her leg a little squeeze. "We are. As soon as we get home, we need to pack our bags and head out."

"Where are we going?"

The emergency signal was sent, and the replies are trickling in. No one questions. They provide their ETAs because this is what we do. We never let one of our own fall, and Liv is one of us now. "Beacon."

38

Noah

WE RENTED AN SUV, and I drove us back to Beacon. Since Loch and Tuesday, Lark and Harbor are flying in together, I thought it was best to get on the road instead of waiting for the helicopter to retrieve us. It also gave me time to think and sort through what just happened.

There were so many topics to cover with Liv that I almost didn't know where to begin. I just want her safe.

At a gas station about an hour from my parents' home, she was coming out of the store with Max wrapped around her front like a monkey and a bag in her hands. I left the vehicle and hurried to help her, happily taking that little monkey. Max clung to me the same. It's been a long and busy day even though it's only early afternoon.

Walking back, I say, "We need to talk about the meeting."

"I wanted to ask but didn't know if it was my business."

I stop in front of the SUV, staring at her in disbelief. "You don't get it, do you?"

"What? What are we talking about?"

"Us, Liv. We're talking about us." Rubbing Max's back, I look into her hazel eyes that stirred more than my libido that night in the Hamptons. They woke me up entirely. I knew then that I'd never be the same after meeting her, and that's come to fruition. "My business is your business, and I hope you feel the same. I have nothing to hide from you. You can check my phone. You can spy on me. You can riddle me with questions about my whereabouts, but you won't find anything incriminating because I love you, and we're in this together. To me, our lives have already become one."

She opens her mouth and then closes it again, choosing to wrap her arms around us instead. I wasn't planning on saying all that, but I'm glad it's out there, and she knows how I truly feel about her. "I love you so much."

I wrap a forearm around her, kiss her on the side of the head, and then whisper, "I should have saved that. It would have been a great proposal speech."

Bursting out laughing, she steps back and nods. She wipes under her eyes as the tears breach her lids. "That would have been." She's still laughing when she says, "I'm glad you didn't. I don't want our proposal story to start with, 'We started pumping the gas . . .'"

Chuckling, I say, "I wholeheartedly agree."

We get back into the SUV, and once we settle in, she says, "You really meant that."

I look at her as she stares out the window, seemingly deep in thought by her faraway gaze. She turns toward me and says, "Every man I've ever known has let me down, except for you. Not once have you questioned anything I've told you. You never even asked for a paternity test. You just stepped in and became Max's dad." She takes an unwavering breath. "You stepped into my life like we were made for each other. Your perseverance and dedication have been nothing less than incredible to witness and receive. I don't know why you were in the Hamptons the night we met, but I'm so glad you were." She leans over to kiss me, but I will always go the distance for her. Our lips meet, and though it's short, it says so much more about her commitment to me.

Max squeals at the top of his lungs, startling us and causing us to both look back at him. I ask, "What is it, buddy?"

Kicking his feet, he laughs, looking back and forth between us. Liv says, "Oh, I know what he wants." She reaches for the bag she bought and pulls out an applesauce pouch. She sets him up, and he's fast to take it and to start sucking that goodness down. Glancing at Liv, we share the same amused smile—one of love and pride, joy and appreciation. Content in the moment.

Although I'm aware of the trouble ahead, I let her revel in the feeling for the time being. Whatever lies ahead, we'll tackle it together.

"First, let me just say that I don't think anyone can deny this kid is mine. Just look at how handsome he is."

When she begins to laugh, I relish the sound. "No, there really is no denying it."

I lean closer again. "And secondly, I will always be a man you can depend on. I will do anything for you, babe. Thirdly, we fit like a glove together. Not just sexually, though that too, but soulfully. I have no doubts that you're my other half."

Melting against the seat, she sighs so sweetly. When she pops up suddenly, she playfully rolls her eyes. "Dammit, you just one-upped me again."

I shrug. "Oops, sorry."

The tips of her nails scratch gently along the back of my neck. "It's okay. I'm happy to be romanced by you any day."

We share another quick kiss. I'm about to shift into drive, but a voicemail notification pops up on my phone. I play it back. *Fuck.* I missed a call back from Leslie. I push play and hold the phone to my ear. "Hello, I'm returning your call. Unfortunately, I won't be available to answer any questions regarding the Torres account, Bancroft & Lowe, or Chip Lowe. If you have further inquiries, you can contact my attorney, David Speckle at Speckle Manhattan. Good luck."

I look back at the screen, wondering why I would need to contact her attorney to ask her questions . . . *And then it dawns on me.*

"Everything okay?" Liv asks, settling in next to me.

Since I have a few attorneys in the family, I know if someone redirects you to their lawyer, they have something to hide. I put my phone down and shift into drive. "All good."

My brother is the best attorney in the city with an impressive track record. I'd trust him with my life, but more importantly, I trust him with the love of my life's entire future. Her life is what matters most.

Liv plays peek-a-boo with Max until he falls asleep in his car seat. She angles forward again and says, "Fear has always been a driving force behind so many of the major decisions I've made."

"What did I miss?" I ask as the statement hits me out of the blue.

"I was always trying to please my father and not disappoint him. I followed a path I desperately wanted him to approve of and dated a vile excuse of a man because I knew it would make my father happy. I even stayed at the company and endured so many years of toxicity for fear of losing him." She laughs, but I haven't missed the tremble in her tone.

Nothing I can say will give her back the time she's lost trying to win his love. I'll do what I can to help her recover from him, though. "Most people would have stopped trying a long time ago. You have such a loving heart, Liv. It's his loss that he'll never get to experience your sunshine."

I find she nods when she's too overwhelmed to speak. She looks down at her fidgeting fingers and takes a few shallow breaths. "Everything I do now is with Max at the forefront of my decisions." Turning to me, she adds, "If anything bad ever happened to him—"

"I'll never let that happen."

She pulls her knees to her chest and wraps her arms around her legs. "Or if anything happens to me . . ." She allows that to lie between us long enough for me to know she's worried.

Liv is an intelligent woman. She can connect the dots from this morning without me guiding her through each step. I reach over and take her hand in mine, our fingers falling together. "Nothing will happen to you, Liv."

"The sudden emergency meeting with your family has to do with the files I sent to the cloud."

I once omitted some details of what was happening in the office to protect her. I can't do that again. I won't. She needs to know everything, but the only way we can make sure she's as protected as Max is to have the full picture of what's been happening. "Yes."

She goes quiet, eventually dropping her feet back to the floorboard again. Turning on some music, she keeps the volume low enough for me to hear her say, "I'll cooperate."

There's no tremble to her voice anymore. She sounds surer than I've heard her. "What do I need to do?"

Wanting Loch to represent her, I walk her through the same steps I took this morning to establish the attorney-client relationship. I feel better knowing she's being advised by the best.

WATCHING Max run free without worrying about strangers grabbing him, or invading someone else's space, or having to contain him even in the wide-open parts of Central Park rewires an aspect of my heart.

I want this for him.

I want to give him what I had growing up—the freedom to explore, to make dumb decisions without major repercussions, to know the feeling of grass under your feet, and allow him to be a kid without teaching him the rules of living in a concrete jungle.

Hell, I want that for me now.

With Tuesday playing with Max and Lark sitting near the pool, which has a new child safety fence installed around it, I turn back to the group in the living room where Loch has been going through the options with Liv. They'd met privately in my dad's office for several hours until they reached a point where the family could be included.

We are Liv's family and are all willing to do what we can to help her reach the best possible outcome.

After Liv decides to go on record and file, Loch leaves the room to call the appropriate authorities. Liv eats one of the remaining crackers from the platter on the coffee table. Food will help her think more clearly, so I'm glad she's eaten.

My mom sits beside her on the couch, saying, "I think that's the right decision, Liv. I'm just so sorry you're being forced to make it in the first place." She rubs her back. "If it helps, we'll be there for you."

"It does help to know that. Thank you, Delta." The warmth in the hug she gives my mom reaches me across the room.

Her eyes latch onto mine while a small smile crosses her mouth. She gets up and comes to me. Exhaustion has gotten the better of her pretty face, and dark circles have appeared along with her eyelids hanging a little lower. I envelop her in my arms and kiss her temple. "How do you feel?"

"Numb."

"Warranted. It's a lot, and nothing you were prepared for when you woke up this morning." I tilt my head to catch her gaze. "Why don't you nap while Loch does what he needs to do?"

"What about—"

"Max is having the time of his life. He's in good hands."

She peers out the window, and a sweet smile appears. "He slept a lot on the ride here, so it's good he's getting to run around."

Loch returns, his eyes directed on Liv. "They'll be here in the morning. Nine o'clock."

She looks up at me with questions in her eyes. "Max has his stuff for the night and so do we. We'll stay here, in my room."

Delta says, "We might have bought a few things for Max and switched up the spare room across the hall from Noah's bedroom."

My dad gets up from the couch and laughs. "It's a nursery. Max is the first of hopefully many grandkids to come. It's a better use of the space than to keep unused rooms."

The pride hitting his eyes from the thought of a whole new generation of little ones running around is one I never imagined. I wasn't even able to broach that mindset before Max. Now I'm all for it. He says to Liv, "The three of you always have a place of your own in our home."

A tear hits the front of my shirt right before she turns and walks to him. When they embrace, I realize how overwhelming it must be for her. Although I know she's touched by my parents' acceptance of her and our son and the nursery setup, just as I am, I can't help but think this is all she ever wanted from her father.

Fuck him.

She'll get all that and more from mine. My family is one hundred percent behind her.

If I don't cut in now, it will be a cry fest in here, and I think we've had enough tears for today. I say, "How about we rest before dinner?"

Harbor gets up from the barstool where he's been sitting in the kitchen. "We've got Max covered. It's uncle time."

Loch heads to the back door with him, adding, "It's time to teach our nephew the rules of basketball."

Just before the door closes, I catch Harbor saying, "I was thinking we could teach him to drive."

"They're not serious, right?" Liv rushes to ask me.

I'm honestly not sure. They can be sarcastic bastards, but they might not be joking. I catch her hand just as she starts for the door. "He'll be okay and probably have the time of his life. Don't worry, they'll take care of him."

She looks between the door and me a couple of times before she exhales. "You're right."

"Nap?"

That wipes the concern right off her face. "Yes, please."

I should have figured she'd be more invested in

exploring my room than sleep. I get it. I might do the same if I was in her childhood bedroom, so I undress and climb under the covers and watch her. Even though it's been one hell of a day that's taken a toll on both of us, she's fucking gorgeous. Knowing who she is on the inside only makes our connection and the chemistry we share more potent.

So much of my life is on display that her eyes travel the walls and tops of the desk, over the shelves, and she even pokes her head in the closet. Every part of the room has been thoroughly inspected when she strips her shirt and jeans off and slips into bed next to me. Lying her head on my bare chest, she rubs the tips of her fingers over my abs. "I love seeing this part of you, babe," she says, seemingly more awake than ever.

"What do you love about it?"

"Seeing who you were before there was a we, an us. You did so much from playing baseball to working on the student foundation league for your university, president of the marketing club, and voted most likely for basically everything."

"Including stealing another guy's girlfriend."

"I pretended I didn't see that award." Her laughter breezes across my stomach. Sliding her head up next to mine, she asks, "Did you steal many girlfriends?"

Running my hand over the soft skin of her arm, I shake my head. "I wish I could say no. There were a few over the years. My thought was can you steal something if it's not yours in the first place?"

"No." Her eyes stay fixed on mine, two lines deepening between her brows. "What do you think happened to the piece of paper with my number written on it?"

"I'm not sure, but I would have called you if I could have." As I think back to that night, the connection we shared—emotionally and physically—has always over-ridden all else. I remember the moon appearing brighter than usual, the dunes built up from lack of trampling, and the wind active that night. I close my eyes, and the details become clearer.

As sleep sweeps us under, one memory shoots to the forefront. My heart starts racing just as my eyes crack open. "The duffel."

Under a drowsy haze, Liv says, "Huh?"

"Marina." I close my eyes to rub them awake and slip out from Liv's side. "Marina came to warn me that my parents were coming."

Liv pushes to her elbows to watch me rush to my closet. "What are we talking about?"

"The night we met," I reply from inside the closet. I reach up and grab the old bag I haven't used in years from the top shelf. "I woke up when Marina had come to the house to warn me my parents were going to be there short-ly." I return to the bed and set the bag down next to her legs. "You were already gone."

"Okay, but what are you doing with the bag?"

"This is the bag I used that weekend." I sit, the reason I was in the Hamptons by myself returning as well. I look at her. There's no part of me I can't share with her. The disap-pointment I felt that day comes back as if it were today. "I was asked to try out for a minor league team. It could have led to playing for the Yankees if I got pulled up to the majors."

She lies back, smiling. "Really? That's amazing. When was that?"

On the surface, people will always think the best, but knowing I failed . . . I still feel the humiliation seeping in when I fucked up my chance to play professionally. "The week we met. I had a final on the morning of tryouts. Tired from staying up to study all night, I was late to the field and performed like shit."

She sits up, resting her chin on my bicep and watching me. I look at my feet on the floor. "What eats you up most about that event?"

"I know it's nothing compared with what you endured with your father, but I'd never failed at anything before." I glance at her, and say, "I was told I had the Midas touch. Everything I touched turned to gold, especially those awards I was accrueing. I felt invincible, but track record couldn't save me. I choked when it mattered most. I failed under pressure. They cut me right after that. No second chance."

"It was one time, Noah."

I'm not sure why this is hitting me so hard. Being in my room again? Opening my heart? "That's all it took." It feels good to get this off my chest though.

"You've achieved so much to fall prey to one failure. It made you fight harder. Look at your GPA, the job offers." Her hand sways in front of her. "Look around this room at all of your success, babe."

I know my greatest success isn't in this room, but playing in the grass outside.

She asks, "I'm the first person you're telling this to?"

"My little sister was there, but we've never spoken of it."

"I love that you invited her."

"I didn't. She just knew. I don't know how. She was always in my business, but I'm glad she was there that day." I clear my throat. "Other than Marina, no one knows about the tryouts or that I went to the house in the Hamptons to get away from it all and think."

"Thank you for sharing with me. I'm sorry you didn't

make the team." Wrapping her arms around my ribs, she smiles. I chuckle and then ask, "Are you enjoying my failure?"

"No, not at all. You could have been playing professional baseball, but we would have never met. You could have your name in lights at Yankee Stadium or be Max's dad." She massages the back of my neck, and says, "Everything happened exactly how it was supposed to. You're in our lives, and we're grossly entangled in yours." She laughs to herself. "All because destiny knew where you were needed."

I caress her face and kiss this woman. And then again because I fucking want to. "You're right. I don't need thousands of fans screaming my name. I have more than I could have ever dreamed of with you two calling me your boyfriend and Dada."

Boyfriend? That's just not going to do for much longer . . .

I look deep into her eyes, always finding comfort there. "I love you."

"I love you too." She giggles. "Now what's in the bag?"

"Right." I dig my hands in the bag, stretching out the empty compartment to look inside. *Nothing.* Running my fingers along the edge of the removable base, I pop it up and search the insides.

And there it is.

I don't know how to feel—happy she left me her number or gutted that I had it all this time and didn't know. I pull it out and see her smile return. It's not smug as if she needs to rub my nose in the fact that she was right. It's relief in seeing the small piece of paper.

"I'm not sure what to say other than I'm sorry for not calling."

This time, she caresses my face. "The number didn't matter. Nothing was going to keep us apart."

39

Liv

When Loch walks into the coffee shop, I stand. I'm not sure why. Nerves? Yes, anxiety has kicked in today. I rub my hands down the front of my jeans, and ask, "How'd it go?"

"Uneventful." He finally cracks a smile resembling Noah's when caught up in the day's business. "Uneventful is good news. All three men pleaded not guilty. We didn't expect otherwise, so the cases are moving forward."

I sit down, unsure how to feel. "What does this mean?"

Loch sits, setting his briefcase on the floor beside the chair. "I ran into one of the DA's at the ballet last night. We got to talking, and they have no intention of charging you. They also have enough evidence to see how this was set up. Noah," he says, looking away and shaking his head.

Clasping my hands on my legs, I lean forward. "What is it?"

His eyes return to mine. "I'm glad he never signed that contract. It would have led to an indictment, and we'd be fighting this out in court. The Torres's are being extradited from the UK because of their signatures and the terms of the contract."

"Were they in on it?"

"I have no idea. It's hard to say. They'll need good attorneys since there's enough evidence to charge them."

"I'm glad Noah's in the clear."

"Me too." There's a pause that causes a lump to form in my throat. "I need you to be prepared to testify against your father."

"Is that a done deal?"

"It is. We have people to help you prepare for court, but I need to know where your head's at with this."

Taking the paper coffee cup, I spin it around with my hands. Although I barely drank any since I was too nervous to stomach it earlier, it's too cold to consider drinking now. Memories populate my thoughts as I stare at the cup. I can still see my father's anger when he saw me getting out of the car and the disappointment when he heard about the sailing accident. I never riddled through if he was upset that I'd survived or disappointed in me for it happening in the first place. Are either of those acceptable responses? No. But his lack of emotion when he laid eyes on Maxwell was the final line to cross for me. He stepped right over it as if he could come back from it any time.

I look at Loch, and reply, "I want justice served. I want to be free from them, and my name kept clear of any wrongdoing."

"Okay." His eyes are steady on mine. "Let's do this."

When we stand to leave, I ask, "Did you really run into the DA at the ballet or was that coincidentally on purpose?"

"Let's just say . . ." We start for the door. He holds it open for me, and when I pass him, he says, "I have my ways, and Tuesday got a surprise night out at the ballet. Double win, wouldn't you say?"

"I would indeed."

No one would ever doubt Noah and Loch are brothers. Or Harbor, for that matter. But now Harbor and Loch are mine as well in all the ways that count. I'm a very lucky woman to have this family in my corner.

———

One week later . . .

"Babe?" I gently shake him. "Wake up, Noah."

He looks at me over his shoulder and then rolls suddenly, tugging the sheet off me. "What is it?"

"Your phone has been going off—buzzing with calls and texts."

Mine vibrates on the nightstand. We reach for them at the same time.

"Lark's having the baby!" I turn so fast that our phones crash into each other.

He jumps out of bed and starts toward the closet. "We need to get to the hospital."

There's never an inkling of hesitation for him to include me. It's always "we" together. *God, I love this man.*

I get dressed and then slip into the guest room where my mom's been staying to let her know we're going. We wanted to be able to dash at a moment's notice, and she volunteered to stay this week just in case the baby came. Since it's only three o'clock, Max can sleep in and join us after breakfast. I tell her, "Thank you for being here."

.L. SCOTT

"Of course, any chance I get."

Noah and I make our way to the elevator just as the adrenaline starts to wane. I look at him, and he looks at me. We exchange smiles, but we don't need a bunch of talking to know how we feel about each other. I tuck myself against him. His arm comes around my back, and after we step on the elevator, he says, "I'm excited."

"Yeah?"

"I'll be an uncle."

I smile to myself. "A new baby in the family is so special."

He kisses my head and says, "They're really something special. We're so fortunate that Max is healthy and happy. He's going to love his new baby cousin."

"I'm so surprised she didn't find out the sex. I had to know all the details so I could plan."

The doors open, and we cut through the lobby. "Have you ever done anything spontaneously, or is everything in your life always perfectly planned?"

I start laughing. "Yes. I was spontaneous once in my life." Glancing over at him, I add, "I ended up pregnant. You and that super sperm of yours weren't going to let my birth control stop your plan."

He chuckles, taking my hand as we head outside. "My plan, huh?" He hails a cab.

"Your plan to tie us together forever."

"You're giving me ideas." My knees get a little weak just from the innuendo alone.

It's not the time . . .

Standing beside him, I say, "For the record, you were never a rebound, Westcott. I truly believe we came into each other's lives when we needed each other most."

He turns to me and runs his palms over my shoulders

and the sides of my neck. "If you're trying to romance me, Ms. Bancroft, it's working wholeheartedly."

"Good." I lift on my toes and kiss him just as a cab pulls to the curb. Figures. It's the only time in history of the city that a taxi volunteers to pick us up.

We share our disappointment in our mutual sighs but get in the back seat and go to the hospital.

———

WITH HER ARM around the back of Harbor, Delta is in tears, taking in the sight of the baby in her mother's arms. "She's so beautiful."

Harbor clears his throat. "Like her mom."

Delta smiles. "Beautiful like her mom."

On the other side of the hospital bed, Lark's father says, "She looks just like you did when you were born."

Although she looks tired, Lark can't stop smiling while staring at her baby. "Really?"

"Yes," he replies. "You had that same tuft of hair on top but were bald for months everywhere else."

Lark's laughter sounds like a melody whistling through the air.

Delta touches that little tuft, and adds, "Her name is so beautiful, too. *Mavie.* Mavie Westcott. So pretty."

Harbor comes around, and Lark hands her to him. Tucked in his big arms, this baby couldn't be smaller or more perfect. "You aren't upset that it's not water-based?"

"No, not at all," Delta replies. "I love that you're starting your own traditions. Mavie follows in the tradition of Lark."

Harbor places a kiss on her little head, and adds, "And it means *my life* in French."

I say, "It's so pretty."

"Thanks, Liv," Lark says, smiling from the bed.

We've all been in rotation for quick visits, but it's our turn to hold her. I can't wait, but I'm more excited to see Noah and his niece together. I get my phone ready to take photos.

"I'm kind of nervous."

"Why?" I ask, watching his brother place baby Mavie into Noah's arms. My heart soars seeing him hold such a sweet little thing. "Other than my sister when I was two years old, I've never held a baby before."

My soul shatters.

I move to the nearest wall, needing the support. If I could run out of here, though, I would. I can't leave without being noticed. Holding my phone up, Noah catches my eyes. I see how the light dances with joy inside his irises and the way he holds the baby with so much care in his cradling arms.

Flashes of Maxwell in my arms or my mom's return. That was it. The two of us. It was enough . . . I always thought it was until now. A tear escapes the threshold of my lower lid as I stare at him, wishing Maxwell had had the same opportunity, feeling gutted that Noah should have been there for him.

So much was stolen from us.

I excuse myself quietly, slipping out of the room. I need fresh air after being cooped up in the hospital for several hours. After walking outside, I go a few feet away from the door. Resting against the brick, I text my mom:

Checking in.

My mom texts back:

> Having coffee and then waking Maxwell up shortly. All good. Did the baby arrive?

I love that she makes it sound like a stork delivery. I reply:

> Yes, a little girl named Mavie.

Her next text comes quickly:

> That's sweet. Congratulations to them.

"Liv?" *Noah.*

I wipe away the traitorous tears ruining this special day and then control my voice when I look up to say, "Hey."

He comes to my side, leaning against the red bricks next to me. Staring ahead, he says, "It's okay."

"It's not, though. You know it's not."

He turns to look at me at the same time I face him. "We can't change it. We can't turn back time. We can wish we could, but that won't fix it. We're doing our best by making up for lost time and filling his life with so many good memories that he'll never know my absence existed. That's my plan." He kisses the apple of my cheek, and says, "Pictures will show his mind, but his heart will never know I wasn't there all along."

"Promise?"

"I'll make sure of it. Swear on my life."

I throw myself in his arms and breathe him in. Although I'm still not sure what I did right in another life, I'm so glad I get to share this one with him. I look up at him and smile. "Mavie, she's beautiful."

"She is." Kissing along my cheekbone, he lands just shy

of my ear, and whispers, "I can't wait to have more kids with you."

I lean back to see his eyes, which are already steady on mine. "We've never talked about having more."

"We should. What do you think, babe?"

The old me would have been spinning, thinking this is too soon to talk about that. But that was before I met Noah, prior to falling head over heels in love with him, and preceding the three of us becoming a family. Now, I don't fear the future we're creating together. I run toward it. "I think we should have that conversation as well. I never thought more kids was a possibility, but I'd love to have more babies with you."

Our future.

Our love.

Our family.

When we kiss this time, it's forever.

40

Liv

"I have two job offers. Both are lucrative, but I'm not sure if I like the companies." Noah finishes filling two glasses, then grabs the wine bottle before returning to the living room, where most of us have been hanging out tonight. "I'm looking for something to challenge me."

Harbor takes one of the glasses and then a sip. "If you're really up for it, I have a lead for you."

Noah tops my glass, then Tuesday's glass with wine before sitting in a chair at the opposite end of the coffee table from me. "What is it?"

"Join the Formula 1 Westcott team. We're at the stage where I need to build a marketing team. It only makes sense to ask you. Are you experienced? No, but you have the know-how, and I know you have the drive to succeed."

"Are you kidding me right now?"

"No, I'm not." He grins and then clinks his whiskey glass against my very sexy boyfriend's glass.

Noah's eyes are wide despite the amount of liquor he's consumed this evening. "Are you asking me to help build this team, to work on it, or to consult? What are you saying, Harbor?"

"I'm saying you can be involved as little or as much as you like. I need an insider to keep the team's best interest at the forefront and to keep the Westcott name clean."

He sets the glass down as he edges toward the end of the chair cushion. "Are you fucking kidding me right now? If you're pulling my leg, I'll fucking pummel you, dude."

We're laughing because of the entertainment factor, but if I've learned anything about the Westcott family, they take care of each other.

Harbor is still chuckling when he replies, "I'm not kidding you or pulling your leg. I've been meaning to talk to you about it for a while, but with Mavie being born, I've been a little busy."

Noah flops back in the seat, his eyes set on mine. "This is nuts, right?"

"I don't think so," I reply. "I think he's serious."

Whipping his gaze back to Harbor, he asks, "Where would we be based?"

"I'm not going to be involved in the day-to-day, so I need a strong team. We need a location where we can buy a sizable plot of land and set up a corporate office, maybe a test track. It would be a great place for my clients to drive their new cars for the first time. In the vicinity of New York City would be beneficial since that's where my operations are based, and Lark will have the opportunity to return to work if she chooses." He sits forward, resting his arms on his legs. "Lark's father is the best mechanic out there. He's local.

He can build out a solid team of mechanics right here in Beacon. Since Westcott Law has been retained as a legal partner, I need my little brother to hit the trifecta to make our racing team dreams come true. How do you feel about returning home?"

Noah's eyes find mine again, the question marks set inside. Like I would ever say no to him or this beautiful town. He once mentioned he'd like to see Max have the freedom to live outside without the confines of concrete—I want that too. He asks me, "What do you think?"

"I think the three of you working together is a force to be reckoned with."

Instead of going to his brother, Noah comes to me. Pulling me to my feet, he looks at me with the same smile that melted my Ice Queen heart many months ago. "Thank you."

Kissing him, I close my eyes to enjoy the sweet pressure, though it's only briefly. We don't mind packing on the PDA, but we also don't need to make a scene in front of the family. "So you're taking it, right?"

He glances back at his brothers on the couch. "The dream team?"

Loch stands first and then Harbor. All three brothers are toe-to-toe. I shoot a look at Marina sitting in a chair next to mine, who rolls her eyes. "Hug it out and get it over with, guys," she teases.

Lark comes into the living room and stops. "What's going on?"

Tuesday raises her arm behind her, reaching out for Lark. "They're having a silent standoff or something. Who knows?" When Lark takes her hand, she asks, "What can I get you?"

"I'm good. Mavie's asleep, so I get a few hours to play

with the grown-ups and the Westcott brothers." She laughs and shakes her head. "Here we go again."

Loch exchanges a look with Harbor, and then it happens so fast that Noah doesn't see it coming. Loch scoops his legs up from under him, and Harbor holds him under the arms. While Noah threatens to get revenge, Marina opens the door for them to run through. She says, "Brr. That pool is going to be cold."

"Wait, what?" I rush for the door.

"They do this to each other at least once a year," Lark says. "They're so competitive, but it's all in good fun. We just let them get it out of their system."

Tuesday follows us outside, closing the door. "What comes around goes around with these guys."

Noah is laughing but reaches his arm out for me. "Save me, babe." He's tossed in before I can reply.

I laugh, and then ask, "Should I get him a towel?"

Lark wraps her arms around herself. "They're all going to need one tonight."

We watch as Loch and Harbor start running across the lawn with Noah in fast pursuit. "Your helicopter can't save you now."

Harbor yells, "Want to bet?"

Lark laughs. "I think he forgot that we're staying the night and sent the pilot to a hotel. Yep. He just remembered." As Harbor legs it toward the woods, she looks at us. "Want to go inside?"

I reply, "I'm hungry. Anyone up for a snack?"

Tuesday says, "I'd love pancakes."

I rub my stomach. "Mm. Me too."

The four of us return to the warmth of the house and start digging through the pantry for the ingredients. Working together, we get the first batch mixed. While I start cooking the pancakes on the griddle, Marina leans against the counter next to me. "How's it going with my brother?" She pops a blueberry in her mouth.

With the spatula in hand, I anchor my hip on the counter to face her. "Really well. We haven't been together for that long in the scheme of things, but it's also like we've been together our whole lives. That sounds weird, right? I just . . . I've never been so much myself with someone else. He loves me for me. He's an incredible partner, and you already know he's a great dad."

"He is. He's so good with Max." She says, "The first time I met you, I saw you were under his spell."

"The Noah Effect?" I start to laugh, remembering her mentioning it before.

"Yeah. It's all in the eyes. They don't lie. The dilation of the pupils when they gaze upon him and then the flirting begins. It's a whole thing that I used to find so annoying. I even had girls befriend me, hoping to get with my brothers. *Ick*. So gross."

I flip three of the pancakes, then snatch a blueberry from the dish. "I'm sorry you had to go through that. Being used never feels good."

"It doesn't, but here's the thing, Liv. It wasn't one-sided with you." I meet her eyes, and we hold each other's gaze. Her heart is on her sleeve as the corners of her eyes soften. "He looked at you the same way." She pops her shoulders in a casual shrug. "The Liv Effect. He's so in love with you."

I love how easy it is to talk so openly with her. She's warm and inviting, and I love that there's a protective edge to her when it comes to her brothers. "I feel the same about him."

The guys crash in through the door, rambunctious and loud enough to wake the dead three counties over. All three are soaking wet. Their hearty laughter is contagious, though, as Lark shuffles them toward the stairs and sends them up to get dressed. "I feel like we're about to get in trouble for waking the parents."

Marina says, "One more thing. When he asks you to marry him, I hope you say yes. You're the perfect addition to our family."

The spatula falls from my hand as my heart kicks into high gear. "Oh my God, do you know something?"

Horror creases her expression. "No. No. No. I don't know anything. I just know how much he loves you."

"Oh," I reply with relief. "Okay." I catch my breath. "That caught me off guard."

Marina is laughing, but she comes to hug me. "Sorry. It was just me being selfish. I adore you."

Tuesday asks, "What about you joining the Formula 1 team? Any interest, Marina?"

"I don't think they could handle me." She's still laughing when Noah crosses through the living room.

Pulling out a barstool, he asks, "What can I help with?"

Loch isn't far behind. When Tuesday sees him, she asks, "Did you know that Alison eloped three months ago?"

"Who's Alison?" I ask.

The room goes quiet, and all eyes are on me and Noah, but he's suddenly very interested in the veining of the marble countertop. *Ah . . . An ex? A hookup? A friends-with-benefits type of relationship?*

I don't care. I'm not threatened. This man would lasso the moon if he knew it would make me happy, so I have no intention of making this a thing between us.

Tuesday replies, "My best friend. She's been living in paradise and, I guess, has been a newlywed this whole time."

Why create upset when there doesn't need to be any?

I stack the finished pancakes on a platter and work on the next batch. As soon as they're cooking, I go to my man, rub his shoulders, and then kiss his back. Spinning around on the stool, he takes hold of my hips. "Do you want to talk about it?"

While the others busy themselves with things to do in the kitchen, I focus on him. "Four or five months ago, maybe. Now, I have no interest."

He smiles before tucking hair behind my ear. "We've both come a long way, babe."

"We sure have, and I couldn't be happier." Wrapping my arms around his neck, I kiss him. No surprise, it quickly turns heated. The spatula is pulled from my hand, and Loch mans the stove by tossing burnt pancakes into the sink.

I say, "Sorry." But it's hard to be sorry when kissing him is so much better than cooking.

Noah stands and tosses me over his shoulder under a fit of laughter he's elicited from me. "I'm not." He waves. "Good night!"

Giggling, I slap his ass. "I was hungry."

"I am, too, sweetheart. Starving. That's why we're heading to the bedroom."

Ohhh! My appetite grows. I'm now famished and not for pancakes.

HE JOKED that he wanted seven figures and a stake in the team prior to starting, but Harbor didn't blink an eye. I don't even know how to process that information.

I just know he's been working for months now, building the marketing team, making connections with sponsors, and putting together the blitz material for the reveal of the team drivers and the first car off production for next season.

After consulting for a few months on corporate accounting, I took a chance and applied to the team under a pseudonym. I made it through three rounds of interviews before I ended up on a zoom with Noah. I recognized the pride in his eyes as he discussed that I'd been winning HR over, and he was looking forward to meeting me. They like my ambition and enthusiasm.

As for him, he took it seriously and interviewed. I was upfront that I have a family I have every intention of expanding and am currently only looking at the part-time position they have listed. I sealed the deal that day. I now work twenty hours a week, currently out of Manhattan. But based on the email I just received, that could soon change. I jump up from the dining chair. "We got it."

"We got what?" He glances up from his laptop but looks back to finish typing.

"The property in Beacon. Oh my God, Noah. We got it."

That grabs his attention. His eyes widen in surprise when he asks, "We got it? We got it!" He launches from his chair and kisses me. I'm lifted, and we're turning as our lips stay connected. The spinning slows, and he carefully sets me down again. The reality of what this means for our family sinks in by the change in his expression and the ease I see in his body. "We're going to build our dream home."

"We are." As I caress his cheeks, my eyes well. I feel like I'm always crying these days, but dammit, there's a lot to celebrate. The neighbors next to Delta and Port were selling ten acres that bumped up to his parents' house. We jumped at the opportunity, and now we'll own that piece of serenity.

The peace that place possesses. The clean air. The wide-open spaces. It's paradise in my eyes.

This feels like the perfect time to share the good news I was saving for later. I get up to retrieve it.

"Oh shit," he says, "finally."

"Shit," Max says, not breaking his playtime with his cars. I gave him a replica of Noah's Aston Martin, and he is addicted to that toy. Boys and their cars . . .

"Noah!"

He cringes. "Sorry. I forget he's at the mimicking stage."

I huff with a quick roll of my eyes. "What finally?" I ask, walking to my bag in the entryway.

He's staring at his screen but looks at me, our gazes linking across the distance, and then says, "It's official. You're an equal owner of this apartment."

"What? Since when? How?" I return with the large envelope and set it between us.

"I added your name. We just need to sign the paperwork."

I don't sit in the chair, though. I make myself at home on his lap with my arms draped around him because it's my favorite place to be. The shock of what he's saying isn't seeping in fully. What does he mean by equal owner? "I don't understand. Why'd you do that, babe?"

"Because I never want you to feel less or trapped in any way. What's mine is yours. You can take all of it as long as I get you. I'm all in, baby."

Pressing myself against him, I stare into his eyes. No lies are detected. I hug him so tightly, needing to be as close as I can to this man. "I don't know how to thank you. Thank you doesn't feel like enough."

"This is it. That's all that's needed. You and me together."

I kiss his cheek and then whisper, "I love you."

"I love you, too."

Keeping the good news rolling, I say, "I have a surprise for you, too."

"Does it involve my old baseball jersey and nothing else?"

I grin. "No, is that something you would be into?"

"Fuck yeah, I'd be into that." He licks his lips, and I kiss them just to steal a taste of him. I'm becoming him, and I don't mind that he's rubbing off on me or rubbing on me, either.

"All right. When we go to bed, I'll give you a few minutes head start, and you can put it on." I'm dying of laughter inside, but I hold my expression as neutral as I can.

"Wait." He's shaking his head. "No. I meant you would be wearing it with nothing else underneath."

Tapping his chin, I pout. "But now you have me fantasizing about seeing you in your jersey."

He rubs the back of his neck, and confusion pinches his brow. "How did we get so off track?"

"Right." I hop from his lap and get Max from the living room. "Ready, big guy?"

He takes my hand and holds the car in the other while I lead him back to Noah. Handing Maxwell the envelope, I say, "Give this to Daddy."

"What is it, buddy?" Noah takes the envelope and then sets our son on his lap.

This isn't something I took lightly before doing. It's something I've been thinking about for a while. I sit across from them again and watch with rapt fascination as he opens the envelope and pulls out the papers.

His eyes scan the top page several times before he drops his head to the side and into his hand. Noah and I have gone through so much, more than many couples, and have always come out together.

What feels like an obvious gesture to show our love has him struggling to even look up. I get up. I felt the same emotions earlier, but I haven't regretted it. I know it was the right decision. I come behind him and wrap my arms around them.

He asks, "When did you do this?"

"The appointment was today to change his name and add yours to his birth certificate." I move around in front of him and rest down on my knees. Rubbing his legs, I say, "I hope that's okay."

"Okay?" he asks, looking at me like I'm asking if the sky is blue on a sunny day. "I'm his father on paper. A recognized parent and guardian now. This is more than I could ask for, Liv."

"That's why I did it. I knew you wouldn't. Not because you didn't want it but because you still feel indebted to me when it comes to Max. You're not. We're Max's parents. *Together.* Anyway, he's more a Westcott than he'll ever be a Bancroft."

Tears well in Noah's eyes. I didn't expect this reaction over the name change. I don't know what I thought would happen, but I knew I wanted this for our son, for Noah, and for me.

Noah reads the paper aloud, "Maxwell Noah Westcott." He looks at me. "The best gift I could ever have. It's fucking beautiful."

Max says, "Fuc—"

"Max. No."

He giggles, looking at Noah like he has no intention of listening.

I sigh. "Oh good lord, help us."

Noah kisses Max's head, not putting weight in the swear

word because we know it will backfire, but he then slides off the chair to kneel on his knees in front of me.

Although Max's feet are now on the ground, Noah still holds him with one arm. Taking my hand with his free one, he adds, "Thank you for doing this. Thank you for giving him my last name."

"You're welcome. He was always meant to have the West-cott name, and now he does, officially." Our kisses are gentle, and our smiles are wide for each other.

"There's only one greater gift you could give me."

"What's that?"

"Your hand in marriage."

I gasp, now the tears are really threatening. I blink, and they begin to fall. "Noah," I reply, half in caution and partly in awe.

"I don't want to waste another minute without strings fully attached to you. You've given me your heart, your trust, and your unconditional love." Noah's smile still shines as he tickles Max. "You've given me this guy. I want nothing more than to be married to you, to spend my life loving you every day and night while we raise our family, and then rock ourselves in chairs in our old age." He kisses my hand, and then says, "I'll honor our love in duty but with care. I'll cherish you emotionally and physically because if there's one thing I know, it's that I was born to love you, babe. Will you marry me, Liv?"

Max jumps up. "Yes."

"There's your answer."

I never denied my attraction to Noah, six-feet-something of sexy man, a face I was drawn to with his natural hand-someness, those hazel eyes that the sun reached down to personally bless, and lips that I find myself kissing not only because I can but because that's where so much love is given. His broad shoulders and muscular build protect the gentle heart that he'd sacrifice in a heartbeat for me if asked.

When it came to us, he was never guarded. He knew exactly what he wanted.

So do I.

Taking his hand, I kiss his palm with my eyes locked on his. There's no reason to hide how I feel about him. He's always allowed me to be exactly who I am, to grow into who I want to be, and to pursue exactly what I want as well. "Yes, babe. I'll marry you and I'll love you deeper than the ocean and longer than forever." I kiss him and then again for good measure and just because I want to. I let the tears fall where they may because I'm going to marry my soulmate. "Yes. Yes. Yes, Noah Westcott. I cannot wait to be your wife."

41

***

Noah

Five days later ...

I wasn't kidding when I said I didn't want to waste more time.

Fortunately, I have a fiancée who agreed with me. We were either going to elope or have a last-minute wedding at the crime scene.

Liv laughed that the crime was against her heart when I stole it.

My side of the story plays out differently. The criminal moment that stands out in my mind is waking up to that empty bed. From either perspective, we got back here as quickly as we could to serve our time—a lifetime of companionship, loyalty, and above all else, our unwavering love for each other and our little family.

We only had one requirement when choosing our date

and to make it special. Our families must be able to attend. All eleven and a plus-one were there on the shortest of notices. Not one person complained that we changed their weekend plans. They just showed up for us like they always do.

My mom fusses about my tie as I stand at our end of the aisle. "You look so handsome, honey."

Tilting my head down, I whisper, "I think we're starting." I'd never ask her to stop caring about us.

Her eyes soften as she looks into mine. "So proud of you."

"Thank you, Mom."

She returns to her seat just as my dad steps out of the house. With the sound of the ocean behind me and the Hamptons house in front, I stand in the dunes where we met under a full moon on a summer's night. Two strangers brave enough to talk to each other and bold enough to fall into bed came together on this very spot.

And here we are again . . .

My bride steps out of the house, wrapping her arm around my dad's extended elbow. Breathe, Westcott. I slowly inhale, drinking in the vision of my soon-to-be wife as she walks toward me.

My heart pounds in my chest, but when I get choked up, I realize I'm staring through a watery haze. I swipe away the fiendish devils invading my eyes, wanting to stare at her instead.

She's spectacular. Two braids drape like a halo around the crown of her head while the rest of her hair flows down in soft curls, the ends getting caught in the wind. She wears her hair more golden than brown these days, but either way, she's fucking gorgeous. Her makeup draws my eyes to hers

—the green and gold are radiant in the diffused light of the setting sun. The softest pink hue of the dress flattered against her skin, the flowing material in contrast to the fitted top that hugs her amazing tits. I feel like I should apologize for having that thought during such a ceremonial event, but I'm okay with noticing such things. Damn, she looks good. She's making it hard to keep my hands off her when she finally reaches me.

So I don't.

Taking her hands in mine, I bring the left to my mouth, kiss it, and then do it to her other hand. I didn't expect this moment to be so emotional. We live together. We've already had a child. You wouldn't think the traditional act of us coming together would be so poignant, but I feel everything about this moment with her—the breeze, the warmer air, and the salt that lingers in the humidity surrounding us.

I feel everything because this woman came into my life and taught me.

"You look beautiful." It's easy to get caught up in her and our life. I never knew I needed it until she showed me what I'd been missing. Our life—it's my favorite place to be with my favorite humans ever.

"You're so handsome, Noah." Glancing at Max sitting in the front row with Cassandra . . . and her plus-one, Halden. Liv smiles at him. "You're my handsome little guy."

Max runs to throw his arms around her legs. Bending, she kisses his head and whispers something that has him smiling while looking up at her. He turns to me and holds out a hand to shake. I shake it but then lift him into my arms and hug the little silly. When I set him down, he runs to Cassandra and climbs on her lap.

The justice of the peace clears his throat. We both glance

at him and then back at each other with smiles. Liv and I
didn't want stuffy or too formal. My mom and Trudy wanted
to handle the food, my dad took care of stocking the bar
inside, Marina took care of the flowers, and Tuesday and
Loch handled the setup. Harbor was out of town, so Lark
and Mavie assisted the moms in the kitchen.

This wedding was a true family affair. But even treated
more casually, I suppose we should get this moving. The
sooner we're married, the sooner we get to honeymoon. And
I plan to honeymoon the hell out of her.

The justice asks, "Are we ready for the vows?"

Staring into my eyes, Liv replies, "I'm so ready to marry
you."

We recite the lines after him and stand there, the humor
gone as the love swallows us completely. Her lithe fingers
are bare until I slide the wedding band and then an impressive diamond ring—if I do say so myself—onto her hand.
Since I didn't have a ring a few days ago when I asked her, I
made up for it today.

But when she slips a platinum band around my finger, I
feel the weight of the metal and the commitment we're
making. I didn't just choose her. She chose me—*then and
now*—always willing to go the distance for each other.

As tears build in her eyes, I caress her cheek, moving
closer, unable to keep my hands from comforting her. The
tip of her nose turns pink as her emotions well up inside. I
kiss it and then her cheek, the corner of her mouth, and her
lips.

Her mouth opens, and as our tongues reunite, the
warmth of her hand slides around to the back of my neck,
holding me to her. She doesn't have to hold on so tight
because I'm not going anywhere.

"I pronounce you husband and wife, equal partners on the deeds of life, and all in. I guess you can kiss—Pfft. You're already kissing. Carry on."

The applause brings us back to the wedding, our eyes opening, and a new fire burning inside—one lit by our passion and devotion to each other. She says, "I love you so much, babe."

"I love you more than you'll know."

We seal our ceremony with a chaste kiss this time around.

She wipes her bottom lip as we laugh with our family, including Trudy and Lark's dad, John, who I've seen grown closer more recently, and Leanna, who sits in the back row with a tissue in hand.

Cassandra holds Max's hand while Halden stands on her other side. Max breaks free again, like the little escape artist he is these days, and comes running into my arms. I catch him, pushing him into the air like a bird with his arms as wings at his side. He closes his eyes, and I know at that moment, he's flying.

I understand the feeling. Married to Liv, I understand more now than ever.

We were already a family of our own, our souls connected long before we realized, much less said vows. Bringing her hand to my mouth, I kiss the top of it just before we walk down the aisle as that same family accompanied by a new perspective—a deeper commitment that works for us on a new level. I wanted to be tied to her in as many ways as possible. This just makes our bond legal. *Check.*

Although it was mostly only family, small and intimate, we had a blast at the reception, and I collected two-hundred bucks on a bet my brothers made when I was twenty-one that I would never get married. Like how I won by bringing the first grandchild into the family, I kicked ass by marrying years before either of them.

My brothers hate to lose, so I'm curious what they'll come up with next.

Since my mom offers to take Max for the night, once everyone leaves, I charm my bride upstairs to the bedroom, hold her in my arms, and dance to the music of nature. We're slow and steady tonight, making love with our eyes as much as our bodies. "Like a thief in the night, you stole my heart when I wasn't looking."

Liv smiles, shattering the remainder of any preconceived notions I still carried around from the years prior—one that made me think I didn't deserve her and another that had me questioning if I'd find her again. I found her . . . as she said, we found each other when we needed each other most.

We kiss until her lips are swollen and make love until our orgasms hit so hard that we need sleep and time to recover. Though it never takes long or much with her. Sometime in the night, she dipped beneath the covers and went down on me. I happily returned the favor, my wife always my favorite flavor, before holding her in my arms until we fell asleep.

When the sun started peeking in, I cracked open my eyes. The dread I felt the first time I woke up in this bed fortunately evades me this morning. Tucked in my arms with a purr of a soft snore is my girl. My girl, the woman who captivated me the moment we met, the mother of my child, now my wife, and my soulmate. This is what forever looks like and feels like. This is love in its purest form, which is how we created Max.

Yep, birth control couldn't stop our love from expanding.

The theme is never wasting time, so we stand in a long line that doesn't seem to budge the following Monday. I'm trying to entertain Max, but he's almost two, so I'm beginning to lose this battle. He's wiggling and antsy to run. Even his Aston Martin isn't keeping him occupied this time. "You sure you want to do this today?" I ask, rocking him to see if it will settle him down.

"Positive. I want the paperwork filed and approved as soon as possible, especially before we travel anywhere."

The wedding came fast and is now a memory of the past weekend. This is not how I imagined spending our honeymoon. "Speaking of travel . . . You sure you want to put off the honeymoon?"

She shakes her head. "I don't know. I don't want this trial hanging over our heads. Is it wrong to wait until we can move on knowing the outcome?"

I agree with a lot of her thinking, but it also feels like we're allowing them to control our situation. "I don't want to live our lives according to what's happening in theirs."

She stands on her tiptoes to try to see ahead. She could just ask her husband since I'm towering over most of the people in line. Turning back to me, she places her hands on my chest. "We're not going to, but there was no closure. I know him. My father will want that. He wants the last word, and we didn't give it to him."

"No, but I gave him the middle finger." I pop a smirk, still feeling good about that decision.

Patting me on the shoulder, she laughs. "And as fun as that is, he won't come after you."

"I won't let him near you, and the restraining order was granted months ago."

She looks at Max, her hand rubbing the back of his leg. "It's not me I'm worried about. He tried his best to do me in and didn't win."

The rage that wars inside me when I think of her father daring to talk to my son will be unleashed one day. It will either take him out or get me locked up in prison. "The restraining order was also secured for him." I'm the only target Bancroft, Chip, or Lowe can come near. On purpose. I dare them.

"Why haven't you shared any of these concerns with me?"

"We had a lot going on. You were busy—"

"I'm never too busy for you." I lift her chin so her eyes meet. "Are you sure you're okay?"

The tension in her forehead loosens, and she replies, "I am. You're not having second thoughts about me becoming a Westcott, are you?"

"You already are." I wrap my arm around her lower back and hold her to my side. "But I'm not the one changing my name, so how are you feeling about it?"

"I don't have doubts about making the change. I don't want to be a Bancroft. It never fit who I was on the inside. That name carries too much baggage and pain with it. It's a burden I don't want to be saddled with any longer." She grins, and I swear I detect notes of a smirk around the edges. "Don't you think Westcott will suit me better?"

"Abso-fucking-lutely. I can't wait to call you Mrs. Westcott."

As she rests against me, her calm relieves my concerns. She says, "I love the sound of that."

The number on the sign changes, and a woman calls out, "One fifty-two?"

Liv holds up the number. "That's us."

"Bingo!"

Two months later . . .

I didn't think my wife could look more stunning than she already is. I'm in awe every day that I get to love this woman and care for her in all ways.

This morning, Liv wakes up looking more relaxed than I've ever seen her. Once she's dressed, she could be vacationing in Italy or St. Tropez on a spring day, by the looks of her casual chic appearance.

It's unexpected to see her so at ease in her body on the same morning that we're going to court to watch her father's trial start. I'm keeping my mouth shut. She's a key witness, so I can only attribute it to the fact that it's moving forward again. And I'm all for getting us one step closer to the other side of this mess.

There's a fervor in the air when we arrive. News stations are covering the steps and asking for interviews. Loch and two of his associates have become bodyguards and our mouthpieces. "No comment," is heard repeatedly until we make it inside.

Liv turns to me, gripping the lapels of my suit. "Something's not right."

The media's interest in such a small case seems to be overblown. I ask, "Why is this suddenly being covered by so many outlets?"

Loch pulls us off to the side. "Chip's camp called them. It's a PR stunt that will backfire."

I catch Liv rolling her eyes just before we make our way inside the courtroom. We're not there ten minutes before the defense drops the news of an accepted plea bargain like a ticking bomb on the floor.

Fuck. I'm shaking my head, eyeing the asshole when he looks back at us. I worry about my Liv and how she feels right now. I give her a nudge. "You okay?"

She leans over and whispers, "How can he get offered a plea deal without everyone knowing?"

Loch leans forward from the other side of me, and says, "It's standard procedure. They need information more than they care about his involvement."

I ask, "How much time are we talking?"

The gavel bangs, ending the proceedings, and Loch stands. His phone buzzes with text messages. He reads, "Fifteen months deducting time served, so just over a year, and they considered our request. It's in here as part of the deal."

Liv says, "That's good."

Reading the rest of the agreed punishment, Loch says, "No contact with any of you unless initiated by you, Noah, Max, or any other children you have. We covered everyone now and in the future."

Her small smile grows, and I see a spark of joy return to her eyes upon hearing that. "That's a victory." Turning to me, she says, "We can now live our lives without his interference."

"We should go," I say, guiding her with my hand on her back. "This will cause a media frenzy."

Only walking a few feet, Liv stops, her eyes locked on her father's while he glares at her. No matter what has happened, I try to remember that he's still her father and a part of her will always miss what she hoped she'd have in a dad.

With his hands cuffed in front of him, he says, "I want to see my grandson."

"No," she replies with no room to wiggle. Proud of her.

"I have a right to him," he says. Not to *see* him, but access. Guess what, fucker? *Access denied.* "He carries my name, Olivia, like you do."

"No, he doesn't. Not anymore. Just like I don't."

Bancroft's eyes shift to me as if I'm the villain. *That's fine.* I'll take the heat if it removes it from Liv. But he's a persistent gnat. He looks at her and gives her a once-over with disgust written all over his face. "You realize that you will never see a dime of my money or that trust fund if you don't bring—"

"I got into Yale."

The words are so powerful and unyielding in a setting built to be formidable. *Go, Liv.*

"What are you talking about?"

"For college." There's a lightness to her tone that's been missing the past few months anytime the topic of her father came up. "I got into Yale. I chose NYU because I wanted nothing to do with you. That still stands. So keep your money. It's all you ever loved anyway, but never come near my family, or you'll regret it."

She walks away without looking back, leaving the courtroom with Loch and I trailing. "I'm impressed," I say as soon as we push through the doors. "I'm not sure that threatening him in court was the best way to go, but it was effective. Two thumbs up from this critic."

With his phone in hand, Loch says, "Chip and his father have now asked for their own plea deals. The best part is that they've turned on each other. Looks like you won't have to testify, after all."

Liv's smug grin says it all. We push into the morning air and keep walking until we're tucked safely in the back of an SUV and on our way home. Sliding her hand in mine, she says, "I'm ready."

"Ready for what?"

She grins like she's up to the no-good I like best—the kind that takes place in the bedroom. "I'm ready to go on our honeymoon."

Fuck yes!

EPILOGUE

Noah

"Remember when you forgot to say goodbye?"

I'm grinning like a fool because sometimes getting her riled up is fun. Especially because we always end up in the bedroom afterward. What's not to be happy about? I'm married to this incredible woman, and our problems are not only behind us but thousands of miles away as we enjoy the turquoise waters of the Maldives.

With her head resting on my shoulder as we lie in bed with the water not ten feet from the end of the mattress, she says, "I didn't forget. Love like ours is rare. No way was I walking away unscathed." She shrugs her right shoulder. "It was more of a see you later and a kiss on the lips since I knew we'd always find our way back together again."

"You kissed me goodbye?"

"You were like Sleeping Beauty lying there—"

"Funny." I laugh without amusement entwined.

Although she's pretty good at teasing, I slow blink at her

until she says, "Fine. You were still stupidly sexy even sleeping, so I couldn't resist kissing you again."

"That's more like it." My ego gets drunk off the compliment. Holding her a little closer, I take her hand and rub it over my sheet-covered cock.

"Pfft." She giggles. "Are you ever not horny?"

"With you, Mrs. Westcott? Never. We've got to make the most of our honeymoon since we traveled halfway around the world."

Pushing up, she reaches for something bedside before settling on top of me and straddling my legs. She bends to kiss me, and then says, "Good. I'll never tire of you either, Mr. Westcott. What are your thoughts about having another baby?"

I grin, rubbing the sides of her hips. "I'll make a baby with you."

She kisses my neck and then my jaw before kissing me on the mouth. I dig my fingers into her hair and deepen it. She pulls back just enough to catch her breath. Lifting, she says, "We're a few steps ahead."

"What do you mean?"

"Remember that night in the Hamptons?"

I smirk. "Which one?"

"The only one that matters—our wedding night."

Caressing her face, I lift to steal a kiss from her lips. "I'll never forget."

"Neither will I." Something cold is slid between us.

When I lie back, I see the test she's holding and the screen that reads, "Pregnant."

Pregnant. "You're pregnant?"

She nods as tears fill her eyes. Not an ounce of doubt enters my thoughts, only happiness fills my heart. And a few tears threaten the corners of my eyes as I look into hers welling. "You're amazing, my love."

Her smile brightens my day along with this news. "We're always better together." Laughter escapes her as if she'd been holding it in for months. I guess she has. She asks, "You ready to be a daddy again?"

I give her a wink. "I was born for this, babe."

Biting her lip, she then releases and says, "Yes, you were."

You just met Harbor Westcott, Noah's brother. Now you can read a sneak peek by turning the page.

YOU MIGHT ALSO ENJOY

Recommendations - Three books I think you'll enjoy reading after *Forgot to Say Goodbye*. All are stand-alones that will grab your heart and have you falling in love along with the characters.

**Turn the page to read a sample of Swear on My Life

Read in Kindle Unlimited and Listen in Audio

Swear on My Life - You met Harbor in Forgot to Say Goodbye. Now read the captivating and emotional journey that will break and heal your heart. Free in Kindle Unlimited.
  READ NOW

Never Saw You Coming - You met Loch in Forgot to Say Goodbye. Now is the time to jump into this unexpected amnesia journey that will have them discovering who they want to while figuring out the mysteries that surround them. Free in Kindle Unlimited.

READ NOW

Best I Ever Had - You will be on the edge of your seat with your heart on the line as two soul mates fight for the future stolen from them. Free in Kindle Unlimited.

READ NOW

SWEAR ON MY LIFE

New York Times Bestselling Author
S.L. SCOTT

You are not a drop in the ocean;
you are the entire ocean in a drop.

~ Rumi

PROLOGUE

Numbness beats the pain I endured, but I realize the next stage is death.

I close my eyes, too tired to hold them open any longer. *So tired . . .* I just need to rest to save my energy. My breath stalls in my throat as darkness takes hold. Despite what you hear, there is no light to guide your soul.

There's music.

My breath returns as a melody calls me back. I open my eyes to a cloud-laden sky and trees that bend to the will of the stronger winds. Roots creep over the edge of the cliff above me while a bird sings from a low-hanging branch.

Broken, I lie there, captivated by the brown-feathered bird and its yellow mask keeping me company. I grin, but the pain that has returned is too much to maintain, so I listen for hours, waiting for my date with destiny.

An ambulance shows up instead.

CHAPTER 1

Harbor Westcott

Room 156.

   Row 14.

   Seat 20.

I recognize her the second I see the back of her head. *I should.* I've stared at it enough to memorize every subtle strand of brown and golden blond that weaves through it, even when it's pulled and twisted on top of her head like it is now.

She's a nice reprieve from the memories that haunt me, like sunshine shining through a crack in the blinds and the first warm spring day after a long, dreary winter.

As I walk toward her, this is the first time I've been this close. She's five-three, maybe five-four on a good day, though I would have guessed a little shorter, sizing her up in the auditorium.

Usually, I see her dressed in a pair of faded exercise pants with a baggy T-shirt hanging over her waist. Today, she's looking damn good in the denim cutoffs hanging on the swell of her hips, and the shortened shirt doesn't dare brush against the top of the shorts, leaving the slope of her waist exposed.

Though, I'd always wondered what color her eyes were, I'm now given the privilege as she looks up as if caught in a thought. Green and bright despite the shadows of her dark lashes under the fluorescent lights of the convenience store. Her sneakers have hit the pavement a few times, judging by the scuffs and black asphalt staining the bottoms that leave the slightest of prints on the white linoleum.

I've always thought she might be a runner by how toned her legs are and her chosen wardrobe in the past. I like that they're not sticks and hold strength in muscle.

It's not that I'm *not* a tits man, but I do love a great ass. *Hers has been noted.*

I move down the aisle from her, eyeing the groceries lining the shelves. There's nothing I need here, but her sweet scent and my deep-seated hunger to be near her draws me closer.

What am I doing?

Why am I acting like a fucking idiot?

I see her in class all the time, at least on the days I go. But I've never craved her company, not like I do now. Sure, she caught my eye. Lots of chicks do. She's different though . . . seemingly oblivious to my existence inside—and apparently, outside—the classroom, judging by her lack of awareness of my presence.

My ego isn't fragile.

I like a challenge, but I *love* the taste of victory.

My life's been boring walking a straight line for too long. This woman is just the detour I'm looking for. *At least for a night or two.*

I imagine she has a boyfriend, probably some schmuck

back home, wherever she calls home, who's waiting for her to return after graduation. I'd bet a day's work that doting middle-class parents who saved every penny to send their only daughter to an East Coast university are a part of her story, along with a hand-me-down Subaru with another good fifty-thousand miles before the odometer rolls over for the third time.

Such a charmed life she must lead.

My assumptions don't do her any favors, but I never claimed I wasn't an asshole. I was never good at balancing bad deeds while looking the part of an altar boy. Not like Lucas was. My cousin is probably laughing beyond the grave, watching me act like a nervous pre-teen having a brush with a middle school crush.

He might have laughed, but he'd also know that hitting on girls isn't my usual MO . . . Opportunity usually presents itself and hits on me first. We never had trouble turning the heads of the fairer sex.

My innuendoes aren't subtle. She's either playing hard to get or is wholly consumed by the can of Beans & Franks in her hand. I'll assume the latter and make the effort. "Don't get hurt," I say. Not my best work, but we're in a convenience store, so I'm certain the bar is already pretty fucking low. When I latch my gaze onto the pale-pink hem of her shirt, a flash of skin is given when she moves. But I catch her gaze just in time to see it sliding up my chest until her eyes meet mine.

Tilting her head up, she studies me in silence, making it hard to read her thoughts. *Did I screw up?* Is she going to give me the time of day or a tongue lashing . . . must rid that wicked thought from my mind or start praying she's into that kind of play. I straighten my shoulders, debating if I should grab the requested diet soda and move on.

But then a half-hearted smile graces her lips. "Is that a warning?" She furrows her brow as her eyes narrow in the slightest. "Have we met?"

I shove my hands in my pockets, eyeing the full package. *She's cute. Innocent, like prey that doesn't recognize the danger around her.* Not sure she would stand out in a crowd, but she stood out to me prior, even in an auditorium full of people.

"No."

"Are you sure?"

"I'd remember." I'm too quick with a response. If I'm not careful, I'll show my cards, and I'd rather her reveal her thoughts first.

Her expression eases, soaking in the compliment. "You would, huh?"

"Absolutely. I'd never forget you."

She laughs, the sound ringing in the air. "Very charming." Her gaze slides down my chest and back to the can as if it's much more interesting.

"I try."

Sighing, she does the slightest of eye rolls before I'm on the receiving end of her glare. "I have a feeling you don't have to try at all when it comes to girls."

Not seeming to break through her cooler composure, I finally realize I have no game with this girl.

"It was a warning," I reply with full intention.

"For you?" She holds up the small can with an all-knowing grin and sees right through me. "Or this?"

This girl.

Fuck me.

What was I thinking? I just hit on her in a gas station convenience store in the middle of the day like she'd fall at my feet. *What did I expect, for fuck's sake?*

I'm arrogant enough to believe I'm worthy of her attention, so I keep my eyes on her. "If you're wise."

"What happens if I'm not wise?" Her voice is as steady as her eyes are on me, which are locked in place.

Call me impressed. The girl can stand her ground, but I'm also starting to think she might be into me. "You might get hurt."

Her gaze shifts, lengthening to a back corner of the store before she looks at me again. "Sometimes the pain is worth the risk." Her body fills with attitude, shoulders straightening and chin held high. "Don't you think?"

"Guess it depends on the risk."

Biting her lip, she smiles to herself and looks back down at the can in her hands. "You're probably right, but I'll take my chances."

Rubbing the pad of my thumb across my lower lip, I then say, "Don't say I didn't warn you."

"Don't worry. You won't be held liable for any damage in the aftermath." She starts to leave but turns back a few feet away. "We're talking about the beans, right? Like, this isn't our meet cute?"

This girl. *Fuck.* She's got my full attention and couldn't care less. "I don't know what a meet cute is."

"It's how they meet in the movies."

"Who's *they*?"

"The main characters," she replies like everyone knows what she's talking about.

I'm still staring at her, trying to figure out what the fuck we're going on about when I realize what she means. "You're really into movies, aren't you?"

"I am. It's a nice escape."

"From what?"

"Life."

That has to be one of the most honest answers I've ever been given, and I've never felt more understood before.

With straightforward honesty like that, I'm determined to find out why this fascinating woman needs an escape from life. "I get that." There's a pause as her eyes look into mine, seeming to search for answers to questions she hasn't asked.

The last thing I want to do is pour out my heart under the stench of gas or show that side of myself that I've worked fucking hard to bury. I need to get over it. I need to get on with life.

I say, "Did we ever decide what you wanted to discuss? The frank and beans or how we met?"

"Quite frankly, pun intended," she says, laughing lightly, "I'm not sure." I have a feeling that's the only thing she's ever been uncertain about.

She has me competing with beans, for Christ's sake. I'll do it if it gets me closer to her. "How about we find out? You can eat that alone, or we can discuss the virtuous qualities of canned meat and beans versus our meet cute over something we didn't heat in the microwave. What do you think?"

She takes me in unabashedly, not seeming the least displeased with what she sees, but then says, "I'm good," and walks away.

Damn.

I played this all wrong . . . *I played her all wrong.*

But when she starts back to me like she's on a mission to settle a score, I know I've gotten to her. Guess I played this right, after all. She holds the can up and waggles it in the air. "And who said I'll be eating this alone?" Cocking an eyebrow in challenge, she knows she scored the winning point. The rubber bottoms of her sneakers squeak against the linoleum tiles as she heads to the register.

I cover my wounded heart. Okay, not really, but I fucking hate to lose. Throwing my arms out to the sides, I ask, "So is that a yes?"

Shooting me a glare that buries any chance of redemption I thought I might have, she says, "It's a no."

They say you can't win them all, but my record remained undefeated until now. I look around, glad there are no witnesses.

I grab the soda for Marina, almost forgetting the reason I came in here, and head to the counter.

"Hey, how are ya?" the guy asks my current fixation . . . *Is that what she is?* Am I fixated or fascinated? I might side with fascination more than fixated, which borders on obsession. Though by how I've watched her over the last month in class, obsession might not be far off.

I don't like the way he's staring at her with his smarmy smile after a quick rattle of his fingers across the register keys. He dips down on one elbow and smacks his lips together. "I get off in an hour if you wanna . . ." Clicking his tongue, he continues, "You know. I'll even let you come behind the counter. There's lots of room down here."

What the fuck? I move to her side, staring the fucker in the face. "What'd you say?"

"Mind your own fucking business, kid," he snaps.

Kid? He's what? A few years older than I am? *He's got some fucking nerve.*

As if I'm the one in need of defending, she edges her shoulder in front of mine. "First of all, you must be new here." Can't say I'm not impressed and a lot amused. The girl's got bite.

He replies, "Just started Thursday."

Leaning closer, she says, "Secondly, ever talk to me or any woman like that again, and you'll be looking for work elsewhere. I know TJ doesn't take kindly to creeps working his counter." She slaps her money on the counter. "And for the record, I am his 'fucking business,' and I want my change for the soda and beans." Turning to me, she adds, "You good, babe?"

I chuckle under my breath. "Yeah, all good, sweet cheeks." I lean in for a kiss because I'm a fucker like that, but I'm met with her middle finger pressed to my lips.

Tugging me by the beltloop of my jeans, she pulls me close, our bodies pressed together, and whispers, "Save it for later. When we're alone."

Fuck. I think I'm in love.

The change clangs against the counter, all twenty-three cents of it. She slides it into the palm of her hand, skipping the tip jar, before taking the bean can from the counter and walking to the door.

Just outside, the door closes, and I say, "I take it you're not friends with that guy?"

She bursts out laughing as we clear ourselves away from the entrance. Eyeing me, she grins. "Can't say we are."

I shove my free hand in my pocket and look at her as if I'm seeing someone entirely different than the girl inside the convenience store. "It's too bad you have to deal with shit like that."

"Part of being a girl." She tries to shrug it off like it was nothing. It was something and made me want to punch his fucking face.

Although I have no doubt she can take care of herself, a vulnerability entangled in her strength causes my chest to tighten. "He was out of line," I say, keeping my voice low between us.

"It is what it is." She starts to back away. "Enjoy the soda."

The soda reminds me of Marina, who's sitting in the car waiting on me. I can barely make out her silhouette behind the tinted window, but I'm really hoping she can't make me out at all, or I'll be hearing about this over the dinner table at every major holiday meal and then some.

"Hey," I say just to the beauty in front of me. "I owe you for the soda."

"My treat." Her shoulders pop up and then down before I'm met with her back as she nears the corner of the building.

I don't go after her, but I make a last-ditch effort. "For real, let me give you some money."

Glancing back over her shoulder, she shakes her head. "It's a soda. It's no big deal."

"But . . ."

"Really. It's okay," she replies, stopping under the awning of the sketchy gas station. Even the potent smell of gasoline and oil slicks on the ground don't make her any less pretty.

Stepping out on a limb, I close the gap by half, leaving enough distance for her to make her own decisions. "Okay, no money, but what about dinner sometime?"

The corners of her lips slope just high enough to back her entertainment, but her eyes reveal a gleam of interest in the way they shine for me. My breath gets caught somewhere between telling her she's gorgeous and reminding her to steer clear of the trouble I bring.

"You don't even know my name, and you're asking me out?" There's no offense to her tone or in her stance by how relaxed she appears.

I should probably take the opportunity she's giving me to prove I'm not a total asshole. Holding out my hand, I say, "People who know me call me Harbor. You can do the same."

She comes a little closer, the heat of her proximity reaching me. As she slips her hand against mine, her chest rises as her lips part. "Are we friends now, Harbor?"

Since not one PG image crosses my thoughts, friends aren't what I had in mind. I'm not friends with anyone these days, but she might be worth making an exception. "It depends."

I'm not sure why my directness puts her at ease, but her smile reveals only intrigue. She should probably run, get away from me as fast as she can without giving me a second thought. "Depends on what?"

"What happens next."

She laughs, rocking back on her heels. "I have to go, so I guess we'll leave it to the fates to decide."

While the distance we had just closed widens, I throw my arms out wide. "You're not going to tell me your name?" In a class of almost two-hundred students, her name is one of the few things I've not caught. I was hoping to remedy that.

The afternoon sun shines on her. "Isn't it more fun this way?"

"Fun is subjective." I watch as she turns around, her shoulders rattling with laughter. "But I'll play along." *Helps that I know I'll see her in class.*

Glancing back, she says, "I had no doubt you would."

"Do you ever have doubts?"

"All the time. See you around, Harbor." She gives me a little wave before she disappears around the corner.

I could chase her down and ask for her number, but two rejections from the same girl is enough for one day. I pull my keys from my pocket and spin the ring around my finger. Anyway, she's right. It is more fun this way. Just wait until she sees me on Monday.

I walk to my pride and joy—my Ghibli Modena—and open the car door. I don't have time to get in fully before Marina asks, "What took you so long? I thought I was going to die of thirst while waiting."

"I didn't think you'd notice since your eyes are always glued to that screen."

"Okay, Dad," she says in a deep mocking voice.

Handing over the soda, I look at her, knowing one day, if she hasn't already, she'll face assholes who will treat her like that guy in there. That's not a conversation to have now, but one we need to have soon. "Don't ever go to this station."

She looks up briefly, her eyes looking at the building behind me. "Ew. I wouldn't anyway." *Good.* "I don't even know where we are."

It's true, this isn't my usual store or gas station, but it's close to downtown, so I made the detour. I reach over to ruffle my little sister's hair, but she blocks me. "You're welcome, by the way."

"Thanks," she replies, pushing my hand away. "Long line?"

"Yeah," I lie, knowing firsthand that sixteen-year-old girls can be ruthless when it suits them.

I start the Maserati, acting as casually as I can. We don't even hit the street before she asks, "Did you at least get her number?"

The last thing my sister needs to hear about is how I hit on a woman with great legs, an even better ass, and a mouth I wouldn't mind occupying for a night. *And then got rejected.* "You saw that?"

She's at least polite enough to keep her laughter under wraps . . . *until she can't.*

"Everyone saw it."

"I didn't ask for it." *Not a lie.*

Her phone is now the least interesting thing in the car when she angles toward me. "Why not? It seems a shame to let all that flirting go to waste."

"Eh," I say, "I think I'll leave it to the fates to decide."

"If the fates have their way, you just met your soul mate."

Surprised to hear the seriousness in her tone, I glance over at my sister. "Why do you say that?"

"Because you weren't the only one flirting."

I return my gaze to the drive ahead, but there's no stopping the stupid grin on my face. I'm not sure about anything when it comes to the gorgeous girl I just encountered, but she's got me thinking about her and this main character business.

I may not believe in fate, but I believe in myself. Wonder what it takes to be the hero of her story?

***

To continue reading *Swear on My Life*, it's available on Amazon, Kindle Unlimited, in audio, paperback, and in special edition hardback and paperback form.

ACKNOWLEDGMENTS

Thank you so much to this incredible team:

Andrea Johnston, Content Editing/Beta Reading
Jenny Sims, Copy Editing, Editing4Indies
Brittni Van, Content Editing, Overbooked Author Services
Kristen Johnson, Proofreader
Michele Ficht, Proofreader
Cover Design: RBA Designs
Photographer: Mark Mendez
Back Image: Depositphotos - Cavan
Model: Mr. Novak
Audio: Erin Spencer, One Night Stand Studios.
Narrators: Savannah Peachwood & Jason Clarke

Thank you to my amazing Super Stars and my awesome SL Scott Books members. To my friends who are not only peers but also friends. I adore you! Adriana, Andrea, Heather, and Lynsey.

My husband and sons are everything to me. I adore you so much! Love you. XOXOX

Made in the USA
Las Vegas, NV
29 October 2023

79935905R00277